JUST SING
THE SONG

A Story of Redemption and Love
Based on Actual Events

TONY DALE

United Writers Press
Asheville, N.C.

United Writers Press
Asheville, N.C.
www.UWPnew.com
828-505-1037

ISBN: 978-1-952248-55-9 (trade paperback)
ISBN: 978-1-952248-56-6 (ePub)

Cover art created from an author photograph and historic view of the NYC skyline
circa 1930s. All other images provided courtesy of the author.

Printed in the U.S.A.

for my wife, Pernilla,
my muse and the melody that inspires me

Prelude

A gentle morning zephyr caressed my cheek. I stood on the threshold, peering through the sliding glass door at my father as he lay sleeping on hills of pillows. A shaft of morning sun fell on the gnarled hands folded on his chest. I was hesitant to wake him, yet I'd come far and time was short. This was likely the last time I'd hear that magnificent voice and gaze into those wise hazel eyes.

Slipping quietly into the room, I pulled a chair up next to the bed. The smell of age and decay tainted the air. As I took in his noble weathered face, his eyes opened. He inhaled deeply as he came to himself and smiled when he saw me there.

"Son, what a treat to awaken and find you here. I know it was an effort, but as I told you on the phone, I won't be around much longer. Your mother came to visit me and told me she would be back to take me home. Oh, my, she was as breathtaking as the first time I saw her!

"So, considering the brevity of time, there are some things I feel compelled to share with you. There is a whole chapter of my past you know nothing of. To truly appreciate how God has blessed me, you need to understand what he redeemed me from. Had I not been through the catastrophic events that I survived, I would not have found your mother or had the joy of being a father to you and your two brothers. Nor would I have accomplished what I did and influenced as many people as I have.

"The path I was on promised great success, fame, and wealth, yet it was leading me to a shallow and dissolute life. The events that befell me were truly my saving grace and the most wonderful thing that could have happened to me."

"Dad," I said, "knowing what I do about what you went through, honestly that's hard to understand."

"To better understand, you need to know that the man I became is completely different than the one I was before. I was like the Prodigal Son from the Bible. I led a life that will likely shock you when you hear it. But you need to hear it." He paused. "Son, would you pour me some water from that pitcher? This may take a while. They say confession is good for the soul. So, let me share the untold story before I go to heaven and dance with your mother…"

JUST SING
THE SONG

Chapter 1
1918

A mockingbird trilled songs into a sultry San Antonio morning. Allan sat on the couch with his mother, enjoying the birds' concert. He watched from the window as his older brother and sister chased their friends around a pecan tree.

"I'll never get to run like that, Mama," he said.

"Nonsense, Allan. You will most certainly walk and run," she replied.

Georgia's heart filled with compassion for her son. Polio had struck down her bright enthusiastic child. Now her mission was to get him as healed as possible and able to walk unaided, even if one leg would be withered. She believed that she could guide him to a better outcome. Better to walk with a limp than to depend on crutches for the rest of his life.

"But I heard the doctor tell you that I would have to use crutches the rest of my life."

"Yes, and I told him he was full of cow dung. Mark my word, you will walk unaided. We'll make it so."

Countless hours of grueling effort began as Allan learned to walk without help. When he fell, his mother would force him to try again. "Stand. Walk. You can do it. Make yourself do it," Georgia demanded, her heart longing to lift him when he cried at times from her discipline. It was excruciating to watch him pull himself up from the floor, but she resisted the urge to help. She trusted her guidance and persevered.

Gradually, over weeks, then months, Allan at last cast aside the crutches. He was now able to walk with a limp, due to his withered right leg. Each day he forced himself to walk further. Although the atrophied leg would never fully recover, his left leg grew stronger and gradually his limp became less pronounced. With his newfound confidence, Allan began to work on strengthening his upper torso.

As his mother guided him in rehabilitation, his father, a concert violinist, opened Allan's eyes to the joy of making music. Each day, he taught Allan how to play the guitar while his mother insisted on classical singing lessons. Allan's natural talents developed, as did his confidence and power of will.

Over the course of months and years, Allan began to develop in ways he could improve himself. To compensate for his weak leg, he started doing pushups and pullups and lifting weights. By the time he reached high school, he could walk fifty feet on his hands.

Georgia taught him to believe in God and himself, that faith was the great equalizer, telling him, "Anything that doesn't kill you outright will make you stronger." Hardship became a worthy opponent to be defeated.

Allan embraced the power of possibility. Soon, there was no stopping him.

It was in his early days at Harlandale High School that Allan's true gifts emerged. The music lessons and hours of practice were getting him noticed. He won the talent show his sophomore year and soon he was playing guitar and singing at parties and sometimes at church. His popularity grew and his limp became less important to him as time went on.

Georgia was thrilled with his development in singing the opera songs he was learning from his voice coach. She could see him one day standing in front of an orchestra—maybe at the Met in New York. She believed in his gift and was prepared to spend every penny she earned raising her parakeets and canaries to give him the training he needed. With her husband's growing stature as violinist and concertmaster with the symphony, and his contacts in the business, anything was possible.

⌢

1927

HIS FATHER'S VIOLIN GRACED the house with the achingly tender strains of Debussy. Higher and higher leapt the notes, fit to reach the angels. The music seemed to hover at the frontier of heaven itself. Allan's heart rode the melody as his father's fingers drew from wood and sinew sounds of indescribable passion and fire.

"Get ready for school, Allan," Georgia called from the kitchen.

Even as he pulled the pants over his legs, he dreaded the ridicule that awaited him. Randy Bonham and his pack of coyotes would no doubt be lurking with the usual ridicule, "Hey Gimp Boy, give us a dance," or whatever fresh insults they'd come up with that day. Allan's older brother Sam came to his defense when he was around, but he wasn't around this morning.

Were it not for the Brown brothers, he would be nervous about facing down the bully. Jessie, Joe, and Willie treated him with kindness and were very protective when someone made cruel remarks. Reading assignments in history and English made school at least endurable, though he dreaded algebra.

However, knowing that his guitar and singing lessons awaited him afterward was the real incentive to navigating school. At least it was Friday and the weekend awaited. He had a birthday party at which he was to perform on Saturday at the home of one of the loveliest girls in school and he was going to get a dollar as well. Things were looking better all the time.

That following Sunday morning was frenetic. Sam Sr. was still tired from his late night with the symphony. His sister Louise, the eldest of the three, controlled the bathroom, leaving scant time for the boys to get ready. After a rushed breakfast, the family headed to church. They were all sweating as they arrived late to find seats in the last pew. Allan was pleased he didn't have to limp all the way down to the front.

After an opening prayer, the choir began. Allan's favorite part of church was singing along with the choir. When they came to "The Old Rugged Cross," he felt unusually caught up in the song. As he sang, the music captured him, and he found tears on his cheeks at the song's ending. His mother noticed and patted his arm when he sat down. He couldn't quantify the feeling but something about that song had really gotten to him.

The pastor began to talk about the power of words. "Christ is the Word made flesh." "In the beginning was the Word." Then he explained that just as there are three components of God: Father, Son, and Holy Spirit, there are three embodiments of the Word. Jesus the Word made flesh; the Bible, the Word written; and the Holy Spirit, the Word spoken. We need to incorporate all three in our lives but remember that the power in is the Spirit, he said.

Allan thought the words of that song had connected to words he had felt within but not expressed. He was struck with the idea that the spoken word had power, and so too, the word when sung.

While normally inattentive to the preaching, this Sunday he was fully engaged. The message concluded with encouragement to boldly speak to God with gratefulness as you make your requests known. Speak to others in love and truth and learn to wait on and listen for God's voice through the Holy Spirit.

This was the first time he had felt a deep understanding of the preaching. As the choir began to sing "Jesus is Calling," the pastor asked congregants to invite Jesus into their hearts. Allan felt a pull, as of a rushing tide, drawing him to the altar. The pastor took his hands, asked if he understood what this gift of grace truly was and what this decision meant. Allan realized that he did feel something powerful entering him and was overwhelmed with a feeling of peace and joy he'd never experienced.

The people at church congratulated him, and his parents and his siblings joined in. Allan appreciated it but took no pride in their words. He did, however, feel something he could not articulate percolating within him. He felt different—changed, new. Whatever he was experiencing gave him a sense of confidence and empowerment that was new and exhilarating.

In the weeks that followed, Allan joined the choir and even sang "The Old Rugged Cross" and accompanied with his own guitar. He felt a lightness now that lifted him above the insults and name calling. He found himself singing just for the joy of it, not just practicing.

The voice lessons and the classical songs in his instructions weren't as inspiring as some of the old hymns and the negro spirituals he knew—in particular "Swing Low, Sweet Chariot." He was also learning the new jazz and popular songs to impress his friends. It was such a joy to sing songs from the radio to his friends. He was becoming more popular, and this new music was giving him a grander perspective on what he might be able to accomplish.

One Wednesday in October, Allan found himself walking home at dusk. He heard voices singing in the distance. Drawn to the music, he discovered a large tent filled with a swaying, singing crowd of Black worshippers. They were raising their arms, shouting "Hallelujah!" while a choir, backed by organ, drums, bass, and guitar belted out the music. Allan was entranced.

Heads turned as the young white boy walked in but smiles followed. The music was infectious, inspiring, intoxicating in a way Allan had never experienced. He moved with the rhythms as hands clapped, tambourines jingled, and their voices became a single breath-borne instrument. The singing lasted for much longer than it did at his church.

When it ended, he realized it was full dark and he was very late for supper. People shook his hands and patted him on the back as he left, feeling like he just gained a new understanding of singing.

—

Hazy May heat greeted Allan and Sam as they emerged from the Majestic Theatre, where they'd watched their father rehearse with the symphony. The soupy air was redolent with fumes from automobiles, horse manure from the lorries, and the muddy funk of the San Antonio River. Houston Street moved to the soundtrack of horse-drawn wagons with the percussion of the mighty drays' clopping hooves as counter point to the automobiles and trollies occupying most of the space.

"Dad gave me some money for lunch...want to go over to the plaza and get some Mexican?"

"You bet. I could eat a coyote raw 'bout now."

"Hey, Allan, maybe we can stop by Garza's gym after and watch some of the boxers. You can learn a lot watching those guys sparring. Wait 'til I'm eighteen and you'll see. I could be a good fighter. Nobody at school can whip me, that's for sure!"

As they neared Losoya Street, they heard a guitar playing something very strange. As they got closer, they saw a shabbily clad Black man sitting on a crate in the shade of an awning, playing a beat-up guitar. The case lay open with a few coins littering the red velvet lining.

"What kind of music is that? I never heard the like."

"Heck if I know or care for that matter," Sam replied.

"Let's listen a little while. Maybe I can learn something new."

"You and that dang music. Okay, but just a little while. I'm starving, Hermano."

Allan watched as the man bent the strings, slurring the following note in a way he had never heard. The man began to sing. It was a raspy voice filled with sorrows, steeped in the pain of love. He played mostly with his eyes closed, and the wrinkles at the corner of his eyes looked like tributaries of a river that had carried many tears. Long thin fingers slid up and down the fretboard with ease, as bittersweet pain poured out of him.

Baby dun lef me
kick me right out the door
just me and my bottle
she won't see me no more.

The slow 4/4 beat featured an occasional run up the neck to grab a string, which he attacked with his thick thumbnail. Allan could hear the heartbreak, feel the release of it through the music.

Finishing the song, the man opened his eyes and smiled up at them. Allan reached into his pocket, retrieving a nickel which he pitched into the open guitar case.

"Thank'ee young squire. Got a favorite song I could play for y'all?"

"No, but I'm real interested in what kind of music you call that and that thing you do where you bend the strings into next note. What you did before you did that arpeggio."

"Arpeggio, is it? Heh heh. Seems you gots you sum musical learnin' under yo young belt."

"Well, I'm learning guitar from my dad. He's a musician...a violinist...but he can pretty much play any instrument."

"This here music is da blues. I be comin' over here from Mississippi to see my aunt. We be playin' and singin' da blues a good long time over dere. Ain't had me no learnin' 'cept what my cousin Ezekiel show me, and I been steady playing ever since."

7

There weren't as many Black people in San Antonio as there were Hispanic and white, so the man was the darkest color of black Allan had seen, almost purple. The skin on his face stretched taut from his cheekbone down to his jaw. He was reminded of the wooden Indian statue in front of the Buckhorn Saloon—the man's eyes were black and shiny as a raven's wing and glistening with both mirth and sorrow.

"Could you show me how you go from a chord to that string bending thing?" asked Allan.

"Don't see why not...surely I don't. What's yo name?"

"Allan. This is my brother Sam."

"Howdy," Sam replied with an impatient tone.

"Howdy do. Name's John Hurt. Sounds kinda painful, don't it? Don't hurt at all long as I'm playin', though. Heh heh heh. So lookee here, when I be done singin' sum, I jes run my hand up the neck here and bend the string when I catch holt of it and pull it into the next one." John demonstrated the move.

Allan took in what John did with his fingers. "Could I try that?"

"Sho nuff can. Sit down here on my beat-up old carry sack."

Allan sat down, took the guitar, and strummed an open E chord, switching to A as he'd seen John do, trying to play the song he'd just heard. Attempting the run up the neck to catch the A string on the higher fret and bend it, his fingers fumbled and only a muted thump emerged. "You know that's harder than it looks...tricky." Shyly, he handed the guitar back to John.

"Well, you jes keep on a keepin' an' you sho nuff get it. I can tell you been playin' some. Show soma yo stuff."

"Mostly what I'm learning is classical from my dad and some Mexican folksongs from some of his mariachi friends. But I really like the new music and especially the jazz. I play at parties and at school. I know *Sweet Georgia Brown*."

John handed him the battered Gibson. Allan lovingly took it, checked the tuning.

He played the popular song and gave himself over to the feeling of it. Before he knew it, the song was over. He gave the guitar back to John.

John grinned. "Son, I reckon you be a fair guitar player if you keep practicin', but you sho nuff can sing. Shoot...you need to learn soma deeze here blues songs. You be breakin' dem lil' girls' hearts. Dat's a natchel fact."

It was at that moment that Sam's hunger caught up with his natural impatience. "All right, then," he said. "Best be movin' on. Nice to meet you, Mr. John."

"Why, it's been rightly my pleasure. Y'all come back here any ol' time, and I'll show you some more blues."

"I just may take you up on it," said Allan.

Proceeding on toward Alamo Plaza, the two brothers noticed several people giving them scowls for spending time talking to the Black vagrant. Allan never could understand the way so many white people felt about the negroes. His dad, on many occasions, played music with them and never spoke ill of them.

Chapter 2
1928

⌢

By the middle of Allan's junior year, he had become Harlandale's "Troubadour" — in demand for parties nearly every weekend. For the first time, he well and truly lost all self-consciousness regarding his limp. And that is when Allan's fortunes took an unexpected turn. He was approached to audition to sing and play guitar with a popular working band. Two weeks later, he started his first professional appearances in a trio called "The Moonlighters."

They played popular tunes and some blues songs Allan had learned from John Hurt. He could play and sing as well as many performers on the radio and records, and he believed this was his chance to demonstrate his skills professionally. It was the band's first time playing at The Embers, a dancehall frequented by mostly high-end clientele seeking out the new music or looking for a bit of "hootchie koo." There was plenty of booze being drunk in spite of Prohibition.

They arrived Saturday at dusk and offloaded their gear in the cool early November evening. It was the first hint that the hot weather was at last over before its all too rapid return in April. By the time they started their first song, the room was already three-quarters full of people keen to cut loose. They were on their feet and dancing in earnest by the third song and responding with enthusiastic applause after each number.

Allan had never performed before such a large adult crowd. He felt completely at ease and more confident with each song. This was the most thrilling experience of his life, and he knew that this was what he was made for.

As they finished the set, he caught the eye of a pretty redhead sitting at a table to the left of the stage. She seemed interested, smiling at him. Stepping down off the stage, he walked up to the table, interrupting a guy whispering to her.

"Howdy. Got any favorites I can do for you?"

"Well, shoot," said her date, "ain't that special? What do you want singer boy?" The man's glare burned from small dark eyes, reddened by drink and smoke. He was older than she and seething with menace.

"Pipe down, Benny!" said the girl. "I'm Amanda but call me Mandy. Just love the way you sing. Do you know 'S *Wonderful*?"

"I think we sorta' know it. See what we can do."

"Hey kid, beat it. You're too young to be here anyway," Benny snarled.

"Benny, be quiet."

"Long as we keep em coming in, the owner doesn't care," quipped Allan.

Sensing Benny's ire, Allan stepped out the back door where his bandmates were smoking and passing around a flask. They smiled and patted him on the back, welcoming him with compliments. Jig Adams the bass player and bandleader was effusive and chatty while Kurt the drummer kept his own counsel, rarely initiating conversation.

Jig handed him the flask. "Care for a nip? Might need some fortification for that redhead upfront. Been eyin' you all night, she has. Boyfriend ain't diggin' it either. Better look out for those older women...she's gotta be at least twenty. Bet she's a handful."

"No, thanks," said Allan. "Have to pass on the whiskey. Maybe the girl too. If I come home with booze on my breath, my mom won't let me out for gigs. As it is, she's not a big fan of this music. She wants me to be a classical guy like dad. Pretty thin ice already. Think I'll hit the bathroom and catch you on stage."

As he turned the corner into the men's room, Allan ran straight into the redhead's boyfriend on his way out.

"Well, what we got here? The singer boy. You best watch yourself padnah. Might end up with your head in the toilet. Stay away from my gal, hear?"

Allan felt adrenaline flood him. "Look, she wants a song, I sing her a song."

Benny grabbed him by the collar and threw him into the wall. Years of tussles with his older brother and all the things the boxers at Garza's gym had taught him suddenly took hold. Without thinking, Allan threw a left into his solar plexus and followed with a right uppercut, catching his jaw as he bent over. Benny rolled on the floor moaning as Allan rapidly headed for the bandstand. Seeing Randy, the bouncer, he stopped to tell him what had happened.

"Don't worry kid, I'll take care of it."

As they were getting ready to start the next song, he saw the bouncer drag Benny out of the bathroom and throw him in the alley. Mandy rose to leave with her friends, but on her way out, she surreptitiously dropped a note on the stage in front of Allan.

When the last song ended, he quickly picked up the beer-dampened paper. "I work at Joskes in the women's wear department. I get off at five. Meet me Tuesday after work."

"Hey there, stud," teased Jig. "Looks like the older gal's got a thing for our rising star."

Allan blushed. "Knock it off. 'Sides, I don't have a lot of extra time and, for sure, no car, so she'll lose interest even if I do meet her."

"Don't be too sure...probably got herself a nest you could bed down in. Hot little Chickadee. Have some fun, man. Gonna be a lot more where that came from. We could be playing on the radio here soon. Be playin' live just like they do in New York and St. Louis. Think we're goin' places."

Kurt uncharacteristically chimed in as he was sitting down behind his drums for the last set. "Only place I wanna be going is Mi Tierra for some enchiladas."

The crowd was well lit with bootleg and danced with abandon in the smokey haze. The trio played their best three songs at the last and took one encore before finishing to rousing applause. Allan was spent but ecstatic.

As the room began to empty, they broke down their equipment. Allan helped carry the gear to Jig's Ford panel truck, already partly filled with plumbing tools for his day job. Allan's bad leg ached from standing on stage for three sets and carrying equipment. His knuckles were also sore from the uppercut to Benny's chin.

"Hey, maybe I need to get home. Mom said don't stay out long after the gig."

"Ain't no problem," said Jig. "Have you home in a jiffy. Right after we eat. Were takin' you to get Mex."

Mariachi music wafted over Market Square. At 1:00 a.m., it was nearly as busy as at noon. Exotic spice-scented air drifted from Mi Tierra, growing stronger as they neared the entrance. A stout Mexican with a huge handlebar mustache greeted them at the door.

"*Señor Jig...Que pasa, hombre?*"

"Nada, Carlos. Got a table for us?"

"*Cierto amigo...Pase.*"

He led them to a booth in the corner. The adjacent booth was occupied by a well-dressed and drunk gringo with a hot little señorita, likely a hooker, draped all over him. The booth across from them held three young Pachuco gang members, loaded and looking for trouble.

Mi Tierra was open 24 hours daily. This time of morning one could rub shoulders with every level of San Antonio culture. It was as close to going to Mexico as you could get north of the Rio Grande.

An overly painted middle-aged waitress dropped menus on the table. "*Que queres a beber?*"

Jig patted the flask in his coat pocket. "*Agua y cafe para nosotros por favor.* Gotta offset the lightning I got with a little coffee. Call it Irish/Mexican coffee."

"Hang on," said Allan. "I told you I can't go home with booze on my breath."

"Ya gotta enjoy the moment, man. We had a great night. Nobody messed up…you wowed 'em,'specially the redhead. And we got paid twenty bucks. That's five dollars each and ten for me as the leader. Hey man, live a little." Jig smiled with teeth resembling a picket fence that a herd of cattle had broken through.

Why not, he thought. *I'm out with the musicians.* His dad always drank—in fact, he drank a lot. Especially when he sat around jamming for hours with his fellow musicians.

Allan knew of his mother's dismay at his father's drinking. Sam was never mean or sloppy. Sometimes a little maudlin, but never obviously in his cups. Nonetheless, Allan had seen the concern on her face.

Allan felt grown up, exhilarated, yet still filled with a niggling trepidation. He was a working musician. He was his father's son. Wherever that river took him, he was well and truly bound to follow the current. He took a drink.

Allan noticed a trio of mariachis drifting their way. A tall thin guitar player, obviously the leader, stopped at their table, the other guitarist and the guitarrón player arriving as bookends either side.

"*Queres un canción amigos?*"

"Shoot, yeah," said Jig.

They began to play a song Allan had never heard. It had a plaintive melody with recurring chorus: "Cooo-ko roo-koo roo, Paloma." Their harmonies poured like warm honey over his heart. There was something ineffably sad and happy about the song at the same time. Although different from the blues of John Hurt, it had the same poignant pull, achingly sweet yet melancholy. Their music touched off a spark in him, illuminating him with a soft warm glow. Even the rough bunch in the booth across from them were caught in the web of it. *God*, he thought, *I love this moment. This music.* The waitress arrived as the song ended.

"*Que queres ala comida?*"

"*Enchiladas para mi,*" said Jig.

"The same," Kurt replied.

"Sure, me too," Allan added.

Jig tipped the mariachis, declining another song. As he and Kurt engaged in a postmortem of the night's performance, Allan sat back in the booth, relishing his autonomy, his part in this world of adults. Reaching beneath the table, he surreptitiously took the flask which they all shared in turn, followed by a sip of the water. A waiter passed them with a cast iron skillet of steaming fajitas. He savored the scent of seared meat, onions, and jalapeño as he took in the room.

Although Christmas was long past, strings of colorful lights stretched along the walls just below the ceiling. Piñatas in pastel hues swayed gently in the muggy, fan-blown air. One o'clock in the morning and few empty tables. The music from three separate groups of mariachis competed with conversation and raucous laughter.

"Hey, man, where you at?" quipped Jig to Allan. "See somethin' you like? Cute señoritas over in the booth by the door."

"Naw, just taking it all in. Wow, Jig, don't think I ever felt so free. When is our next performance?"

"Couple of weeks we got a good payin' gig at a wedding for some Alamo Heights swells. Tell you what, I think The Moonlighters are headed for some good times."

Nearly two hours later, Jig deposited Allan at home. He did his best to be stealthy but that one loose board on the porch betrayed him with a rude squeak. The door was locked and by the time he found the keyhole, it swung inward. His mother stood there glaring.

"Know what time it is, young man?"

"Ah…think maybe three?"

"Which would be two hours later than I told you to be in, correct?"

"Yes, ma'am."

"I know all about musicians so I'm way ahead of you. If you want to continue performing, you had best abide by the rules. You are not a grown man, so until that time, you will adhere to them… understood?"

"Yes, ma'am."

"Fine. Try not to wake your brother when you go to bed."

"Yes, ma'am."

Even at this tender hour, he was still too amped up to sleep. Plopping himself down on the living room couch, he shrugged off her scolding, savoring his night singing with a real band at The Embers. Allan was sure that he was the only one there under eighteen and probably the youngest musician to have played there.

In the quiet sanctum, visions of big stages with huge audiences, him in the spotlight, beckoned. He could hear the breeze caressing the big live oak in the front yard. A dog barked, but all else lay still, save the torrent of visions that bore him away. His father had been teaching violin at Peacock Academy and performing at seventeen. Allan felt sure that were he in Allan's place, he'd be out playing this popular stuff and not just the old classical pieces.

There was a scent of change in the air as sweet as mesquite smoke at a barbecue. The new music was the increasingly popular jazz of mostly Negro musicians. New Orleans, Saint Louis, New York, all were the creative hotbeds of a new, exciting life. Young people were flocking to cities for jobs, excitement, and escape from the drudgery of country life. Radio stations were broadcasting this new music and radios allowed them to hear all the music, as well as news, radio plays and other entertainment. Prohibition had little power to prohibit the dreams of excitement waiting in the cities.

Exhaustion finally felled him. Allan brushed his teeth and climbed as quietly as he could into the top bunk of the trundle bed above his sleeping brother. In that twilight between wakefulness and the land of twisted faces, Allan saw himself dressed in a tux, singing in a sound studio at a radio station. One day...one day. But then there was his mother.

Georgia gave no quarter when it came to lessons and practice. As Allan grew in his skills, she recognized that there was the potential for him to be a great baritone. She had a vision of her son with a withered leg, becoming an opera star or, at the very least, a concert guitarist. That was her dream.

But it wasn't Allan's. The same mother who empowered, encouraged, and drove him to ever newer heights was becoming the greatest impediment to his own dreams.

—

GEORGIA'S PARAKEETS AND CANARIES were cacophonous. His brother was already up, chatting away in the kitchen. Groggy from the drink and lateness of the prior night, Allan was in no hurry to get out of bed. He would have rather drawn the covers over himself and returned to the lovely dream he had been enjoying. But the smell of bacon wafting through the house finally gave him the impetus to rise and face the day.

"Pleased you could join us," said his brother.

Allan sat without answering.

His father put down the Sunday *Express*. "How was the performance last night?"

"Ah, it was alright. As Jig put it, 'Nobody got kilt.'"

"Were you happy with your work?"

"Yeah, I guess. Seems the only things that I remember are the mistakes."

"That's the way of it. We are our own worst critics, which is, in part, good. Makes us work harder, practice more. But there is a point at which you have to be willing to forgive yourself the mistakes. Perfectionism can become tyranny. You can end up so focused on perfection that you perform self-consciously for fear of mistakes. The truth is that there *is* no true perfection. We get close when we develop our skills. But as you grow, the more you come to realize how much there is that you haven't yet achieved. That's the beauty of the music. It's an endless river that, if you let it, sweeps you away to places you have never been. But arriving at perfection…? It is the voyage that matters."

Allan's dad folded his paper. "So, if you will excuse me, I will get dressed for church. Oh, by the way, darlin', some of my friends from the vaudeville show are coming 'round this evening after dinner. Have a little jam session after their performance. You kids are welcome to hang around. Some good players and maybe a singer named Eddie Cantor, I believe as well. They say is very good. Should be fun."

The older Sam's chair squeaked like a struck dog as he unfolded his angular six-foot-two-inch frame like a concertina. Allan loved his father's fluid movement, his walk drifting ghost-like, as if he was walking on deep Persian carpets. Sam was self-effacing, rarely noticing his own reflection, uncomfortable with compliments. His wavy brown hair, hazel eyes, and chiseled cheekbones drew women's attention. He seemed oblivious.

People were calling his father a genius. His violin playing was already gaining widespread acclaim. Now in his first position as concertmaster, he was being watched in anticipation of positions with larger orchestras. Yet he preferred the company of boxers, bartenders, and musicians to the society mavens who funded the symphony. And he loved San Antonio.

Sam would no doubt spend hours tonight drinking, playing, laughing with the rowdy touring group from the vaudeville show. Prestige seemed not to matter a wit to him. He frequently brought home musicians to jam with, exploring jazz, blues, and popular tunes which he seemed to enjoy as much as the classical music he played.

His mother, on the other hand, held the classical music world in high esteem. She had grown up in the home of the most prosperous ship chandlery owner in Galveston. Her vision of proper music was clearly and narrowly defined. She had little time for the jazz her husband dabbled in, nor the nonsense her son was wasting his time on. She saw Allan's talent as way to achievements that would eclipse his physical disability. Always there flowed the undercurrent of her ambitions being roiled by countercurrents of this silly new popular music that seemed to infect both her son and husband.

—

EVERY WINDOW WAS THROWN wide to allow the evening breeze. The curtains caught the last pink light, casting a roseate glow over the players. Allan sat in the corner watching as the musicians tuned to the notes struck on the piano in the parlor.

The room was already hazy with cigar and cigarette smoke. Without preamble, the piano player kicked off a rolling barrelhouse bassline with his left, followed by a syncopated countermelody with his right hand. The bassist waited to catch the groove and dropped in. The guitarist joined in with some kind of crazy chords riding a rolling strum, and then his dad drew his bow across the violin strings.

Allan was mesmerized. The group established a melody and then took turns riffing variations on it. It was infectious, hilarious, joyful. He closed his eyes and beat out a rhythm on the arms of the chair. Whatever this stuff was, he wanted more of it. When at last they ended, he took a few moments to come to himself.

"Jeepers!" he blurted.

A few beats of silence then everyone broke out laughing.

"What was that song?" he asked.

The piano player took the cigar out of his mouth, smiled at Allan. "Don't have a name. Just came on us. Is what it is."

His dad laughed and took another sip of whiskey. "My boy here is a budding guitarist and singer. Plays in a trio. Does some popular stuff. His mom wants him to be a classical man, so you boys may be a bad influence."

For the next few hours, the walls reverberated with music and Allan marinated in the rich melodious stew. Whereas classical music could take him to an ethereal realm, this music pulled him along in a current of childlike fun. It was a non-stop sonorous celebration. He knew he was hooked, wanted to play like that, wanted to sing along with it.

Allan became aware of his mother's presence in the arched entrance to the parlor. She was not smiling. It took a few minutes before his father, now well into his cups, noticed her.

"Well, hello, Georgia. Ain't we just kickin' up some dust!"

Georgia smirked. "Yes, Sam, you most certainly are. Would you think me inconsiderate if I suggest that you enjoy some conversation with your friends? It's getting a little late and perhaps our neighbors might appreciate some quieter pursuits."

"Why, yes, dear. I believe we were just getting ready for a break. Would you be so kind as to bring another bottle from my cupboard?"

Allan saw the look. She would fetch the whiskey politely, but her tight jaw was a dead giveaway as to her true feelings. Then she turned her gaze on her son. "I think it's time for you to round yourself up for bed. Say goodnight to your dad's friends. I'll see you in your room."

He wanted to stay and join in the camaraderie of the musicians, but he knew that was out of the question. "Thanks for letting me listen," he said to the musicians. "It was something else. Goodnight, gentlemen, I really enjoyed your music. Goodnight, Dad."

With great reluctance, still floating, he headed for bed, knowing sleep would be slow in arriving.

———

IT WASN'T JUST THE smell of burnt biscuits. The normally voluble breakfast chatter was missing. Silence hung like ground fog—the only chatter was from the canaries and parakeets. His mother's slight frame was hunched over a tray of bacon and eggs she was placing before his dad, brother, and sister. She spoke without looking at him. "Slept in after your big night with the musicians?"

"Ah, yes, ma'am."

"It's a good thing you are awake. I was going to roust you, this being a school day."

His dad caught his eye and gave him the merest grin.

His elder sister Louise joined in support of their mother and couldn't resist. "Hope you finished your homework. Two weeks before final exams." She was an imperious one, he thought, bossing him around.

Last night, he had tasted something intoxicating. He felt it still. Like a sailor called to the sea, he wanted to set sail to the far shores of where the music took him. That spontaneous joy he had witnessed as the players created music that had never existed before nor would ever be repeated called to him.

"If you will excuse me, I will repair to the study to work on arranging the Mendelssohn score." His father rose without looking at his mother. Yet the disconnect between them hung in the air like the carbon stench of the burnt biscuits.

"Allan." His mother gave him the look he knew too well, the one that meant he was going to be tasked with something she had decided that he was required to do.

"I have arranged for you to take opera lessons this summer from Miss Spoetzal. We will begin week after next, Tuesdays and Thursdays."

"But...but...we practice on Tuesday nights."

"That will not be a problem. She will see you at three in the afternoon."

"I'm already taking classical guitar from Mister Garcia on Wednesdays. How am I supposed to learn and practice what he shows me, plus the opera stuff, and still have time to rehearse with the band?"

"You will focus on the lessons. The band is but a lark. You don't want to end up playing in some vaudeville pit band. You have gifts that are destined for better things."

He stared at his uneaten bacon and eggs, torn between obedience and passion. She had slaved over him during his rehabilitation, driven him, encouraged, cajoled, and demanded that he strive through the pain, suffer whatever was needed to improve. Now for the first time he saw a divergent path from the road upon which she had placed him. Before he realized what he was about, he was speaking.

"I'm sorry, Mother, but I won't be able to do both the guitar and voice lessons. I have a band to sing with and that matters most to me."

Sensing the approaching squall line, his brother and sister excused themselves, leaving the two of them in the murky silence.

She spoke slowly in a low voice, always a bad sign. "I have not spent all these years helping you become what you are capable of being to no avail. You think those cigar smoking drunks banging away last night are something to aspire to? I will not have it. If you do not take these lessons, I will no longer allow this nonsense with your little band to continue. If you can become as accomplished in classical music as your father, then like him, you can play about with others. I am committed to your future, and you will do as I say as long as you live under our roof."

He started to argue but he hadn't the words to express his perplexity and frustration.

"May I be excused?"

"You haven't eaten a bite."

"I have to get ready for school."

"Off you go, then."

He fumed as he brushed his hair, steamed as he put on his shoes. With every step on the way to school he tried to untangle his knotted feelings. He was sixteen, almost seventeen. Boys a year older had gone off to fight in the war and he was being treated like a child.

He decided he needed to talk to his dad and get his perspective. Perhaps he could sort it all out. After all, he was a musician. At least his dad would understand. Allan felt better and prepared to face the challenges awaiting him at school, not the least of which was the usual pack of bullies, no doubt even now working up new torments for him to endure.

—

THE SCHOOL DAY DRAGGED. He could barely pay attention in class thinking about Mandy. He was to meet her after she got off work that afternoon. Did she really mean what she said in the note she'd left on the stage? Would she think him a silly young fool in the cold light of day? His stomach churned at the thought of it, but he would be there. Even if it cost him.

He was supposed to study with Miss Spoetzal, the voice coach, after school. Georgia would be furious if she knew about his assignation. He had no choice. Every time he pictured Mandy with her red hair and green eyes, her sly grin, her long white neck, her ample curves, his breath quickened. Finally, after an interminable length of time, the final bell rang.

Now he had an hour and a half to kill. He decided to stop and watch the fighters at Garza's gym, might even see his brother there. Afterward, he would head over to Joskes to meet Mandy.

Allan loved to walk downtown by the Alamo Plaza. He could smell the Mexican food from the Chili Queen's carts. Somewhere a woman was singing a Mexican folk song accompanied by the rhythm of trolley wheels clicking along the tracks. He opened the door at Garza's and the rat-a-tat-tat of a speedbag grew louder as he descended the stairs. Nothing else smelled like this. Sweat soaked canvas, mixed with leather, blood, and tears.

Two boxers, a white boy and a Mexican, were going at it in the ring. It took him a minute to realize the white boy with the black headgear was his brother Sam. The Mexican had a quick vicious left jab and Sam was eating a good bit of leather, standing in the middle of the ring trading punches. The problem was, he was missing most of the punches he threw, as his opponent bobbed and weaved. Bobby Garza yelled out, "Move your head, use your jab, Sam."

As if from nowhere, Sam landed a solid right cross followed by a left to the body that dropped his opponent to the canvas. The bell rang and Sam helped the other fighter up.

"Sorry, didn't mean to hit you so hard."

"Forget it, man, it's what you're supposed to do. But I'll give you a taste next time."

They struck gloves and Sam climbed down through the ropes. Garza unlaced his gloves and poured out nonstop advice. Finishing his instructions to Sam, he greeted Allan, then was off to work with another fighter.

"Wow, you looked great in there. You nailed him!"

"I got lucky. He landed twice as many punches, and I did a lousy job of moving and defense. I've just got heavy hands and saw an opening. I've got a lot to learn. What are you doing here? Don't you have a lesson or something?"

"Well...you see...I'm sorta going to see a girl instead."

"Are you crazy? Mom will kill you if you miss." His brother shook his head. "So who is the mystery woman you are risking your life for?"

"Her name is Mandy. She works at Joskes and gets off at five. She was at our gig last weekend and asked me to meet her."

"Hope she's a beauty since you are going to catch hell for it."

"Oh, she is. A redhead with green eyes."

"Anything I can to do cover for you?"

"Don't think so. I'll be home for dinner. In fact, I should probably get going. It's after 4:30 and it's at least a fifteen-minute walk."

"Well, good luck, my little Valentino. I want all the details when you get home. That is, if you survive."

"Don't mention you saw me."

"Oh, believe me, I don't want any part of this little mess."

Allan walked up the stairs and onto Houston Street, his breath quickening. He wasn't really sure what to expect but the possibilities made his heart race. Allan arrived a few minutes early and sat outside the Menger Hotel, watching the front door of Joskes Department Store, scanning the departing shoppers and workers for a girl with red hair.

And suddenly there she was, laughing and chatting with another girl. He wasn't really sure of the protocol so he forced himself to intercept her as she crossed over to his side of the street.

"Hey...I...Do you remember me? From the Embers? You left me a—"

"Of course," she said. "I wasn't sure you'd come after all that nonsense with Benny and our being asked to leave. I'm so glad you came. Tell you what, we'll go to the Menger Bar and see what we might cook up for some fun. They only serve Coke and stuff, but I have a little juice in my purse."

"Oh yeah...great...I mean...well, sure."

"The bartender's a friend and he won't even ask."

Grabbing him by the hand, she led him through the doors of the Menger and down the hall to The Rough Rider Bar. Allan had never been inside but had always wanted to see the place where Teddy Roosevelt had held court and recruited men for his Rough Riders during the Spanish-American War.

The smoke hung at head level, a thick mixture of cigars and cigarettes. There were more men than women, but it seemed a lively and jovial group. Allan was surprised by how small the place was. In his imagination, he had visualized high ceilings, chandeliers, elegant furnishings. Instead, it was small, dark, with very low ceilings. The crowd filled every available space. The dark wood paneling reflected little light, giving it a cave-like aura. Not even the massive mirror behind the bar helped to expand the perceived size.

Mandy waved to a couple of girls sitting at a small table while several men turned toward her as she approached the bar. The bartender smiled and came over to greet her, though the smile was mostly lost in his enormous handlebar mustache.

"Howdy. How's my favorite redhead?"

"I'm fine, sugar. But I'd be better with a Coke and a glass with a little ice and room for something extra, and whatever my friend here is having. Let me introduce you to Allan Ezell. The dreamiest singer in San Antonio. He sings over at the Embers with his band. He's the bee's knees!"

He looked at Allan with a raised eyebrow for a few seconds.

"Okay. Name's Lefty. What's your poison?"

"Same as what she's havin'."

"Comin' right up."

Mandy eased up close, sliding her arm through his and whispering. "Maybe we could grab a taco from one of the chili queens and take it to my apartment for dinner. My roommate's gone for the next couple of days. We can get to know each other better."

Allan felt himself redden. He wanted to be a part of all this grown-up world but suddenly felt lost at sea. Still, he had put himself here and if he was going be a sophisticate he would have to figure out what he was supposed to say next.

"Here ya go. Enjoy." The bartender winked as he placed the drinks in front of them.

"Whoopee!" Mandy took her glass, pulled a flask of bootleg gin from her bag, pouring two fingers, filling the rest of the glass with Coke. She smiled expectantly at him.

It took him a few beats to realize he was supposed to pick up his glass so she could pour gin into it.

"Oh, yeah. Cheers," he blurted as he raised his glass.

"So tell me, handsome, you got a girl?"

"Ah...no not at the moment."

"Well, ain't that grand. I just gave Benny the bum's rush. Guess we're free to explore the possibilities."

Allan took a large gulp of his drink, nearly choking on it. Mandy's perfume began to envelop him, her gauzy tan blouse revealing a hint of cleavage.

"So you like that idea?"

"Gee, that would be dandy."

As soon as the words left his mouth, he felt foolish. But he remembered that she had sought him out and he was in fact a good singer. So who cared if he was just short of seventeen? If boys his age could go to war, he could be in a bar with a pretty girl and go to her apartment, and what would be would be.

Mandy stroked his cheek and whispered, "Why don't you settle up and let's skedaddle."

It had not occurred to him until this moment that he would have to pay the tab. Cokes were three times as expensive at the Menger. He had more than enough—the problem was that he was supposed to pay for voice lessons which, at this very moment he was missing. Tipsy from the drinks, he quickly dismissed his concerns, paid the tab, and left the bartender a generous tip as well.

As they wove across Alamo Plaza, they stopped to buy tacos from a food stand. Ten minutes later, they were entering Mandy's small guest cottage behind a stately home with columns in the King William district.

As the door opened, Allan took in his surroundings. Two bedrooms and a small kitchen/dining/living area. It smelled of old grease and new perfume. Clean dishes sat in the drying rack. There was no clutter other than house slippers by the door.

Yet there was an aura of something exotic, an enticing essence of femininity. It made his breath short and his heartbeat quick. He'd never been in a woman's place.

Allan felt her slide up behind him, encircling him in her arms, feeling her breath on his neck. Then he sensed something else. It was not a voice, more a cautionary feeling. He couldn't justify what he was doing. He was breaking so many rules. But his senses and body were intoxicated. He longed for the promise of all the unspoken fantasies roaming the dark corners of his dreams. Everything he had been taught—his faith, family—all of it now seemed so unimportant. All that mattered was this moment.

He turned to her. Her green eyes locked onto his and he found her lips, her tongue probing his own. It was like the waves in which he had frolicked on Padre Island, dragging him under, tossing him about, thrilling him with a vague fear of drowning, yet knowing he'd survive.

He had never experienced such passion. He willingly succumbed. All the teaching, all the obedience, all the still small voice was whispering…all lost in the mad rushing surge of the moment with Mandy. Then it was over.

It was like the stories of the hurricane his mother had told him. Furious screaming torrential rain and wind…and then calm. He lay in the quiet eye of the storm. Her warm skin, their sweat commingling, their breath rising and falling in unison, bathed him in a warm broth of timelessness, forgetfulness, blissfulness. But somewhere deep in his consciousness he sensed the eyewall of the storm approaching. Even as Mandy stroked his chest and kissed his ear, as he succumbed to the glory of the moment, he could hear the wind rising in the distance.

He awoke realizing he had fallen asleep, and it was now dark. The whisper of Mandy's breath as she slept was the only sound. He looked around the room for a clock, heard one ticking, but could not see the time in the darkness. With elegant effort, he slid his arm from beneath her head in a way that would have made a snake proud. Stealthily creeping, he found the clock, pulled back the curtain, and in the twilight saw to his horror that it was almost eight o'clock.

His life was over. The storm named Georgia was building up even now and there would be no escaping the devastation.

Quietly gathering his clothes, he dressed in silence. Should he leave a note, wake her to say goodbye? In turmoil he quietly slipped out the door into the muggy gloaming.

He had a forty-minute walk ahead of him. Were it not for his afflicted limb, he could do it in thirty. Striking off as fast as he could manage, his thoughts were as imbalanced as his gait. His mind was a miasma of exaltation and recrimination, satisfaction, and loss.

He was at war with himself. All the while he had been with Mandy, a soft whisper in his ear murmured... *Is this right?* So distracted was he that he nearly stepped out in front of a Pearl Beer truck. The evening was still tepid as the day's heat relinquished its grip. Sweat from exertion and emotions conspired to soak him within the first five minutes.

Lost in a stew of feelings, he was surprised to find himself standing before his front door. Heading in stealth toward his room he saw the one thing he most dreaded—Georgia sat at her pedal sewing machine, mending one of the endless articles of clothing needing repair. Her eyes lifted from the cloth before her, focused on him.

Time took a breath. As with a lit fuse on a firecracker, so the anticipation simultaneously sped up and slowed down. The explosion came in stages. First Georgia arose, removing her spectacles, and stared at him, mouth thin as a thread. "I'm certain you have a compelling reason for missing dinner and arriving home at this late hour. One would hope it revolves around the inspired time you had learning how to sing with Miss Spoetzal. However, my intuition leads me to believe otherwise."

His heart raced like a captured rabbit's. His mouth was so dry from drink and fear he hardly trusted himself to speak. He had but two choices: fact or fabrication. "It was awful, Mom. If you could have seen poor Billy, you'd have done the same thing.

"He was crossing the street and didn't look both ways, like you taught me. Next thing, he gets hit by an automobile. He wasn't terribly injured but I think he may have some broken ribs and he is bruised like anything. The man driving the car offered to take him to the hospital. By the time we got there and Billy was seen to, it was already dark. So I headed home. But it was a long walk and I don't walk so fast."

"Who is this Billy? I don't recall you mentioning him."

"He's just a guy I know from school. Don't know him well. He's a couple of grades below me. But he recognized me and called out for help, so I felt I had to come to his aid."

He was shocked at the ease with which he wove the lie. There was not one scintilla of fact involved, yet it sprang whole cloth to his mind. The thought of facing the truth and the consequences of it were untenable, so he plowed on.

"Oh, yeah, I missed my voice lesson because of all of this. I was on my way there when it happened."

She appraised him in silence. He was glad he was already sweaty from the long walk. Hopefully, she wouldn't notice his nervousness or smell the booze on his breath. He moved toward the chair furthest from his mother, hoping the distance would put her out of olfactory range, but caught the musky scent lingering on him from his evening with Mandy.

Pursing her lips into the crumpled shape of a prune, Georgia considered all she had been told.

30

"Very well, I guess there was nothing else you could've done."

He felt the freedom of a prisoner released.

"Well give me back the money for the lessons. I will re-schedule although I know she will be quite put out at the missed lesson."

Caught off guard, he quickly blurted out.

"Oh, that is the other thing. I forgot the money, left it in my room. Just a sec and I'll get it for you."

Taking the opportunity for flight this afforded, he rushed to his room, retrieving money from a cigar box in which he saved the earnings from his singing jobs.

She was waiting with an unnerving calm. Like two headlamps on a new Model T, her eyes cut through his haze as she quietly regarded him. He heard his dad practicing violin in the study. Heard the neighbor's dog barking, heard his heart rattling as she stared mercilessly at him. He handed her the money which she accepted silently.

"It is remarkable that the very thing you wanted to avoid was spared you because of a tragedy. I suppose opera is largely about tragedy so perhaps you can use this experience to help you emote in the great singing you will learn. Now clean up and go to bed."

He crept into the room he shared with his brother, hoping he was asleep. It was not to be.

"Ah the distant wanderer home at last. So let's hear it, how did it go?"

He was torn between braggadocio with respect to his first romantic conquest, and what would happen if the truth were revealed. Sam had always been good about keeping secrets. He had to talk to someone, and his big brother seemed the best option.

"Okay. Here's the deal. If you ever tell anyone and I mean ANYONE, I will share the little tidbit about you and pastor McGee's daughter after the football game with Alamo Heights last year."

"Wha...how the...what are you talking about?'

"Two love birds in a rumble seat under a pecan tree in Brackenridge Park."

"Who told you about that?"

"Jesse Brown and some friends were just down from you having a little get together. Curiosity got the better of them. I made him swear to keep quiet."

"Mum's the word, I promise."

"You remember the girl from the gig who left me a note to meet her after work?"

"Oh, yeah, the redhead."

"Well, I spent the evening at her place and…oh, my."

—

IN EARLY MARCH BY fortuitous chance, Allan arrived home within minutes of his father returning after a performance. Allan and the Moonlighters had sung at a private party at a big ranch estate outside San Antonio. It was after one in the morning, and both seemed relieved that Georgia wasn't awake to greet them. The fact was they were both a bit lit.

The dynamic between them had grown into a hybrid of father/son and fellow musician. As Allan's reputation had grown, his dad had heard good reports about his son's talent. Sam went to the bookcase and pulled two volumes of Shakespeare from the shelf, removing a bottle of whiskey hidden behind them. "Just between us kids," he said with a wry smile, winking as he pulled the cork out with his teeth. He took a dirty glass that sat on the coffee table, cleaned it with his handkerchief, and poured two fingers. "How'd it go tonight, son?"

"Well, it was kinda' crazy to tell the truth. The host had gotten hold of a case of tequila smuggled in from Mexico. By the second set, the party crowd was well-lubricated. We were in the groove and we got them to cutting the rug like anything. We were outside on a huge patio on the top of a hill surrounded by a rock wall. Some gal was dancing on the wall and fell into a cactus. Next thing I knew she had her dress off and was being attended to by several willing thorn pullers." Allan shook his head. "That was before the piñata got broke. The host had filled it with Mexican candies and beaded necklaces. Two of the flappers got into a catfight over the baubles. The crowd cheered as they tore each other's dresses to shreds. That's when we took a long break."

"That sounds more entertaining than our concert," said his father. "At least these boom times are funding the symphony and we have a busy season ahead. I've put away a bit even after buying your mom the Frigidaire and I figure with the symphony pay I can buy a new Ford, maybe before Christmas."

They sat down in the living room, lit only by the streetlights and a shaft falling from the kitchen. In the companionable silence, they listened to the peepers and crickets singing in the big oak in the front yard. They shared the post-performance comedown, as the adrenaline seeped from their tissues. Sam struck a match with his thumbnail and lit his pipe, setting shadows dancing in the brief flare. Allan took a long slow sip of the bootleg whisky.

"Dad, can I talk to you about something?"

"Well, of course, son. That is what I'm here for."

"It's like this. I know you and Mom want me to go to the university in Austin to study music. But I don't know if I've got it in me. The only time I really feel alive is when I'm singing, and I don't mean opera stuff." He took a deep breath. "It's not that I don't like the classical music. I do. I've learned a lot from my voice lessons and it's made me a better singer. But what really gets me is the jazz and blues stuff, especially what the Black cats are doing. I think that I can sing as well as the guys on recordings—at least that's what people are telling me, even musicians. And we're going to get a shot on KTSA—the radio station—soon and there will be a lot more opportunities since radio is taking off. Stations are going to be popping up like dandelions. I just have a feeling about it. So here's the thing…Mom will have a conniption fit if I head off to pursue this in New York or wherever instead of going to college.

"You must have felt like this when you were young. You followed your music and you have done well. Surely you can make her see that it's better for me. Who knows, maybe I'll end up singing opera if this doesn't pan out."

Sam's pipe glowed as he took a deep drag and blew smoke rings into semi-darkness. He ran his fingers through his hair and sighed, savoring another sip of whiskey. "You know it's gonna tear her up if you leave. But I'd be lying if I didn't admit that I know how you feel.

"It was different for me. I just took to the violin. Came as naturally for me as running does for horses. Next thing I knew I was teaching at Peacock Academy and getting offers from orchestras. It just sort of picked me up in the current and swept me on. My folks were happy with the free college and paid performances. Didn't really have to think about it. I couldn't conceive of doing anything else. The Lord gave me a gift and blessed me by letting me earn a living playing music. So yes, I understand. But, what's your plan? Do you have one? Might be a bit rough striking out to New York without having some contacts and a place to land."

"Well, there just may be an opportunity for me. A friend of mine knows a fella in an up-and-coming band, The Russel Rhodes Orchestra. They are looking for a male vocalist and my friend thinks he can get me an audition." Allan leaned toward his father. "And here's the really great part. They are going to be traveling and performing at dance halls all over Texas, Oklahoma, and Louisiana. Then maybe St. Louis. There is a great jazz scene in St. Louis, and I hear there are some new sounds coming from guys blending blues and jazz. That's why I need your help. If they offer me the job, Dad… well…I'm going no matter what. Even though I've only been with The Moonlighters for a few months I know I'm ready."

His father chewed on the end of his pipe. "You probably know this. I've told you enough times how proud I am of you and what a fine singer I think you are. Thing is, being in a traveling band at your age can be pretty rough. But you have my blessing. I know you will do well. You have the looks, personality, and a great voice. I too believe that radio is going to change things and especially how people get to listen to music.

"If you get the job, give me a couple of days to talk to your mother. I'm not saying this will be painless. She will be crestfallen that her budding opera star won't be singing La Traviata at the Met. But I believe I can bring her around. And frankly, I'm a wee bit envious of your dreams and the excitement that awaits you. I will also be praying for guidance through all the trials and pitfalls that come with the territory."

—

ALLAN'S BEST FRIEND, JESSIE Brown, drove him to the Gunter, one of San Antonio's finest hotels. The audition was at three p.m. As they drew near the hotel, he became anxious. Who was he, at his young age, to presume he would out-perform older, more experienced singers?

The convertible top was down, the houses and buildings flew past in a soupy haze. He saw the new Tower Life building in the distance and before he knew it, they were pulling up in front of the Gunter.

"There she is, padnah. I know you'll knock 'em dead. Go get 'em."

They entered the sparkling lobby and inquired about the location of the Grand Ballroom. The clerk called a bellman who led them up a broad curved staircase to the mezzanine floor. Nearing the ballroom, they heard a piano. When they entered the cavernous room, they took in a sweeping bar, numerous tables, and a bandstand large enough for a full orchestra. Only a piano player and one other man on the stage.

The smaller of them turned at their approach. He was wearing a blue and white seersucker suit, no tie and torturing a very large cigar held between his full lips. Lifting a bushy brow, he said with a slight grin, "Ah, the next pretender to the throne has arrived."

Not quite sure how to respond, Allan hesitantly replied. "Yes, sir. I'm Allan Ezell. We are a little early. Sorry. We can wait if you're not ready. This is my friend Jessie. He drove me. He's not a musician."

The man slowly appraised him with a slight smile and removed the cigar. "Howdy, I'm Russell Rhodes. What do you think, Jake? We ready to hear from young Mister Ezell?"

The large Black man at the keyboards smiled widely. "Yassah, I believe we is purdy much always ready for de next star to be risen on up." He looked down at Allan, cocked his head, and took him in. "He be a handsome young buck. He able to sing as good as he look, well den, might jes got us a new singer for dis here band."

"Got something in particular you want to sing?" asked Russell.

"Yes, sir. I brought music for *You Took Advantage of Me, With a Song in My Heart,* and *The Birth of the Blues.* But I can sing whatever you would like."

Rhodes turned to the piano player. "Jake, do you need the sheet music to accompany Mr. Ezell?"

"Nope, don't need it."

"Well then, step on up here."

Russell noticed Allan's limp as he climbed the four steps up to the stage. "Hurt your leg?"

"No, sir. Had polio when I was little. But it doesn't bother me."

"Fine then. It don't bother me as long as you can sing. Need to warm up?"

"I guess I'm alright if you want to begin."

"What would you like to start with?"

"*The Birth of the Blues,* I guess."

"What key?" asked Jake.

"G would be good."

"*Blues* in G it is."

Jake began the intro with a strong left hand bass line underlying the melody. Allan liked the feel of it. He waited for his cue and started to sing. All of his nervousness and insecurity vanished as soon as he began. He closed his eyes and bonded with the piano, rode it like sitting a frisky stallion. By the time the bridge arrived he was well and truly lost in the song, and as quickly as it had begun, it was over.

Russell took the cigar out of his mouth and looked at Allan for several beats. He turned to look at Jake and they exchanged a few silent gazes. "That was not bad, son. Let's see what else you've got."

"Okay. Can you play *With A Song In My Heart* in D?"

"Sho nuff," said Jake, and he began the intro.

Allan liked to sing this song and now felt completely within himself, enjoying the moment and the interaction with such an exceptionally good accompanist. When he finished and opened his eyes, they were both staring at him with grinning faces. They turned to look at each other and Jake gave an almost imperceptible nod to Rhodes. "Let's hear one more," said the band leader.

Allan sang his last song and the room rested in silence.

"As fate would have it," said Rhodes, "you are the last audition. Give us a moment to confer. Jake, would you care to join me for a few minutes?"

"After you, boss."

As they exited backstage, Allan breathed deeply, turning to Jessie, who was smiling like the Cheshire Cat. Somewhere deep inside, Allan knew his life was getting ready for a big change.

Fifteen minutes passed. He wandered around the room, looking at the set up for the band on stage, catching his reflection in the room length mirror behind the bar. He looked so young yet felt so much older than his peers.

These last months singing with The Moonlighters had opened a very grown-up world. He had been with a few girls since his brief fling with Mandy and had had his share of booze. He found himself seeking ever more excitement. What he was contemplating now, a singer with a band on the road, was as challenging as it was exciting. Allan was so absorbed in his thoughts that he hadn't seen or heard Russell return.

"Sorry, sir. Come again?"

"I said that after careful consideration, my colleague and I have concluded that you should be our new vocalist. Pays one-fifty a month plus meals and accommodation."

"Well, hot dog!!" said Allan.

"I'll take that as an affirmative response. Listened to more than thirty singers over the last couple of weeks. None of 'em had a patch on you. You got nice pipes and sing with deep feeling. Couple of things. Gotta furnish your own tux and white dinner jacket and whatever other wardrobe you need. No drinking while on stage, no showing up drunk for the gig or rehearsals, no entanglements with married women, and no drugs of any kind on the bus or in the rooms. That work for you?"

"Oh, yes, sir."

"Fine then. We are leaving for a three month tour a week from Monday. Our first engagement is in Austin. Since you live in San Antonio and we have gig here for a big society wedding this weekend, think you can get up to speed with the songs by then?"

"You bet."

"We have rehearsals tomorrow at ten. Jake can give you the song list and sheet music today so you can get a feel for the material."

"Great. See you tomorrow, then. And Mr. Rhodes, thank you for the opportunity. I will give you my very best."

"I'm sure you will. And it's Russell."

The big piano player sidled up, laid a massive hand on Allan's shoulder, and smiled. "Done real good, son. You sho nuff can sing. I'm gonna be lookin' out for you, this bein' yo first time on de road."

"Jeepers, Mr. Jake, thanks."

—

ALL THE WAY HOME, Allan and Jessie basked in the joy of Allan's success. They regaled each other with tales of a future of fame and fortune...recordings, radio appearances, even movies.

As they approached his home, Allan's enthusiasm drained from him like water over a fall. He was going to have to deliver this news to his mother. Things had already grown strained between them as he spent ever more time out singing and ever less taking lessons.

They arrived and Jesse pulled the emergency brake. The ratcheting sound put him in mind of a drawbridge he was preparing to cross, a final crossing to this life, before departing for the one that beckoned.

"Oh, Jessie. I am dreading this so. I'm afraid I'm getting ready to break Mom's heart. Dad and I have talked and he's a musician, so he understands. He'll be fine. But I hardly know how to start this conversation."

"Well, padnah, you can't sit here all night. Better to just get at it like you're yankin' off a bandage."

"I appreciate the support. But you're right. Thanks for taking me to the audition."

"Oh, it was one of the best things ever. It was something watching you sing and seeing those guys' faces. You are gonna be a big hit. That is if you survive the wrath of Georgia."

Allan stepped out into the muggy afternoon air and began the death march up to his front door, hoping she was gone but knowing she would be there. As he walked in, his dad greeted him.

"Howdy, son. How was your day? Were you at rehearsal?"

"Well...ah...not exactly. Dad, I auditioned today with The Russell Rhodes Orchestra for the job as vocalist...and, well I sorta got hired."

Laying aside a book, his father rose. He walked over and wrapped Allan in his arms and held him for several seconds before speaking.

"I am torn between my pride in what you have done and the havoc this will wreak on your mother. I have as you asked, broached the subject of your ambitions. It was not welcomed with enthusiasm, a gross understatement. I fear there is little likelihood of her acceptance of this. But it is your life and I will not interfere. In fact, speaking as a musician, I will tell you that I have heard marvelous things regarding Russell's band. When are you to depart and for how long?"

"A week from Monday. From what I understand we'll start in Austin and tour Texas, Louisiana, and Oklahoma and be gone for three months or so. Oh, Dad, I am so excited. The pay is more than I could have hoped, a hundred and fifty bucks a month plus food and lodging. I get to start this Saturday with a big wedding at the Gunter."

"I must admit, I was aware of this possibility. Figured I'd just let things fall as they might. But I want you to be aware of the magnitude of your decision. You are stepping into a world far removed from the one you have known. There will be many temptations, many pitfalls to avoid out there. Some advice. Never forget who you are. Be true to yourself. Don't try to please everyone or be someone you're not. Don't try to copy someone else's style. Become the best Allan you can be, and no one can match you.

"Now, as for your mother...she will see this as a betrayal, I fear. You will be the prodigal son, turning your back on her after she has spent more time on your care and development than both of your siblings combined. It's understandable because of the polio and considering the care and rehabilitation she went through with you while maintaining our home. It was a Herculean task. You are her baby who nearly died, her miracle boy. Her dreams for you have informed her thoughts for so long that your future has to some degree become her own. And the healing will be long and tortuous for her.

"She is on the back porch feeding her birds. Go and do what you must but do it gently. I love you son and will welcome you back always."

As he turned down the hallway, his thoughts rattled like a cup of marbles in his head. His throat closed like a bent straw as he reached the door to the porch. He rested his hand on the knob, then rested some more. Finally, he inhaled, turned the knob, and stepped down onto the screened porch enclosing twenty bird cages.

The cacophony of parakeets and canaries tweeting shot like sharp treble arrows, pierced his ears in the small enclosed space. His mother's back was turned as she filled the water tray and put birdseed in the feeder of a canary's cage. He thought that it might be the canary in his coal mine warning him of impending danger.

Georgia turned with a start, her hand covering her heart. "My word you gave me a fright. Glad you're home. We will be eating in half an hour or so. Made some stew and cornbread. Better wash up. I'll be along shortly. 'Bout done with my birds. I sold two of them today and look to have at least another sold this week."

She smiled, then noticed his expression. "Are you all right? Look a bit peaked to me. Maybe you should have a wee lie down before lunch."

"Mom, I need to talk to you about something."

"Very well, go into the parlor, and I will be in directly."

His dad caught his eye and cocked his head in question. Allan shrugged his shoulders, passed by him, and sat down in the parlor.

He loved the smell of the room—old wood lathered in lemon oil, worn velvet furniture that had been there longer than he. Through the window, Allan saw the house across the street, his neighbors laughing at a shared story. He envied their harmony, knowing that he was shortly to destroy the harmony in his own home.

He heard the porch door close, followed by the sound of Georgia opening the oven. Then the dull clang of a metal spoon against a cast iron pot. He could smell the stew—onions, garlic, beef—as well as the cornbread. He realized he hadn't eaten since breakfast. He should be ravenous but his stomach was as bitter as gall.

Georgia arrived, her footfalls echoing off the hardwood floor. She sat down on the couch across from him, wiped her hands on her apron and folded them in her lap. "You seem upset. What is it, son?"

"Mom, you know I love you and I always try to make you happy. You have helped me learn so much and grow and overcome so much and I appreciate everything you have done for me."

"This sounds like a preamble to a speech I don't want to hear."

"I'm not sure how else to say this. I have been offered the position of vocalist in a band, The Russell Rhodes Orchestra, and I have accepted."

"So, you are quitting the boys you are playing with now and joining this new bunch?"

"Yes, ma'am. But the thing is this…band…well, you see, they don't just play around here, they sorta play all over."

"All over where exactly?"

"Well, actually…uh…Texas, Louisiana, and Oklahoma."

She turned her head away, staring into space for a few seconds, then dropped her chin and looked down at her careworn hands. Allan waited in air as thick as quicksand.

At last, she looked up at him. He was expecting the fiery temper that revealed itself on occasions. Instead, he saw something even more unsettling. Her soft gray eyes glistened and a lone tear rolled down her cheek. His dad's glass clinked against a bottle in the next room, the clock in the hallway chimed. He could stand it no longer.

"Mom, please don't be sad. It's just for a little while and it's a great opportunity and they are really good musicians and I'll make a hundred and fifty dollars a month and…and…I want this more than anything."

After an interminable pause, Georgia turned to him. "I've spent my life around musicians. Married one, of course, and I've got a pretty good understanding of that life. Now, with Prohibition, all the speakeasies, bootleggers, flappers—I know the swamp you're getting ready to wade into. You're a good boy. Lord, you're not yet seventeen. I know you think you are pretty grown up. But I quake at the thought of you out amongst the riffraff you will be mingling with." She wrung her hands. "So, it's my blessing you're wanting, is it?"

"Well, yes…yes, ma'am."

Georgia cleared her throat. "As much as I love you, Allan, the answer is no. There will be no such blessing. I cannot in good conscience do so. I have spent much of my life guiding you toward the fulfillment of your gifting. You are on your way to being a remarkable prodigy in opera, exposed to the finest elements of society. But you will cast all aside to play in dancehalls and Lord knows where else, rubbing elbows with the baser strata of humanity? No, I will not have it."

The color rose up her neck and spread to her cheeks. Her anger hurdled toward maximum velocity, her volume rising and the speed of her words increasing as they spewed forth.

"Oh, the hours I nursed you when you were young, The pain I felt as you struggled with your therapy. The hopes I held high as I watched you grow in your talent. I felt with certainty I would one day watch you singing with the New York Metropolitan Opera. I spent my bird money to pay for your lessons. And this is my reward. Well, so be it."

The tirade stopped as soon as it had begun. "When are you embarking on this grand career?"

"We leave a week from Monday."

"And you will be gone how many days?"

"Actually, we'll be gone about three months."

Georgia sat in stunned silence, then said softly, "Three months? Lord, have mercy." She rose, turned her back, and without another word, went to the kitchen.

Chapter 3

One voice, one guitar, one suitcase. His sword, his shield, his armor for this grand adventure. Cicadas crooned in the oaks and pecan trees shading him. Humid Gulf-scented Southeasterlies whispered like a drummer's brushes over the leaves.

Allan hummed to himself, watching folks on Alamo Plaza bustling in the morning light in hopes of beating the steamy torpor that would kick the struts out of all activity by afternoon. The Mexican siesta made a lot of sense.

Still savoring his last home-cooked breakfast and dealing with the tension of his fractured departure, Allan considered the admonitions his mother had hurled at him. It was distressing to leave on such discordant notes. Still, deep in his heart, the inexorable pull of the music was a riptide sucking him into the maw of the unknown. It was the kiss of a mistress too tempting to flee, her embrace as rough and intoxicating as cheap mescal, yet tender as a lover's whisper.

He smiled as he rolled his new name on his tongue. Allan Dale. He got the idea from Alan-a-Dale, the bard in Robin Hood's merry band. The moniker still squeaked and pinched like a new pair of boots. Yet the name was an essential element of his new identity. He was no longer the son of Sam Ezell, master musician and concertmaster. He would not have to stand in that shadow. A new life, a new name.

He heard the bus beating out a tortured complaint long before he saw it turning from Presa onto Alamo Street. It rolled to a stop in front of the bullet-scarred Alamo, sacred cradle of Texas liberty. The converted school bus sported bright yellow letters announcing "The Russell Rhodes Orchestra" emblazoned on a peacock background. The accordion door squeaked open, disgorging Jake the piano player. The other musicians and Russell followed, garnering the stares of pedestrians who would have been no less intrigued had a chariot full of Roman legionaries arrived.

Allan picked up his suitcase and guitar and crossed the street to greet Russell and Jake.

A grinning Russell offered his hand. "Howdy, been waitin' long?"

"No, sir. Maybe an hour or so."

"Well I'd say you're chompin' at the bit to get here that early. Say, how's your dad? Seen him play down at the Majestic once. Fine musician. You got half his talent, you'll do him proud."

Without waiting for a reply, Russell began introducing him to the band members. Each in turn shook Allan's hand, openly assessing this young singer they would be living and performing with. He came at last to Jake.

"Good to see you again. Did you just tell them your last name was Dale? Shoot, I done forgot 'yo' name already?"

"No. I changed it. Thought Allan Dale makes a better stage name. You know, like the bard in Robin Hood?"

"Well, alright then, Mr. Dale. Glad to have you aboard de bus what carries de Rhodes boys. Heh heh. Surely be de way, surely be de way."

Jake revealed gleaming white teeth set off with a gold rimmed front tooth, against his obsidian skin a ferocious smile. His deep voice as soft as he was large. "Hey man, I'm mighty hungry, are dem food stands any good? Ain't really had me none o' dat famous San Antonio Mexican food."

"Tell you the truth, Jake, if you have the time, I'd go over to Mi Tierra by the Mercado."

Jake turned to Russell. "Hey, boss. You said we had an hour 'fore we check in, right? This young hoss say he gonna show me where the real Mex food is at. Wanna come along?"

"Naw, think we'll just hang around the Plaza then get checked in at the Gunter. Reckon on rehearsal at three in the Grand Ballroom."

"Alright, den. Lead the way, Mr. Dale."

Allan stowed his gear on the bus, then set off toward Mi Tierra. Jake hummed and walked, tattooing a rhythm with his shoes as they walked, arriving ten minutes later.

"Man, dere be some potent smells 'round here. Reminds me of Piedras Negras down cross de border. Always liked that name. Means black rock, me bein of the darker persuasion and all. Been down dere once. Lordy the Mexican senoritas sho nuff love Big Jake, surely be de way."

Allan hadn't been to that southernmost border town but figured it was about the same as Laredo, ragged and rich in temptations. He'd visited "Boystown" with Jessie, Joe, and Willie Brown but managed to pass on the forbidden fruit his friends had sampled, settling for a solid bout of inebriation on Carta Blanca.

"It does call to mind the border towns. I reckon half of these folks are wetbacks. Don't blame 'em for wanting to come up here. Things are pretty rough down in Mexico. Funny thing about Mexicans. It doesn't matter how poor they are, they will share their last tortilla with you even if it's all they've got. White folks treat 'em pretty bad. Guess that's something you know plenty about."

Jake turned slowly and looked down on Allan. He didn't speak but his dark eyes reflected the sad truth of his experience. This was still the South and he lived in a world of discrimination with the Klan still making their evil presence known.

Allan opened the door of Mi Tierra to the cacophony of mariachi music, loud conversation, and laughter. Jake assumed they would be eating in separate sections. He was surprised when Allan asked the man at the door for a table for two in the white section. The small Mexican host considered them with furrowed brow. "You are sure, señor?"

"Si, cierto."

They followed him past a sea of white staring faces to a booth in the far corner. Jake looked around. "You bein' mighty bold here. Sure dis is a good idea?"

Allan nodeed. "San Antonio may be in the South but it's a lot looser here. We've always been a stew of gringos, Mexicans, Germans, Poles, and—of course—Negroes. Some of these folks will be none too happy but they won't make a fuss like they would in Alabama or East Texas." He leaned back in the booth. "Look, Jake. I know how it feels to be different. You walked in here with me and people stared. They've been staring at me since I was little 'cause of my bum leg and funny walk. Been called a gimp plenty of times, at least till I learned how to scrap. I can't possibly understand what you've had to put up with but I know the pain of being treated like you're less than everyone else. My dad taught me that it's what's inside a man that matters. He plays music with Negro musicians and brown ones and white ones, heck... he'd play with green ones. All he cares about is how well they play and the nature of their character. He says if they're good enough to make music with, they're good enough to break bread with.

"I know I'm young but I feel like I know better than a lot of the old folks running the action in this world. By God, I aim to make my mark as a singer and when I do, I'm going to let them know what I think about all the high-minded hypocrites who sit in church hearing how Jesus loves ALL people on Sunday and cursing Black folks and calling them 'niggers' the rest of the week."

Allan's volume had increased, which made the waiter a little nervous as he arrived to take their orders.

"Que queires señores?"

The two placed their order and when the waiter disappeared, Jake looked at his young friend. "This be yo first time on de road."

"Yep."

"Ain't all dat shiny some a de time. Be some rough joints out there. Specially dem oil towns. We playin' down near Port Arthur while back, seen a man gutted right in front of the bandstand. Happen so fas' I didn't see the blade or the man what dun de cuttin'. He was split out de door while the other fella was tryin' to tuck his tripe back in his trousers. Crazy. Seemed like he was more embarrassed to have his guts spilled out than he was scared 'bout dyin'."

"Well now Jake, that's right pleasant dinner conversation. Glad I didn't order Tripas."

Jake poured out deep laughter, shaking the table and making the ice in the glass tinkle like Christmas bells.

The meal arrived and was attended to with great dispatch. Jake went after his food as if it were the Last Supper, sighing in satisfaction and breathing with some difficulty. "That sho nuff de best Mex I dun ever ate. Since dis is yo first day with de band, I be mighty pleased if you let me buy dis here meal seein' as you ain't earned yo first dollar singin'."

"Thanks, Jake. I'd be honored."

As they stood in line to pay, a group of four young white men in the line glared at them. They paid and walked out into the building heat and began their walk to the hotel. Arriving at an intersection, they found themselves waiting at the light with the same bunch who had given them hard stares at the restaurant. A tall rangy tough with close set eyes turned to them. "A gimp and a nigger to boot. You boys from the circus? Hell, it's enough to make me lose my lunch."

Allan stared back unflinchingly.

"Anybody but a gimp look at me like that, I'd bust 'em up good."

"Well, don't let that stop you."

Jake put his big hand on Allan's shoulder and said, "It ain't necessary. Let it ride. Nuthin' to prove and we gots to get to rehearsal."

At that moment the light changed, and Jake took him by the arm and turned him toward the intersection leading them across the street with the four hooligans taunting them.

"Ain't no thing, son, ain't no thing."

They arrived at the door a few minutes later. Allan was still awed by the venerable old hotel. The heavy furniture, the sweeping staircase with gilded balustrade. He felt his imminent departure, the threads that bound him to this city loosening. When would he see his family again, living the itinerant musician's life? What hotels would he call home, what relationships would he form? His fear and uncertainty were offset by the anticipation of the unknown.

It seemed somehow fitting that the first performance with this new band might be his last in his hometown. It was a wedding reception celebrating the union of two of the most prominent families in town. He'd met the bride a few months before at a cotillion where he had performed. She was from a wealthy Alamo Heights family, and he doubted she would remember him.

The grand ballroom was being decorated as they arrived, the band already setting up on stage. Suddenly, he felt the merciless butterflies that arrive to taunt every performer. Now he would have to sing with skill equal to musicians that were above his level of experience. Allan stepped up on the stage as the musicians were tuning. Russell smiled and pointed to the microphone. "Here's the song list. You ready?"

Allan glanced down at the sheet. *I know these songs*, he thought. *I've sung most of them before and I was meant to be here.* The affirmation took the edge off his terror.

Jake sat down at the piano and waved him over. "Gonna be great, son. Just be yo self and have some fun."

Russell raised his hands and the band kicked in. Allan waited for his cue, and then his demons were cast aside. Free as a mustang running across the plains, he let his voice have reign. The Creator's first instrument—the human voice, capable of expressing the collective emotions of all humankind. An instrument of wind, muscle, soul, and blood, enchanting and transcendent. Allan sang, fleet of heart, riding the cascading melodies.

He turned to see Jake smiling, gold tooth aglitter, saw Russell nod his head in appreciation. He felt at home, would always be at home, when he was singing. He felt more powerful than had he the fastest pair of legs. Allan only needed to refer to the sheet music on a few of the songs. The rest of the rehearsal passed smoothly as a bullet through a barrel.

A few of the musicians stopped to pat him on the back or give him an "atta boy." Had it been gold nuggets they handed him, it would have meant no more. Finally, Russell himself wandered over to pass along his appreciation. Could it get any better?

The best part was Jake's blinding smile and his words, succinct and succulent. "That right there's what I'm talkin' 'bout. Done real good. Surely be de way, surely be de way."

———

HE WAS ASSIGNED A room with the bass player, Rick Henderson. Rick had already decamped, choosing the bed nearest the window. Allan unpacked, hanging his tuxedo and white dinner jacket on the shower rail to be steamed while he showered.

Rick seemed pleasant but quiet, the conversation passing between them perfunctory and brief. No matter—Allan was soon engrossed in his second favorite passion, reading. The three hours before dinner and the performance were passed in the world of *The Moon and Sixpence* by Somerset Maugham.

When Rick began to get ready for the evening, Allan put down his book, dressed and followed his roommate to the dining room. He looked for Jake and then remembered the Black musicians would be dining separately with the Negro hotel staff. Allan would have preferred to be at Jake's table, but he made the effort to connect with the other players.

After the meal, he took the opportunity to wander out into his last balmy San Antonio evening. He decided to stroll a couple of blocks over to the Majestic Theatre, where he'd watched his father perform and seen the best of Vaudeville. It had been his inspiration and playground. It was an old friend soon to become a memory.

He wandered to Travis Park, sat on a bench, and listened to the grackles cackling in the trees. Tonight, he would launch himself into the ocean of chance and find out if he could swim. He took leave of the small park with its stately live oaks and fountain, heading back to the Gunter for his debut.

The band was setting up when he arrived with half an hour to spare. Jake waved him over to the piano. "How you be, young Squire? what you been up to?"

"Just wandered down to the park to say goodbye to some old friends."

"Listen here. Me and Ezra, the sax player, goin' ova' to blow some jazz at Eastwood after we done. You know Eastwood?"

"Heard about it. Never been there. I know they get some of the best jazz and blues players in there, but I don't think white folks go much."

"Well, depends on who they show up with. Be a few white players show up. It be you and me and Ezra the sax player. You wanna' come after the gig?"

"Shoot, yeah!" said Allan. "Always wanted to hear some of those blues and jazz guys."

"Dun be settled den."

Russell walked up and looked at the young man. "A little nervous, are you?"

"Yeah, I guess. First time with you guys and all."

"That's a good thing. First time you don't get a little nervous before you perform, it will be the worst singing you do. Bein' a little scared means it matters. Ain't worried about you, son. You'll knock 'em dead."

The bride and groom's families and a few guests began to arrive in a slow trickle. Russell made sure the band was ready, raised his arm and kicked off with an instrumental arrangement of *Bye, Bye, Blackbird*. A few songs later as the room began to fill with guests, Allan stepped to the mike. He felt the sweat running under his tux as he began to sing *It's Wonderful*. Soon he was caught up in the singing, barely aware of the faces of the listeners. As the song was ending, the bride and groom arrived to applause and whoops from the groomsmen. Russell seamlessly led the band into *Here Comes the Bride*.

Angela Arthur was stunning in her wedding gown. He'd thought her fetching in his brief encounter with her. Tonight, she was breathtaking. The groom seemed to shrink beside her, filling out his morning suit like a sack of pecans.

William Rowan Caldwell III was imposing only regarding the holdings he would inherit. Wild Bill, as he was known to friends, was the only son and scion of a family whose fortune was writ large in oil, cattle, and banking. With a father in failing health, Billy was likely to take the helm in the near future. He had a cruel mouth and a weak chin. His arrogance went before him like a moldy odor.

The first break found Allan searching for something to slake his thirst. He headed for the massive crystal punch bowl, glowing in the success of his first time on stage with the band. He had just swallowed a sip of the spiked punch when he felt a light touch on his shoulder. He turned to discover the bride's beaming smile. "You sing so beautifully!" she said. "I didn't know you were with the Russell Rhodes Orchestra. You may not remember, but we met at a cotillion where you were performing."

He remembered all right. She'd been so sweet and so unassuming. He'd been slightly abashed. "I certainly do remember. You make a lovely bride. This must be the happiest day of your life."

Something flickered just behind her blue eyes, a chimera too slippery to catch. "Yes, it was a lovely wedding."

An uncomfortable silence lay between them.

"Well, Angela, I wish you great happiness. Is there something special I could sing for you?"

"I'm quite enamored of Mr. Gershwin. Do you know *Lady Be Good*?"

"I love that song. It's not on the set list for tonight but I'll ask Russell if the band knows it."

"That would be divine. Tell me, are you traveling with this band now?"

"Yes, actually, we are leaving in the morning. We're playing at a club in Galveston for a week. After that, I'm not sure. We're on the road for a few months. Tell you the truth it's a bit overwhelming. First time I've been away from home."

She smiled. "It sounds wonderfully exciting. How I envy your freedom and sense of adventure. And much more your talent. I think you have a rare gift."

"I'm amazed you even remember hearing me. I'm flattered."

Allan sensed movement to his left as the groom arrived, well in his cups, unsteady on his pins. "Come, my dear, I want you to meet some of my old fraternity chums."

Without awaiting her reply, he seized her arm and dragged her off to his waiting entourage.

She turned to Allan as she was whisked away. Her conflicted smile held a trace of Black Strap molasses—sweet, strong, yet slightly bitter.

—

THE FINAL SONG HAD been played and the guests had dwindled. The band began putting away their instruments. Jake and Ezra came over to Allan, Jake's gold tooth sparkling in the chandelier light. "Mighty fine, mighty fine young buck! Sho nuff dun yourself some croonin'."

"Did too," added Ezra. "You gonna be good, yes, suh."

"Me an Ezra headin' over to Eastwood with a friend of his now. Still wanna come along?"

"You bet! Let me run up to the room and change. Meet you in five?"

"Yes, suh. We headin' on up to get into our party rags too. We'll see you in the lobby."

Following a lightning change of clothes, Allan found them in the lobby, dressed to the nines in vested suits. "Gosh, I feel underdressed."

Jake laughed. "No need. You lookin' jes fine in yo shirt and slacks."

"For a white boy," added Ezra with a wry grin.

They walked out onto streets still jealously hanging on to heat held there from the long hot day. A sticky breeze gave scant relief. Ezra waited on the curb impatiently looking up and down the street. "Bless my soul where dat boy be? Zeke, he be famous for bein' late. Likely layin' up with some fine young thing." Ezra said shaking his head. "Zeke believe women be his own flower patch and he be the king bee. He do love de nectar. One a deez days somebody gonna cut dem wings and stomp de bumble right on out 'a dat bee."

Ezra appeared ready to help his friend in harvesting the pollen. His processed hair glistened in short curls, cleaving tightly to his scalp. Starched white shirt, burgundy jacket and black shoes with white spats bespoke a strong vein of vanity. Each finger sported a ring reflecting the glow of the streetlights.

By comparison, Jake seemed positively dull in his burgundy suit, white shirt, and blue silk tie.

The wait was rewarded with Zeke's arrival in a hunter-green Ford. His long, lanky frame emerged, leaned on the roof, and smiled. "Evenin' gents. Sorry to keep you waitin'. Seems I was occupied helpin' a young lady home, ya see."

Zeke walked over and threw his arms around Ezra. "Good to see you, my man. Let me introduce you to Jake Galvan, the piano man, and our new singer, Allan Dale."

"Pleasure. We'll step on into de carriage and we be off to Eastwood to see what be shaken'."

Driving through the East side was a novel experience for Allan. It was smaller than the Mexican neighborhoods or white enclaves and had a distinct atmosphere. Music could be heard blaring from radios. The residents sat on porches or stood in small groups chatting, laughing, and even dancing to the music. There were people of all ages unselfconsciously communing with joyful abandon, in spite of the deep poverty evident in the small, weathered houses.

They drove until they came to a gate opening onto a gravel road. Zeke turned onto an unmarked road, continuing a half mile or so before a pink glow appeared above the mesquite and live oaks. The road opened to a parking lot with dozens of cars parked in front of a large barn-like building with bright neon signage announcing EASTWOOD COUNTRY CLUB. They could hear the band even over the car's engine as they searched of a parking place. Strings of Christmas lights lead to the entrance.

Zeke parked then spoke to Allan. "Best let me 'splain the situation. Don't get many white folks here. I'll square it with big Mike at the door. You be alright but it might take a while for people to loosen up 'roun' you. All right den."

Ernie smiled and they all climbed out onto the caliche gravel and walked to the door.

Big Mike was aptly named, looking well north of three hundred solid pounds. He sat imperiously perched on a bench that seemed unlikely to make it for the long haul.

"Evenin' Zeke. Who you got with you here?"

"Well, howdy do, Big Mike. Let me introduce you to some of the boys from the Russell Rhodes Orchestra. This here is Ezra Charles.

Blows a mean sax. Jake Galvan here is a fearsome piano player, and Allan Dale is the singer with the band. Thought we might get them up on stage to jam a little."

Big Mike eyed Allan. "Be fifty cent cover."

They fished out the money and stepped across the threshold and into a whirlwind of sound and motion. The music rolled off the stage like combers on Padre Island. Allan's eyes adjusted to the dimly lit interior, covered by a moving carpet of dancers, arms raised, skirts twirling wide, in a sea of smiles.

The band was laying down a boogie beat that stuck to his bones. Zeke led them to a table against the rear wall. Within seconds a waitress arrived, smiling at Ernie as she leaned in for a hug.

"Well, hello, shuga'. Been missin' yo handsome face sho nuff. Who yo friends be?"

"Why, Ruth, you got prettier since I was here. How dat be possible? You is already the finest lookin' woman in this joint."

"You lyin' devil. Jez keep on talkin'."

"Rose, this here is Ernie, Jake, and young Mr. Allan. Dey with the Russell Rhodes Band. Maybe get around to jammin' later."

"I look forward to dat. You boys need some set ups?"

"Yes, ma'am. Bring us some Cokes and glasses with ice. I got the rest," Ernie said patting both the side pockets of his jacket.

"Be right back."

Ernie smiled. "Got us some decent bootleg whiskey and some tequila, which ever suits yo' fancy. Tequila is two dollars. Whiskey is three for the bottle."

They each kicked in for the booze.

Allan turned his attention to the stage. Five musicians and a female singer were putting out music such as he had never heard. It was less structured and had a loose spontaneous unruliness that was thrilling, like a saucy flirt. The seductive sound captivated him.

Leaning into Ezra, he loudly asked, "What would you call this stuff? I hear jazz, blues, boogie."

"I don't know it got a name 'xactly. It be all dat stuff. Sho is inspirin' dem dancers. Got a good rubbin', huggin', crawl goin'. Jes enough bottom and groove to keep it movin' but dem brushes de drummer usin' keep it sexy."

The drinks came as they played a song Allan knew, *Rockin' Rhythm*, a Duke Ellington tune. Jake poured a stout shot over the ice in Allan's glass and filled the rest with Coke. Allan ignored it as he felt the energy change into a higher gear. Flaring skirts revealed strong black legs as their partners swung and guided them around the floor. The dancers surrendered to unbridled joyous abandon.

Zeke stood up. "Boys, I got me some business to attend too. Be around if you need me." He headed for a door in the rear.

Two songs later, the band took a break and Ezra went up to the stage to talk with the musicians.

"Ezra be settin' us up to sit in," said Jake. "They a song you like to sing? Figure we can play during the break, me on piano, Ezra on sax and you singin'."

"Do you know that song Louis Armstrong recorded a year or two ago...*St. James Infirmary*?"

"You are in luck. Indeed I do. Ezra can vamp with anything. We can start with that. Maybe do some we know with the band."

Ezra returned, ring-encrusted fingers fluttering. "We in boys. Dey be happy to take a long break and let us hold down de fort." He took his sax out and put a reed in his mouth to wet it down before fitting it into the mouthpiece. Jake stood up and grinned. "You ready for somethin' different?"

Allan nervously replied, "I reckon."

Feeling a dry feeling in his throat, a flitter in his belly, he followed his friends up onto the stage, still running lyrics in his head as Jake laid down the intro. Inhaling, he sang, "I went down to St. James Infirmary, and I saw my baby there..." The song poured forth, gliding on the slow blues of Jake's keyboard. Abandoning himself to the lyrics, Allan let the pain of loss pour out in deep purple hues. When the verse ended, Ezra's sax framed the words with soulful notes. Opening his eyes, Allan found the crowd deep in the feeling, swaying to the groove. Ezra tore loose with his sax and soon the crowd was all smiles and nodding heads. Returning to his vocal, he felt tears rolling down his cheeks, lost in the heartbreak of the blues.

The song ended to great applause, whistles and amens. The drummer and bass player mounted the stage. Jake waited for them to get set and counted off *Hardhearted Hannah*. The crowd went back to dancing and the rest of the break took on a life of its own.

Allan had never experienced such abandon. From the stage into a sea of backslapping happy people shouting, "Nice," "You got it," "Amen, cool," and "White boy gots him some soul."

The band started back into their set when his reverie was broken by shouts, cursing, and the crash of tables and breaking glass. He turned to see their friend Zeke backing away from a large man in a brown leather coat. The man slashed at Zeke, light glinting off a blade. A woman screamed as the straight razor sliced the coat sleeve on Zeke's upturned arm. Zeke circled around a table putting it between himself and his assailant. The music stopped and a ring of spectators gathered around the two.

Allan got his first good look at their friend's attacker. His shaved head was mounted on a massive neck. His leather coat stretched tightly, revealing a thickly muscled back. Though much shorter than Zeke, he outweighed him by thirty pounds or more.

Allan's breath caught as he watched his friend backed into a corner. The blade swung but Zeke moved, catching the man's wrist, and sweeping his feet from beneath him. As he fell, Zeke jerked and twisted the arm at an acute angle. The bone sounded like a splintering branch as the man screamed out in agony. Zeke seized the razor and kicked the man in the head, putting him well and truly out.

Suddenly the crowd parted before the towering Big Mike, carrying a Louisville Slugger. "What goin' on here. Y'all move back."

Taking in the scene, he turned on Zeke. "What you done here boy?"

"Hey now, he done pull de blade on me. Ain't got me no weapon. Jes' protectin' myself."

"Take yo sorry black ass outta here now. Don't allow no fightin'. No excuses. Couple you boys help me drag dis boy off de floor. May need him a doctor."

Jake took Allan by the elbow and whispered, "Believe our evenin' dun ended. Ezra, best get your sax and let's get Zeke out before some of this boy's friends wants some more of him."

Blood seeped from a towel covering Ernie's forearm. The flow didn't seem heavy enough for it to be arterial. They'd just reached Ernie's car when they heard the sound of swiftly approaching feet.

Four men approached from the darkness forming a semi-circle around them as they backed against Ernie's car. A tall wiry man stepped in close to Ernie. "You gots yourself two choices. Pay me the twenty bucks you cheated off my brother in that craps game, or some dark night, Mr. Colt gonna pay you a visit."

"Well now, Mr. Colt, maybe get a chance to meet Dr. Buckshot," growled Zeke.

Silent as a spider, Big Mike stepped from the shadows. "All right den, you all are outta here...now!"

They climbed in the car and drove away, no one speaking until they reached the hotel. Jake and Allan got out of the back seat and Ezra leaned out the window. "You boys settle in. Gonna go with Zeke. He know a nurse what can sew him up and doctor him. See you in the mornin'."

Allan turned to Jake as they entered the lobby. "What a crazy night. Like *The Tale of Two Cities,* "It was the best of times. It was the worst of times."

Jake cocked his head inquisitively.

"Just a line from a story. Jake, thank you for taking me along. I never enjoyed singing that much. And the excitement was scary but thrilling."

"Maybe not the last time you see some of dat. But you dun sang yo ass off, boy. Mighty proud of you. Truth is Ezra, he not so keen on takin' you. But you dun me proud. Okay, now get some sleep. We be pullin' out in the mornin'."

Allan undressed quietly, trying not to wake his roommate, and slid between expensive sheets as the last dregs of adrenaline seeped away. Suspended in anticipation of his first day on the road and the foretaste of homesickness, he stared at shadows from light falling through the blinds and began to whisper a prayer.

"Lord, I'm so scared and excited. I know I've been doing some things I shouldn't. Forgive me for the girls and the drinking. But thank you for giving me this chance to follow my dream. Help me to not fall into bad things. I know where I'm headed there are going to be temptations. I'll do my best. Watch over my family while I'm gone. In Jesus's name, amen."

He drifted into sleep smiling, lulled into slumber by the soft whisper of the curtains blowing gently against the windowsill.

Chapter 4

The bus pulled away from the hotel on a steamy Sunday, rolling past churches where well-dressed families poured from the doors, heading for Sunday dinners.

Allan sat next to Micky O'Herlihey, the trumpet player. Watching the city began to thin out into countryside, old established neighborhoods transitioning into rundown shacks, and eventually farmland. As he dwelled on the last look at his home and his first time away, he was interrupted by his seatmate.

"Bet ol' Jake's been fillin' your head full of visions of the grand life on the road. Let me tell you, it ain't all swank hotels and champagne. So, your first time out, huh? Well good luck. Some guys don't last a month."

Allan appraised the small man with close set, watery-blue eyes. He was only four or five years his senior but already the effects of drink were written in the broken blood vessels on his nose and in his bloodshot eyes. He emitted an odor like raisins soaked in witch hazel.

Jake leaned across the aisle.

"Don't let Little Mary Sunshine over dere be puttin' no disillusionments on you. Dat boy dun come outta his momma complainin'."

They traveled for a couple of hours before reaching the town of Columbus, nestled in green rolling hills, decorated with spreading oaks and southern pine. The town square had the obligatory stone courthouse and county seat, complete with a doughboy statue commentating WWI at one end and a Confederate soldier at the other. They stepped down from the bus, stretched, and found a suitable restaurant for a lunch break where a sign on the door read *Whites Only*.

Russell turned to Jake and Ezra. "Sorry. Guess you'll have to eat on the bus. We'll bring it out to you. What would you like?"

They shrugged resignedly, ordered fried chicken and trimmings, and waited on the sidewalk. Without thinking, Allan spoke up.

"Hey, tell you what, Russell. I'll order the same and eat on the bus with them if that's all right."

The band leader cocked his head, gave a small grin.

"We'll get seated and I'll come back with your food."

Jake sidled up next to Allan. "Don't have to be doin' dis. We used to it."

"Well, *I'm* not. 'Sides, I wanted to find out what happened with Zeke after you dropped us off, Ezra."

Russell returned to the shaded bench where they awaited their lunch. Several passersby gave them hard looks. East Texas clearly had far more animus about Black and white interaction. They decided it best to eat on the bus and avoid the locals. Between bites, Ezra gave an account of Zeke's thirteen stitches and the compliant nurse whom he managed to talk into more extensive comforting.

"Dat boy got him a two-track mind. Girls and gamblin'. Sum of dem gals is married—which is gamblin' with his life—but dat be Zeke. Dat de onliest man I ever see be dat lucky. But de cat jess loss hisself one of his nine lives. Sooner or later, his luck be runnin' out."

After lunch, they watched their bandmates saunter out of the restaurant. Three teenage girls now occupied the bench where they had been sitting. As Sam Vanderbruggin, the trombone player, neared the girls, he leered and stopped to chat. Allan couldn't hear the conversation but could tell that the girls were offended as they quickly turned and left, walking quickly away from the grinning musician. First on the bus, Sam came and sat down next to Allan.

"Pretty little town eh. Specially them tender little buds. Be a dandy little place to spend a couple of days. Young and sweet. They ain't been handled much, them little fillies. Way I like 'em."

His raspy whisper and hyena breath made Allan squirm. It sounded like the hide being torn off a deer carcass. He considered his sister. What might Sam think about her? She'd probably use him like a heavy bag, but that didn't lessen the uneasiness Allan felt.

"A might young, don't you think?"

"Younger the better." Above his twisted grin, dark eyes gleamed. Somewhere behind them a cottonmouth slithered out of a swamp.

"'Scuse me, Sam. Got to ask Jake bout a song I'd like him to learn."

Moving around Sam, he went to Jake two seats back. "Okay if I sit with you?"

"Sure, but I be asleep fore you know it. Best you get a wink in. We be up late tonight. That place in Galveston where we playin', it go on till the wee hours sho nuff." With that, Jake put a rolled-up jacket against the window, leaned his head on it, and was asleep within a minute. Allan heard the bus door close, the engine fire, and they were away, headed for the coast.

The excitement of beginning his quest to become a singing star didn't leave him immune to thoughts of what he was leaving behind. He already missed his family and, as the youngest member of the group of seasoned adults, he battled thoughts of insecurity.

The humming of the engine and rattle of the bus lulled him into a hypnotic reverie as he watched the Texas landscape slowly change from hills to flat coastal scrub. He let his imagination transport him to huge venues in New York City where he sang before a famous orchestra and saw himself in a studio broadcasting his music on the radio. His imaginings became dreams as he rested his head on his own rolled-up jacket and drifted into sleep.

Chapter 5

Two years passed in a blur of dancehalls, speakeasys, and roughneck honky-tonks. Allan had grown into his role as front man, gaining the respect—if not the friendship—of the other musicians. The only ones he'd gotten close to were Jake, Ezra, and the guitar player Rod Maguire. Being a fellow guitarist, Allan spent an increasing amount of time jamming with and learning from him.

Rod's abilities far exceeded his own and he was gaining a whole new vocabulary on the guitar. Rod taught him about the gypsy jazz of Django Reinhardt and showed him some of Reinhardt's wild techniques. Rod shared tales of jazz clubs in New York and Chicago where he'd played with many famous musicians. Allan expressed his envy at Rod's talent and experiences.

"Tell you somethin'. I've heard some great players. Don't hear too many great singers. I have what, eight, ten years on ya? I reckon I play guitar 'bout as well as you sing. That's sayin' somethin', 'cause I ain't no slouch. But I think you got a gift's all I'm sayin'."

"Gosh. But you're a better musician than me."

"More polished maybe, been doin' it a long time. But it's what you ain't got yet but you soon will have that I'm talkin' bout."

"Rod, it means so much to hear that. We should make a pact. Hit the road for New York or St. Louis, get our chance to swing with the big leagues. Radio is hungry for something other than the boring fare they're getting for the most part. Folks want—no, *need*—the music, especially in these rough times. You play as well as Rhinehart. Today is a great time to be something different, something unique that people love. So it's what, March 1931? March of next year is our deadline. We save a grubstake and leave as soon as we have the dough, one year from now. No matter what, we fly the coop. Maybe even write a song…who knows? Go where it's happening."

Allan followed his own advice. Half of everything he made, he saved. He was stunned how fast the cash grew. In these tough times, he knew he was blessed. He urged Rod to follow his example and was assured that he was doing just that. Allan knew that with their combined talents they would have a very real chance of breaking into the higher echelon of the business.

The road became his classroom. He listened to the radio every chance he got, followed the programs, heard the newest songs. Some he liked, but there was plenty of drivel to be heard. He and Rod started to learn some of the latest songs but create new arrangements. Soon they had a burgeoning repertoire of new songs from great players. They encouraged one another daily while riding the crazy wave of life on the road.

Allan had departed on this journey in a world gone crazy with wealth. Everyone had been getting rich on Wall Street. But following the Crash of 1929, more than fifteen-hundred banks had failed. Average people were losing jobs, homes. Even so, people still came to dance, party, and drink away their troubles. There was now a new national anthem, and the tallest building in New York, the Empire State Building, opened as if its mere presence could tame the primal forces set loose on the economy.

In spite of the economic uncertainties—or perhaps because of them—people sought escape and found it in booze, music, and wild abandon. The Roaring Twenties had created an appetite for escapism and for a working band that created opportunities to satisfy peoples' need for entertainment.

Allan was reading the paper when Rod came through the door to join him for a late breakfast in the hotel restaurant. "What a shocker, Allan Dale reading," said Rod. "Well, what's the latest bad news?"

"Seems Al Capone was convicted of tax evasion for selling hooch without paying the revenuers, but he beat the rap on the Valentine's Day Massacre. Rest of the country is still fumbling along in this murky mess. You know, Rod, we're lucky we got a job 'cause lots of people don't. I called home yesterday. They've shut down the symphony and Dad's getting by on vaudeville and other gigs."

"Cheery stuff."

The waitress arrived, took Rod's order, and poured coffee for Allan.

"It's not all bad news. Looking more likely prohibition gets the axe. That would make it easier to get booked in bigger more legit rooms."

The Russell Rhodes Orchestra was gaining a regional reputation in part because of their singer. They traversed Texas, Louisiana, Arkansas, and Oklahoma, playing venues from the sublime to the scurrilous. One night a cotillion in a swank hotel, the next a dancehall filled with oilfield workers plowing through cash they made cheating death in the oil patch.

They had not performed on the radio as yet but at last, the opportunity arrived. In their first live performance on KPRC in Houston, they would be the opening act for the famous Fletch Henderson Orchestra from New York. Allan was keen to do well, in hopes that he might be noticed by Henderson and perhaps get his foot in the door for grander opportunities. His confidence had grown to just south of arrogant.

Allan considered Rod staring into space, his hands wrapped around a cup of coffee. Rod looked like he'd been rode hard and put up wet. The previous night he'd acquired a Chicken Cock, a pint of bootleg in a can, which he drank mostly by himself. When the waitress placed the plate of bacon and eggs before him, he recoiled as if it were noxious.

"You gonna be all right, padnah?"

"Just a little hungover's all."

They chatted and Rod picked away at his food. Allan continued reading *The Houston Chronicle* until Russell arrived at their table and placed his hand on his shoulder.

"Mornin', boys. Rod, you look like somethin' the cat drug up. Allan, Fletch Henderson came to see me. He's got a problem. His singer's gone and got himself thrown in the pokey. Seems he was caught with somebody's wife and ended up beatin' the daylights out of the husband, who is some rich oilman. He pulled some strings, but it looks like it could be a while before Fletch's singer is cut loose. He was wonderin' if you could fill in for him after we finish our set. He asked if it was square with me and I said as long as you were okay with it. I know it'd be a lot of singing, two full sets, strain on your voice and all."

Allan's thoughts quickened at the idea of singing with Henderson's band. Was he good enough, would his voice hold out, would he know the songs, arrangements?

"Sure boss, I can do it. No problem," he replied with false aplomb. "'Course I'll need to get with them right away to learn the songs and rehearse."

"Great. Just one thing, Allan. Remember you are *my* singer, and we got a lot of good gigs lined up. I figured you'd say okay, so I have you set up for rehearsal in the ballroom at one this afternoon. By the way, on top of the extra twenty you're getting from me, Henderson is paying you a full c-note. Enjoy your breakfast...and Rod, I hope you survive." Russell smirked and walked away.

"Well," said Rod, "it seems like a four-leaf clover's been dropped in your lap. Could be a great connection for our dream. You'll wow 'em."

"Hope so. But what if I blow it?"

"Ain't no way. You got it, man. Just be yourself and have fun. How many people get to sing with the Henderson Band on live radio?"

Allan wished that his parents could hear him, but unfortunately the signal wouldn't reach San Antonio. He called to tell them he'd be on the radio to mixed responses—pride and encouragement from his father, indifference from his mother.

—

ALLAN WALKED INTO THE cavernous ballroom promptly at one. A middle-aged Black man, cigarette dangling loosely from full lips, sat at the piano. Fletch Henderson stood nearby looking up from a music stand stacked with sheet music.

"You the singer?"

"Yes sir. Name's Allan Dale."

"Pleased to meet you. Thanks for covering for me. Not sure which songs you know, but here is our playlist for tonight."

Allan looked over the set list. There were, in fact, only six songs he didn't know well. Indicating as much, he requested the sheet music. Henderson introduced him to the piano player whose name was Mose.

"Can we run through these so I can get a feel for the arrangements?"

Fletch pointed to Mose. "Show him," he said.

Mose removed his cigarette, placing it in an ashtray on the grand piano. "Okay, which ones you don't know?"

Allan handed him the sheet music.

For the next three hours, he immersed himself in the songs. By four, Allan said, "That's enough. Think I got this down."

"I'd say you sho nuff do. You gonna do jes fine son. See you tonight."

They were the shortest hours he could remember. Eight o'clock crept upon him and suddenly he was on stage. The room glittered in refracted chandelier light, imparting a glow to the well-dressed patrons. He'd never seen so many stunning women in one room. The crowd was brazenly open with their drinking, with flasks and bottles on the tables. They obviously knew which palms to grease.

The band struck up and, as he sang, he watched the dancers and revelers abandon themselves to the music as if this might be the last great blowout before the reaper arrived. For many, financial ruin might await on the morrow but tonight was all that mattered.

An array of microphones was placed strategically around the bandstand, attached by cables like strings of black spaghetti, connecting to a soundboard in the back of the room, and manned by serious looking engineers. He thought about the fact that his voice was now being heard by who knew how many people sitting in front of their radios. What an amazing miracle.

It struck him that instead of picturing all those listeners, he would imagine himself singing to one person. For some reason, Mandy sprang to mind. Allan began to sing as if into her ear alone—warmly, intimately. The set ended with uproarious applause, and he realized that they were finished and soon he would step before the mike with the Fletch Henderson Orchestra on live radio. Even though he knew he had done well, he was nervous. During the thirty-minute break for the bands to switch out, he found Rod putting his guitar in the case.

"Hey man, you sounded great," said Allan. "Loved that lead on the last tune. Got any advice before I do this?"

"Yep, just sing like you did tonight. Never heard you sound better. Come find me after. Should be around here, hopefully with a cute broad or two well into their cups."

"See you after. Wish me luck."

"Don't need it. You got the gift."

Thirty minutes blew away like beach foam on the wind. He mounted the stage, Mose smiling at him from his perch at the piano.

Fletch Henderson acknowledged him with a nod as he walked to the mike. Allan looked behind him at the appraising eyes of the band. These guys were big time. He was overawed to be fronting a band of national standing. His flesh felt like it was shrinking around his bones. Then he remembered his dad's words, "Never forget who you are." He wanted to sing with the big-time bands…here was his chance.

They kicked off the set with an instrumental. He watched the dancers, heard the laughter and music bouncing off the ceiling. He got lost in the music and then the song ended. Henderson raised his trumpet and counted off the intro to the next tune. Allan closed his eyes, took a deep breath, and let the music have its way with him. The band was incredibly tight and he rode their music like a rocking canter. His nervousness evaporated as he found the groove and held tight to it.

The song ended to rousing applause. Mose beamed at him from the piano. He felt exhilaration not only from the applause but from singing with such a fine band. Still savoring the moment, he watched Henderson count down the next song.

In quick succession, the set flew by. Hoping for Henderson's approval, he decided he'd nail the last song in the set with a full three-octave treatment. The intro for *I Got Rhythm* started, and he jumped on it. Letting himself go, he began to add little flourishes and variations to the melody. As the song built, he jumped up an octave testing the higher reaches of his register. Soon he was off to the races, improvising, giving himself free rein. The song ended with Allam at the top of his range, holding the note to the bitter end of his breath.

Opening his eyes in pride at his delivery, he expected thunderous applause but was surprised to receive a tepid response. Mose motioned him over to the piano. When he leaned down, the piano player looked at him with a stern, yet kind expression.

"Just sing the song, son, just sing the song."

He turned to see Henderson glaring at him.

He was bemused. He had given it all he had. He thought it the performance of his life. The band took a break, and he went to chat with Mose. "What's up, man?' I get the feelin' you guys weren't happy with the last song. Heck, I gave it all I had."

Mose laid his hand on Allan's shoulder. "Too much butter on the biscuit. Good music is as much about what you leave out as what you put in. Gots to lay down the melody the way it was written 'fore you go addin' gewgaws to it. Like I said, just sing the song like it's wrote first 'fore you start jazzin' it up. Understand?"

"I guess."

"Well next set, jes' keep it simple. Fletch get over it if you finish right."

He located Rod in the back of the room during the break. He had lassoed two girls with whom he was sharing his flask when Allan walked up.

"Hey padnah," said Rod. "Sounded great. Ladies, this here's Allan Dale. Sings with our band but he's on loan to these guys. Best singer in Texas, I reckon."

The inebriated girls grinned at him with overly painted faces through glazed eyes.

"This here's Mazey and Loretta. Loretta wants to spend some time with you when you're done."

They wore short flapper dresses, long strings of pearls, gaudily painted faces, and seductive smiles. Allan tried to smile and be pleasant, but he was shaken by his overreaching performance.

Rod picked up on his mood. "Scuse me ladies. Gotta chat with my friend. Help yourself," he said, handing Mazey the flask.

"You don't look real good. What's up?"

"I think I overdid it on that last song. I wanted to impress Henderson, but I got carried away. He didn't look real pleased."

"Yeah, maybe you did a little. But hey, man, you are a fine singer. Just keep it simple, don't get too busy. These guys are killer musicians, tight, slick arrangements. You just need to be more straight up, blend with their groove, not your own. Hey, it's cool. We got a party waitin' when you finish the next set. Them gals is hot to trot."

He spent a few minutes with Rod and the girls, returning to the stage early for the next set. While contemplating what he needed to do in the upcoming set, the band leader tapped him from behind. "Just so we understand each other, I'd appreciate you sticking with the arrangements as they are written."

"Yes, sir, Mr. Henderson. Sorry, I got a little carried away."

Allan focused on sticking with the song as written and was surprised when the set was over. Fletch approached him with a bland expression, reached in his pocket and handed him an envelope. "Thanks for filling in. Here's the hundred as promised. Best of luck to you."

"Thanks, I..." Too late to be heard. Too late to make the connection he'd hoped for. He watched the crowd dispersing. The chandeliers still glowed upon the elegant celebrants, the smoke still hovered, the laughter still echoed of expensive wallpaper. He saw none of it through his miasma of disappointment.

He found Rod and the girls waiting by the door. Loretta giggled and put her arm in his. "Oh, you were just dreamy."

"Thanks. Rod, let's head up to the room. Got a bucket of sorrows to drown."

When he had been full of himself as a child his mother would remind him not to get too big for his britches. Tonight, he'd tried to stuff ten pounds of singing in a five-pound bag. "Just sing the song," Mose had said.

That would be his new motto.

Chapter 6

Dawn hurled red shafts of light, painting the barren landscape of west Texas in more beauty than it deserved. Some of that sun fell through the slats of blinds onto Allan's face. He clawed his way out of a murky dream, jaded, taking in the remnants of last night's party. Allan opened the door of the motel room, tongue furry, feeling wretched. The stench of crude oil was on the breeze. "Midland. Been here way too long," he said to no one.

"Whassit?" Rod answered groggily.

"Nothing. Go back to sleep."

Oil derricks dotted the flat landscape like miniature Eiffel towers. Khaki scrubland spread as far as the eye could see. The constant sound of the running pumps and music from the always-open bars competed with the constant whisper of wind in the eaves.

The band had been playing at the biggest club in this oil boomtown for six weeks. The money was incredible. He'd made more in tips than Russell paid him. While he'd grown happy with the money, he suffered like a horse with a poorly fitting saddle after each performance. By now, he should have saved a bundle for his escape to the big city. Instead, his money had evaporated like water on the hard pan, spent on fast women, bad cards, and hard liquor.

The club catered to roustabouts and roughnecks. It was so

rowdy, in fact, that the owners had put up a chicken-wire barrier in front of the stage to protect the musicians from hurled bottles and chairs launched by drunken patrons during the frequent brawls. He understood the wild abandon, the need to escape. These men had jobs that were dangerous and often lethal. He'd read that thirteen million folks were out of work. The Depression was causing hundreds of businesses to fail. Wages were cut in half. Even President Hoover took a 20% cut in pay. He understood the willingness to take the risk. Allan was thankful for such a great gig. But he wanted so much more.

In clothes rumpled from last night's revelries, he walked out of the room into the arid scrub, watching the ground for rattlesnakes, which were as numerous as the cactus. He urinated on the dry ground as the sun rose to the ceaseless mechanical rhythms of oil pumps, spread like a legion of praying mantis dipping and rising endlessly, sucking up more of the black gold the world thirsted for. At least that thirst could be satisfied legally. People were increasingly fed up with the Prohibition of their other thirst.

Allan was no closer to his dream of singing in New York than when, months ago, he and Rod had made their pact to save money and split for the big time. They were sidetracked, stranded in this thirsty wasteland, held by chains of money and the pleasures it provided. He felt adrift. He decided that today would be the day he and Rod made the break, gave notice, took their savings, and hit the road for New York.

Coffee was needed. And breakfast—specifically huevos a la Mexicana at Rosalita's. He walked down the raised boardwalk and watched Midland wake up and go to bed simultaneously, as night shift workers passed the morning crews on their way to the rigs. Arriving at the cafe, he spotted his friend Jake alone at a booth. Jake's head rose from his cup, white smile beaming. "Well now, young Master Dale. What you be doin' up at this tender hour?"

"Couldn't sleep. Figured to go on and start my day."

Jake caught the waitress's eye. "Ruby, bring that coffee pot on over for my young friend. Turning to Allan, he asked, "So tell me what kinda mischief you dun' got you self into last night when we was finished playin'?"

"Tell you the truth, I don't remember much. Couple of dames, bottle of tequila. I guess we must have had fun." Ruby arrived with the coffee. Allan ordered, took a long slow sip from his mug, and looked out the window.

"Somethin's gnawin' at you, boy," said Jake. "Seen it clear. Powerful changes happening in you since we been here." He lit a cigarette, letting the comment ride on the smoke.

"I don't like myself much at the moment," said Allan. "I'm livin'' like I'm hogtied to the crazies. Feel like I'm walking backward. Fact is I've been lyin' to myself about how much fun I'm havin'. I'm doing nothing to follow my dream."

"What dat dream be?"

"Just between us, a few months back I made up my mind to save some dough and head for New York, sing with a really big band on the radio, record records. Rod and me, we made a pact. We'd stay with Russell till we saved a grubstake, maybe a few months but not too long. Well, here we sit, not one inch closer. I've saved a little and I think Rod has too."

Jake looked down at his coffee, then lifted his head, arched his eyebrow and looked deeply at Allan. "Well now' 'dis ain't like a big surprise for me. You a way better singer than this outfit deserves. I would miss you but you sho' nuff need to hit the road and chase down that dream a yours. So, here's ol' Jake's advice. Stop playin' poker, stop getting loaded, stop chasing de women, save yo money and go."

"Thanks for that, Jake. You've been a good friend to me. I appreciate the advice. I'm gonna talk to Rod and put away all I can. Maybe get out of here sooner 'stead of later. Thanks, man."

"Ain't no big thang. You keep me posted. Don't be sneaking off without sayin' goodbye, heah?"

They parted after breakfast, Jake to meet a woman, Allan to his room to discuss his renewed vision with Rod. The heat was already radiating from the street. His uneven gait on the boardwalk beat a counterpoint to the heavy boots of his fellow pedestrians.

A door flew open in front of him and a man erupted from it and fell into the street, followed immediately by a larger man shouting. "I'll kill you for what you done to my daughter!" the big man yelled as the other cowered at the foot of the wooden steps.

"Don't. I swear I didn't know how old she was," he cried. It was a voice Allan recognized. Sam Vanderbruggin, the trombonist. The one who leered at all the young girls.

Allan stood paralyzed as the large man pulled a revolver from his belt. "You ruined my Margie, you worthless scum, and you're gonna pay."

As if propelled by some unseen force, Allan felt himself converging on the gunman, grabbing the man's wrist and twisting, just as the gun discharged. He managed to grab it from the assailant's grip while sweeping the man's feet from beneath him. The big man fell hard, his head smashing into a lamppost. Two horses tied out front of the saloon spooked, a crowd was gathering, and several cars had stopped to observe the unfolding drama.

Allan found himself standing over the man, holding the gun on him. "Now hold on. I don't know what's going on here but there ain't no cause to shoot anyone," he said.

"Somebody call the sheriff!" a voice cried out.

The gunman reached around to feel the wound on his head, taking away a bloody hand. Looking up at Allan he said, "I'll get you for this. It ain't changed nothin'. I'll kill him for what he done, then I'll kill you for interferin'."

With the gun still trained on the man, Allan spoke to Sam as he lay in the street.

"What is this all about, Sam?"

"Nothin', I didn't do nothin' wrong. She told me she was eighteen. She wanted it. She was showin' off with the musicians. Know what I'm sayin'?"

As if on cue, the crowd parted before a tall, rangy man with a long gray mustache, a gold star pinned on his chest, and a Colt 45 Peacemaker slung low on his belt. The sheriff took in the scene and in a deep gravelly voice said, "Put down that hog leg, son. Now, what we got here?"

Dropping the gun, Allan spoke up. "Not really sure what caused it, Sheriff, but this fellow was attempting to shoot my friend here who is unarmed. I stepped in just as he pulled the trigger and took the gun away. Don't think anyone got hit."

The sheriff took the still warm revolver from him and spoke to the man on the ground. "Get up, Jeremiah. 'Splain to me why you was tryin' to plug this hombre."

"He took advantage of my little Margie. I'll kill him, Sheriff!"

"Ain't nobody dyin' lessen a judge and jury say so. They decide to fire up Ol' Sparkey, so be it. Now git on up, both of you. The office is a block down the other side of the street." He pointed with the pistol. "After you, boys." He looked at Allan. "You too, young feller."

Something felt all wrong about this. Allan didn't like the look the sheriff gave him, nor the familiarity between the sheriff and the aggrieved father.

Sam grabbed Allan's arm, breathlessly thanking him for his intervention. The man's face was streaked with blood and dust. He reeked of fear, sweat, and urine, a stain spreading across his crotch. Allan found himself wishing he'd let the events unfold. He'd disliked Sam since the first day they'd met, watching as he'd leered over the teenage girls in Columbus.

The hinges squeaked a doleful lament as the door to the sheriff's office swung wide. A corpulent deputy sat at an ancient, weathered desk, boots propped on the top, reading a *True Detective* magazine. He nearly fell over backwards at the sudden entrance of the sheriff and detainees. "Mornin', Sheriff."

"Sit back down, Roland. On second thought, get me some coffee."

"Yes, sir," said the deputy departing in a welter of obsequious boot-falls.

"Y'all sit down. Let's see if we can get a rope around this mess." Motioning to a line of hard wooden chairs against the wall, the sheriff laid the revolver on the desk and stared down at them for a full minute. The lawman then turned and sat down at his desk, withdrawing a pad, and dipped a pen into an ancient, stained ink well.

"What's your name?' the sheriff asked Sam.

"Vanderbruggin...Sam Vanderbruggin. I'm with the Russell Rhodes Orchestra down at the Bon Ton."

The sheriff appraised Sam with unblinking eyes as the clock ticked a staccato beat. His gnarled fingers tapping slowly on the desk for a minute or more before he spoke. "Musician huh? How 'bout you, sport? What's your story?"

It took a moment for Allan to realize he was being addressed. The expression on the sheriff's face was just a few degrees south of menacing. He felt his anger rising. Sam had almost been murdered. Yet the assailant stood beside the sheriff as if he was the assistant inquisitor. He could have been shot by the man, yet there he stood, uncuffed beside the lawman.

"Excuse me, Sheriff," Allan pointed at the gunman, "that man tried to shoot Sam. Seems to me you ought to be questioning him."

Sheriff Will Patton was a force to be reckoned with. His voice dropped an octave. "You'd best be ridin' herd on that mouth, boy. I'm the one asks questions 'round here. Now what's your name?"

"Allan Dale. I'm the vocalist for the Russell Rhodes Orchestra."

"Another musician. Thought you seemed like you was a tight pal to your friend here."

"Look, we're not pals. We just play in the same band. I don't have any truck in whatever Sam may or may not have done. I just didn't want someone to get plugged. That fellow beside you was a whisker away from drillin' a hole in Sam. I didn't even know it was him. I was just doin' my civic duty tryin' to prevent a murder."

The sheriff's gray eyes bored into Allan's, holding his gaze, unblinking for several quiet seconds. Then he turned to the gunman. "Well let's hear it, Jeremiah. How come you were tryin' to shoot this fella?"

"He raped my little Margie!" Spittle spewed as the man pointed a finger pointed at Sam.

"That right, mister? You try to sully his child?"

"No-o-o-o, sir. I mean, I *did* sleep with her, but she led me to believe she was an adult and that's what she wanted. You know how it is. Sometimes a girl fights a little, just havin' a game of it, you know. It's all it was. She said she was of age."

"Weren't no game, you low life," yelled her father. "She come home, dress tore to shreds, bawlin' like all get out. She ain't never been no hussy. I swear it."

The sheriff nailed Sam with a piercing stare. "'Round here... we don't hold with no rapists. Matter of fact, some of them have disappeared 'fore the judge got around to tryin' 'em."

Allan had no fondness for Sam. Given the man's predilections, he knew it was quite possible that he was guilty of rape. However, either there was justice and a legal system or there was vigilantism.

"Now, hold on," blurted Allan. "This man was attempting murder. So far we have no proof one way or the other. It's one man's word against another."

The sheriff twirled one end of his mustache. "Tell you what, counselor. If you want to represent your friend here, you're more than welcome. 'Cept I ain't seen a shingle or sheepskin proclaiming you to be a lawyer. Why don't you go think about your client while you rustle up a law degree? If I need to talk to you, I'll come on down to the Bon Ton and fetch you. Bye now."

Allan stared in stunned silence, his thoughts swarming like angry yellow jackets. "This is not right or just. I'll talk to Russell. We'll get you a lawyer, Sam."

"Don't leave me here," Sam begged.

The sheriff rose with a ring of keys in his hand and looked toward Allan. "You'd best watch yourself, sport. Lots of laws and statutes to observe around Midland. We are a law-abiding community. Hate to see you run afoul of any of them laws and end up in the cell next to your friend."

In stunned disbelief at the abrupt detour his life had taken, Allan finally left, missing the smirk shared between the sheriff and the aggrieved father. He was torn between the need to help his bandmate and hitting the road for New York.

If the morning's events weren't enough to rattle him, Russell Rhodes's reaction set his teeth on edge. Rather than springing to his trombonist's defense, the bandleader saw the event as a personal offense and bad publicity for his band. "That man always worried me," he said. "He's always struck me as a lecherous old fool. And you...you defended him? The sheriff probably thinks you're cut from the same cloth. Bad for the band's image, all of it. Better call my agent and see if we can line up a trombone player pronto. Midland may be ruined for us now."

Allan was aghast. "Russell, you get it!? The guy was already pulling the trigger to shoot Sam when I grabbed the gun. What else could I do? We have to make sure justice is done."

Russell ran his hands through his hair. "You gotta understand these small Texas towns. Folks all stick together. Don't trust strangers. 'Specially musicians. This could bring down a lot of heat on us. Some of these boys is holdin' illegal booze, reefer, coke..." He shook his head and thought for a minute.

"Shoot! We been rolling in dough. Now I reckon we better find a new gig fast, as well as a new trombone player."

"So you're not going to bail Sam out? Just let him rot in the slammer?"

"Shut your trap or you'll be lookin' for work."

"Well, I'll tell you what, Russell, You're a heartless piece of crap. For all you know, Sam is innocent. But you only care about your own welfare. Sam's been with you for years. Guess it's obvious your only loyalty is to yourself." The words shot from Allan unbidden. "Fine, consider this my notice. I'll sing through the weekend and then I'm gone."

"Gone where, Mr. Big Shot? I know every club owner and agent in Texas. All the bandleaders too. You ain't never gonna get another job singin' if I can help it."

"Well, I'm not planning on stickin' round here anyway."

With that he slammed the door and headed for the room he shared with Rod. Rod was still sleeping off the prior night's party, so he kicked the bedpost. "Get up, Rod. We got things to discuss. Big problems goin' on."

"Wha'? Huh? Can't it wait?"

"No! Sam Vanderbruggin is in jail. An angry father tried to shoot him for supposedly raping his daughter. I intervened and stopped him, now the sheriff is siding with the father, and to top that off, Russell isn't lifting a finger to help. We just had it out. I quit. Told him I'm leaving after the weekend."

Rod shook his head, grabbed a glass of water on the bedside table, poured some in his hand, and splashed it on his face. "Let me get this straight. You quit the band?"

"Yep. First, I'm not working for a guy with no loyalty to his musicians when they are in trouble. Second, I've come to the conclusion that we ain't gettin' anywhere in this flyblown manure pit. It's time to fish or cut bait. We made a pact to head for New York.

Let's take what we've saved and head on out. Maybe all this is a good thing. Make us get up off our duff and do something 'bout our dreams."

Rod retrieved a cigarette from the pack of Lucky Strikes on the nightstand, lit it, and stared out the window. Releasing a series of smoke rings, he turned to Allan. "Look man, truth is I'm broke. Ain't been savin' nuthin'. I need some time to put together a grubstake 'fore we leave. Just not right now."

Allan shook his head. He was learning a great deal about commitment in a very brief time span. "Rod, I meant what I said about wanting to go for the big time. I've saved a little under $600 bucks. I was hoping you had at least that much. We're fritterin' away our time here. That's plenty to get us to St. Louis. There is a big music scene there. We could find work, save some more then head on to New York. 'Sides, things are sliding sideways for me in this town with the sheriff."

"What did you do?"

"The right thing. I just asked for justice to be done. But it appears the sheriff and the father are friends and don't care much for musicians."

"Look, let me think about it for a few days, a week or so. Maybe things'll sorta settle down and such. I don't wanna go rushing off halfcocked. Sides, I'm really enjoyin' that gal Martha I've been seein'. And her girlfriend sure took to you last night. "

"You sorry no-account toad. We've been plannin' this for months. Made a pact. Now that I need to move, you're hitched to this place like a hog at the trough. One way or the other, I'm leavin' soon as I help find a lawyer for Sam. I can't stand the man but he doesn't deserve a lynchin'."

A taut silence hung in the fetid air. Finally, Rod spoke. "I'm goin' to get some grub, a cup of coffee, try to think about this mess. At least consider my side of this deal."

"Rod, I pretty well have your side of the deal figured out. Bon appetit...and adios."

That afternoon Allan bought an old Model-T for $150. Although the paint was faded by the West Texas sun, the engine and transmission were sound.

Chapter 7

The two-lane highway to Dallas was a black snake slithering across an undulating sere landscape. Not another car to be seen. Nothing but mesquite, chaparral, and spiraling buzzards above. The dry wind poured over him with the odor of crude oil. The flatness of the land was broken only by derricks and pumping stations.

He was driving his first car, the best he could afford on his way, at last, to St. Louis. Jake had given him a few musician contacts and convinced him to spend some time checking out the music scene, hopefully making money to help him on his way to New York.

His first time alone, Allan sang along with the song on the radio as he drove. He relished the delicious new taste of freedom. Though he had left behind a well-paying gig and suffered disappointment from Rod's failure to live up to their plans, he was filled with hope and ready to tackle St. Louis, confident a gig awaited.

It was dark when he arrived in Dallas. Having passed through the stockyards of Ft. Worth, he wanted to put as much distance as possible between himself and the stench of Cowtown. Worn out from driving, Allan found a Mexican restaurant on the eastern edge of Dallas and asked the waitress if there was an auto camp nearby.

As luck would have it, there was one ten miles or so down the road. It sounded like a good place to spend the night.

The auto camp was packed with other cars. Families were gathered around small cooking pits, the fires reflecting on tents and faces. He found a small parking place in the rear and turned off the engine.

Allan's hands vibrated from the hours of driving—he felt his exhaustion as the cooling engine ticked sporadically. He found the outhouse and while walking back to his car, noticed a family sitting around a large fire, laughter filling the night. The father saw Allan as he passed and called him over. "Howdy. Saw you pull up. You all alone? Come on and sit a spell. Got some coffee left."

Surprised, Allan wandered into their camp. The family sat in front of a tent, husband, wife, and three small boys.

"Come sit on that there water barrel. Ain't comfortable as a chair but it'll do. Name's Joe, Joe Tucker. This here is my wife Ellie and my boys, Andy, Earl, and Bruce."

"Pleased to meet you. I'm Allan Dale. Thanks for asking me over."

"Where you bound?"

"St. Louis. How 'bout you?"

"Well, guess I don't have to tell you times is tough. Lost my job. Heard there's a lot of work out west. Thought we'd give Midland a try."

"Midland. Well, Joe, I just came from Midland. There is work in the oil patch but it's hard and the town is rough as gravel. Don't think it'd be a safe place for your family."

"Don't say," he replied. "Well, we was thinking 'bout California too."

"Heard there's a lot goin' on there. I just know 'bout Midland and with your family and all..."

As they conversed, the three boys sidled up and surrounded their guest. "Hey mister. You hurt your leg?" asked the oldest boy.

"Naw, just have a bad leg from polio when I was a kid."

"Elmer, don't be rude," Ellie scolded.

"It's okay. Is what it is. "

"How you like your coffee?"

"Black is fine, ma'am."

"Good. We ran out of milk and we're low on sugar."

"I appreciate it."

"St. Louis?"

"New York, eventually. St. Louis first though."

"Huh. Lots of folks headin' west but you're headin' east. What kind of work are you lookin' for?"

"I'm a singer. There are a lot of bands in St. Louis, so I hope to work a while there and save up for New York."

Ellie sat beside her husband and took his hand. Turning her brown eyes on him she asked, "You sung in some big places, been on the radio?"

"Well, a few big venues. On the radio in San Antonio and Houston. That's why I'm headin' for New York. That's where the big bands and radio opportunities are." He drained the cup. "Thanks for the coffee and the company. Been driving all day and I'm tuckered out. Gonna hit the road early. If I don't see you, thanks again."

Bacon, coffee, and mesquite smoke blown on a freezing wind drew him up from a restless night, vivid dreams, dark images. Campers huddled around fires, huddling up against the vicious wind. People think Texas is hot. It is. But not in late November. Not with the first Blue Norther of winter blustering down unhindered across the plains.

Stiff, shivering, Allan kicked the coat he used as a blanket aside. He found the outhouse, enduring a frosty morning constitutional. He decided to thank the family again for their kindness the previous night.

Greeting him, however, was a rectangle of weeds where the car had been parked, a dry spot now surrounded with morning dew. Disappointed, hoping for a last glimpse of the love and tenderness that he'd shared, Allan climbed into his car and continued his journey.

As he drove, the fierce rising sun pierced his glazed windshield. The landscape began a subtle change from flat terrain to rolling hills decorated with oak and pine.

He had never spent this much time alone. It was freeing, but after witnessing the loving family from camp, a bit lonely. He began to sing torch songs, some blues, laments to capture the mood.

Upon reaching Greenville, he stopped at an ESSO service station. He asked the attendant for a fill up and headed inside to buy a Coke. Walking back to the car he noticed a diner across the highway, and realized he was famished.

Late morning found the place serving, but only a handful of customers. He took a seat at the counter, ordered coffee and a large breakfast. Sensing a presence, he turned as a shabbily-dressed man approached and sat next to him. Allan nodded politely. The food arrived, and he began to eat. A few mouthfuls into his meal, the stranger spoke.

"Where you off to? Seen ya pull in. Looks like you're packed up for a long 'un."

"Yep. On my way to St. Louis."

"Ya don't say. Don't that beat all. I'm on my way to Memphis. Got a line on a job. What would you say 'bout takin' me far as Texarkana. I can head east, and you keep on north to St. Lou."

Allan took stock of his diner-mate. Late thirties, unshaven, ripe— but not rank, glacial blue eyes darting furtively from beneath red caterpillar brows. Nervous energy radiated from him like the hum of a power line.

"See, bud, I'm a bit down at the heels," said the man. "Been out of work for a good while. Just thought you might like a bit of company and I sure could use the help."

Hard times were making most people a little more compassionate. *There but for the Grace of God go I*, Allan thought. "Don't see why not. Have you eaten? Be happy to spring for a meal."

"Now, that's right neighborly of ya'. Fact is I ain't et since breakfast yesterday." He smiled with the merest corner of his lip, his eyes unchanged.

"Hey, miss, bring me some coffee," he called out to the waitress. He pointed at the menu. "Farmer's Breakfast too."

Turning to Allan, he shot out his hand. "Name's Neal. Friends call me Red cause of the hair." He removed a sweat-stained fedora revealing a thick carpet of curly red locks."

"Howdy. Name's Allan."

"So, what takes you to St. Lou?"

"Hope to find work. Got some names of folks that can help me."

"What kind of work you do?"

"I'm a musician—singer, actually. Just left the Russell Rhodes Orchestra. Lookin' for bigger opportunities."

"Hear there's good money in that—if you're with the right outfit. Specially if you sing on the radio."

"That's my hope. How 'bout you?"

"Hell, done lots of stuff. Bit of this and that. Last job was a bust. I was a driver."

"Well, hope you find what you're lookin' for."

The waitress brought the heaping Farmer's Breakfast, placing it on the counter before Red, who proceeded to attack it like Grant did Richmond. When he was done, Allan paid the bill.

Climbing into the Model T, he and his new companion were away. They drove in silence for an hour or more.

Red looked in the backseat a few times at Allan's belongings. "Play that guitar pretty good, do ya'?"

"Well enough to accompany myself and jam a little. But I'm not up to being a guitarist with a band."

"Pretty expensive, that thang?"

"Probably. It's a Martin my dad gave me, so I'm not sure, but Martins are great guitars."

"Hum. Always wanted to learn how to play one a them."

"Well, it's never too late. When you get a guitar, take some lessons. You'll always be able to make music and entertain yourself."

"Most of my friends don't cotton much to music, lessen it's the rattle of dice or the clack of pool balls. Say, that's a right nice lookin' watch you got there."

"Thanks, my dad was given this in honor of his work with the San Antonio Symphony."

"Come from some culture, do ya'?"

"Naw. Just musicians."

"Don't know 'bout that. Bet you rubs shoulders with folks in the high cotton."

Allan turned his attention back to the road, relishing the silence. Something nagged at him. There was a ferret-like edginess about his passenger. When the sign ahead read Texarkana, 65 miles, he was glad to be nearing the place of their parting.

Over the next two hours the conversation died and Red napped for a while. As they entered the outskirts of Texarkana, Allan asked Red where he'd liked to be dropped off.

"Just keep on into downtown. Your turn off to St. Lou is on the other side of town. I'll show you where."

Texarkana seemed to be weathering the hard times well. Lots of cars and pedestrians in the busy downtown. When they reached the other side of town, a large, wooded park appeared on their right.

Red pointed to a road into the park. "Pull on in there for a minute."

Allan glanced at him. "You're meeting your friends here?"

"Not exactly. Pull up under them trees. I'll 'splain my situation."

Something twitched in Allan's spirit, but he rolled up under a spreading oak grove. Fast as a cottonmouth, Red whipped out a gleaming blade, pressed the point against Allan's neck. "Here's what's gonna' happen, sport. You're gonna give me all your money, that watch and that there ring too."

"Hang on a minute. I tried to help you out. I'm out of work same as you. Tell you what—how 'bout I give you twenty bucks and let's part on good terms?"

"Hah! I'm the one settin' terms here. Terms are give me what I want and you live. Don't, and I'll slice you like a ripe watermelon and take it all and the car too."

Allan had hidden the bulk of his cash in his sock. Still, at least a third was in in his wallet. Seeing no way out, he handed it to the robber.

"Now the watch. And that ring. That from school?"

"Listen. The watch is a gift from my dad and the ring is so tight I can't get it off."

"I'll have that watch and you either slide that ring off or I'll take the finger as well."

He unbuckled the watch and handed it to Red. The ring had been stuck on his hand since he'd gained a few pounds. He twisted it, spit on his hand, twisted some more.

"Give you ten more seconds. Then I'm cuttin' it off."

Suddenly, as if by magic, the graduation ring slid free and was immediately seized by his tormentor.

"Now then, give me them car keys, get out and walk into that thicket."

He complied and soon they were hidden in a copse of trees. "Take off your belt and hand it to me," said the man. "Now back up to that tree and sit down agin' it."

When he complied, Red bound him to the tree, secured his hands behind him with his belt. The robber stood over him and grinned. "It's your lucky day. I dun drove for two bank jobs and shot myself a copper. I'm letting you off easy, boy. Figure it'll take you least ten minutes to get loose. I'll be long gone. Goin' to the cops ain't gonna help neither. Ain't caught me yet and ain't gonna. Adios."

Allan sat in shock, bound to the tree. When he heard his car fire up and drive off, it hit him. Now he had a little more than three hundred dollars, no car, and all of his belongings including his beloved Martin gone. He began to work against his bindings. It took more than ten minutes, but freed at last, he stood and walked out of the trees, heading for the bus station.

First, he placed a call to the police, who arrived quickly. After giving them the information, the senior cop told him he was lucky to be alive. Red was on the FBI's wanted list and considered highly dangerous. Cold comfort, he thought, considering all he had lost. They said they'd put out an All-Points Bulletin, asked if he'd stick around for a few days to identify the perpetrator if caught.

In the end, he told them he'd call from St Louis, then walked to the counter and bought a one-way ticket. Two hours later, he boarded a crowded Greyhound.

As evening fell, Allan watched the landscape pass as they traveled north. The vibration and engine noise calmed his frayed nerves, but he was overwhelmed by the loss.

He had a choice. He could wallow in his anguish or consider his opportunities. He chose the latter. He still had enough to buy a tux for performing and pay for a couple of months' rent until he found a gig singing. He was confident it would take less time than that but at least he had enough to get started.

Drowsiness crept upon him. As he drifted off, he prayed, "Lord, it's been a rough one down here. I haven't been following your guidance. I pretty much lost everything I own. Guess I deserved it. But I'm rolling on. Give me the strength to do what I need to. Help me get started quick with a good band. And Lord, help me find the kind of love that family back in the road camp had. I'll try to do better. Amen."

Chapter 8

Allan awoke when they arrived in Cape Girardeau, Missouri. It was a little after ten p.m. when he stepped down from the bus into a frigid wind he had not expected. His fellow passengers seemed equally assaulted. Like a tribe in flight, they headed for the warmth waiting inside.

Wandering about the small depot left him feeling adrift. He bought a candy bar, a Coke, and a newspaper and returned to his seat. A new passenger was sitting in the aisle seat next to the rumpled coat Allan had left behind in his window seat.

"'Scuse me." A middle-aged man looked up through bushy brows and rheumy grey eyes. He stood to allow Allan entry without a word.

"'Preciate it."

The driver arrived, followed by the bass thrum of the engine and the whoosh of the closing door.

An hour passed and then the man unexpectedly reached out his hand. "Name's Wilbur. Wilbur Jennings. Where ya' bound, young fella'?"

"St. Louis. You?"

"'Racine, Wisconsin. Transfer in St Louis. Been in Washington till they chased us off. Part of the Bonus Army." The man's grizzled beard, threadbare wool army coat, and rank odor augured for a long trip.

"Yeah, I read about that in the paper. Not real clear on the details."

"Us veterans are sufferin'. We need the bonuses we are owed now during this Depression. Can't wait till them government boys want to turn loose of it. We are hurtin'. Lots of us wounded in the war. Just want what we been promised. We need it now to survive. There was at least a couple thousand camped out till they called in the troops to chase us off. Ain't right, I tell ya."

"Sorry you've been through all that. I appreciate your service. Country's a mess for sure. Least it looks like Prohibition is likely to be repealed. Hasn't done much good for anyone 'cept the gangsters and politicians."

"Seems to me more people drank more booze than ever when they passed it," Wilbur replied.

"Yep. Guess in a way it's been good for me. Lots of people wanted to have a good time at speakeasies and dancehalls and needed music. Being a musician, I've worked pretty steady while many folks have lost their jobs. My hope is they still need the music when the booze is legal."

"'Spect they will. This new music on the radio is gettin' wilder and wilder...jazz and nigra music creepin' in. What kinda music did you say you play?"

Allan avoided smiling. "Didn't say...but lots of that jazz and nigra stuff." The man turned a wary eye on him but said nothing. "Believe I'm gonna get a little shut eye before St. Louis. Hope you get your army bonus, mister."

It was nearing two a.m. when they finally arrived at the Union Terminal in St Louis. Allan had to find a room but had no idea where to go. A kindly desk clerk directed him to a hotel a block away with "reasonable rates." When he checked in, he found the rates were three times what he was used to. He took the elevator up four stories to a bleak room with a narrow bed and a faded bedspread. *Oh well,* he thought. *It'll do till I get the gig and a decent place.*

Worn out, yet still abuzz from the trip, it took him a fair while to succumb to slumber.

The next morning, Allan awoke with a start in the unfamiliar surroundings. The east-facing room poured piercing spears of sunlight over him. Surprised he'd slept till nearly ten, he headed to a bathroom barely large enough for a sink, toilet, and shower. He dressed and prepared to take on his first day in St. Louis.

Following a sparse but pricey breakfast in the dining room, he found the house phone and called the first of Jake's contacts. Emil Landreau was a New Orleans trumpet player that Jake said knew everyone. After ten rings, Allan was getting ready to hang up when a gravelly voice answered.

"What y'all want? Ain't even noon, ah guarantee." The Cajun patois carried an edge.

"Sorry. Is this Emil Landreau?"

"Who dat be askin'?"

"I'm a friend of Jake Galvan, the piano player. Said you played together in New Orleans. My name's Allan Dale. I sang with the Russell Rhodes Orchestra where Jake was the pianist. He thought you might be of some assistance in helping me get an audition with a band here. Or maybe help me find an agent who can."

"Jake, huh. How dat ol' catfish?"

"He's good. Playin' a gig in Midland, Texas, the oil patch. Steady work, good money."

"That's just grand. Jobs is sparse round here, but I'm playin' with a band that couldn't get arrested in N'awlins. Money ain't great but I'm gettin' by, ya understand."

"Well, I'm a pretty good singer. Anybody you know of lookin' for one of those?"

"Not off the top of my head. Tell you what, let me get some java under my belt. Maybe we can meet up this afternoon. Friend of Jake's is a friend of mine."

"That'd be great. Where and what time?"

"Place called Big Mo's down by the Eads Bridge. Ask someone. They tell you how to get here."

"What time?"

"Gotta be at the club at eight. Say six or so, yes?"

"Great. Thanks, Emil. Look forward to meeting you. Jake says you blow a mean trumpet."

"Well, I do my dangdest for an 'ol Cajun swamp rat. See you round six."

—

THE EADS BRIDGE WAS large and well known. Built in the late 1800s, it connected St. Louis and East St. Louis. Allan located Big Mo's and found a bench. Having arrived early, he sat gazing at the Mississippi rolling by. This was where it joined with the Missouri.

Dangerous looking currents roiled the muddy water. Riverboats, barges, and countless boats plied the expanse. Allan was reminded of Tom Sawyer and Huckleberry Finn stories, borne on the currents of imagination, back to the wild days of riverboat gamblers and pirates.

What he observed now was a ragged populace, closed shops and businesses, more evidence of the hard times befalling the country. Clapboard buildings, unpainted, listed in weathered abandonment. Aging warehouses sat empty. He watched a rat scurry across the wharf and a rank river funk filled his nostrils.

He tried to stay optimistic. After all, he had what would be a few months' wages for the average person, as well as the possibility of a position with a band. Emil hadn't been overly encouraging but it was a start. At least he had a foothold on the mountain he was climbing.

He was reminded of a Mark Twain quote:

"Twenty years from now you will be more disappointed by the things you didn't do than the things you did do. So, throw off the bowlines. Sail away from the safe harbor. Catch the Trade Winds in your sails. Explore. Dream. Discover."

Allan breathed in the cold river's odor and smiled. He left the bench and headed to Big Mo's for his meeting with Emil. When he arrived there, he found a booth in the corner. Out a window, he watched the river traffic until his reverie was broken. A curiously dressed man carrying a trumpet case was walking in the door. Even without the instrument, Emil's appearance screamed "musician."

Tiny in stature, no more than five feet in height, he walked with the bearing of a prizefighter. He wore an ensemble of taupe pants, a grey shirt, a purple brocade vest and a buff corduroy coat, topped with a dove grey riverboat gambler's hat.

Allan rose to greet him. Emil smiled, offered his hand. "Guess you must be the singing sensation sent from my ivory ticklin' friend. He say you good, you be good…I guarantee. Glad to meet you."

Emil's Cajun accent disarmed Allan and brought a sense of mischief to the meeting.

"Howdy, I'm Allan Dale. Good to meet you."

"I don't be goin' to play for a while yet so let us see what we can explore here, eh?"

Big Mo's warm air, the smell of food, and his new friend brought a sense of peace he'd not had for a few days. Emil produced a small black cheroot and lit it. "So…. tell me all 'bout yo' self an let's see if Emil maybe he got some help for you."

Emil listened patiently while Allan spilled out the drama that had brought him to this point. Expended at last, he leaned back and took a deep breath.

As if on cue, the waitress arrived, and Emil lit up with a blinding smile. "Delores, ma belle. You are lovely as the first butterfly of spring.

This is my new and hungry friend, Allan Dale. He would steal your heart with his song, but I have already claimed it."

She smiled knowingly, slapped his shoulder with a menu, and turned her smile on Allan. She was a fading beauty weathered by hard miles, yet maintained a lovely visage. Her brown eyes bore hope and hopelessness in tenuous balance but Allan could see the sixteen-year-old girl that would always inhabit her even in her dotage.

"Well," she said. "I don't know how he sounds, but he looks mighty fine."

"Oh, you would break the heart of your admirer with so little care?" chuckled Emil.

"You are a caution. What you boys want to drink?"

"We wish for champagne, but the gendarmes will not have it. We will settle for Coke."

"All right, shugah."

Emil turned back to Allan. "So, my friend. You have blown in on a west wind in hopes that Emil can open a door, yes? But you have arrived in a time of difficulties, no? So, I will reveal to you the picture. First however, we share in some of the local moonshine mixed with the exotic Coca Cola, yes?"

"Sure, that's fine. So Emil, where are you playing tonight?"

"I am in a quintet led by Lonnie Johnson, a crazy guitarist. We are down at a club on Biddle Street, a speakeasy. Don't have a vocalist but sometimes Irene Scruggs or Alice Moore sit in and sing some. The blues and jazz here is way different from back in N'awlins. You're welcome to tag along, check out the scene. Ah, here comes my angel now."

Delores brought two Cokes, glasses with ice, and a wry grin.

"Are you gentlemen eating as well as drinking this evening?"

"I will have a bowl of your gourmet stew, and I recommend it my young friend."

"Yep, sure," said Allan. "That will be fine."

Emil poured two fingers of clear liquid from a silver flask into each glass. He filled the rest with Coke, as did Allan.

"Sante." Emil clinked his glass against Allan's and drank half in one gulp. "One must fortify one's inspiration, *oui*?"

Allan took a sip and nearly choked. He had tasted a fair bit of bootleg, but this was potent brew.

Emil chuckled. "You are looking a little green around the gills. I should have warned you. I have a friend in transportation. Occasionally a few bottles are, sad to say, lost or dropped. He has the privilege of catching them before they fall and are wasted. A noble endeavor, no?"

Once recovered, Allan smiled. "So, Emil, what is the lay of the land here? Do you know anyone looking for a good singer? And with some modesty, I am good, as I hope you will hear if given the chance."

"My friend, the scene here is very tight. One must make inroads with the locals. It took me a few months to be offered regular work. Also, we must consider the problem of you being a singer. There are more spots for instrumentalists but only one for a vocalist." The musician observed Allan's face. "But do not be discouraged, my friend. Emil will reveal to you the first open door tonight. Perhaps we may hear your voice and be captivated. One must have hope and one must have patience. Ah, and our patience is rewarded as I see the lovely Delores bearing our dinner."

Emil dominated the conversation and Allan learned much about the Cajun life, New Orleans, and Emil's prodigious accomplishments—in particular, those regarding his romantic conquests. Pushing his plate aside, he called Delores to the table. "Well ma passion, the time for us to part has arrived and already I am lost. There is music to be made and laughter to be shared. Please bring me the bill as I'm treating my fellow musician to dinner. And oh, yes, when you are off, come by Biddle Street—you know, the green door. There will be a party waiting for you."

"'Preciate the invite," said the woman. "Don't believe I'll make it. Maybe another time?"

"*Merci*, ma belle. Perhaps another night, yes?"

Emil paid their fare and led the way to Allan's first taste of St. Louis nightlife. They arrived at a large green door in a commercial district where Emil knocked twice, waited, and then knocked three more times. A peephole opened, followed by the door opening to a scene of intrigue and music. The doorman, broad as a bull and hard as an oak, welcomed Emil and his guest with a tight tip of his head.

"Evenin', Emil."

"*Bon jour*, Charlie. Keepin' the joint safe from the gendarmes?"

"Think enough of the city council is here to keep them from showin' up. Who's your friend?"

"Why, this here is the next big singing sensation, Allan Dale, fresh in from Texas."

"Welcome. Enjoy."

Allan followed Emil to a small dressing room filled with musicians getting ready for their set. "Emil," said one, "'bout time you showed up. We go on in five."

"Ah, Lonnie. Never too early, never too late...Emil is always ready to blow. Lonnie, meet Allan Dale, recently the singer with the Russell Rhodes Band in Texas. My friend Jake Galvan tells me has pipes for miles."

"Evenin'. Hope you dig our set. Come on, Emil, let's give 'em what they come for."

Turning as he spoke, Lonnie picked up a sunburst Gibson F-hole hollow-body guitar and headed for the door, followed by the rest of the musicians.

Emil called out as he left, "There's a table up front for friends of the band. Find a chair and I'll catch you after the first set."

Allan joined the exodus, last out behind the drummer, twirling his sticks as they headed for the stage. The light was a muted smoky purple hue, giving the room an eerie fog-like ambiance.

Allan spotted a chair at a table with several ladies who had been in the dressing room. Enveloped by invisible tendrils of several perfumes as he approached, he received questioning looks from a couple of the ladies at his inclusion at the band's table.

"Good evening. I'm Allan Dale, a friend of Emil. Mind if join you?"

A striking Black woman studied him for a few seconds, then broke into a beautiful smile. "Why sure shuga'. You a friend of Emil, you be welcome. I'm Irene Scruggs. I'm singin' a few songs with Lonnie tonight."

"Really? I'm a singer as well. Just arrived from Texas. I was with the Russell Rhodes Orchestra until a week or so back. Came to see what opportunities St. Louis might offer."

Her sparkling eyes glittered over high cheekbones, a wry smile animating her lips. "What kind of singin' you do?"

"Mostly popular stuff. It was an eight-piece outfit I just left. We were booked solid. It was just time for me to move on. Look forward to hearing you."

She smiled and turned to the lady next to her and continued a conversation as he watched the band take the stage. Lonnie welcomed the crowd and kicked off with an upbeat instrumental that was a mélange of blues and Django jazz guitar style.

Allan was knocked back by unique style. By the third song, he was captured. Whatever this sound was, he loved it.

Then Lonnie invited Irene up to sing. She elegantly unfolded herself from the chair and walked like Cleopatra herself up onto the stage. The band did a long intro with Lonnie leaning on his blues bends and phrasing. When Irene began to sing, as if by magic, everyone else onstage disappeared. Her smoky voice pulled you under like a riptide.

Allan was entranced. She sang with such depth, such passion, such pain. He knew that he had made the right decision in coming to St. Louis. This was a place where he could tap into a whole new energy, a novel, unfamiliar musical landscape. His reverie was broken when the set ended and Emil sat down beside him.

"Amazing!" was all he could say.

"Cool. I'm glad you are enjoying it. Did you like my solo on the last number?"

"I've loved every note of everything I've heard. This is another sound, another approach. It makes what we were doing seem as dull as old brass next to fine gold."

Irene descended the stage like a lioness sated by a fresh kill. Applause accompanied her. She absorbed the adulation as would a thirsty rose. Her friends poured more appreciation on her as she luxuriated in it.

Allan was struck by a realization. As were all performers, Irene was fed by, and addicted to, applause. He understood as never before the seductive power of approval that all performers crave. This powerful force drove them, inspiring them to devote untold hours perfecting their art. They were drawn like bees to pollen to the applause given in appreciation of the release of their creative force. Those blessed with the gift of music awaited their turn to feast on the praise and devour the compliments.

She turned to him, her smile broadening. She nodded and looked deeply into his eyes. "You sing like an angel."

"Means a lot from a fellow singer."

Several flasks appeared to further lubricate the group and joy poured over them as they drank in the delicious moment of connection. An hour passed and Emil stood and motioned to Allan. The two left, Allan still filled with the music, and shared fellowship with other performers.

They walked in silence until Emil spoke. "What you think, hey? You like The St. Louis Blues?"

"Oh, Emil, that stuff just knocks me out. Thank you so much for inviting me. Man, I'd love to sing some of that music."

"Well, I tell you what...Old Emil, he put his mind to helping you. Maybe tomorrow I get some ideas."

They parted at Emil's stop, leaving Allan simultaneously fulfilled and empty.

Climbing the stairs to his spare quarters, he was overcome with conflicting emotions of hope and loneliness. He realized the tenuousness of his situation as he opened the door to his tawdry room—all the ambition, the dreams of success, were diluted by his realization of how much he had to learn and how uncertain were his prospects. It was a difficult admission, but he felt intimidated by the level of skill he had witnessed.

Did he really have what it took to make it? Would his funds last long enough for him to find a gig?

He brushed his teeth, pulled back the worn bedspread, and lay down to sleep with his doubts.

Chapter 9

A month spent visiting the clubs, hearing the bands, getting to know the musicians had so far produced nothing. Allan sat in the chilly air, on a bench by the river, contemplating the last few turning leaves remaining on skeletal branches. Smoke drifted from listing houses joining the low gray clouds crowding rooflines. Bare trees bereft of leaves held no promise of Springs return. Smoke from a trash barrel mingled with Mississippi mud hung in the air.

He found solace watching the river and the craft borne upon it. Loneliness and worry stalked his thoughts. His funds were dwindling at a shocking rate. With his current spending, he could only keep fed and housed for a few more months.

He picked up a newspaper someone had left on the bench. With nothing else to occupy him, he began reading. Not cheery stuff. Southern Pacific Railroad had kicked more than 700,000 vagrants off their trains. The Children's Bureau had announced that upwards of 200,000 children were roaming the country as vagrants. The Depression was devastating to all but the wealthy and those working in government jobs. It was not a great time for him to be unemployed.

Tired of the dreary news, he happened upon the society pages. Here were the scions of St. Louis in celebration. He saw announcements for several cotillions, receptions, and society functions. Having played at such events he could picture the sumptuous foods, in elegant hotels, entertainment by orchestras.

The seed of an idea sprouted. He owned a suit, a tux, and a dinner jacket needed for performing, bought with the money he'd hidden when he was robbed. Could he not arrive at such an event as if an invited guest? With a little research on the families, the proper attire, and the willingness to brass it out, perhaps he could at least stay fed.

Allan began his elegant subterfuge. Each week, he combed the society and announcement sections of the paper. With charm and clever conversation, he began to rub shoulders with St. Louis's leading citizens. This led not only to a stomach filled with gourmet delicacies but several assignations with attractive debutantes. He also began to meet some of the top musicians performing there.

One icy Saturday night in mid-December, he found himself at the punch bowl next to Al Lyons, the leader of the band. Both of them had been properly lubricated and hit it off. Allan revealed the truth of his position and Al, after gales of laughter, complimented Allan on his ingenuity and aplomb. Seizing the moment, Allan asked if he knew of anyone looking to audition a singer. Al's lips parted in a crooked grin.

"As fate may have it, this could be a bit of fortuitous timing. As a matter of fact, Donnie, our singer, whom you have been enjoying this evening has been a pain in the ass and I am looking to replace him. We rehearse on Tuesday at four. Come around three. I'll have my piano man there. I'll give you the address. Show me what you got. You never know your luck in the big city."

As a result of Allan's societal survival skills—and his singing—he landed his first foothold in the St. Louis music scene. Over the next few months, he began to build a reputation and following.

New Year's Eve found Allan and the band at The Meadowbrook, one of St Louis's most prestigious venues. It was festooned with balloons and streamers, the crowd glowing in reflected chandelier light. Gentlemen in tuxes, ladies in the most daring and stylish evening wear swanned about in the pleasure of the esteemed company they shared. The electricity and prestige of the live radio broadcast on KMOX made all present feel part of a momentous event. Perhaps this would be the end to the brutal days since the Crash. Maybe President Roosevelt would return America to greatness.

Allan had never felt more alive nor more certain of his ability to deliver his best ever performance. From the first note, he soared as never before. He poured his soul into each song, growing in enthusiasm as the first set rolled on. When the radio announcer broke in with commercial, the band took a break, and Allan found the bar where set ups were passed out like an assembly line, soon to be united with waiting flasks of booze. He found himself surrounded by adoring fans, mostly female, offering him a taste of hooch and the hint of something more enticing.

Focused on the next set, he politely disengaged and found a quiet alcove near the terrace doors. Sensing someone approaching, he turned to see a striking woman in a black off-the-shoulder gown. She bore a wry smile, an inquisitive expression shining from bright green eyes. She cocked her head—hair the color of aged maple fell around her face.

"Do you remember me?"

Caught by surprise, he took a few beats for her face to register.

"Angela? Angela Arthur?"

"Well, *Williams* actually, as you may recall since you sang at my wedding reception. As usual, your singing is divine. You have grown in your gifting. I have always thought you were destined for great things and now here you are in St. Louis singing on the radio."

"Angela, you are too kind and give me more credit than I deserve."

"How did you end up here?"

"Billy's business associate invited us. He said it would be the best New Year's party ever. So far, I'd have to agree."

Allan had always found her lovely but now she radiated an

animal attraction which seemed irresistible. Resist he must, and the upcoming set gave him an exit line.

"It is grand to see you. You are lovelier than ever. Sad to say, but I have to get up on the stage."

"Perhaps we could visit sometime. Billy is playing golf tomorrow. You could meet me at the Magnolia Hotel. I'm told they have a lovely brunch. Say eleven? See you in the morning."

She was gone before he could reply.

The wild abandon of the dancers increased. He imagined couples dancing as they listened to the broadcast ringing in the new year in their homes or on some remote farm. Small groups huddled in front of radios, as much a part of the music as the crowd before him. This is the future, he thought, bringing music to hundreds, no, thousands of fans. He resolved to make 1932 his year of ascendancy, the stepping stone to New York and national recognition. Perhaps he'd start with a clandestine brunch in the company of the fetching, if married, Angela.

—

LATE MORNING SUN WOKE him. Groggy from having gone to bed intoxicated at four, his first thought was what to do about Angela's invitation. His enthusiasm over their encounter was brought up short by the impropriety of meeting.

He didn't know how to contact her and knew she would expect him. He resolved to tell her he wasn't up for a tryst with a married woman. He crawled out of bed discovering, to his shock, a clock reading ten-fifteen.

Throwing himself into some semblance of order, he bolted to catch a bus that would take him near the Magnolia. Arriving twenty minutes late, he found Angela stewing in her own juices. He rushed to her table and bowed. "I'm so sorry to have made you wait. We finished so late that frankly I only awoke about an hour ago. I arrived as soon as I was able."

Her smile disarmed him. Instead of anger, she greeted him with a countenance showing only joy at seeing him.

"I wasn't sure that you would take me up on my invitation. It is a bit scandalous, I suppose. The fact is I have always thought you enormously intriguing and found myself emboldened enough to seek you out."

"Well, I'm flattered and have been intrigued as well. But you being married and all, I wouldn't want to cause any problems."

"Ah, I have a fair few of those in my basket anyway. Tell me, then, how it is you ended up in St. Louis?"

For the next hour they shared their stories, laughed at their foibles and mistakes, and found desire sprouting between them, desire that could create a conflagration. A voice within him warned Allan to depart, but the voice grew quieter as they grew more enlivened in one another's presence. He was valiantly attempting to rein in his longing and to find a graceful way to exit when she began to reveal the disturbing details of her situation.

"Our families envisioned a practical union. Two established families joined through their children—a marriage to create a dynasty. It's a story so old as to be a cliché. The problem is that Billy is riddled with self-loathing and cruelty. He has never accomplished anything on his own. He feeds off the teat of his family's wealth. Though I also come from wealth, I have never regarded it as a worthwhile reason to feel superior to others. We are like chalk and cheese, the two of us.

"What was at first mild irritation has grown into ever more cruel behavior. He is careful to attack with puerile insults or when he *does* actually strike me, to do so in places where the bruises cannot be seen. My family is of little help. The merger, as it were, is of such extraordinary potential that my mother's best counsel is to soothe his ire with affection. Not the easiest thing to do if you are a proud woman.

"So, I find myself here having brunch with you. I have been drawn to you since I first heard you sing, but not because of your talent alone. I sense a quality in you. Your eyes hold a tenderness that beckons me. I know it is scandalous, yet I could not but follow the current that pulls me to you."

He was stunned. Her frankness, her sadness, her situation called to the rescuer within him. His heart went out to her and his body longed for her. Was there anything as seductive as a beautiful woman in distress?

Yet this was not a one-night adventure with a flapper. This was a woman of substance. A wounded, vulnerable soul. Whatever choice he made would have unforeseen and likely dire consequences. Moreover, it was a moral dilemma of great import. Adultery was clearly proscribed in his faith.

"Angela, my mind longs to help you. My heart longs for you. Yet my spirit whispers resistance. Were the circumstances different, were you not married, I would be honored to court you. You are an exceptional woman and deserve far better than the shoddy treatment you receive from your worthless husband.

"Nonetheless, I feel it would be a mistake to embark upon a journey that, one way or another, will leave a string of crushed hearts and disappointments in our wake. "There is also my own situation to consider. I have no prospects. Only ambitions. You are accustomed to a life of ease and privilege at a time when many are in wretched straits. I can offer you nothing. Therefore, I must step away from all the allure and beauty that you embody, hoping that you will leave this cruel, selfish man. Perhaps, if we meet in the future, we may have a chance to write a new and beautiful chapter in our lives."

Tears welled in her eyes as her chin dropped. She looked up at him. "I should have expected no less. It took no small amount of drink for me to make the suggestion that we meet. Yet it was your obvious goodness that drew me to you. Well, in truth, it was your singing that got my attention, but I see in you a deep reservoir of kindness as well as passion, two things that Billy cannot give me. So, I should thank you, I suppose, for your rejection, although, in truth, no woman can stand the thought of it. Yet I must, and will accept it, and while I hate it, I admire you for your honesty." She kissed him chastely on his cheek and parted.

Allan walked out of The Magnolia, lost in thought, and found a bench by the river. The city was quiet and in the chilly midday light, the breeze carried the wet smell of the river. A distant boat horn and the chatter of crows were the only sounds. Alone on this cold first day of 1933, he considered where the river of time might take him.

The sound of voices floated on the dank air. Turning, he saw four raggedly clothed children huddled around a barrel fire. Watching them laughing amongst unpainted tenements and dirty snow brought him out of his self-absorption.

Hunger stalked a country suffering with twenty-five percent unemployment. As he had been enjoying a sumptuous brunch, the brutal truth of life was demonstrated by the condition of these little ones. Yet as children do, they laughed and frolicked in the only reality they knew.

He thanked God for his success, feeling good about overcoming the temptation of an affair with Angela. Watching the boats and barges passing on the river, he envisioned a life with someone as lovely as her, yet someone of the steadfastness and purity of his mother. He rose and walked to the bus stop. He paused, to give a dollar to each of the children warming themselves by the barrel.

"Happy New Year," he said, handing each a bill. "I think it will be a great year for us all." He hoped that it would for these and the countless other waifs suffering the privations of the Depression.

On the bus ride back to his room, he took in the human wreckage passing by outside his window. Men with vacant expressions, trudging aimlessly toward an ephemeral future. Women carrying frightfully small sacks of groceries home to feed their families. While he contemplated a grand future of fame and fortune, most people hung on the cliff edge of disaster.

—

ALLAN ARRIVED EARLY FOR the Saturday night radio broadcast. He was excited to have landed the permanent position as vocalist. The band had been invited to be a regular on the show to be heard on KMOX from the Meadowlark. Engineers were still fiddling with the sound as he wandered backstage to check in with Al to go over the set list and make any needed changes.

"Evening, Allan. Got a big crowd tonight. Bunch of high rollers in the oil business in town. Expect it will get lively. Just want to add a couple of upbeat numbers in the first set, get things jumpin' early. Here's a new set list. You know these tunes so it shouldn't throw you for a loop."

"Sounds good, boss. I'm rarin' to go."

An hour flew by and suddenly they were taking the stage. The announcer welcomed the crowd and the radio audience, introduced the band, and they kicked off with *I Got Rhythm*. It seemed to Allan that they had just begun when the first set ended.

As he stepped down from the stage, someone grabbed him by the lapel and turned him halfway round. At first, he didn't recognize the man, who was obviously drunk and had blood in his eye and murder in his heart. "Remember me from San Antonio? You sang at my wedding. Now I find out you're having your way with my wife Angela. Well, let me tell you, you've plowed up an acre of snakes."

Suddenly, William Arthur was winding up to throw a punch. Allan's boxing instinct took over and he threw a straight right with his full weight behind it, landing it squarely on the chin just as Williams' looping punch was just getting started. The blow dropped him like a steer in a slaughterhouse.

Three of his friends joined in, cursing and swinging. The crowd began to panic as the security man at the door waded into the fracas.

William's friends dragged Allan down and were beginning to kick at him. He managed to get hold of the leg of one of his attackers and drop him into his companions. Finally, the security man prevailed and began to break up the brawl. He helped Allan to his feet while holding his tormentors at bay. William was now standing, blood streaming from a cut lip, framing an empty space where a tooth once resided. Held at bay by his friends, he spewed venom as he yelled.

"You no good wife stealing S.O.B. Do you know who I am? I will see that you never get another singing job. You'll be lucky to get hired as a garbage collector when I'm done with you!"

"What the heck are you talking about? I never touched her, even though she deserves better than you."

Allan saw Al and the band staring at him in horror. Al came over from the stage. "What's going on here?"

"I'll tell you what's been going on. Your singer has been having an affair with my wife. I'm William Arthur the third, and I will not be cuckolded by a gimp singer. You should fire him or I'll see that your band gets enough bad publicity to ensure you'll be playing bar mitzvahs and birthday parties if you're lucky."

"Hey, no reason to get crazy here. I'll have a talk with my singer and get to the bottom of this."

Two police officers arrived asking witnesses who threw the first punch. Several pointed at Allan and the larger of the two cops grabbed him and began to march him toward the door.

"Al, do something. I was just defending myself."

"Listen here, you have ruined this performance. I'll have to get by with instrumentals the rest of night. You've put me in real bind and hurt my reputation."

"Fine. If that's all the loyalty I get from you, I quit," he yelled over his shoulder as the cops drug him out the door.

—

THE STENCH OF MOLD, urine, vomit, and fear greeted Allan as he was unceremoniously thrown in the cold "drunk tank" with a gaggle of bedraggled miscreants. Finding an open space on the bench running along the wall, he returned the dark stares of the prisoners wordlessly appraising him. In his bloodied tux, he stood out like a diamond in a sow's ear amongst the wretchedly clothed group.

Contemplating the turn of events that had brought him there, Allan was stunned at the unfairness and disloyalty being visited upon him yet again. Though he had some money stashed, who could he call to loan him bail until he could get to his savings? Aggravated assault was the charge. Serious enough, but more consequential was the loss of his job with the band. What would this do to his aspirations? Was he now to be a pariah, unwanted by other bands? Was history repeating itself?

With no bedding to be seen, he took off his shoes and made a hard pillow. Allan removed his jacket, lay down, and pulled it over him for a crude blanket as he tried to figure out how to navigate this unseen development. *No good deed goes unpunished.* In spite of his innocence, he was where he was. And so, amidst the grunts and snoring, the funk of fellow inmates in his nostrils, he drifted into a shallow, troubled sleep.

The jangling of keys, the squealing door and a looming guard brought him awake. "Dale. Your bail has been posted. Let's go."

At the front desk, he was informed that Angela Arthur had sprung him. He was relieved to be freed but disappointed that Al Lyons hadn't had a change of heart and come to his aid. There were, as well, the unseemly implications of Angela paying his bail.

He bought the morning paper and waited at the bus stop. Halfway down the first page in large print he read, *Scandal Surrounds Radio Singing Star! Arrested For Assaulting Oil Magnate.* The copy was tawdry.

It framed him as a cad who attacked the husband of an adulterous wife and ruined the broadcast of the popular Al Lyons Band.

He finished the article on the bus, beset by the sinking feeling that his career was over, at least in St. Louis. It was history repeating itself, undone by circumstances not of his doing just as had been the case in Midland. Well, he thought, if that led him to St. Louis and the success he'd had here, perhaps this was a blessing in disguise. The fact was that New York was where he wanted to be. He just had to end this chapter, deal with the legal ramifications, and head for where he'd been aiming all along.

That afternoon as he was preparing to see Al about his last paycheck, there was a knock on his apartment door. A tearful Angela greeted him. "I'm so sorry for what Billy and his friends have done. I have paid your bail and convinced him to drop the charges. I told him the truth, that we were not involved. I don't know if he believes me. Considering his frequent indiscretions, it is the least he could do. Forgive me for dragging you into this. Is there anything I can do to help you gain the good graces of your band leader?"

"I appreciate your bailing me out. Not sure what the deal is with Al. In fact, I'm on my way to see him to pick up my last check. Honestly, I just want to move on. I'm going to New York as I've been planning to do anyway. Hopefully, we can part on good terms and he can give me a good reference or some contacts with musicians in New York. We'll just have to see. Angela, I'm sorry for your situation, but it's best we part."

"Allan, since I'm the reason you've lost your job, please take this small token with my apologies. Perhaps it will help you get established in New York. It's the very least I owe you."

Allan took the envelope and headed for the club where Al would be rehearsing. He arrived to looks of opprobrium and avoided the glances from his band mates. Al turned to him with furrowed brows. "What do you want? Seems you've managed to sully our reputation in one fell swoop."

"Al, just give me five minutes. I know you're angry and I don't blame you. But the charges have been dropped and I truthfully did nothing I was being accused of. I am just here to get my last check and move on, but I want to part on good terms."

"Very well. Excuse us, boys. I'll be right back."

They stepped backstage into a dressing room where Al turned stiffly to him.

"I know how hard you've worked to build your reputation," said Allan. "But I swear to you I was not having an affair with the man's wife. He and his friends accosted me. It was ugly and I hate the bad press. Frankly, I'm disappointed you didn't support me but that's as may be. All I ask is that we part on good terms and that perhaps you would be kind enough to give me some names of contacts in New York to help me get started there."

Al's features softened. "Well, I guess I was a little quick to judge. You've caused me no trouble and been a great addition. I will miss your fine voice. You won't be easy to replace. Come by tomorrow around five and I'll have your check and some names for you. Fair enough?"

"Fair enough," he said as they shook hands and parted.

—

THE COOING OF A pigeon on his windowsill woke him. Through his blurred vision, the bird appeared to be a moving part of the grey morning. He heard the traffic and somewhere a radio playing. His mouth felt like the Russian army had camped there as he spotted a half full glass of bootleg booze on his dresser. He dragged himself from the bed to the bathroom and took in his bedraggled features in the mirror. He splashed water on his face, took a drink from the faucet, and walked to the window.

Allan stared out at the street below, appreciating what he had acquired in his time in St. Louis. A tux and dinner jacket for the stage, a suit, a few shirts, and a new Gibson guitar. Most importantly, he had saved enough to buy a cheap used car. And Angela's five hundred dollars would give him a reasonable grubstake.

There was no telling how long it might take to get a foothold in the music scene in New York. Suffering no illusions, he knew that it would be a rough climb up a steep hill.

Chapter 10

The frigid northwest wind was at Allan's back as he drove away from St. Louis in his newly acquired used Ford. He was on his way to New York at last. The trouble was blowing heavy snow, falling from a bruised, charcoal sky. The road was becoming increasingly slippery as visibility dropped. *Lovely send off.* At least the long drive to Indianapolis was mostly flat and straight.

The windshield was fogging up, forcing him to wipe away the condensation every few minutes. The sound of the engine couldn't override the wind. He reminded himself that he was on the journey to fulfill his dream and soon he was singing. Sing, wipe the windshield, sing, wipe, repeat.

By late afternoon, traffic had dwindled as the blizzard grew in intensity. He considered pulling off the highway but there was nothing but farmland. Terra Haute was hours away with very few small towns in between. Nothing for it but to motor on.

The snow grew deeper as the light began to fade and the first inklings of worry began to invade his thoughts. Could he survive the night in this rag top with no insulation with a heavy coat and a couple of wool blankets? He rounded a curve to be confronted by a car approaching in his lane, causing him to swerve. It happened so quickly that by the time he came to a stop, he was stuck at a steep angle in a deep snow bank. The other car continued on as if nothing had happened.

Retrieving his heaviest coat and his blankets, he prepared to create the most effective cocoon possible. The wind pulled at the convertible top shaking the car with relentless gusts. Even though sealed, cold drafts crept in with freezing teeth. Traffic seemed to have ended with the falling night and now the seriousness of his situation gnawed at him. He began to pray that he would survive the night.

He awoke suddenly, having dozed without realizing it. In the distance a light was slowly growing. Perhaps, it might be dawning but in the east? As the light approached Allan understood it was an approaching car and threw himself out into the storm flashlight in hand.

As the vehicle neared, he saw it was a truck. Standing in the road waving the light wildly, he prayed he would be seen and not flattened. Seconds before a dive for safety was needed, the truck slowed to a stop a few feet from him. The door opened and a dark figure stepped down, approaching through the blowing snow.

"'Appears you in a pickle here, sho nuff. Ain't likely to be nobody along. They done shut down de road. Onliest reason I'm here is I gots to get on to my place 'bout ten miles up de road. Name's Abel."

"Well, Abel, you are my angel of rescue. I was dozing and in this weather that could lead to the big sleep. I'm Allan. I got run off the road hours ago and was praying for someone to show up."

"The Lord he do work in mysterious ways, that He do. Well, let me get my chain and see if we can get you pulled out of there."

Abel looked to be six foot four, at least, with a smile as white as the blizzard shining from his black face. Within minutes, he had hooked Allan's car to his truck and thanks to the chains on the truck's tires, was able to drag it from the snowbank and onto the shoulder.

"Abel, thank you. Can I pay you for your effort?"

"No suh. Figure the Lord done put me here to help you out. But listen here, it ain't safe you be drivin' in this storm. You be back in the snow fore you know it. Hop up into the cab and come on to my house till the weather clears and I'll bring you back. Mazie, my wife, loves to take care of strangers. Say the Bible speaks of entertaining angels."

"Abel, I don't want to impose."

"Get yourself on up in that truck. It ain't gettin no warmer out here."

Twenty minutes later they pulled up in front of a small farmhouse. Abel set the brake and turned off the engine. "Well, grab your bag and come on in and meet my Mazie."

Allan followed Abel through the door and was immediately enveloped in warm amber light and the smell of food cooking on a wood stove. Two small squealing children sprung from behind a table, wrapping their arms around Abel's legs, as a small woman turned from the kitchen, radiating joy.

"Baby...I'm so glad you're home! I been steady prayin' you safe out de storm. Who dis we got here, Abel?"

"Mazie, meet Mr. Allan Dale. Someone dun run his car into the ditch, and I come a long and pulled it out...but it way too dangerous to be drivin' so I brung him home 'til dis mess be over."

"Well you showed up jes' in time for some chicken stew and corn bread. This here is Ezra and Sarah. Say hello to Mr. Allan."

Disengaging from Abel, the children eyed him curiously, then approached him cautiously. Allan put his suitcase and guitar down, took off his gloves, and held out his hand.

"Howdy. Your daddy is a hero...probably saved my life and I'm mighty grateful."

Ezra, the eldest, tentatively shook Allan's offered hand, and Sarah quickly followed suit. Pointing at the guitar, Ezra asked, "Dat be a guitar in dere?"

"It is. Maybe I can play and sing you a song later, okay?"

Grins painted both small faces as Mazie stepped up to shake his hand. Though a young woman, creases from years of smiling already graced her face. Light seemed to emanate from her dark eyes. She bore a sense of repose in her upright carriage. Allan felt an atmosphere of peace he'd not experienced since leaving home. Mazie smiled pointing to the rough-hewn table and bench seats as she laid a steaming cast iron pot and a tin of corn bread on the table.

"All right, y'all, let's dig into this meal I dun cooked up."

Abel sat, inviting Allan to sit beside him as Mazie and the children took seats facing them. Allan felt Abel's large, callous hand taking his own, even as he reached his other across the table to take his wife's hand. Little Sarah leaned half way across waited for Allan to take hers. All properly joined, Abel began to pray,

"Oh, Lord, we be 'specially grateful you brought me up on Mr. Allan at jes de right time so as I could hep him out of dat storm. You be de best guide all de time. Thank you for this fine meal Mazie cooked up and for your blessings over dis family. In Jesus name.... Amen."

The stew was savory chicken and rice with vegetables complemented with piping hot cornbread to rival Allan's mother's. Watching the family sharing their contentment, he realized this was the first sit-down home-cooked family meal he had shared since leaving San Antonio. It was pure ambrosia. As they ate, he listened to them sharing their days, laughing, teasing, questioning one another with tender fondness. Mazie finished first and rose, taking her dishes to the sink. "Who wants some canned peaches for dessert?" she called over her shoulder.

The children squealed in affirmation, and Abel and Allan nodded in agreement. Allan turned to Abel. "How can I ever thank you for saving my life and sharing your wonderful home and hospitality? Mazie, the meal was marvelous. Someone should write a song... Marvelous Mazie!"

She threw her head back and broke out in laughter, joined by her family.

"Well, Mr. Allan, maybe you reward me by writin' it for me on that guitar."

"Don't know about that, but I can sure play some tunes for you. Maybe some we can sing together."

"That sho nuff be de way to end dis evenin'," added Abel.

As Mazie cleaned up, Allan opened the case and removed his rare 1919 Gibson O-Style guitar, a unique instrument that he'd won in a high stakes poker game in St. Louis. The rich tobacco/sunburst finish set off the unique mandolin style recurving, scalloped top with a Florentine cutaway on the lower part of the face below the round sound hole. Allan loved to admire it as much as he enjoyed playing it. He took out a tuning fork and began to tune. Abel sat down beside him, and the children gathered on the floor. Once the guitar was tuned, Allen began to noodle around with some chords until warmed by the fireplace and cast in the amber glow, Mazie joined her expectant family. Allan smiled and began to play.

"Grab your coat and snatch your hat, Leave your worries on the doorstep. Just direct your feet, to the Sunny side of the street."

As Allan sang, they clapped their hands in rhythm, laughing and enthusiastically applauding as he ended the song.

"More! More!" squealed the children.

Allan sang *Ain't Misbehavin'*, Louis Armstrong's popular *When You're Smilin'*, and Charlie Patton's *Pony Blues*. Then he asked if they had any requests. Mazie asked if he knew the spiritual, *Swing Low, Sweet Chariot* and Allan started to sing.

"Swing Low, sweet chariot. Comin' for to carry me home." Mazie's sweet voice joined in harmony on the next verse with Abel adding a lower one. Joined together in praise, they blended and soared together.

When they finished, the room was quiet for a minute or more.

"Wow, that was spectacular!" Allan blurted out.

"We love to sing the spiritual songs. Know any more?" asked Mazie.

"I know *Go Down, Moses* by Marion Anderson."

"We sing that at church," said Abel.

For the next hour the small house was washed in song, warmth, and happiness.

"Got one more," said Allan, "then I've gotta call it a night. Been a rough day for me." He started to play and sing ad-libbing the lyrics.

"You may say I'm crazy when I sing you my song
Bout Marvelous Mazie, who can do no wrong.
Fills her house with laughter; they all smile with praise…
Marvelous Mazie, we love your ways."

They sat looking at Allan in stunned silence. Finally Mazie cocked her head. "Did you jes make that up here and now?"

"Oh, it was just a bit of fun…a little ditty for the little lady."

Tears formed in her eyes. "Ain't no one ever wrote a song 'bout me. Dats one a de bes things ever anyone done. Thank you, Mr. Allan. Well, guess dat be 'bout enough music and fun for de night. Time for you two to get them pajamas on and climb into yo bed. Sorry we ain't got no bed for you but I gots spare blankets we can lay down on the floor for you."

"That'd be wonderful, Mazie. Goodnight, Ezra and Sarah."

Abel got the children tucked in the small bed they shared while Mazie saw to Allan's bedding. As they said goodnight, Allan looked up from the floor and whispered, "This is a night I won't forget. Making me a part of your family, feeding me, sharing the songs. If I'd known what the car mishap would lead to, I'd have done it on purpose. See you in the morning."

"Oh, forgot to tell you, outhouse is 'round back. Be careful, likely slick as spit on a doorknob. See you in the mornin' and we'll get you on the road again."

Allan lay down on the rough pallet, watched the dancing shadows cast by the dwindling fire, and lifted up a prayer of thanks for his good fortune. His thoughts drifted to the comfortable bed and warm family he'd left behind in San Antonio and wondered how they were faring. He'd last phoned them several weeks earlier and gotten the impression they were getting by better than some but struggling nonetheless. Likely be a long while before he'd be home, he thought, as he drifted into sleep.

He opened his eyes to the smell of bacon and two small faces staring down at him. It took a few seconds for him to remember where he was. Rising on one elbow, he smiled at Mazie and the children. "Mornin'. How's it goin'? Boy something sure smells wonderful."

"You awake, Mr. Allan? Got some bacon 'n eggs and grits acookin'. Abel, he out checkin' on de truck. You have to take care of your needs, now be a good time. Gonna be ready here directly."

"Thanks, Mazie, I'll be back in a jiffy."

Gathering himself up from the floor, Allan made his way to the door. Opening it, he was greeted by clear blue skies and an arctic landscape. The frigid air burned his nostrils and his fingers tingled as he shoved them into his pockets.

Abel was standing on the running board, reaching up to clear snow from the truck windshield. "Mornin', Mr. Allan. getting her ready go find your car and get you rollin'. Good thing I put them chains on 'fore this storm hit. They should be out clearin' de roads by now. Hope you don't got no more delays."

"Thanks, Abel. Gotta visit the outhouse and I'll be back for breakfast shortly."

He nearly slipped twice before experiencing the coldest morning constitutional he'd ever endured. The warm room enveloped him upon his return where the family awaited him. Not realizing how hungry he was, Allan had to fight a desire to inhale the breakfast. They ate quietly and when finished Mazie announced, "Well, chillen, don't reckon dey any school today, so you gets to play in the snow. Maybe make you a snowman."

"Mr. Allan, you 'bout ready?" asked Abel, rising from the table.

"Won't take a moment. Miss Mazie, where do I begin to thank you? This has been the loveliest evening I've enjoyed in a very long time. The car trouble was a blessing in disguise."

"Weren't nothin. But them songs, specially the one 'bout me... well that was special sho' nuff. I be prayin' you make you big success in New York. Maybe I hear you singin' on de radio one day. Dis here some lunch for you when you get hungry later. You ever back by here you stop by and sing some more with us. Lord bless and keep you now. Hey, Ezra, Sarah, come say goodbye to Mr. Allan."

They sidled up, shyly hugging him around his legs.

"You be de best singer everest I heard," said Sarah softly.

Allan knelt, wrapping his arms around them. Reaching into his pocket he gave them each a quarter, which they stared at with astonishment. "Look Mama!" shouted Ezra. "Most money I dun ever had. Can I keep it?"

"Mr. Allan give to you so you sho nuff can. You best thank him." Which they did with such enthusiasm that Mazie had to pry him free.

"Well, off I go into the frozen tundra. I feel like *Sgt. Preston Of the Mounties.*"

They made slow progress on the secondary road leading to the main highway, arriving to the welcome sight of a plowed road. The problem, however, was that when they located Allan's car, only the top half was visible above a snowbank left behind by the plows.

"Alright, then, Mr. Allan, I'll get the shovels."

An hour and a half later, with the use of a tow chain, Allan's Model T stood ready for the journey to resume. Allan pulled Abel close in an embrace and handed him ten dollars.

"I ain't doin' this for pay," said Abel.

"No, you did it out of kindness and because the Lord sent you. I'm doing this out of appreciation and because I've been blessed with the resources. Please Abel, give me this opportunity to thank you."

"Well, I guess if you say so. Mr. Allan, be safe and don't get caught up in no nonsense in New York. I know they be some crazy wildness goin' on there. I'll wait to make sure your car starts up."

"I'll do my best to keep it on the straight and narrow. God bless you and your family."

Allan set the choke, walked to the front of the Model-T, and wrapped his hands around the crank. Even with heavy gloves, his hands tingled with cold. After more than a dozen cranks, the engine coughed to life. He ran to the door and took off the choke. Although he'd scraped the windshield free of snow, it began to fog up from his breath. Finally, he put the car into gear and slipping the clutch, he resumed his journey, waving a last goodbye to Abel.

The stew of clouds was breaking up, allowing the low-angled winter sun to glare off the white snowscape into his eyes. His cold hands gripped the steering wheel as he navigated the icy road. So focused was he on his driving that two hours passed unnoticed as he found himself entering Effingham, Indiana.

The town was having as much trouble getting started as his car. Although many of the shops appeared to be closed, the diner across from a filling station appeared open. First things first, he thought, pulling into the station to fill up. Following this, his need for a fill-up of breakfast and coffee struck him. He parked in front of Alfie's Diner, mounted the steps, opened the door, and inhaled the enticing smell of bacon, hash browns, and coffee. As he sat on the stool, a rotund middle-aged woman in a pink uniform arrived and leaned toward him.

"Mornin', handsome. You look like you could use some coffee. Anything I can get you besides?"

"I reckon three scrambled eggs, bacon, hash browns and some biscuits, if you have them."

"Best in town! Alfie...three shook, bacon, biscuits and browns," she called while pouring the most inviting coffee Allan had ever beheld into his cup.

By the time his breakfast arrived, he was, for the first time that day, feeling almost warm. As he ate, he took in fellow patrons. One, in particular, struck him as a likely long-haul truck driver. Upon finishing and paying for his meal, he gently tapped the man's leather jacket. Putting down his cup, the man turned and appraised Allan.

"Pardon me for disturbing you," said Allan, "but I thought perhaps you're a truck driver and might have an idea of the conditions between here and Terre Haute."

Spinning around on his stool and cocking one bushy brown brow over a pair of bloodshot blue eyes, the man offered his hand. "Sure, kid, name's Howard. Just come down that road and it's still a bit slick in spots. Few cars off the side in the snow but she's passable. Probably take you four or five hours. If you're plannin' on spendin' the night, there's a motel just the other side of downtown. On the left. Can't miss it."

"Gosh, Howard, thanks so much. Hope you have safe travels."

"Headin' to Chicago and I expect it's pretty rough goin' till I hit the Lincoln Highway. Drive safe, son." He turned back to his coffee.

Following a long slow slog to Terre Haute and a fitful night in a seedy motel, he made much better time to Columbus, Ohio where he joined the Lincoln Highway. This much-traveled route spanned the country more than three thousand miles from San Francisco to New York. From this point onward, he could expect much faster travel all the way.

Chapter 11

Allan's first view of the New York skyline left him breathless. After three days of travel, he gazed at the city of his dreams. The newly completed Empire State Building and the Chrysler Building dominated the skyline. Late afternoon sun cast Manhattan in honeyed golden hues, constantly changing as the dance of shadow and sunlight washed the vista in constant motion. The air smelled of the Hudson River, exhaust from factories and vehicles, with a base note of rotting garbage.

Pulling off the highway he looked at the George Washington Bridge and contemplated the new life this portal would lead him to. Excited, expectant, anxious, he pulled back onto the road and began the crossing. Watching the ships and numerous vessels below made it hard to keep his eyes on driving in the heaviest traffic he had ever encountered.

At last, he entered the great canyon of tall buildings. That's when he realized he didn't really know where he was or where he was going. Plodding slowly with the flow of traffic, he saw a parking place beside a smaller building and pulled over.

Allan retrieved his address book to begin seeking out the contacts he'd been given by his former bandmates and leader. He had but seven names. Not much to start with, but it was a beginning. He spotted a phone booth, occupied at the moment, and waited in the car for the caller to finish. After what seemed an interminable amount of time, the man hung up. Allan jumped out, locked the car, and rushed to the booth. The first name on the list was a piano player, Billy Briggs, that his friend Emil had given him. He was reputed to be well connected and last thought to be playing with the Will Osborne Band at the Hi-Ho Club. It was nearly five p.m., but he likely hadn't left for a gig. He put a nickel in the slot and dialed. A rather gruff voice with a Brooklyn accent answered.

"Yea, whaddya want?

"Howdy, my name's Allan Dale. Emil Landreau, the sax player, gave me your number. Said you might be able to give me some ideas on the music scene here. I'm a singer looking to find a spot with a band and thought perhaps you might be able to help."

"Did you say howdy? You a western singer?"

"No, just from Texas. Been singing jazz and popular stuff with several bands, most recently with The Al Lyons Band in St. Louis."

"Ain't heard a 'dem. Tell ya what bub...I'll keep my eyes open. Hear of somethin' I'll let ya know. You got a number?"

"Ahh...well not yet. I just got into the city."

"Okay. Where ya stayin'?"

"Well...ahh...nowhere yet, but I hope to find a place today."

"Look, get yourself squared away and give me a call." Before Allan could answer, Billy hung up.

Allan felt very alone in the fast-moving sea of cars and pedestrians. First, he would have to find a place to live and a way to be reached before he could even begin to find work. He drove around until he found a newsstand, bought a paper, and asked the vendor if he knew of a reasonably priced hotel in the area. The man told him he might try the Hotel Lexington on 48th Street and gave him directions.

Allan was overwhelmed by the traffic, the noise, the sheer volume of humanity around him. Carefully following the street signs, he at last spotted the hotel. As he pulled in, a liveried doorman greeted him, opening the door.

The lobby was sumptuous. Chandeliers, large potted plants, huge Persian carpets. The smell of cigar smoke and the sound of a piano floated from the bar. He took it all in as he waited in a short line at the desk.

"Pardon me sir, are you checking in?"

"Yes, thank you. A room for one."

"And how long will you be staying with us?"

"Oh, a week, I guess."

"Our daily rate is three dollars, but the weekly is just nineteen."

"Okay."

"Please sign the register, Mr...?"

"Dale, Allan Dale."

"Very well, Mr. Dale. Here's your key. You're on the fourth floor, Room 408. Do you need a bellboy to help with your luggage?"

"Certainly."

After getting the luggage unpacked, Allan walked to the window and observed his new city. He could see an edge of Central Park from the window, surrounded by more buildings. Below, the sidewalks flowed. Cars and pedestrians were like schools of fish in a human sea. *Nearly twenty dollars for a week*, he thought. With the money he had, he'd not be staying there for long. He picked up the *New York Times*, skipped the news and found the rentals section. The prices were vastly more than he'd envisioned. But he wouldn't give up. "I came here to become a singing star and I will do so!" he said aloud.

An hour later, he'd narrowed his search down to a couple of boarding houses and a possible roommate situation that he felt were affordable. Determined to investigate them the next day, he realized that he was famished. He threw on his coat, headed downstairs and struck out to see what culinary possibilities he might discover.

The cacophony of the street buffeted him from all sides. A miasma of exhaust fumes, garbage, and food cooking washed over him. After a few blocks he found a small Italian restaurant around the corner on 53rd St.

The smell of garlic and spices drew him to La Taverna. The posted menu looked to be moderately affordable, so he stepped inside to be greeted by a round, mustachioed, smiling Italian man. "Welcome, senore, to La Taverna. You are alone? I have a quiet table for you." Without waiting for a response, he led the way to a small table with two chairs near the kitchen and waiters' station. Handing Allan a menu, with a beatific smile, he said, "I am Luigi. My family share our recipes from home here. We are the best pesto in New York but everything issa best. My daughter she come to take your order."

As if on cue, a lovely young woman arrived with a smile and glass of water. "I am Angelina. Would you like something to drink while you are deciding?"

Allan was so taken with the tenderness in her dark eyes and the music of her voice that he took a few beats to respond. He caught himself staring at her.

"Oh...well...sorry. Ah, yes...I guess a Coke and maybe this pesto chicken."

"It's one of our best. You will like it. Is this your first time here?"

"I just drove in today. Still trying to get my feet on the ground. I'm staying at the Lexington. Gotta admit, I'm a bit overwhelmed by the city, but I'll figure it all out."

"I'll be back with your drink," she said with a smile.

"Well," he mused, "New York is famous for beautiful women. Never know your luck in a big city, as they say."

Angelina brought his drink and lingered. "You are here for a visit?"

"More than that. I'm here to find work. A gig singing in a band. If I'm to break into radio and the big bands, it's gotta be here. But first I need to find a place to live and settle in."

"A musician. There are a few who come here. I know one who is a piano player. Maybe you could meet him? You are handsome. If you sing as good as you look, you will do well, I think. I'll go check on your food."

Encouraged by her attentions and the comment about other musicians, he sat back and took in the room. Candles set in straw bound wine bottles, resting upon red and white checked cloths, graced each table. The smells prompted his salivary glands in anticipatory action. Soft guitar and accordion music issued from somewhere and the first sense of peace he had felt in days fell on him. He smiled and breathed it all in, releasing all his concerns.

Angelina arrived with a large oval plate of pesto and a basket of warm bread, then leaned closer than necessary as she placed them on the table. He could smell her perfume mixed with the ubiquitous garlic and spices issuing from her hair and clothing.

"Enjoy. I am near if you need me," she said with a flirtatious wink.

The meal was unlike anything he'd ever tasted. He had to force himself to eat it slowly, savoring each mouthful. At last, he lay his utensils down and leaned back in sated bliss. No sooner had he done so than Angelina arrived at his elbow.

"You like? I think yes. There is nothing left but your smile. Maybe you'd like some dessert or some cappuccino?"

"Wow. Angelina, you really are an angel delivering me heavenly food and a heavenly smile with it. I think I will have some cappuccino. I'm in no hurry...nowhere else to go."

"I'll bring it to you right away." It seemed the door to New York was just cracking ajar with a peek at the possibilities.

Angelina was soon back with cappuccino and biscotti.

"What is your name?"

"Allan, Allan Dale."

Placing the check before him, she softly said, "You must come back. Very soon. It would make me very happy."

"Well, I would like to make you happy, so I promise I will come back, maybe tomorrow."

"I will tell the piano player about you. Maybe you two can meet?"

He walked back to the hotel. Streetlights cast shadowed fingers from leafless trees. It was a leisurely contemplative stroll. Although still intimidated by the enormity of his ambitions and the obstacles before him, he found an inner resolve and certainty which overrode his doubts. He could see himself standing before a microphone in front of a huge crowd, broadcasting live on the radio. No matter what it took, it would be so.

—

AFTER FIVE DAYS AT the hotel, Allan had his first bit of good fortune. Upon his third visit for dinner at La Taverna, Angelina greeted him and led him to a thin faced young man in a worn brown leather jacket. He sat at the same table Allan had on his first visit.

"Allan, this is Ira, the piano player I told you about."

"Howdy. Allan Dale."

"Ira Brenner," he said, offering his hand.

"Must be from out west, what with the howdy. Angelina tells me you're new to town and a musician. What kinda stuff you into?"

"I play guitar, but I'm mainly a singer. Been with several bands, most recently in St. Louis. Al Lyons Band. Looking for any opportunity for an audition or just to sit in and get a feel for the scene here."

"Gotcha. Well, at the moment, I'm playing at the Bull and Bear Bar at the Waldorf. Good dough but a dead end. I'm lookin' for a band as well. Have a seat."

For the next three hours, they discussed musical passions, war stories, dreams and aspirations. They discovered shared tastes and passions and basked in the rare camaraderie.

The next day Ira helped him find a comfortable, less expensive rooming house and took him around to show him the city. Allan had never felt so close to a friend so quickly.

That Saturday evening Allan went to The Waldorf to hear Ira play. The room was filled with a moneyed crowd, dressed for a promise of exciting evenings on the town. Ira acknowledged him with a nod from the baby grand as he played. Allan sat at the Triangular Bar and ordered a Coke. Never had he seen so many gorgeous women in one place. Cigarette and cigar smoke lent a gauzy mystery to the room, commingling with competing scents of expensive perfume. Through the haze, he marveled at the ornate marble columns, rich dark oak paneling, and dignified appointments.

As Ira played, Allan was struck by his deft touch, imaginative phrasing, and his fearless abandon. This was a profoundly talented man, one of the best piano players he had ever heard. His genius was every bit a match for the grandeur of the room. Ira finished his set and walked over to Allan.

"Glad you could come, man. Quite the layout, huh? And that piano, it's a Bosendorfer. What a joy to play."

"And, man, can you ever play it! I've heard some great pianists but what a touch you have. You're bound to get on with a big-name outfit."

"Well, it's a tough game here. Lots of killer players. But that's why we came. Course I'm from upstate New York, not all the way from Texas, but the city...well, it's another world. Hey, man, would you like to sing a song or two?"

"Are you sure? I mean...you don't have to. You've never heard me. I could be lousy."

"Hey, they love it when a singer drops around. What would you like to do?"

"Hmm...how 'bout *Walkin' My Baby Back Home*. In G?"

"Sounds good."

"Well let's hope so, Ira. Wouldn't want to get you canned."

Ira left for the restroom and returned to the piano. He pulled the microphone close and announced, "Ladies and gentlemen. We have a treat tonight. One of New York's newest up-and-coming singers is with us. Fresh from wowing them in the City of the Blues, St. Louis. Please welcome Allan Dale."

The faithful butterflies of doubt whispered their wingbeats, as Allan approached the piano. Ira began a gentle intro and Allan stepped behind the mike. A deep breath, a quick silent prayer, a nod from Ira, and he began. Through the first verse he focused on the singing. By the chorus, he was beginning to relax and flow with Ira's intuitive accompaniment. Allan took in the crowd, most of whom were wrapped up in chatting with and impressing one another. Allan didn't care. He embraced the joy of sailing on the melodic vessel Ira fashioned.

Light applause and a smattering of smiles issued forth at the end of the song. Allan nodded in appreciation and began to step back to the bar. "Not yet, old son," said Ira. "They liked it. Let's do another."

"Are you sure?"

"Oh, yeah," Ira said with a grin.

"Well...okay. Do you know *St. James Infirmary*...in A?

"Good call. A little blues comin' up." Ira began a slow soulful intro and Allan closed his eyes and sang.

"I went down to Saint James Infirmary.
And I saw my baby there.
Stretched out on a long white table.
So sweet, so cold, so fair."

Louis Armstrong's tearful lament poured out of him, and a purple poignant mood crept over the room. Heads turned, feet tapped to the slow rhythm, and conversation tapered off. Allan and Ira were on a hypnotic vessel that drew all ears to the cargo it bore. The deeply moving melody and words penetrated hearts with the impermanence of life, of death and loss.

Ira took a lead after the third verse. His playing was to music what

Matisse is to painting. Allan ended by repeating the first verse with slow almost conversational phrasing. Ira followed with a stylistic flourish. The room was momentarily silent. Then scattered applause grew to a respectable level, considering the room and the crowd. Ira beamed, Allan smiled and nodded in appreciation.

Not wanting to overstay his welcome and to end on a high note, he thanked Ira and went back to the bar.

A striking young couple sat next to him and welcomed him back. "Marvelous, old man! Might I refresh your drink, sir?" When Allan nodded, he pulled a silver flask from his dinner jacket and poured a generous shot into Allan's half-empty glass, then offered his hand. "Ronald van Damme, and this is the lovely Veronica Smythe."

With a sultry smile, she raised her hand to be kissed.

"Are you performing elsewhere?" asked the man. "You have an exceptional voice. I'd love to hear you with an orchestra."

"Well, Mr. van Damme, I just arrived here a few days back and am looking for opportunities. I have high hopes some band leader will share your enthusiasm."

Pulling a gold cigarette case from his pocket, he offered one first to Veronica and then Allan, lighting both with a matching gold lighter.

"Thank you for the smoke and kind words, Mr. van Damme."

"Ronald, please. And the words are sincere. I'm a bit of a music aficionado, and I'm a big fan of that pianist. One of the best I've heard around town. In part why I like this bar...and of course the steak house here is divine. We're dining at the Peacock Alley tonight. We're not staying at the hotel. I have a place across the park." Rising to help Veronica from the barstool he said, "I have a friend or two in the music and radio business. I'll have to tell them to come give a listen."

"Ronald, that would be great, but I don't have a regular gig here. Ira just invited me up for a couple of tunes."

"I'll mention you to Eric, the manager. They should consider hiring you. I'm confident you'd enliven this somewhat staid lounge.

Splendid meeting you. All the best 'ol chap. Hope to hear you again."

Ira finished his set, wandered over and took the seat Ronald had warmed. "Allan, I was taking a flyer that you could sing, having never heard you. Wow. That was a winning bet. You, my friend, have some amazing pipes, but it's not just that you're technically proficient. You sing from the bottom of your heels, man. I felt every word, like you were an actor. Come up and do couple more!"

"Ira, I appreciate your praise more than you can know. Coming from someone with your skills, I'm humbled. But I think I'll 'stand pat', as the lyric in *St. James Infirmary* says. Gotta pretty big task ahead and want to start putting together a plan to get my foot in the door. Are you up for lunch tomorrow?"

"You bet. There's a great little place on the Lower East Side called Katz Deli, on the corner of East Houston and Ludlow. Best in town. Oldest too. My people know how to make a bagel and the brisket is to die for. One o'clock is good for me. You?"

"Yeah, great, and thanks again for all you've done to help me get my feet on the ground. Tonight was just the best. I needed to get started on trying to make my way here. See you tomorrow at Katz Deli."

Allan pulled his coat around him in the biting February wind. Barren branches accompanied him as he walked, whispering like brushes on a snare. His thoughts vacillated between the compliments he received singing with Ira, and the stark reality of his dwindling funds and lack of any real foothold in the most competitive entertainment city in the world. He sang as he walked, as always, unaware of it until someone looked at him oddly.

—

ALLAN INHALED THE DELIGHTS of Katz Deli as he opened the door to a large crowded room. Conversation enveloped him. Toward the back, he spotted a smiling Ira waving *The Times* and beckoning. He rose as Allan arrived, taking him by the elbow and leading him to the counter. There, beneath long glass shelves, lay an array of Jewish delicacies, only a few of which looked familiar.

"First time in a deli?"

Allan nodded. "Yeah, Texas isn't famous for them."

"Well, may I suggest you start with the house favorite, pastrami on rye. Katz makes the best in the city which, considering they are the oldest, makes sense."

"Sounds good."

"Great! I'll order. Extra pickle for you? Best kosher dills too. Coke okay?

"You bet."

Ira paid and they found a table where Allan fell in love with his first taste of Katz's trademark favorite.

Between mouthfuls, Allan began to tell his story and to reveal his recent disappointments. Ira listened intently, sympathy in his eyes. Allan paused and looked down at his empty plate.

Ira cleared his throat. "Well, my journey to the city wasn't as long as yours but we're on the same road and it's not an easy one. Like you, I have big dreams. So far, the Waldorf gig is the first real smooth part of the trip. It pays good and helps keep my chops tight, but it sure ain't what I want to be doin' for long. I'm looking every day for a band gig or maybe at least a small trio at a jazz club. I know it must be a lot harder for you with no gig and no income. You need to come back to sit in. I know that fellow told you he'd suggest to the manager to consider hiring you. He's in pretty regular. Old money, lots of pull. Maybe you ought to spend a little time back at the Bull and Bear. You never know."

"I appreciate your encouragement. Truth is, I feel a little out of place in that swank place and I can't afford the prices for long. Heck, a Coke is four times what it is here at Katz. I'm pretty good at puttin' on the dog for brief conversations but I run out of success stories pretty quick."

"Tell you what. Thursdays are good nights to come. Lots of regulars and a fair few have started to come hear me play. I've got a free tab for my drinks and a meal. I'll spring for your drinks and food, and you can sing a few songs. In fact, we could work up some arrangements, put on a little show. I can't sing, but you have a gift. Let's put it out there."

"Gee, Ira, that'd be swell. When do you want to get together and practice?"

"What are you doing for the next couple of hours?"

"Well, nothing really...practicing...I guess."

"That's the ticket! Nothing like makin' music to get your spirits up. Come to my place. It's just four blocks from here. Leave your car. We'll walk."

That afternoon they worked up several songs. Allan sang three of them that Thursday as he did the following weekend. His acquaintance with Ronald van Damme began to develop and soon he was feeling more at ease in this rarified atmosphere.

Allan sang there for the next couple of weeks but there was no offer of a singing gig. He continued to hope as he and Ira bonded more in their music with each performance.

Chapter 12

Day upon day passed, filled with disappointments, accreting over his hopes like drops of mud, hardening and encasing him in doubt. Within the first three weeks he'd called every contact on his list, read the entertainment section of the paper to learn the scene and look for openings, and had begun to consider trying to find an agent. At the current rate of expenditures, Allan would burn through his savings all too soon. As it was, he was eating minimally and preparing to sell his car.

It was a fairly mild day for mid-March and he decided he'd give Ira a call and see what he was up to. Were it not for those Thursday nights and their practice sessions, he would be truly lost at sea. He put on a light jacket and headed down to the pay phone on the corner. It was only ten-thirty, early in musician time, but the day was too lovely for burning daylight.

On the fifth ring, a groggy Ira answered.

"Hello?"

"Ira...Allan. You up yet?"

"Am now. What's shakin'?"

"The breeze in the leaves on the trees with the bees. Well not many leaves, but it's the nicest day since I've been here. Thought I could buy you a cup of coffee."

"Too early for bad poetry, man. Funny you callin', though. I have some news to deliver and was gonna run you down. The manager has been getting more than just your friend van Damme's requests to hear your singing. He's going to make time this Thursday to give you a listen. La Taverna opens at eleven. Meet me there. We'll drink some of that eye opening espresso and plan our campaign."

It was Allan's first time back in a while and Angelina's smile told him he'd been missed. Stepping quickly to the door, she took his hands in hers. "The sun was shining through my window, and I say to myself, 'Angelina, today will be beautiful for you.' And here you are. I asked your friend Ira where you've been. He said you will come back soon and now I am happy."

"As am I to see your smiling face. Ira is meeting me here for coffee and a chat."

"Sit at the table where you met. What do you want?"

"Some of that espresso. That'll turn me every way but loose!"

Angelina brought the coffee, then laid her hand on Allan's shoulder with an arched eyebrow, and a slight pout. "So...why you wait so long to come back? I look for you for days."

"I had to find a place and get settled and make some calls and my place isn't so near and...no excuse, I guess. Now that I behold your beautiful eyes, I am hypnotized, and think I will have no choice but to come back more often."

Ira's voice interrupted the flirtatious moment. "Hey man, hi Angelina. Can you get me an espresso fast? I'm dyin' here!"

"Where have you been keeping him, Ira? Okay, I'll be right back."

Ira sat down and removed a black homburg, releasing a tangled nest of black curls over his large ears. Ira's infrequent grin tilted up as his eyes caught Allan's.

"She asks about you every time I come in. It would appear you have quite an admirer. You should proceed with caution, however. Her dad and her brother, the cook, watch her like hawks. And rumor has it her other brother is involved with some shady friends in the, shall we say, entertainment and supply industry. But, oh my, if she fluttered around me like that, I'd be sorely tempted."

Angelina returned with their espresso and stroked Allan's shoulder as she left.

"Okay, let's pick four or five songs—ones you do well, different tempos and styles. A little swing, a ballad or two, a blues number, maybe something popular, cute. Today's Monday, so we have four days to pick them and polish up the arrangements. Got any suggestions for songs?"

"Hmm...Let's stick with newer stuff. Hold on...summoning Angelina. Darlin', may I borrow a pencil and a piece of paper?"

"Anything you want."

"Great, thanks so much, and can you keep the espresso coming?"

"As long as you wish."

Allan began to create a song list. A few minutes later he handed it to Ira who studied it as he sipped.

"I like these and know them all. Never heard you sing *Georgia on My Mind* or *April in Paris* but we'll polish them up till they shine. I'm off tonight and tomorrow so let's meet at my place...say five or so. We'll practice and then grab some dinner and—I'm buyin', no arguments. You can reciprocate when you get the gig."

"Ira, you're the best."

"Since we're here we might as well have an early lunch or brunch or whatever."

—

FOUR DAYS OF PRACTICE behind him, Allan dressed in his freshly pressed dinner jacket, hopped in the car, and headed for the Waldorf. The crowd was sparse when he arrived at 6 p.m. Ira stood by the piano chatting with Mr. Carlson, the manager. Both turned as Allan came up and Ira introduced Allan.

"I've heard great things about you. As I told Ira, we haven't considered hiring a vocalist but I'm willing to listen and gauge the patrons' responses. There should be a fair pre-dinner crowd here by seven. I shall return then and give you a listen," said Mr. Carlson.

"Thank you, Mr. Carlson. I look forward to it."

The hour dragged by. He was encouraged when he saw Ronald van Damme, who had brought four friends along. By the time Mr. Carlson returned, Allan was anxious to perform.

Ira welcomed the crowd and introduced Allan with a few too many accolades, then began the intro to *How Deep is the Ocean*, and Allan began to sing. By the third song, he knew he had them. Even Mr. Carlson was tapping his foot and smiling. He followed with the upbeat *I Got Rhythm* saving his best for last. *Georgia on my Mind* was both a great crooner's song and had special meaning since it was his mother's name. He drifted on the lazy beat as Ira laid down some intoxicating riffs, then lost himself in the joy of singing.

The applause lasted for a long time with Ronald calling out, "Encore!"

Mr. Carlson came up grinning. "Very impressive. You are quite gifted, and the audience seemed engaged, Especially Mr. van Damme who, of course, recommended you. Let me consider this and how it might fit in the budget. May I let you know Monday?"

"That would be great. And thank you again for giving me the opportunity. I hope you can fit me in."

"How much would you be expecting for Thursday through Saturday?"

"Actually, I'm not sure since I don't know the scale here. I would consider any offer you think is reasonable."

"Very well, then. I must be off. I'll arrange to get back with you through Ira."

Ira's lopsided smile awaited him. "Spectacular, Allan! You had the room eating out of your hand. You even made me play better.

Accompaniment is a skill of its own and I dig the way we flow, man. My guess is it's just a matter of how much dough he can scare up. Heck this place is makin' plenty even in these hard times. Folks that come in here, they ain't got no worries."

"So how much do you think is a fair amount to ask for?"

"So, you're not in the union which means you can ask less although you'll likely need to join it before long and that will kick up the scale. But for now, ask for fifty and settle for forty-five a night. It's less than union and it's less than he's paying me. We'll see what shakes. Gotta get back to playing. You sticking around?"

"Yep. I want to go thank Ronald and his friends. And Ira, thank you for all you've done to help me."

"Say nothing of it. You're the cat's meow and like catnip to those gals at the end of the bar."

Allan was greeted by an already well-lit Ronald who enthusiastically welcomed him, handing him his flask. "Capital, old bean, we all loved it. I shall put in a word with Carlson. You would liven the place up, no end."

The rest of the evening's celebration involved too much hooch and plenty of laughter. Allan, at last, had a foot in the door.

—

THE OFFER TURNED OUT to be sixty dollars a night, ten more than he'd expected, and the next three months proved to be a great investment as The Bull and Bear saw increasing crowds. With numerous clubs and music playing on the radio, the city was in a lather. Patrons loved to hear popular songs sung well. Allan was not only making more than enough to save some. Mr. Carlson was now a hero to *his* boss as the nightly take increased.

Six months passed in a New York minute. Even with this lovely turn of events, though, Allan began to feel restless. That same smoldering desire to sing with an orchestra on the radio whispered.

One evening, Allan finished his first set and wandered around the hotel to see who might be performing in the main ballroom room. He arrived to hear the intriguing sounds of swing from a large orchestra. Peeking in the door, he saw the signs on the band stand. LARRY CLINTON ORCHESTRA.

He'd heard of them. They were broadcast sometimes on radio from the Glen Island Casino in New Rochelle. Allan introduced himself as the singer in the hotel and asked the door man if he could listen to a few tunes. "Well Mr. Dale, this is the gala for the museum but I'm sure it would be alright...for a few songs."

He walked up close to the stage, drawn by their arrangement of *Forty Second Street*. The female vocalist was stunning and sang as good as she looked. The band leader, Larry Clinton, took a trombone solo, the singer finished, and the crowd applauded from the dance floor.

"Thank you, ladies and gentlemen...and once again...let's hear it for the lovely Bea Wain."

Allan checked his watch and realized he was cutting it close and headed back to the lounge thinking that was exactly where he belonged, singing with a big band. After two more sets, he decided to spend a little time at the bar sharing some quality hooch from his flask with Ira. A small crowd gathered around them offering flasks of their own and showering Allan with praise. Allan noticed an odd expression on Ira's face.

"Hey, Ira, want to take a walk down to the main ballroom and see if the Larry Clinton Band is still at it. Heard them while I was on a smoke break. Great stuff."

Ira shrugged. "Yeah, why not?" he said with scant enthusiasm.

"Something buggin' you, man?'

Ira shrugged his shoulders again. "I don't know. Don't get me wrong. Things have really been hoppin' since you started and that's great. People are diggin' your singing and I guess, I don't know, I just sorta feel like the cork on the champagne bottle...popped and forgotten."

"Ira, none of this would be happening if not for you. I hope you know that I think you're the best pianist in town."

"Well, I'm not, but thanks. Hey, man, just ignore me. It ain't your fault. You're good and getting better fast. I expect you'll be moving on to sing with a band before long."

They arrived in time to hear the last couple of songs and the ample applause that followed. The crowd began to leave and the band put away their instruments. The singer stood beside the stage smoking and decompressing from her performance. Allan knew the feeling as the adrenaline drained away slowly, replaced by a creeping weariness. He and Ira walked toward her.

"Pardon me, Miss Wain," said Allan. "Don't mean to intrude but I just wanted to tell you how impressed I was by your wonderful singing. I love the sultry slant you put on *Bidin' My Time*. Great breath control on that last note. Oh, forgive me...I'm Allan Dale and this is Ira Brenner. He plays piano and I sing down the hall at the Bull and Bear. We just finished up and caught the last couple of tunes."

"Pleased, I'm sure," she replied, turning to watch the band breakdown.

"So...if you ever find yourself at the hotel again drop by the Bull and Bear. I'll buy you a drink."

She turned and appraised him. Took a pull on her cigarette and cracked a slight smile. "You know, I might just do that next time I'm over this way. Spend most of my time at the Casino over the bridge, but I'll keep it in mind."

At that moment, Larry Clinton stepped up beside her, eyeing Allan. She gestured at the two of them. "Couple of musicians from the lounge down the hall. Say they dig our stuff." She looked at Allan. "What did you say your name is?"

"I'm Allan Dale, this is Ira Brenner. The best piano player in town. Well, with the possible exception of your own. Really a great sound you have. Very tight."

"Thanks. What do you play?"

"I'm the singer."

"You sing elsewhere?"

"Not at the moment, but I hope to find a place with a great band such as yours."

"Well, best of luck to you both. Bea, shall we depart?"

"Sure, Larry, I'll be right along."

Larry took a beat, looked again at Allan, and walked away. Bea turned back to the two of them. "A pleasure to meet you both. Maybe I'll drop around. Always like to hear other singers. Ta," she said as she walked away.

—

THREE WEEKS AFTER THEIR meeting, Allan spotted Bea Wain take a seat at the bar and turn to listen to him. Allan had just begun the song and started to add some embellishments to impress her. Then he remembered the old lesson. *Just sing the song, leaving a little flourish for the end.* When the song was over, she joined in the applause with a smile. The set ended after two more songs and Allan joined her at the bar. Though crowded, she had managed to save a stool beside her.

"Some mighty nice crooning there. Must say, better than I was expecting."

"Well your presence is better than I expected. I'm very pleased you chose to come."

"I'm a curious kitty, and you have an innocent sort of charm. Had the night off, some time on my hands, and thought 'Why not?'."

"Would you like a little something to freshen up your drink?"

"Indeedy. What you got?"

"Believe it or not, some bonded Kentucky bourbon," Allan said, pulling a flask from his jacket.

"So Allan, as much as you seem to be enjoying yourself, you got any plans on maybe singing with a band? You're sure good enough and cut a dashing figure as well."

"Wow, Bea, how kind of you to ask. Yep, I'm starting to cast about for auditions and keeping my ears open. But, as you know, it's a big city with lots of singers looking for a gig. At least this is steady, pays the rent and a bit more, and Ira is a great accompanist and good friend, so I haven't felt rushed."

"What are you doing to make some connections?"

"Honestly, Bea, I haven't really gotten out that much to any of the speakeasies or after-hours joints to meet other musicians. Ira isn't big on the nightlife and I'm not sure where to start. I've heard of a few places but I've only been here a few months."

"Tell you what...what time you finish up here? I'm thinkin' of headin' over to Harlem. Place called Club Hot-Cha—a lot of musicians hang out there after their gigs. Sometimes there's a chance to sit in. Interested?"

"Boy, am I! Can you wait around?"

"Hey, buster, it was my idea, right? I want to hear more of your singing, figure out your style."

A little after one-thirty a cab dropped them off at 7th Avenue and 134th Street. The sidewalks were surprisingly crowded for the hour with a mélange of well-dressed society swells mixed with scruffy looking men selling reefer and cocaine near alleyways. Widespread inebriation was evident in unsteady gaits and too-loud conversations. Bea led him to a building with a small line waiting by the door. One by one, a doorman spoke to and admitted them until their turn arrived.

Bea smiled at the man through a small window in the door. "Hey, big boy, I need to see Clarence."

At those words, the door opened, and they were admitted into a smoky room filled with people dancing to some fearsome rhythms. They were knocking 'em dead with a crazy sort of swing beat that grabbed you and forced your feet to move, your hands to slap against your knees, and make you want to dance. The bar was packed, the drinks served openly.

Mayor Walker had passed a local law allowing speakeasies/private clubs to ignore national prohibition laws, creating a thriving business for several hundred establishments in New York. Although Prohibition was scheduled to end in February, already regular bars were starting to serve alcohol as well.

The clubs in Harlem were more popular than ever. Bea led him to the only open stool. Allan stood beside her. Bea eventually got the bartender's attention, yelling over noise. "Gin and tonic and..." She looked at Allan and he shrugged. "Make that two." She turned back to him. "You think this joint is hot now? By three or so, they'll have to nail down the roof. I already see a few musicians I know. Let's have a drink and then mingle. You like to dance?"

"Actually, I'm not very good. Had polio as a kid so I limp slightly."

"Oh, nevermind. I find most musicians prefer making the music and leaving the dancing to the audience. See the fellows at the booth in the corner? Notice the two gorillas at each end. That's Dutch Shultz and some of his gang. Thomas Dewey, the prosecutor, has been trying to nail him for years. Best to stay clear of that bunch. At least some of the Italians are handsome and romantic. That one's cold and slippery as an eel."

A pale thin man with slick dark hair stepped close to Bea and whispered something to her. She giggled.

"Oh, Eddy...you're a naughty one. Meet my friend Allan Dale. He's singing over at the Bull and Bear in the Waldorf, great set of pipes."

Eddy shook Allan's hand with a deflated smile.

"What band you with?"

"No band. Just me and Ira Brenner, the pianist."

"Oh, I see," Eddy said with a hint of condescension.

"Believe me, Eddy, this one's going places, betcha anything. Take it from another singer. You heard about anyone looking for a new vocalist?"

"What about Guy Lombardo? He does that big New Year's bash at the Waldorf. Maybe he's lookin'," Eddy said with a smirk.

"Stop beatin your gums. I'm serious. Give it up for my friend here!" Bea snapped.

"Okay, okay, Bea. Don't snap a garter! I heard Buddy Adler was putting a group together. Supposedly for a new joint opening up in Harlem. Not sure but I think he hangs out at The Log Cabin."

"Thanks for the tip, man. I'll try to run him down," Allan interjected.

Seeing he was a third wheel, Eddy said his goodbyes and disappeared into the bedlam. They never saw him again as they immersed themselves in the fun and frolic till four. Between the infectious music and festive crowd, and the lovely and well-connected Bea, Allan had his first deep draught of New York nightlife and music. Eventually, it all began to catch up with him. "Bea, I'm a bit fried. Hope you don't mind but I'm going to have to furl my sails pretty soon."

"Oh, sugar, did that naughty 'ol Bea wear you out? Just kidding. Let's call it a night…well…morning now. Go find us a cab. I'll say goodbye to a friend in the band. Catch you outside."

As they arrived at Allan's place, Bea kissed him on the cheek.

"I'm a bit canned and it's a long drive to my place. Had a fun time showing you around. Maybe another time. I'll drop by the Waldorf soon. Night, handsome."

Allan wobbled like a conductor on a train as he navigated the stairs to his room. The waning excitement of his night with Bea was mixed with a bit of disappointment at not sampling the romantic pleasure he'd fantasized. In truth, he figured he'd be pretty useless anyway. But, at least, he had a possible lead on the Buddy Adler Band.

The mattress absorbed him while visions of microphones danced in his head.

Chapter 13

Life at the Bull and Bear rolled like a lazy river—much too slowly for Allan, who was beginning to feel like a boat becalmed on it. He had visited the Log Cabin Club twice in hopes of running up on Buddy Adler, to no avail.

Ira sat down beside him during a break and opined, "You can tell me to mind my own potatoes, but your chin's so low, you've been dragging three tracks behind you. What's up with you?"

"Ira, you're the best friend and I love singing with you. But you know I want to be with a full band. Heck, you do too. It's like I'm stuck with a flat tire and no jack. I told you I went to the Log Cabin a couple of times. It wasn't just to hear the band or have a good time, maybe meet a dame. Bea, the singer that came in a couple of weeks ago helped me find out about a leader who may be looking for a singer. He's supposed to hang out there, but I haven't been able to find him."

"Well now, there may be a better way for you to track him down. You know, I've been trying to get you to join the union. They will have his contact info for sure. Not only that but they have regular listings of auditions and opportunities for musicians. Why don't you just pony up the dues and join the rest of us? All the big players are in it."

"That's good advice and very kind, considering it might mean my leaving."

"Way I see it, you deserve to be heard by a bigger audience and heck, what kind of a friend am I to want less for you? Oy vey! One day you'll have 'em in a panic and I'll tell my friends I used to accompany you."

The next morning found Allan at the Musicians' Union office. After joining, he studied the posted auditions. There at the bottom of the third page was a listing for a singer, a piano player, and several other positions for The Buddy Adler Band. Waiting until a respectable afternoon hour, he called the number listed. A deep melodious voice answered on the fourth ring. "Buddy Adler here."

"Howdy, Mr. Adler. I saw your listing at the union hall and wanted to throw my hat in the ring for the vocalist gig. I'm currently singing at the Bull and Bear at the Waldorf. The crowd has grown since I started there a few months ago."

"Indeed, I am putting together an orchestra and need a vocalist, preferably a male. Draws more ladies. Would you be available Tuesday next week to audition?"

"Absolutely, I would. I also noticed that you're looking for a piano player. Ira Brenner, who accompanies me at the Waldorf, is one of the best I've ever heard. Since we already work together and have a tight sound, you could kill two birds with one stone. Even if one of us doesn't fit, perhaps the other one will."

"Well, that is an interesting proposition. Tell you what. I've got a rehearsal space over at 10 West 123rd. Would three o'clock work?"

"You bet. We're excited for the opportunity. See you Tuesday, Mr. Adler."

"That's Buddy to you. See you then."

Allan arrived at work keen to tell Ira about the exciting opportunity. He rushed up to the piano where Ira was arranging his music and set list.

"Listen up...I took your advice and joined the union. I checked the listings for gigs and audition and found Buddy Adler's. He is still auditioning vocalists and believe or not, piano players. We have an audition this coming Tuesday. How's that for some good news?"

"Wow...that's a lollapalooza! Wouldn't that be the ticket, playin' in a band together? What time and where? Oh...and what songs do we want to do that shows off both our skills?"

"It's three in the afternoon at number ten West 123rd. He's got a rehearsal space there and he has a piano. I asked."

"Tell you the truth Allan...I've been dreading the day somebody figures out how good you are and hires you away. The chance to stay together and step up to a band, well that's just my game."

They were better than ever. Each night they polished the songs and grew ever tighter. Tuesday found them at Katz Deli having a late lunch, dawdling there till 2:30 when they headed to the audition.

The building was a nondescript warehouse in a block full of them. They arrived at a grey metal door with a buzzer, which Allan pushed. Shortly thereafter, it flew open revealing a small sandy-haired man with a cigarette dangling from below a pencil-thin mustache.

"Mr. Adler...'er, Buddy? I'm Allan Dale, and this is Ira Brenner."

"Follow me, boys—the room's just through that big door."

The tall ceilings, musty odor and detritus of old boxes and discarded furniture cast an orphaned atmosphere. Their footsteps echoed through the cavernous room. Buddy led them into a smaller but still spacious room where a piano, drum kit, and Buddy's trumpet sat on a stand.

"Great to meet you both. So... here's the deal. I'm set to open at a new spot in Harlem called Jewell's Place. It's not as big as The Cotton Club or some of the others. But kind of like the Log Cabin, it's gonna' have its own feel. Jewell has some serious dough behind her from some of the same kinda guys that did well during Prohibition. Now, they're lookin' to get in on this new scene where they can sell hooch to folks legal like and figure they'll be flocking to the joints with good music and great lookin' broads. We'll take care of the music and they'll have a bevy of beauties decorating the joint. On top of the ones that'll come with their guys. Nothin' pulls 'em in like plenty of Janes lookin like a million, plenty of booze to lubricate 'em, and us to keep 'em jumpin'. We're gonna be doin' a bunch of standards, plenty of Foxtrots, Lindy, Charleston, and boogie to keeping 'em sweatin' and drinkin'. Okay, then, show me what ya got.

Allan followed Ira to the baby grand parked in the corner. Ira sat and began the intro to *Night and Day.* Halfway through, the subtle lifting of a cigarette followed Buddy's slight grin. At the conclusion, he nodded for more. The next song painted a larger grin on Buddy's face. Allan was feeling good about his performance and wanted to showcase Ira. "Buddy, I think you should hear what Ira can do besides being a great accompanist."

When Adler nodded, Ira kicked off *Jelly Roll Blues.* Tapping his feet, the leader jumped up, walked over, and grabbed his trumpet, and they were off to the races. They played together, taking turns on the lead for ten minutes or more, both deeply in the same groove.

When they stopped, all was quiet for several moments. Then they all broke out in whoops and laughter, lifted by the sheer joy of spontaneity. "Jeepers!" said Buddy. "Son, you can flat dance on those keys! Really dug that. Why don't you play one more for me?"

Ira served up a delicate lead-in and Allan began, *"Georgia, Georgia..."* When they finished, Buddy walked up to them at the piano.

"That was really sweet. So here's the deal. I still have a couple of other guys to check out, but I tell ya...you are some hep cats. Give me a week and I'll for sure let you know what's shakin'. If you're the ones, we'll talk dough and what not. Guarantee it'll be better than scale. Jewell's backers got some serious cash and don't mind spreadin' it around. Can you wait till then before you make any other commitments?"

"You bet!" they blurted in unison.

The drive back to Ira's apartment was jubilant. Within seconds of arrival Ira produced a bottle of fine scotch he'd been saving, whereupon they proceeded to fall joyously into their cups, reveling in the great future awaiting them as members of the Buddy Adler Band.

The ensuing week made a lie of the adage "No news is good news" as they anxiously waited for a call. Nine days after their audition, they were losing hope. Then, just as they finished their first set at the bar, Buddy Adler walked in and came directly up to them. "Hiya. Hope you don't think I forgot ya. Had to give a fair shot to a couple of guys, but I'm here to find out if you still want to join us. We can talk particulars tomorrow if that's cool. If the answer is yes...we celebrate and I'm buyin'!"

"I think I can speak for both myself and Ira. That would be okay for us."

"Alrighty, then. How 'bout you scoot over to the Log Cabin when you finish up. I told Jewell you might be showin' up to knock back a few and put on the dog. You'll get a kick out of our fairy godmother and I know she'll think you're the cat's meow, Allan. She fancies young handsome lads. You get off what? One or so? See you around one thirty or two, alright?"

"Nifty. We'll see you at the Log Cabin."

Riding an elevation wave through the remaining sets produced inspired music. The audience responded with applause and profligate tips. Two slithery brunettes draped themselves over Allan and Ira inviting them to continue the party but were disappointed when the offer was put on hold. Nothing was more exciting for Allan and Ira than the prospect of celebrating with their new employer.

They got to The Log Cabin by 1:40 and spotted Buddy at a table with a stunning redhead. Her mane fell far down her back, covering most of the exposed skin bursting from a green deep-cut sequined gown. Two other men were at the table, both smartly dressed yet somehow out of place in their suits. Buddy saw them and motioned them over. Skirting the crowded dance floor, they cut through dense smoke to the table. Buddy jumped up, already a little unsteady on his pins.

"Hey, boys, glad you could make it. Let me introduce ya. This here is Mr. Lou Mondini and his associate Roman Cantore. And this is the amazing Jewell O'Conner...queen of the soon-to-be hottest joint in town."

Hands were shaken, drinks ordered as Buddy waxed eloquent about his two talented new musicians. Allan took in his new companions. Captivating didn't begin to describe Jewell O'Conner. Her green eyes brazenly met his, exuding equal parts mirth, mystery, and hypnotic magnetism. Full, perfectly painted crimson lips parted, gracing him with an ivory smile. Though not an ingenue, the bristling energy she exuded belied her years. The scent of Guerlain drifted across the table.

Allan sensed Lou Mondini observing him and a small caution light went off in his mind. Two brutish men arrived, stationing themselves near their table, and began to scan the room. Mondini lit a cigar, appraising Allan through the smoke, dark pupils peering beneath large, black, caterpillar brows. The menace fairly oozed from his pock-marked face.

Having taken Allan's measure, he turned to Jewell. "Hey doll, get youze some champagne? Ya look thirsty."

"That would be delightful, Lou. How thoughtful."

"Ain't nothin. Just sold this joint a case of Bollinger," he said, snapping his finger for the waiter, who was fetched promptly by one of his gorillas.

The dance floor moved in a rhythmical, mosaic wave of dancers twirling skirts, flashing jewelry, in the arms of well-dressed men. The dancing was frenetic, almost tribal, as the twelve-piece band lay down a ferocious beat. It was a small dance floor but no one seemed to mind the intimacy. Allan was so engaged in watching that he was startled by a tap on his shoulder. Jewell peered over her champagne mere inches from his face.

"Buddy raved about your singing and I'm sure the ladies will love your striking features. Did I catch an accent?"

"Well, ma'am, I'm from Texas…San Antonio."

"Please save the ma'am for someone more matronly if you'd be so kind. Okay then, Tex, tell me more."

Allan gave her a short, somewhat embellished history, along with his ambitions. She focused on each word with her penetrating gaze. He felt a bit intimidated, something he wasn't used to in a world where female attention had come to him with little effort on his part. Jewell was of a different order entirely.

"Well, I'm glad the winds of fate have ushered you into my club. I trust it will be a pleasurable and prosperous association for us both."

Before Allan could respond, Lou Mondini broke in. "Hey doll, what's say we dance to this here slow one?"

She winked at Allan, and replied, "Why not? Lead on."

Buddy leaned over and spoke above the noise in Allan's ear. "I'm gettin' the impression Mondini has plans for Jewell. Just so ya know, he's part of the Italian crew. Mob money is what's fronting Jewell's Place. I figure she's gotta play that one just right, but she ain't nobody's push over. She's run a couple of speakeasies and had some of her girls workin' there if ya know what I mean. She's tough, but fair. But if I was you, I'd play it careful like. Mondini ain't no sweetheart."

The band took a break and Jewell sat down beside Allan and turned to Buddy. "You know I'd really like to get a little taste of my new singer. You know the guys in the band, right? Ask if Allan and… Ira…if they can't fill in during the break."

"Hey sure. Why not? I ain't got my horn with me but these two are killer diller. Be right back."

Moments later, Ira sat down at the piano and Allan stepped to the mike. After being introduced, they kicked off a three-song set which garnered vigorous applause. As the band returned to the stage, the leader patted Allan's shoulder and nodded appreciatively.

Jewell welcomed them back to the table with a beaming smile. Buddy was grinning as well, but Mondini smoked his cigar and ignored them. Roman Cantore gave a curt, appreciative nod.

Jewell leaned close to Buddy. "I relish hearing him with your fine band. I predict that Jewell's will quickly become the hottest club around. Just three weeks from now, boys! I'm wildly excited. Aren't you, Lou?"

"Sure. Long as we pack 'em in and the juice flows, that's fine by me."

Chapter 14

⌒

The booze and money indeed poured like a waterfall through Jewell's. It flowed in rivers to the music of Buddy Adler and his increasingly popular singer as the soundtrack. Through the summer and into the fall the crowds grew.

Jewell worked the room like a modern Cleopatra, surrounded by her bevy of beauties. Though not as large as the Apollo or as famous as the Cotton Club, Jewell had created the Egyptian motif with bold murals of the Pyramids and waitresses dressed like harem girls.

A simmering, flirtatious tension was developing between Allan and Jewell but she always pulled back when the heat grew too intense. Mondini's occasional presence helped tamp down the embers. Jewell was tempting and dangerous fruit—both Allan's conscience and common sense helped him focus on his music.

He was soaring in this new band, as was Ira. They were making nearly three times what they had been. Mondini's money made sure everything about Jewell's was first class. Allan kept himself in check with Jewell's girls. They were more interested in working their own business, so it wasn't hard. Allan began to be invited to private parties and eventually, poker games. It was at one of these that he met Michael O'Bannon.

Though Allan had learned to be a fair hand with the cards, he recognized genius in O'Bannon's deft play. He considered himself fortunate to have lost a relatively small amount in exchange for watching the man. The second time he was at the table, he realized that O'Bannon seemed to know every card in every hand. At the end of the game, Allan offered O'Bannon a ride home. It was on that ride that a new friendship began.

O'Bannon began to spend more time at Jewell's, hanging out and taking Allan to after-hours games. Allan never won or lost a great deal but he enjoyed playing and was learning a lot.

One Friday morning in the wee hours, Allan sat at a table with O'Bannon and four others. They'd been at it for an hour or so when a player across the table lost a big hand, and not for the first time. The man had been drinking and appeared a bit coked up. His eyes hardened in his ferret-like face. He stood, his chair falling as he rose.

"You thievin' little mick! I think ya been dealing from the bottom!" he spewed, spittle dousing the table.

With a tight smile, O'Bannon calmly looked up at him. "Careful, ol' son. You be insulting me heritage and me honesty. I've no need to cheat. You have been playin' poorly, you have. Made big bets on poor hands. So I'll thank ye then for an apology."

"Apology!! Why you bog trottin', potato eatin'..." The man charged around the table and reached for O'Bannon's lapel. How the knife appeared in O'Bannon's hand and the speed with which he sliced the man's forearm was a wonder to behold. As quick as a cobra, he threw his attacker to the floor and the dagger's blade was against his neck.

"Now then, laddie buck. You'll be givin' me your apology and you'll be on your way or I'll mark ya with a scar that'll be a conversation piece for your lady friends. What say you to that, then?"

Fully sober now, sweat breaking from his forehead, the man nodded his head. "Yes, sir, mister...no need for any trouble. Sorry I offended you. I'll just be going, if that's okay."

"Fine, then. But don't be draggin' your useless bloody self around here no more." His rapid exit was followed by silence—first one and then the rest of the players bade farewell.

"My word, Mike," said Allan. "Where did the knife come from? It's as if you conjured it from thin air."

"When you earn your livin' with the cards, no matter how fair ye plays, sooner or later someone thinks you're cheatin' and the game is on. I've been accused of keeping a card up my sleeve, but it's my sharp little friend who's up there." Pulling his jacket back, he revealed a spring-loaded scabbard that instantly brought the knife to hand.

O'Bannon gathered his winnings and the two walked out into the quiet pre-dawn of a lovely fall morning. "Some advice for ya, old son?"

"Sure, Mike. About what?"

"Me trade. First off, never cheat. Then, never play for more than you're willin' to lose. When you arrive there, walk away. And most important, don't do it for a livin'. I got a gift—a blessing and a curse. I can remember all the cards played and know the odds and yes, I count 'em. You can sing and have 'em in the palm of your hand. That's your blessing. But it can be your curse if you become proud as Lucifer and get too hungry for the applause. Pride will make a meal of ya, then spit ya right out. I can teach you a few tricks with the cards, but don't get to liking it too much nor get too used to winnin'. I'm likely to end up dead sooner than later, but it's all I know how to do. You're likely to get famous and have a flock of the lasses draped about ya. Be careful who you listen to 'cause your gamblin' for bigger stakes than ya may know."

"Dang!" said Allan. "That's a whole passel of stuff to think about. Didn't know you were an amateur philosopher, as well. But thank you. I do struggle with the temptations of the attention, the ladies, the drink, and other stuff. Right now, I figure I've got two wise counselors—you and Ira."

O'Bannon squinted at him for a moment. "I'd be careful how much stock you put in this Irish card mechanic." They reached a corner and O'Bannon stopped. "Here's where I'll leave you. Got a wee lass that's waitin' on me. I'll see you at Jewell's, probably tomorrow night. Good night, me friend."

Watching O'Bannon blend into the shadows, Allan contemplated his advice. He was probably a good deal older than his sparkling blue eyes and curly auburn hair would indicate. Beneath the Irish banter there was a melancholy seeping through. Allan figured whatever wisdom he'd acquired had come through strife. He thought of something Ira said. Good times never last, but hard times always end.

Boy, I've gained some interesting friends, he thought, *a long-suffering Jew and a scrappy Irishman.*

Chapter 15

Allan felt both blessed and guilty for his good fortune. All around him, the Depression shredded the dreams of countless Americans. He had listened to a few of Roosevelt's "Fireside Chats." His folksy attempt to console and encourage left Allan less than convinced. But there was definitely something to the way the president talked to people.

He had the night off and he and Ira were going to a place called Yeah Man, where musicians came to meet and jam with other musicians. Top players were always attracted.

Nothing would be happening till late, so they agreed on dinner first. He picked Ira up and drove to the place where they had met, La Taverna. Allan began to reflect on the amazing things that had happened in the short time they'd been friends. He'd come to trust and rely on Ira's good judgment. Frequently blunt, but always compassionate, he'd taught Allan that people aren't what they say they are. They're what they do, he said, and that's all that matters. Ira had asked little and given much to Allan. He'd helped him get his first break at the Waldorf. He was pleased that he'd helped Ira get on with Buddy Adler.

"So whaddya think, Allan? Is Angelina gonna be happy to see ya or put arsenic in your wine? You haven't talked to her since we were here last, right? She has a thing for you, and you know what they say. *Hell hath no fury like a woman scorned.*"

"Hey, man, we just flirted around. Besides you warned me about her mobbed-up boyfriend. Pretty girl like that...shoot, she gets plenty of attention."

"Yeah, but she didn't get yours. I guess we'll find out soon enough—here she comes now. You know La Taverna...The Tavern... never got to serve booze during Prohibition. Bet they're goin' through the old Chianti now."

Angelina had spotted them the moment they arrived but waited before coming to their table. Striding toward them without taking her eyes off Allan, she paused without a word, prompting Ira to speak up.

"Angelina, it's so nice to see you. We have been wanting to come visit and have your fabulous food and catch up."

"Catch up?" she said, turning to Allan.

"Well, of course. I've wanted to come by often, but as Ira will attest, we have been playing almost constantly since we saw you last. We're with the Buddy Adler Band at the new hotspot, Jewell's. In fact, we'd love for you to come be our guest when you're free."

"Well, let me show you to a table. Your booth is occupied." She led them to one of the only empty spots.

"We now have wine and beer if you like," she said handing them menus.

"How about a bottle of Chianti, best one you have. That okay by you, Allan?"

"Sure. Hey, Angelique, do you still have that fried calamari? You recommended it the first time Ira and I met here. We're celebrating tonight and seeing you makes it all the more memorable."

"I will bring the wine and order the calamari." She turned and walked away.

"Sorta like I figured," said Ira. "She's a bit miffed. But I've seen the Dale charm work magic on more than one poor dame. Bet she'll be all smiles before we leave."

She returned with the wine and poured it, saying only that their appetizer would be out shortly. Her aloofness spoke volumes, bringing a brief chill to the moment. Halfway through dinner, on their second bottle of wine, their spirits soared once more as they revisited the turn of events since they were last here, and what an amazing journey it had been.

Ira's droll wit kept Allan entertained as always. Ira didn't talk a lot but some of his comments and whimsical retorts could keep an entire bar entertained. Allan shared his vision of the future, his grand ambition to be the most famous singer on the radio. "I knew you wanted to sing on the radio, but I had no idea you were so focused on being the biggest star. So, what are you willing to do to get there? I've noticed that most of the biggest successes have to make some sacrifices, sometimes some dicey compromises. I've been around a couple who've told me they've done whatever it took. The thing that I enjoy...admire...even envy in you is your genuineness. There has never been a false note in your dealings with people. But I saw something, heard something, tonight that sounded like a different Allan."

"Well Ira, I've been talking to some of the heavy hitters who come to Jewell's. They tell me it's not what you know but *who* you know, that you have to cut a few corners, bend a few rules sometimes if you want a bite of the apple. Some of them are in the same business as Mondini and have hinted that they might be able to help me out. They're giving me a broader perspective on what I can be. That's all. Hey, man, I won't forget you when I make it."

Ira finished his meal, took a sip of wine, and stared at his friend. "Look Allan, I know all you've had to overcome, what with the polio and your mom's anger at your leaving and not following her dream.

You've been through a lot to get here. But I'm seeing changes in how you treat people. You used to ask how they were doing and listen, ask if there was anything you could do for them. Seems like I hear you telling people how well you're doing and what they can do for you. Nothin' wrong with being confident. Being self-centered never ends well no matter how well you do."

Allan sat back in his chair, stunned and not a little offended by these forthright observations. He threw back a large swallow of wine, staring at Ira before he spoke. "You don't know the half of it! Most of my life, I've been stared at, ridiculed, pushed around. It was only when I became a singer that I got respect and love. I've got dames throwing themselves at me. Never have to buy a drink. I'm starting to get invited to parties where big wigs and players hangout. What was it Shakespeare said? *This above all, to thine own self be true.* Well it's about time *my* self got what he deserves."

"Well, on your way to the top remember...be nice to the people you meet on the way up. They're the same ones you'll meet on the way back down." Ira drained his glass. "You know I think I'm ready to call it a night."

"WHA'! What are you hot about? I thought we were headin' over to the Yeah Man to hear some jazz and maybe jam."

"Sorry, man. Feel like I want to turn in early. Probably too much wine." Ira caught Angelina's attention, signaling for the check. As she arrived, Allan plucked it from her grasp and kissed her hand.

"Ah, the angel Angelina. How I've missed your beautiful face. I'll take care of this, Ira. I'm plenty flush and there's more on the way. Here doll, keep the change. Oh, and drop by Jewell's some night and see the show. Maybe we can have a drink and who knows what else after, huh?"

"You know," said Angelina. "I remember that sweet boy who used to come in here. I really liked him...a lot. You, I'm not so sure. I'm probably not up to your standards. Goodnight, Ira...and Allan."

He looked at Ira and shook his head. "Well, what's eatin' her? For that matter, what's eatin' *you*?" When Ira didn't respond, he shrugged. "Whatever. I'll drop you off at your place and then head over to Yeah Man. The night is young and I feel like a frolic."

—

THE MUSIC POURED OUT of open windows of Yeah Man as Allan neared the door. His first impression was how small the room was. He'd heard about the place from musician friends. Through the smoke he saw a quartet on stage, laying down some serious jazz. He stepped to the bar and waited for a stool to open, which took a while. There seemed to be a lot more men than women in the mix, which was unusual. Considering that most of the cats were here for the music and not the party, maybe that made sense.

Spotting an opening, he sat, ordered a drink, and turned back to watch the band. The trumpet player was blowing holes in the roof while the piano man laid down the groove. Unlike Jewell's, most were focused on the players rather than the conversation. A few songs later, they took a break and Allan approached the trumpet player.

"Hey, man, that's some mean horn you blow. Do you ever have singers up or is it just instrumental? I'm the singer with Buddy Adler's band at Jewell's. Name's Allan Dale."

"Rex Bonner. Glad you liked my chops. Yeah, I hear good stuff about you guys. I'll try to get by if I'm off some night. Been workin' pretty steady. So, talk to the piano player. He sorta runs the show around here. 'Scuse me, gotta leak some so I can make room for more."

Allan found the piano player and was invited to sing a song or two on the next set. They decided that they both knew *All of Me*.

The style and tempo set by the piano player was a much more upbeat arrangement than the one Allan knew but he fell in with it and soon was snapping his fingers and turning it loose. The crowd, as well as the band, gave polite acknowledgment and the piano player asked if he wanted to do one more. He sang one of his best, which led to extended piano and trumpet leads. Plenty of applause followed and the piano player even told the crowd they could hear him at Jewell's.

Allan had been a bit wobbly when he arrived, but he felt the adrenalin kick in and he ordered another drink. A tap on his shoulder came just as he took his first sip, causing a bit to dribble down his chin.

An expensively dressed man in a dark suit and matching Borsellino hat stared at him with fierce brown eyes. A cigarette dangling below a thin black mustache barely moved when he spoke.

"Hey dere. Name's Joey Castello. Liked your stuff. Heard good things 'bout youze guys from some of the boys from Mondini's crew. You like it over dere?"

"Yeah. It's going well. Place is packed most nights. You should come around and give us a listen."

"Might just do dat. My boss is gonna open a new place. Gonna make deez udder joints look like nuthin'. Mondini is small potatoes. Ever hear of Salvatore Marazano? We're talkin' high end girls, high end business, high end pay, ya get me? So here's the deal. I'll send some of my boys to give a listen. Mondini don't like me so much, know what I mean? We like youze guys, maybe you and Buddy and me, we talk some business. I'll be talkin' to ya. Like the way you sing. Think you'd look good in our joint." Turning abruptly, the man left.

—

A WEEK LATER, ALLAN sat at Jewell's having a drink after their second set. Two large swarthy men arrived, standing one on either side of him. The smaller one spoke out of the side of his mouth.

"Joey Castello sent us to give you a message. Wants ya to meet him and his boss Tommy Lucchese dis comin' Tuesday. Rao's, One o'clock. It's over on East 114th. Wanna talk business, have a little lunch."

"Joey, the guy I met at Yeah Man?"

"Dat's him. You good?"

"Sure, why not? I'm always open to new opportunities."

Three days later Allan parked across from Rao's and sat considering the men he was going to meet with. According to some of his Italian friends, Tommy Lucchese was a lieutenant in the Marazano mob. A brief cautionary ripple washed over him. But what the heck? He already worked at a place owned by a mobster.

Rao's sat on a corner sporting bright red paint, contrasting with the tan brick of the building it anchored. The smells of garlic and Italian spices mixed with cigar smoke enveloped him as he walked in the door. The long bar was peopled by several tough looking men, all watching his reflection in the mirror. Scanning the room, he spotted Joey in a booth in the rear, waving him over.

"Siddown. Glad ya could make it. Like ya to meet my boss. Mr. Lucchese, this here is the singer Allan Dale I tol' ya about." Lucchese took several seconds to look him over. Joey stood, allowing Allan to slide in next to him.

It was Lucchese's eyes that defined his presence. Set in an unremarkable oval face with a cleft chin, his visage held neither smile nor frown lines, as if he had no emotions. The intense brown eyes percolated with a quiet menace. There was the slightest lift of the corner of his mouth as he shook Allan's hand.

"Joey tells me great things about you and your band," he said. "I believe he told you we are opening a supper club over on the Upper East Side. We're gonna throw a load of dough into it and make it the hottest joint in town. We got lots of connections in entertainment and plan to have some big-name guest performers and maybe broadcast on the radio. We need the best house band we can find. Joey says Buddy Adler and you as the singer fill the bill. Interested?"

"Well, *I* am but Buddy runs the show. I can talk to him, set up a meeting. The only problem I see is that Mondini is the silent partner with Jewell. He might not take kindly to our splitting, especially since we've only been there less than a year."

"We can handle Mondini. Small time. Mr. Marazano can convince him of the wisdom of letting you go. So when can Buddy Adler meet?"

"I can ask him when he is available and tell him about your plans, but I'd like to get an idea about exactly what you have in mind. We're getting paid pretty well and like Jewell's and the clientele."

"Whatever they're payin' we'll double it. You seem ambitious. Would getting to sing on the radio live from the club help your career?"

"I reckon it would. When are you planning to open?"

"We are already halfway done with decorating and getting it ready, should open in a couple of months. We're going to call it NOBLESSE. Means classy, elegant in French. Fancy name for fancy people. You're gonna see the best of the best comin'. Bankers, politicians, actors. Like I said, we're well connected. Alright then, how 'bout some lunch? Got the best pesto in the city. You should try it."

Little was said during lunch as both men clearly enjoyed the food, which Allan had to admit was even better than La Taverna. Immediately after paying the check, Joey and Tommy Lucchese rose to leave. "We'll be in touch." Lucchese pulled three cigars from his jacket, handed one each to Allan and Joey, and lit the other.

"We got some business to do over the bridge. Enjoy the cigar. Joey will be in touch for a time to meet your boss."

Driving home, Allan thought about how quickly things had happened since he had arrived in New York. Now it seemed he was closer than ever to singing on the radio. He had to talk to Ira and discuss the unexpected opportunity. Ira usually had a wise viewpoint and would likely come up with a number of concerns with the deal.

Two months would put them into 1934. Probably be their first and last New Year's performance at Jewell's. Nothing ventured, nothing gained. He altered course and headed for Ira's flat.

Allan found Ira in good spirits. Without a great preamble, he laid out all he'd been told. Ira, in his usual way, rubbed his chin and mulled it over before responding. "First off, we've got a great gig at one of the hottest clubs. Jewell gave us a break, as did Buddy. They're good friends and the Mondini money is behind it. He's not a guy you wanna make mad. He don't care much for you as it is and if he gets wind you're behind this, it could be a problem."

"All that's true, Ira, but if you're gonna make an omelet you gotta break some eggs. This could be a chance to get on the radio! It's a huge chance to break into the big time. And don't forget the money. We're already getting one and a half times scale. Double that...that's three times scale. And think of the exposure. Lucchese says top politicians, bankers, actors, and big guest stars will be there. We can make the kind of contacts that will get me heard all over the country. Maybe get a recording deal. Shoot, man, this is too good to pass up. You gotta help me convince Buddy."

"Oh, no. You're on your own. I'm just a piano player. You're the one with stars in his eyes. If you can get Buddy to meet with those guys and he takes them up on the gig, so be it. But you got your work cut out for you. Sometimes it's better to make haste slowly. But I know you and your ambitions, so we'll see how it plays."

After Ira, Allan was surprised at Buddy's eagerness to meet with Lucchese about the offer. He'd been prepared for a bit of a tussle, but Buddy was a money-driven fellow and saw the potential. He also knew about the Marazano crew and their clout. He'd never cared for Mondini and figured if it was all mob dollars, might as well stick with the top dogs.

The meeting went smoothly and within a week, Buddy decided to take the deal. Allan was ecstatic but torn by the thought of hurting Jewell. She had been more than fair and even dropped hints of a deeper personal relationship. But to get where he needed to be, he had to learn to put his future first. It was becoming all he thought about. One day the folks back home would see how good he was. His mother would have to admit that his was the right decision.

———

"MY FIRST THOUGHT WHEN I met you," said Jewell, "was how can a man be that handsome, sing that well, and be that innocent and humble?' Your wavy black hair, those hazel eyes, the permanent tan, and a voice that make's the girls tingle…well, it appears that you have managed to disprove the innocent and humble part. The very things that attracted me to you, the unspoiled nature that made you different…it appears you've learned the me first, New York ethics very quickly."

"Jewell," said Allan. "I didn't mean to hurt or disappoint you. It's just such a great opportunity."

"When I hear you say, 'I didn't mean to,' I hear you lying to yourself and to me. We all are responsible for our choices. You chose expediency over loyalty, ambition over relationship. Well, so be it. I had feelings for you, thought you might be different than the men I'd known. Buddy, I can understand. He's got a band to keep working and he is what he is. You, however, are not who you think you are. Best of luck. I think you'll need it." Jewell eased herself up from the empty bar, gently placed her hand on his cheek, stared into his eyes and walked away.

Allan sat with his face burning. The sting of her words was more painful than a slap. Somewhere within, they resonated. That still small voice, the one he was becoming adept at ignoring, whispered admonitions. Yet a stronger voice called out. The fates were calling. He deserved to achieve his dreams, prove that a man with a limp—but a great voice—could achieve stardom. He regretted Jewell's words but he had to do what he had to do. Sometimes people's feelings have to be put aside. To my own self be true, he thought.

They say life happens fast in the city. Six months evaporated in a breath. "Noblesse" was on fire. In a city avid for the newest, most chic nightspot, the lines aggregating at the door attested to the draw of the Buddy Adler Band and their captivating crooner.

Allan was starting to recognize faces he saw in the *Times*. These were the people that defined power, elegance. And they hung on his every note. The dance floor was packed, the juice flowed, as did the reefer and coke. Lucchese's girls worked the room. Noblesse struck the perfect balance between sophisticated and profane. With Prohibition in the rearview mirror, the mob figured out how to create profitable new ways to grow their business.

Allan was pleased with his progress, but the live radio broadcasts had yet to occur. He knew that the future of music was in radio and recordings. It was that possibility that had swayed him to make the move. The next step was obvious, and he was anxious to make it.

He didn't want to appear ungrateful but perhaps it was time to talk to Lucchese. He dreaded dealing with the taciturn expressionless mobster. His subtle menace had kept Allan at bay. But there the man sat at his personal corner booth. Doesn't fortune favor the bold? When the set was finished, he wandered over.

"Mr. Lucchese, hope you're enjoying the music. Always pleased to see you, and your lovely entourage." A blond and a redhead hanging on either arm, turned their attention from Lucchese to Allan.

"You're doin' good, kid. Word on the street bringin' 'em in. Keep it up," he said, turning his attention back to his girls.

"So, Mr. Lucchese," Allan said, "I was wondering if there is anything new on the live radio broadcasts? I know a lot of the top clubs are having great success because of those broadcasts."

"It's in the works. Just gotta be patient. Tell ya what. This here redhead is Molly. She really likes your singing. Molly, why don't you help our singer unwind after his hard work?" he said, winking at him. Soon after, Molly joined the stream of gorgeous girls and the cornucopia of pleasures that issued forth to him at Noblesse.

Allan awoke one morning to the phone ringing, coming to consciousness sporting a hangover from a night of frolic he couldn't recall. Slipping away from the deeply sleeping beauty of the hour, he placed the receiver to his ear. "Hello?"

"Hey, man. It's me, Ira. Just wondered if you want to have a late breakfast or early lunch. Haven't had a chance to visit for a while. We only chat after the gig for a few minutes. Just wanted to check in, see how you're doin'."

"Hey, Ira. Got a babe in the bed still sleeping. Let me get her outta here and I can meet you. Hey, why not meet at the Waldorf, like old times, but with us as the customers. What do you think?"

"Sounds good. It's what...a little after ten. How 'bout eleven?"

"See you there."

Pulling up in front of the Waldorf for valet parking was a delightful experience. No more parking on the street. Arriving a few minutes early allowed him time to wander through the place where he'd gotten his start. Allan soaked in the moment and realized how quickly he had moved toward his goal. He believed as never before that this was only the beginning.

He walked in the restaurant, enjoying the feel of being an honored guest, not just another employee. Ira arrived just as Allan was being seated, bearing a less than cheerful countenance.

"Hey, Ira, it's nice to see you in the daytime. It's always so busy at the club we never have any time to hang out. You okay? You don't seem your usual self."

"Yeah, there's stuff goin' on that makes me nervous. Let's order, and then I'll tell you what I've been seeing."

They shared small talk as they ate, caught up on what each had been doing in their time off. Allan realized he'd been a bit remiss in checking in and spending time with his closest friend. Ira was the one person he could be totally transparent with. The truth was, on the other hand, he'd become mostly opaque of late.

The waiter arrived and cleared the dishes, pouring more coffee.

"So, let's hear it, Ira. What's the burr under your blanket?"

"First, there's plenty to like about Noblesse—good dough, lots of exposure, fancy joint. But I've been seeing some things that make me nervous. For starters, there's a lot of drugs being sold and used in the bathrooms. I'm not just talking reefer and coke. It's hop heads shootin' up heroin. And it's the guys running the joint pushing it. I know that they control the hookers, but this ain't good. Lucky Luciano and his bunch are the big players but Marazano's bunch are nippin' at their heels. And the Jewish mob are in the mix as well. Those boys play rough. Plenty of people gettin' knocked off in turf wars and I think Noblesse may be a target at some point.

"I was smoking in the alley couple of nights back. Joey and a pair of his gorillas came out the back door. I heard him tell them to keep an eye open for trouble. Luciano's put the word out he may have to teach their bunch a lesson. You remember how out of hand it got when they were all competing in illegal booze. If people want something illegal, it's bigger money for them."

Allan frowned. "Dang, Ira. That ain't good. I know these guys don't mess around. But hey, as long as we keep our noses out of it and just play music, I'm sure we'll be fine. 'Sides, I talked with Lucchese about radio, and he says it's gonna happen soon. I'll do whatever I have to for a shot on the radio. I'll keep my eyes peeled, but it'll be alright, I'm sure. You are prone to worry too much."

Ira shrugged. "So, Allan, how's things with you?"

"Best ever. Diggin the music we're layin' down, meeting some interesting people, especially of the female variety. I think we're on the way to big things. I feel almost guilty for my good fortune. I read all the stories about the Depression and those dust storms out west and here I am actually saving dough for a new car. Got my eye on a Buick. And this suit...Brooks Brothers. Got a Borsellino hat to match. Yep, we're heading for the top, Ira."

"Glad you're diggin' it all. Just watch what's going on. You know that a lot of those politicians and judges and cops are on the payroll. There's another thing that bugs me. This business with framing and blackmailing prominent men with the hookers they're running. It's a nasty little side business and the girls are the bait. Aren't you the guy who said you can't walk around the corral and not get crap on your boots? Be careful where you step, Allan."

"I will. And on that note, I have to cat out of here. Meeting a debutante over at Central Park in about a half hour to feed the ducks and watch the kids sail their boats. Her idea. Family's loaded. Never hurts to make a connection. The opposite of walkin' in the corral. Hang around money and some of it's likely to find its way into your pocket."

"Hmm. Yeah, I guess so. Take care. I'll see you at the club tonight. Thanks for the meal and visiting with me."

"Hey man, you're my best friend. We'll do this more often. What do you say?"

Allan smiled and breezed away to a new amorous adventure.

—

A FEW DAYS LATER he was having a drink at the club with Robert Greenberg, a prominent banker he'd come to know. Robert was well into his cups and began to confide his troubles to Allan. It seemed that one of the girls he'd met at Noblesse had lured him to a hotel room where during their foreplay, a man had burst into the room with a camera, catching them in the act. The girl was obviously in on it, and Robert was contacted the following day with the option of a large payment or pictures for his wife to peruse. The man was beside himself as the demand was substantial, and he'd lost a big whack in the market. Almost tearfully, he asked Allan for advice. He had none.

"The problem is," continued Robert, "it would pretty much wipe me out. Our money, if you must know, is mostly from my wife's trust fund and inheritances. If she leaves me, I'm finished."

"Robert, I'm so sorry. I don't know what to tell you. Maybe you could try to negotiate a lower payment?"

"These guys play rough. Mobsters, I'm sure. I'm not the first victim. I know of several prominent men who have had the same scam run on them. I can't go to the cops. Most of them are on the payroll, all part of the Tammany Hall rat's nest. It's my own fault, I guess. The dames in this place are incredible and this one, Judy, was irresistible and eager. I'm sure you've seen her—blonde, big bust, frequently sits at the end of the bar."

"Yeah, maybe." It was time for the next set, so Allan stood up and straightened his suit. "Thanks for the drink. Sorry for your troubles."

In truth, Allan *did* know the woman Robert had mentioned—had even had a drink with her while enjoying her flirtations. Ira had mentioned the frame-ups and the mob connection but what could he do? It was not his problem.

At closing time, he spotted Judy on the arm of a distinguished looking middle-aged man and something niggled at his conscience. If he was honest, Allan had to admit he was involved with some unsavory characters. But he wasn't personally doing anything all that bad. Okay—the girls, a bit of booze and reefer sometimes—and yes, he was drinking a fair bit and gambling more than ever. But after all, he was a young up-and-coming singer. What could you expect?

The still, small voice became quieter.

—

Noblesse was now THE place to see and be seen. The fame of Buddy Adler's Band and their popular singer spread.

Allan came to work on a chilly fall night to find Tommy Lucchese and a few of his goons waiting at their corner booth, waving him over.

"Hey kid...got some good news for you. We're set up for a live radio show on New Year's Eve. You're the early act, the warm-up for the headliner, but it's great publicity."

"That's spectacular, Mr. Lucchese! You know how much I've been hoping for this. We'll be the best ever. And it's gonna lead to more, I betcha!"

"I know it will. We got some friends over there in the radio biz owe us a favor or two. You do good, maybe we get a regular show. Capiche?"

Lucchese turned back to Joey, leaving Allan savoring this grand news. He could hardly wait to tell Ira. Hopefully Buddy hadn't done so first.

That night, buoyed by the news, the band and Allan put on the best performance of their career. The crowd was wowed, the dance floor was packed, and Allan was soaring. At evening's end, Joey invited Allan to a private party. He was told not to invite the band members, that he'd be driven to the event in the next half hour. It felt like less of an invite, and more like a command, but who knew? Maybe he'd meet some of those radio folks.

Allan sat in the backseat of a Cadillac with Joey and a bodyguard up front. Joey offered him a cigar and a silver flask.

"Good cigar from Cuba, scotch from…well 'dose guys dat wear dem skirts." Joey laughed.

"Thanks. So where are we headed?"

"Mr. Marazano's got him a place over da bridge for entertainin' his friends. He wants to meet this singer he gonna hear on the radio. Whaddaya think about meeting the big boss?"

"Great."

That was the last of the conversation until thirty minutes later when they turned from the rural two-lane road into a gated and well-guarded driveway. Bright lights glimmered from a stone Tudor mansion at the end of a quarter-mile-long drive. The woods gave way to a broad, open expanse, lit by a half-moon and bright security lights. Allan was amazed. This was like the country estate of a prince or oil tycoon. He knew there was a lot of money rolling through the mob's shady businesses, but this was truly impressive.

They were dropped under the porte-cochere, before wide flagstone steps leading to massive doors fit for a castle. All this was under the watchful eyes of at least ten armed men. A valet helped him from the car as another approached from the driveway. Outdoor lighting washed the building's gray stone, casting a medieval ambience.

Joey led them to a large ballroom, brightened by sparkling chandeliers, under which a hundred or more people gathered. Navigating their way through the festive crowd, Joey led them to a small group gathered around Salvatore Marazano. Tommy Lucchese was standing at his side, leaning in to whisper as they approached. Marazano broke off his conversation with a man and turned to Allan.

Allan felt an odd shiver as he was introduced by Lucchese. He took in Marazano's wavy black hair, the high forehead over to arched bushy brows. But it was the impenetrable and ominous eyes, the right of which seemed permanently at half-mast. They were the most disturbing eyes he'd ever beheld. What lay behind the black pupils left no doubt as to the danger and power lurking within.

Allan had expected a much older man, but Marazano was likely in his forties, of medium height and build. Other than those eyes and the almost expressionless face, he seemed unexceptional. His grip was dry and powerful as he shook Allan's hand, his voice a surprisingly high tenor. "So, you're the singer Tommy's ravin' about. Says you're great, even if you're not Italian. You know, we're famous for our singers. You know Caruso?"

The man smiled, but it didn't reach his eyes. "So you're gonna do the first radio from our joint. Thought you ought to come enjoy yourself, meet some of the boys...and some of the broads too. Just keep 'em rollin' into Noblesse and do us proud. We'll take care of you. Joey, take Allan and introduce him around. Nice talkin' to ya."

A trio—piano, bass, and drums—was playing in the corner. The soft easy music drifted over a diverse crowd. Elegantly dressed young and beautiful girls hung on the arms of richly turned out, mostly older, men. A tougher looking group of men wandered about with vigilance.

A disproportionately large number of strikingly lovely single girls wandered in several small gaggles around the room as well. As they moved about, Joey introduced him to several of Marazano's upper echelon men—judging from their attire. Almost all had a cigar in one hand, a drink in the other, and a girl at his side.

Joey waved an arm around. "Make yourself at home. Bar's over there." As Joey left, Allan slid through the crowd to a long mahogany bar with a green marble top. One of the two bartenders poured him a bourbon. No sooner had he taken a sip than someone took his arm. He turned to find a ravishing woman smiling at him. Her parchment white skin stretched over cheekbones sharp enough to carve diamonds, framing eyes the color of Texas bluebonnets. All of this was crowned with a jet-black mane dropping over pale, bare shoulders. "I knew you'd be coming. Why did you make me wait so long?"

"Ah...I'm...I think maybe you have me mistaken for someone else?"

"Oh, no. It's you. My old aunt told me that when I came here tonight, a dark handsome man would be waiting for me. Is it you?"

As struck as he was by her beauty, Allan was captivated by her voice. Deep, rich, and sultry, breathing her words in velvet waves.

"You know, I believe I *am* he," said Allan.

"I'm Elena," she said. "Buy a girl a drink?"

"Certainly. What might that be?"

"Martini, twist, two olives. It's best when round things come in pairs," she grinned seductively, glancing below his belt. He gazed at the cleavage displayed above a low cut, sleeveless red dress.

Taking their drinks, they wandered to a small round table. Their conversation flowed as if they were old friends. They laughed, shared the same humor, liked the same music, enjoyed the same films. Allan was especially pleased that she was not impressed with his singing career.

At one point, she asked him to dance and he took the risk. As they danced, she forthrightly asked about his limp. She was mildly interested but unconcerned with his answer. He was smitten with her unaffected spontaneity. Elena was unlike any woman he'd encountered. She was vague at first about her occupation. "I work in fashion," she said.

Allan lost track of time until Elena looked down at her watch. Looking deeply into his eyes, she placed her hand over his and leaned forward. Holding his eyes without blinking for what seemed to Allan an eternity, she said, "My pumpkin awaits. I must bid you farewell, my handsome troubadour. I have an early shoot and need my beauty sleep. It has been deliriously lovely being with you. Do you have a good memory? Well of course you would, having all those lyrics to remember. Listen closely... TREmont-3107. Call me and let's continue this wonderful conversation."

She kissed him on the cheek and was gone before he could respond. Rushing to the bar, he borrowed a pen from the bartender. He wasn't about to trust his memory on this one. He smiled to himself, realizing that this was the first time he'd been so taken with a woman since he'd come to the city. She was something of an entirely different caliber. He puzzled over her parting words.

He found Joey and asked if he knew Elena. He didn't. Apparently, a wide variety of people were invited to Marazano's parties, including bankers, actors, politicians, and models. And there it was. "She must be a model," he thought, "with that face and figure."

THE FOLLOWING WEEK ALLAN spotted his friend Mike O'Bannon sitting down at the bar. He realized he'd not seen him since the move to Noblesse and felt a stab of guilt for not calling him. He had hoped to run into him at one of the poker games Allan frequented but surprisingly had not. O'Bannon grinned as he watched Allan approaching.

"Mike, where have you been?" said Allan. "I kept thinking I'd see you at a game. Sorry, I could have called you but with the move to Noblesse and all, I've been flat out. So, what do you think of the place?"

"Oh, right elegant, it is. No shortage of high rollers and toffs. Don't worry about not callin'. Been down Miami way. Had a good run down there. Lots of players. It looks like Lady Luck has been smiling on your music career."

"Has she ever. We're set to do a radio broadcast on New Year's Eve. The money is great, and the place is the hottest joint in town. Hey, I've missed your company. I have been playing a good bit. Lady Luck hasn't been real even handed. Been losing more than winning. Maybe a little O'Bannon coaching will get me back on the winning track."

"Word has gotten back to me about your playing. From what I hear, you've lost more than a few quid. Remember what I told you of knowing when to walk when you reach your limit? Seen it more than a few times—a bloke forgets himself and overplays his hand. How much are you down?"

"Mike this is a bit rough. I'm ashamed to tell you but it's a good bit, more than half of my savings. But I know I can win it back."

"My old friend. There is those about who'd have your guts for garters if word is out you're an easy mark. It's different for me. It's my trade and I'm a professional. With you making all this dough you're making it's easy to feel you've nothing to fear. But in the heat of the moment, you can lose and lose big. As your friend, I suggest you take a wee breather. Let's play for fun. Let me show you a few things. But give her a rest, mate."

Allan was surprised and chastened by Mike's words. It was actually worse than he'd admitted. He'd been playing more frequently and in higher stakes games with skilled opponents to whom he had lost closer to three quarters of his savings. Still Mike's comments irritated him.

"Listen man, I can handle this. Just had a bad run is all. I've got a good feeling about this next game coming up."

O'Bannon eyed him. "It's me, Allan. I can read you like I do the cards, boyo. Take it or leave it but I'd sleep better knowing you was givin' it a rest."

"Sorry, Mike. I'm a bit flustered over it and I've got to get up on stage in a minute. I will consider what you've told me. I do love to play, though. You kinda get hooked on it."

"Aye, that's the problem."

"Look, let's get together next week and I'll lay off till then. Fair enough?"

"Too right, me old son. Give me a ring up."

Allan called O'Bannon the following day, but the call went unanswered. He called the next day and the day after. Two weeks of fruitless calls led him to go to Mike's apartment to check up on him. He knocked repeatedly, called out, and finally, in frustration, went to the landlady's apartment to see if she knew Mike's whereabouts. A frazzled older woman in a housecoat answered.

"And how can I help ye, lad?"

"My name's Allan Dale and Mike O'Bannon is a dear friend. I've not been able to reach him for nearly two weeks and we were supposed to get together days ago. He doesn't answer his phone so I thought you might know where he might be."

"Aye, I too have been wonderin' after him. I'm Mrs. Fitzpatrick. He's been nowhere to be seen these last days. His rent is a week past due and it's not like the lad to be late. You're not the only one asking after him. A couple of his mates from over to Killarney's Pub stopped round asking after him. There were also a pair of Italians, shady they were. Truth be told, I'm a bit worried about our Mike."

"Do you know anyone who might have information on him?"

"Those two Irish lads who came by are at Killarney's Pub regular. Mike spent a lot of time over there with his boyos. It's over in Bay Ridge in Brooklyn. Ask around for Tim and Kevin. Don't know their last names but they're usually together. You may have some luck. If they don't seem helpful, mention me. Angela Fitzpatrick."

"Thank you, ma'am. I'll keep you informed on what I learn. Here's my phone number. Call me if you hear anything and thanks for your help."

"I'll be prayin' for him, that I will. Good luck, lad."

Allan headed to Bay Ridge in Brooklyn. It was one of the older Irish neighborhoods and the local pubs were a center of social life. He walked into Killarney's around six to find a good-sized crowd. The smell of cigarettes and beer competed with whatever the kitchen was cooking. He figured he'd start with the bartender since they usually knew the regulars. He found an empty stool at the bar. "Pardon me, could I have a pint of Guinness?"

Returning with the beer, the bartender asked, "Can I get you anything else? We've some fine shepherd's pie and our stew is the best in Brooklyn."

"I'll try the stew and I'm looking for someone. Perhaps you might know Tim or Kevin. Mike O'Bannon is a dear friend and Angela Fitzpatrick told me they might be of help."

"They're not about but they are likely to turn up. If I see them, I'll send them over. Be right back with your stew."

Allan had just finished his meal and having a second pint when the two men arrived together and introduced themselves. They were an oddly matched pair—Kevin a tall rangy redhead with green eyes and Tim a stocky muscular fireplug with an oft broken nose and thinning hair. Allan told them about his friendship with Mike and his concern. They were deeply worried as well and shared some disturbing information.

"Look mate, we all know that in Mike's line of work you can create enemies. Mike never owes money. It's his rule—don't bet more than you can lose. But he was having some games of late with some Italian blokes and had been doing really well. I don't have to tell you those blokes aren't known for kindheartedness. We've been snooping around over in the neighborhood where they was having the games and no one's saying anything. We got us a bad feelin' altogether."

"Tell you what. I'll give you my number and get yours. If either of us finds anything out, we can let each other know. I sure hope he's all right. He is one of my best friends."

"Aye, he was…I mean he *is* a fine lad."

Allan was so busy in the next week that he didn't notice the time slipping by with no word on Mike. He asked Joey if he'd heard anything about O'Bannon. Joey gave him an odd look before answering. "Some things you're better not asking about. I don't know nothin' but if your friend cheated or tried any funny business, he could be at the bottom of the Hudson. I'd drop it if I was you, capiche?"

The disappearance of Mike O'Bannon became a mystery that would haunt Allan for the rest of his life. It did not, however, dissuade him from card games.

Chapter 16

The weeks blew away like the fall leaves. Allan tried several times to reach Elena, but her phone went unanswered. First Mike, now her? His increasingly busy schedule left little time to ponder it. The band's popularity was getting them hired for functions away from Noblesse, increasing their incomes, even as the Depression continued to impoverish millions of Americans. Allan was learning to ignore their hardships. He launched full bore into developing contacts with those who could help him—and to being at the right parties when he wasn't performing.

And he was becoming adept at the practice of willful blindness. The drugs, the hookers, the blackmail, and all the other criminal activities that fueled the mob that owned Noblesse—all these, he learned to ignore. If he ignored other's faults, perhaps he needn't be defensive of his own. As he watched the wealthy and powerful prosper in often amoral lives while in the midst of mass impoverishment, he marveled. He would choose to do what was needed to grow more successful, famous, beloved. If it took associating with a few unsavory people to get there, so be it.

It was coming on Christmas. He thought about his family. Although he missed them when he stopped to think about them, they populated a diminishing portion of his musings. He called infrequently, rarely wrote except to share the latest break in his career, though he knew they were struggling to get by in the hard times. His father was playing for Vaudeville, pit orchestras at the movies, and taking random teaching jobs since the symphony had closed. He did wire money home from time to time.

He wished his big New Year's radio debut could be heard in San Antonio. He decided to send a Christmas card and substantial check to help them. He was making multiples of what the average musician pulled in. The only way to go was up—and he was ascending at an exhilarating pace.

When Allan arrived at the club that evening, he saw the band gathered around Buddy, all wearing somber expressions. Buddy saw him walk in. "Allan, please join us. I've just been telling the boys that Art was found dead last night. Seems he shot up too much horse. Art was a great clarinet man. I don't know who we can get that has his chops. With the big New Year's Eve show a few weeks off, it's lousy timing."

"Pretty bad timing for Art, I'd say," Ira added.

"Oh, well, of course, and we will all miss his friendship. We've contacted his folks back in Cincinnati and we'll help them get the body back there for the funeral. Try your best to not let this get to you. We're on a roll and I don't want this to slow down our momentum. Any questions or comments?"

"Yeah, I got one," said Ira. "I'm pretty sure he was just doing some reefer from time to time till we got here. We all know that heroin is a huge money maker for the mob. And there's a river of the stuff pouring through here. Anybody but me feel a little weird about that?"

"Ira, we're just the band," said Buddy. "We can't do anything about crime and war and poverty. We're entertainers, not moralists. People have been getting hooked on booze, broads, betting and whatever else forever. It ain't our job. But boys, let me remind you, first one I catch doing horse is gone. It's a whole other kind a stupid doing that stuff. I never heard of anyone dying from reefer but as you can see, this stuff can kill you." He shook his head. "Okay, try to shake it off. We gotta play in an hour. Oh, and be careful what you say around here about the drug stuff. Don't want to bite the hand that feeds us. And this bunch bites back."

Allan was stunned by the news. He'd liked Art, a quiet, somewhat withdrawn young man. The likelihood that he'd gotten hooked while at Noblesse nagged at him. Ira came up beside him and threw his arm over Allan's shoulder. "Tough way to start an evening, my friend. I've been worried about Art for the last couple of months. I knew that monkey was riding him, getting fat chewing away at him. I know for a fact he got the stuff here from one of Joey's boys. Don't think Buddy appreciated my comments, but I'm right, for all the good it does."

"Know how you feel. But hey, what can we do about it?"

"Nothing, I guess, except steer clear of it and don't hang out with the mobsters."

Allan excused himself do go to the dressing room to change into his dinner jacket and get a little distance from Ira and the rest. He caught his reflection in the mirror as he walked in. He hadn't noticed it before. His resting expression seemed different. He saw in his eyes an intensity, a seriousness he'd never seen there. The smile lines were fewer, the countenance more constrained. He was enjoying the most success and adulation he'd ever experienced, on the way to greater things.

It wasn't just the news of Art's passing. He realized that *he* was changing. An odd thought popped into his head. *Nothing turns someone into a slave quicker than the need to be liked.* He dropped the self-appraisal and changed for the show.

New Year's Eve was three weeks away. The club was jammed Wednesday to Saturday nights, and they were playing private parties when not at the club. Allan was beginning to get some good reviews in the papers. He liked seeing his picture and reading all the grand things they wrote. Lucchese was making sure the New Year's Eve show was being promoted and, for the first time, Allan felt the buzz of fame.

The Saturday night before Christmas, as he was wowing the crowd with his rendition of *Embraceable You*, Allan saw Elena walk through the door. She turned to smile at him as she entered. He poured his soul into the song, singing only to her.

She sat at the bar, arms sheathed in elbow-length white gloves. Elena's fulsome smile beamed. Though he'd not forgotten her, he had been too busy to call, so this was good fortune. The set ended two songs later and Allan hurried through the crowd, acknowledging compliments and pats on the back, stopping to thank them. By the time he arrived, she was engaged in conversation with two men. As he neared, he heard her say, "Ah, here's my date now. So nice chatting with you."

He slid onto a seat next to her and leaned toward her. "Elena, words can't express my delight in seeing you. I've called several times but no one answered. Where have you been hiding?"

"Paris, actually," she said. "I've been doing some work for Chanel. I just got back a few days ago. I saw your handsome face in the Entertainment section. My, aren't you becoming popular? You probably don't have much time to spend swanning about the town with a lady."

"It's gotten a bit crazy, that's for sure. With the holiday party gigs and the regular shows here, I'm lucky to get a day or two off. But for you, Elena, I will move heaven and earth. We're off Monday. Would you like to have dinner?"

"That I would. Where did you have in mind?"

"I keep wanting to get to Sardi's but haven't been yet. Lots of entertainment types go there. Being an entertainment type myself, it seems appropriate. But if you have another idea, that's fine."

"I love Sardi's. I've been eating French food for days so Italian would be grand. Would an early dinner work? Say 6:30? I have a shoot in Bal Harbour the next morning, so I have to be home earlier than normal. And if it's okay, let me meet you there. No need to pick me up."

"That sounds great. I'll take what time I can get with you. I have truly longed to continue our conversations. You are the most intriguing woman I've ever met. I've been wondering what exactly you do in fashion?"

"I model clothing. I hope to own my own boutique one day, but this is the door that has opened and I'm saving my money to that end. I'm quite fortunate. I have all the work I can handle, the money's great, and I get to travel to some interesting places."

"I guessed that was it. I'm not surprised. I mean look at you—you are stunning."

"I can take no credit for being born this way. And this won't last for long. Aging is kind of like having a dishonest bookkeeper who is very gradually siphoning off your money so that by the time you catch on, it's too late to do anything about it. What do they say? *Make hay while the sun shines.* Besides, at the end of life, it's what you accomplish, what you create, that you'll be proud of. How you look pales in comparison."

"That speaks volumes about who you are. And I want to read all those volumes...call them Tales of Elena."

"Here's a question. What are you doing after you finish tonight? I have nothing tomorrow so I can stay out and play with the big kids. Maybe we can find a quiet after-hours jazz club that's not too loud to talk over." Elena's sparkling eyes held his.

"You are on. I know just the place. I have to get back on stage. Just this one more set and we can saddle up."

"That sounds like the ride for me, cowboy."

—

ALLAN AWOKE ALONE. AFTER an enchanting night with a great jazz trio playing, the only melody he could remember was Elena's voice, and intriguing conversation with never a false note. They parted well after three, with the most hypnotic and satisfying kiss of his lifetime. A lyric from *Embraceable You* played in his mind: *Above all, I want my arms about you.* She'd chosen again to pass on his suggestion to go further. This woman was the most mysterious, the most captivating he'd ever imagined. And, he confessed, "I'm well and truly lassoed."

The events that unfolded over the next few days kept his focus entirely on the most important performance of his life. The broadcast would be heard by the largest radio audience of Allan's career, far greater and more influential than his first in St. Louis. The MBS network would air the show over much of the country. So busy was he, that when New Year's Eve arrived, it took him by surprise.

After dinner, as he was changing into his tux and getting ready, he had another surprise. The phone rang delivering the dulcet voice of Elena.

"Hello, Allan. I just wanted to wish you a Happy New Year early since we won't be sharing in the festivities. I will not be able to enjoy you on the radio as I have been invited to a private celebration, but I wish you all the best. You will wow them, I know."

Allan had two simultaneous reactions—a sting of jealousy and the realization that he should have invited her to be with him. So focused was he on his career that all his thoughts had been on the night's show.

"Elena, thank you so much. I must apologize, however. I should have invited you to be here. I've been so wrapped up in preparing that it never even dawned on me."

"Understandable. I know how important this is to you. Fortunately, I will be among friends. I will be fine. Just wanted to wish you luck. Break a leg." She paused. "Oops, probably not the best choice of words. Break a lung?" She laughed again. "Oh, forget it. Knock 'em dead, baby. Talk to you soon. Happy New Year." And the phone went dead. Allan was a bit discombobulated, but shaking it off, he headed for Noblesse. He had to get there early for the radio sound check and to make sure all was in order.

Buddy seemed even more roiled than usual, while Ira floated on his normal calm pond. Thick cables secured with gaffer tape snaked like black anacondas from the stage to a mixing board. The microphone was one of the new RCA 77a ribbon mikes, the very latest, delivering the purest tone for vocals ever heard. They ran through three songs as the engineers tweaked settings, finally satisfied that all was in readiness.

Allan collared Ira, suggesting a stiff drink before the show to steady their nerves. They were in good company as the entire band was having a tipple at the trough. Buddy arrived and put his arm around Allan.

"Don't want you to get the big head, but I don't think we'd be here without your great singing and stage presence. We're a good band but there are a lot of good bands. Having an outstanding singer gives us our unique sound. Even though I'm a horn player, I know that the ultimate instrument is the human voice and instrumentalists only approximate it. I think together, we are going places. Just wanted to wish you an early Happy New Year and let you know I appreciate you and the fact that you're never a prima donna. Now, let's go have some fun. You know what I always say…makin' music is the most fun you can have with your clothes on!"

The crowd was big, beautiful, and boisterous. Noblesse was festooned with balloons and party favors sported in abundance. The butterflies of anticipation flew away as Allan got lost in the music—in the intoxication singing in front of the power of horns and piano and drums.

He soon forgot about who was listening on the radio as well as the crowd. When he began to sing *Embraceable You,* his thoughts turned to Elena. He felt he was singing to her alone and tears came to his eyes. It took a moment before he came to himself and realized the audience was responding with exuberant applause.

When the time arrived to sing *Auld Lang Syne,* Allan was surprised. It seemed they'd only gotten warmed up. With the countdown in the rearview, the revelry shifted into high gear with an enthusiasm bordering on desperation. Considering the last ten years, everyone was ready for an end to the Depression, and a new season begun with the new year. Allan was hoping for a new acceleration for his career and possibly a new deepening of his relationship with Elena.

Chapter 17

The new year proved both surprising and rewarding. By early spring, the radio broadcasts were now every Saturday night over the MBS Network and heard over a multi-state area. Allan was now the featured singer and voice of the program. Marazano had renovated and opened the second floor with a dining room and a few private rooms for various activities, most of them illegal.

His love affair with Elena had become exclusive and intimate and he now had an agent, Ernie Herzog. He told Allan that he had great potential, foresaw a recording contract, and possibly even film opportunities.

The band had all gotten substantial raises. Allan was now making more than three times the amount he'd started with. The wheels were rolling, greased by Marazano money of dubious provenance. Ignoring much of what transpired around him at Noblesse, Allan flew like an arrow, the bullseye ever before him.

As his love for Elena grew, the time he had available to spend with her shrank, as both of their careers demanded more of them. The band was booked at least five and sometimes seven days a week. Elena was also in constant demand as her modeling career ascended.

Incrementally, troubling currents began to creep into their lives. Elena began to use coke to propel her, booze and pot to relax her. Fissures traced themselves in the smooth surface of the couple's relationship. Allan was increasingly disturbed with her growing use of booze and drugs and arguments between them grew.

Winter found them both too busy to resolve anything and Allan fell into a pattern of quiet acceptance. The year had swept him into a whirlwind and growing popularity. Mutual Broadcasting was talking to Ernie about a possible show featuring Allan as the star. The year was almost over.

The new year came and went grandly and 1935 began with great expectations. Although his life was financially secure, his popularity growing, and his love life manageable though troubled, he found himself impatient with the pace of his progress.

The radio show with him as the star was yet to come to fruition. Ernie assured him that he was being pitched to the right people, reminding him that these things took time. Unfortunately, patience had never been a virtue of Allan's. He watched as other singers like Bing Crosby and Rudy Vallee became stars, and thought he was at least as good. He wanted to make sure he didn't miss a moment to a lost opportunity.

In late April, a glorious spring week arrived. Elena wanted them to get away to the Catskills for a few romantic days. She suggested, reminded, cajoled, and finally hounded Allan about it, much to his irritation. Finally, she let fly several barbed comments about his self-centeredness, his manic ambitions. It seemed to him they were starring in two separate movies with vastly different plots and theme music. His thoughts were turning ever more to evasion and escape.

By Thanksgiving, Allan noticed that Elena was drinking even more than usual, smoking reefer, and he suspected she was using horse. It mellowed her mood, making her both less demanding and less amorous. He decided as long as she didn't overdo it, and ceased nagging him, he'd keep his mouth shut. *Time flies when you're having fun,* he thought. *But it bolts even when it's no fun at all.*

As 1935 drew to a close and Allan prepared for the big New Year's Eve broadcast, he was struck by the fact that another year was almost past. He was essentially treading water. He called Ernie and lit a fire under him, scorching him with demands. Ernie promised that big things lay ahead for him in the upcoming year.

Mollified for the moment, he took Elena for a nice lunch at Tavern on the Green. She became tipsy and suggested they have a little romp in the bushes in Central Park. Her behavior was beginning to give him pause. Although she was far more manageable, she frequently seemed a bit disoriented, her normal rapier wit and keen observations noticeably missing. Still, they were managing to let the good times roll and Allan rolled with them.

Ira joined him at the bar one evening before the show. "Hey Allan. Hardly ever get to visit with you these days. That gal keepin' you busy?"

"Oh, you know how women are. I think she's starting to see rose-covered cottages and little boot chewers in our future. But I'm in no hurry. Ernie tells me things are looking good for the new year and Lucchese says he has a contact in the record business that he can put me next to. Everything good with you?"

"Yeah, what's not to like? Steady gig, great dough, fine band. Only thing that bugs me is some of the stuff I see goin' on around here with Joey and his boys. Guess it goes with the territory, but I see some pretty wigged-out people. Guess that's to be expected since this joint ain't their only source of revenue. But with LaGuardia and Hoover wound up about the gangs, it does make you wonder if something could happen to this gig."

"Ira, you are still a worrywart. Take it easy. They own half the politicians and judges—not to mention the police. Like it or not, they seem to have it under control."

"Yeah, okay. Listen, Allan, you know I'm your friend and I always tell you what I think, not what I think you want to hear. I may be the only one who'll do that. I want you to know I'm proud of you and what you've accomplished since I've known you. You've helped me and been a good friend. But don't spend too much time listening to everyone who tells you how great you are. Pride is a dangerous thing, and it can sneak up on you. At times you seem a little too taken with your popularity."

"What are you talking about? I treat you and everybody fairly, don't I?"

"Everybody that you think is influential or can help you out. But sometimes you're pretty short with the waitresses and the bartenders. You also got up the new sax player's nose when he wanted to chat and you were in a hurry. Just somethin' to chew on. Don't take offense. It's just ol' Ira here. See you on stage."

—

APRIL WAS BREEZILY ARRIVING with the first mild weather of the year. Elena was gone for the week on a fashion shoot. Allan was done for the night when he was invited by an old card-playing acquaintance to a poker game upstairs. It had been a while since he'd played, remembering O'Bannon's' warnings. He still hadn't heard from Mike nor had any of his Irish friends and they all expected the worst. But he was feeling lucky.

Six players were already at the table when he arrived to find two empty chairs. He was dealt in on the next hand—five-card draw. As they played, Allan spoke to a couple of guys he'd met in the club and was introduced by first name only to the rest. It became clear that these were serious players. A waitress offered drinks, which he declined.

The bets were becoming sizable as the evening became morning. Allan looked down to find himself holding three jacks. Upon the table lay the largest pot so far. Calling for two cards, he added a fourth jack in his hand. As O'Bannon had taught him, he let a subtle look of concern cross his face. Deciding to take a chance, he bet his entire week's earnings on the hand. All but one player folded.

All eyes were on him and the remaining player. It was time to fish or cut bait. Allan brought out the last two hundred dollars he had with him, not risking the money he was saving for a new Buick.

A grin spread across the man's face as he called and laid down a full house—three tens, two queens. Allan was taken aback at first, but he began to tingle. Four of a kind was the superior hand. He laid down his cards to audible intakes of breath around the table.

Gathering the pot, Allan stood and prepared to leave. His opponent was not pleased that he wouldn't get a chance to win his losses back. "Seems a little unsporting of you," he said. "Stick around for another hand. Double or nothing."

"Perhaps another time," said Allan. "I promised my gal I'd be home long ago. But I'm here from time to time so I'm sure you'll have another chance. Let me know when you're playing again."

Allan stuffed his pockets with his winnings and departed to the sound of Jack's mumbled curses. As he left, a fellow player warned him. "You played that well, Allan. Smart move leaving while you're on top. He is not a fellow to be trifled with though. Played with him before. He's a lawyer for some of your Italian friends. He'll be wanting his pound of flesh. You're swimmin' with the sharks in that room. Don't get too far from the boat."

"Thanks. Yes, I think discretion is the better part of valor in this case. Thanks for the invite. Drinks are on me next time I see you."

As he drove home, he realized how much he missed O'Bannon. He recalled the times he'd spent learning from Mike. At least twice a week, O'Bannon would meet with him and tutor him at cards.

Mike had an old rowboat in which they would paddle up the Hudson. Tossing lines in the water, they'd spread a blanket across the bench seat between them and fish while they plumbed the depths of the art of poker. No fish were ever caught, but Allan caught on to O'Bannon's techniques. He'd grown more confident and O'Bannon had been pleased with his rapid advancement, particularly in learning to count the cards and get a feel for what had been dealt. Allan missed his friend and still lived in hope that he would show up with wild tales to share about the adventures he'd had during his absence.

Then one night in May, after the last set, the player he'd bested before approached him. "Got a game starting upstairs. What say you join us?"

Allan shrugged. "Okay, why not? I'll be up in a few."

Five men sat at the table when Allan walked in. The lawyer was the only one he knew. He was dealt in on the following hand and put down his five-dollar ante. For the first hour, the winning was evenly distributed, but his adversary started taking more of the hands.

The rhythm changed and Allan began to win. Soon the pot had reached a mountainous pile and only he and the lawyer were left. It was like déjà vu. Allan had a good sense of what cards remained to be dealt.

Allan held four spades and a king and drew one card. He allowed his mouth to turn down in concern as he looked at the matching spade he'd drawn, completing a flush.

Jack beamed as he upped the bet by three hundred dollars. Allan already had at least twice that already sitting in the pile. It was more than he'd been ready to lose but he stood pat and called. Jack lay down an aces high full house.

Allan felt as if he'd taken a shot to the liver.

"Sorry, old chap," said the man. "Guess the goddess of fortune is with me tonight. But I'm happy to continue should you wish to try and win some of it back."

"Nope," said Allan. "I'll pass. I'll catch you next time." He descended the stairs in a daze. Near as he could figure he'd just lost close to $800—a third of all he had saved. Fuming as he drove home, the glare of the sunrise blinding his bleary eyes, he vowed to win it all back.

Elena awoke as he walked in. "Good morning, darling. You're just now getting home?"

"Yep. Go back to sleep."

"Where have you been?"

"Just playing some poker."

"Are you okay? You seem upset."

"I lost some dough, alright? I don't want to talk about it. I just want to get some shut eye alright."

She looked at him. "Fine then, you can cry in your own beer. I have a shoot in a couple of hours and won't have to put up with your surly behavior. You're so busy we hardly see each other anymore, but you add playing cards with the boys to the schedule? The bed's all yours, still warm." She threw the bedcovers onto the floor and stormed into the bathroom.

Allan awoke perspiring. The heat of August had arrived, joined at the hip to her ugly sister, humidity. These days, New York was giving Texas a run for the money.

He oozed sweat as he got ready for a meeting Ernie had arranged with a record company executive. It was the most hopeful thing that had happened in weeks. He needed a change of luck, and a record deal could be just the ticket he'd been hoping for.

Allan's bank account was dwindling in spite of his income so he was counting on Ernie finally coming through—he'd been waiting too long for that big break his agent kept promising.

Crown Records reportedly wanted to meet and discuss signing Allan and promoting him as the "new singing sensation." As he dressed, he felt as if he'd been lifted on wings. He began to envision an album cover and vast crowds waiting to hear him sing. When he arrived at West 42nd for the meeting, he wiped the sweat from his forehead. Ernie met him at the door, and they took the elevator to the fifth floor. Crown wasn't the largest record label but they had Hubie Blake and Fletcher Henderson in their stable. Crown's motto was *Two Hits for Two Bits*, which was printed on the sleeve of their records. A red Crown logo graced the door they walked through.

Following a twenty-minute wait, they were ushered into an office with modest yet comfortable furnishings and a window without a view. Rising from a cluttered desk, the producer, Fred Mann, introduced himself and asked them to sit.

"Fred, I'm glad you could see us," said Ernie. "This is Allan Dale, the singer I've been raving about. Like I told you, he's packing them in at Noblesse and the guys at Mutual Broadcasting love him and are featuring him and, of course, the Buddy Adler Band. Allan could be your shot at the next Crosby. I mean he's got the looks, and he definitely has the voice to boot. I know you said you'd give the broadcast a listen...so what did you think?"

Mann was apologetic. "I'd hoped to get a chance to hear the broadcast but Saturday night proved challenging as I had to attend a function I couldn't get out of." He looked at Allan. "I've heard positive comments and read some reviews giving you high marks. As I told Ernie, we are always open to new talent, though at the moment, things are a bit tight. Nonetheless, I told him I was good to take a meeting and get an idea about your personal presence and what your ambitions might be. I must say you are certainly a handsome young man."

Mann's rheumy brown eyes were framed by creases, etched through decades of frowning and magnified by thick lenses. Allan watched as liver-spotted hands smoothed back his few remaining gray hairs. He'd expected to be intimidated by a big record company executive but for some reason, he found himself envisioning Mann in underwear and black socks held up by garters. He almost giggled but caught himself. He felt his confidence click up a notch. Mann folded his hands on the desk and stared at Allan, ignoring Ernie. "So, tell me, what might you expect from Crown were we to take you on?"

"Well, Mr. Mann, I'm not an expert on your business but I know you make your money through the talent and record sales of your artists. I assume you've invested in recording, distributing, and promoting them to sell their records. I guess I'd like the same kind of deal you gave to, well, Hubie Blake for example. I imagine I would sign an exclusive contract and you would pay me an advance and produce my recordings—at your expense of course."

Mann looked at Ernie and back at Allan. "I see. As your agent may have mentioned, this is just an exploratory meeting. I've yet to actually hear you, but Ernie thought it would be worth a meeting to get a feel for you." He paused. "But to respond to your comments, let me give you a fuller picture of how we work. There are a few different approaches. Sometimes, as with Hubie, we sign an already popular artist, involving advances, recording costs, and pressing and distribution. In the case of talented but largely unknown artists, we create more of a, shall we say, joint venture. The talent pays for the recording, there is no advance, and the percentage on sales we negotiate is based on the risk and expenses we assume in pressing, packaging, distribution, and promotion."

Allan frowned. "And where do I fall in your scenario?"

Ernie stood up. "Fred, let me jump in here and say you really need to listen to this kid. Allan's got more talent than just about any of these chumps tryin' to get you to sign them. Once you hear him— better yet, watch him—wow the crowd, you'll sign him. I'm sure."

"Thank you, Ernie. I appreciate your enthusiasm," Mann said.

"So," said Allan, "out of curiosity, how much would I have to pay for this joint venture?"

"Hard to say, Mr. Dale, without assessing your potential and long-term prospects. I promised Ernie a sit down to establish a dialogue. I am impressed with your looks and obvious growing popularity. I will listen to your radio broadcast and I will come to see your performance at Noblesse, a club I've been meaning to visit anyway. Based on what I see and hear, we'll take it from there. I do appreciate your visit and will be in touch with Ernie after I've seen your performance." Mann rose to shake each of their hands and sat down, turning his attention to papers on his desk.

On the elevator, neither of them spoke. When they reached the door, Allan turned to Ernie. "That was certainly an underwhelming experience. I'd hoped to at least be whelmed if not overwhelmed. A conversation with that guy is like chewing old jerky."

"Now, Allan, you know what they say. *Slowly, slowly, catchee monkey.* I just know when he hears you live and sees how the audience, especially the dames, dig you, he'll want to offer us a deal. Remember, it's the broads who buy the records."

"Ernie, the only deal that will work for me is I get an advance and they pay all expenses. That joint venture is a lame horse I'm not riding."

"Cool down," said Ernie. "It'll be fine. I'm following up to get a commitment on when he can come see you. It'll be soon. Leave it to me, okay?"

"Fine. Just keep me posted. I gotta get back and check in with Elena."

It was early afternoon when Allan got back to the flat. Elena was still sleeping. He planted a kiss on her cheek and gently nudged her shoulder. "Hey, sleepyhead. How 'bout some lunch? Just got back from that meeting with Crown. Want to fill you in."

"Hmm..." she said, turning over. "Hi, baby. A little foggy. Maybe let's do early dinner. I need a few more winks."

Miffed at her rebuff, Allan poured himself two fingers of scotch. It seemed to him that the momentum was shifting. Until now, the opportunities seemed to arrive in waves of good fortune. Now between his gambling losses, the disappointing meeting, and Elena's growing dependence on booze and drugs, he felt like a character in a blues song. He thought about praying for good fortune, then realized he hadn't prayed in a very long time. Now, considering his current way of life, he decided it would be presumptuous to do so.

He had hours to kill before going to the club and was getting hungry. It would salve his sullied spirit to bask in the attentions of the lovely Angelina over a glass of Chianti and a plate of ravioli at La Taverna.

He'd let Elena see to her own business.

Chapter 18

A llan opened the door and the aromas took him back to his first meal at La Taverna. He found his way to the very table at which he'd first dined there. The lunch crowd was tapering off and he saw Angelina waiting on a table by the window. He watched her, marveling anew at her lithe body, the waterfalls of black mane spilling over her shoulders and back, her erect posture. He had forgotten what a stunner she was and how different from the women he saw at Noblesse. It was not an affected or stylish look—it was natural, authentic, and suddenly more alluring than ever.

When she saw him, she paused, stared, and eventually faced him with her blinding smile. "Well, if it's not the famous radio singer. I heard you a couple of weeks ago. You sounded wonderful, Allan. It's so nice to see you. It's been a very long time, but I guess you're busy these days. How is Ira?"

"Ira is great. Playing in the band with me, of course. You have grown more beautiful since we've been apart. Hard to believe that's possible." He smiled. "You know this is where my luck began to change. You introduced me to Ira and it's been off to the races since then. I have missed seeing you, but you're right. We play almost nightly and are either in Harlem at Noblesse or playing at a party at a big hotel."

"I suppose you're hungry, maybe thirsty too?"

"A glass of Chianti and some of your famous ravioli would be grand. And if things slow down and you have some time, I'd love to catch up."

Angelina winked with a flirtatious grin. "Very well. I'll be back with your wine, sir."

Allan took his time over the food, watching the crowd dwindle. As hoped, he saw Angelina take off her apron and head his way. The day might prove to have a better ending than beginning. He rose at her arrival and pulled out a chair for her.

"My, such a gentleman," she said. "Waitresses rarely have the pleasure. I'm usually the one seating people. But I'm off for the rest of the day so I have lots of time to hear all about your exciting life." She rested her chin in her hands and smiled expectantly.

"Well, darlin', it's been a wild ride so far. As you know we're doing regular broadcasts from Noblesse on Saturday nights. The crowds are overflowing, usually with a line waiting at the door. The private gigs are for some of the most prominent folks in New York so the exposure is great. I'm doing what I love and making more than a few pesos.

"Oh, and earlier today, my agent Ernie and I had a meeting at Crown Records. They're interested in signing me to a contract. That would launch me into the big leagues in a hurry. Not much to complain about. How're things with you?"

"Not as exciting as your life, for sure. The restaurant is busier than ever but I'm thinking of going to school. I want more than this family business. I've been reading a lot of books and they have me seeing life differently. I want to explore more of what's out there and find out what I really have a passion for. My boyfriend and I are quits so there is nothing holding me back…well…other than my Italian family. They think I'll just stay here and grow old and run La Taverna with my brothers, but I'm starting to see another future taking shape."

"Are you free this afternoon? Want to head over to the park and watch kids sail boats on the pond and maybe have some dinner later?"

"That's tempting," she said. "Tell you what, my apartment is a couple of blocks from here. Maybe you can wait while I change out of my stinky clothes and we can go for an adventure."

Her place was small but neat. Fresh flowers sat on a small table. Inexpensive prints hung on the walls alongside family photographs. She poured Allan a glass of bourbon and excused herself. Minutes later, he heard a lovely soprano voice—she was singing in the shower.

After a half hour, Angelina emerged wearing a white A-line dress made of a sheer gauzy fabric, cut fashionably short. Her hair was pinned so that black tresses fell over her left shoulder. When she came to him and took his arm, the subtle scent of perfume and pheromones wafted about him.

The afternoon was warm, but the humidity had relented. When they reached the park, they found a bench beneath a large overhanging oak. Children frolicked at the pond as they launched toy sailboats, hoping to startle the ducks. Their conversation was that of old friends, although they'd never actually spent time together away from La Taverna.

After a while they strolled, sometimes wordlessly, her arm hooked in his. Later, enjoying a sunset from a grassy knoll, they decided it was getting on to dinner time. He suggested the Hotel Algonquin as it was a hangout for writers and the literati.

The food was superb, the wine excellent, the pastries—their specialty—otherworldly. As they lingered over coffee, Angelina reached across and took his hand. "What time do you have to be at the club?"

"In about three hours or so."

"Then let's get back to my place. Have an early night cap before your show." The night cap turned out to be Angelina taking him in her arms and leading him to her bed.

What transpired left him dazed and confused. It wasn't what he'd expected, though he knew she'd always fancied him. But her passion took him by surprise. She kissed him goodbye with a smoldering longing that left him breathless.

"Sing well, mi amore. Thank you for the most delightful day I could have imagined. Come to me again soon."

He drove home vibrating with lingering ardor, home to lingering disorder. Elena's inebriated greeting morphed from loving to loathing in the time it took for her to catch a hint of Angelina's perfume. Curse-filled accusations flew, as did a vase of wilting flowers, barely missing him.

Since Allan had no honest explanation, reasoning with her was useless. Instead, he threw back a list of her failures—the drinking, drugs, wasted hours that drove him to his dalliance with another woman.

Elena began to gather her things and Allan poured a drink and lit a cigarette. Maybe it was best for her to spend more time at her place and allow time for the dust to settle, time for him to figure out what he really wanted.

Angelina presented a very different set of possibilities, but she also carried potential risks. Allan remembered the warnings about her boyfriend's mob connections. The fact that he was part of a rival family meant Joey would be of no help with such complications.

Awaiting was the prospect of a night of release in performing, always a cleansing and exhilarating experience. He showered, changed, and poured another drink before heading for Noblesse. Before the show, he had another, and by the first break, all his problems were forgotten. By the second break, he found himself in the flirtatious company of a tall stunning redhead named Daisy. By night's end, Daisy was his blissful escape.

—

THE FLING WITH DAISY played out over the next few weeks with visits to her uptown brownstone, bedecked with priceless antiques and artworks. Clearly well supplied with money, Daisy also came with cold martinis and hot passions. Upon awaking, following nights of abandon, Allan could only retrieve glimpses of what had transpired. Daisy usually shooed him out the door on her way to brunch with her old sorority sisters, but eager for a rematch.

Allan decided that, with all he wanted to accomplish, it was no time to burden himself with relational dramas. He figured he had the pick of the litter at the club, free party favors and hooch, plenty to keep him occupied if in a shallow, egocentric way. First things first—Allan's career, Allan's fame, Allan's success, Allan's pleasures. All of which sounded great in theory.

As he was to discover in the following months, the cleanliness of theory bears scant resemblance to the messiness of reality. As 1935 drew to a close, Allan had left a dozen disappointed damsels in his wake. He knew he was drinking and partying too much and he still found himself no further in his progress in gaining stardom.

The Crown Records deal had come to naught. As before, Ernie kept promising a breakthrough "any day." That day better come in the new year, he thought.

He looked forward to the New Year's Eve broadcast. They expected to have the largest radio audience ever and the show now had a regular sponsor. At least he wasn't trying to make it in Germany—Hitler had banned jazz music played by Jews or Black musicians. He just hoped Germany didn't manage to start another war.

New Year's Eve arrived with dames and dandies tricked out in the finest gowns and garb filling Noblesse. A suspended sheet holding hundreds of balloons hung from chandeliers over the packed dance floor. The band was swinging and it was an hour till midnight.

Allan, lost as ever in the song he was singing, was a bit surprised when it ended. After the last song in the set, he navigated through the river of bodies to the dressing room where a bottle of twenty-year-old scotch awaited, a gift from Marazano.

Ira joined him in a pre-New Year's toast to grand success for them all. "Hope I get more opportunities," said Allan. "Cause this year, all I'd hoped for didn't happen."

Ira shrugged. "We Jews have a saying. *Man plans, God laughs.* I know you were disappointed with the Crown thing and I imagine you saw things with Elena getting more serious. But you sure seem to be enjoying yourself with the broads. Maybe a little too much? You are certainly one for the party. But, hey you're only young once, right? I should be so lucky."

Suddenly several shots rang out in the alley. Rushing to the door and hesitantly opening it, Allan saw Joey and one of his goons lying against the curb with blood covering their shirts. A car made the end of the alley and squealed around the corner. They knelt over Joey who whispered, "Lansky's boys."

Ira left to get help. Allan could see the other man wasn't breathing. Joey grabbed his sleeve and started to speak but all that emerged was a breath that sounded like crumpling paper.

Allan had never watched anyone die. It took him a while to come to himself, to process what had happened. The door swung wide as Lucchese and his gorillas emerged. "What'd you see? What kinda car?"

"Ira and I just heard shots and saw a car turning the corner up on the left. I couldn't tell what kind. But Joey said, 'Lansky's boys.'"

"There's been some disagreements and some heat about who's doin' what and where. But this here..." He grimaced. "There's gonna be some dead jewboys. Get Joey and Louie moved to the warehouse before the cops get wind of this. The mayor is already banging the drum about turf wars. And you two, you didn't see nothin', understand?"

"Sure, yeah, none of our business," Allan answered.

"Hey you, piano player, you're a Jew, right? You know any of Lansky's bunch?"

Ira shook his head. "No, sir. I'm just a piano player. I don't hang out with gangsters...I mean, I'm not associated in any way with those men."

Lucchese stared at Ira. "Keep your lips buttoned, botha ya."

A car arrived and the bodies were quickly put in the trunk. There was no time for discussion—they had to be on stage in minutes. Both of them shaken, they were tentative for the first few bars of the song, but they soon thought no more of it until the balloons had dropped, the champagne was served, and *Auld Lang Syne* had been sung.

Allan and Ira avoided each other after the show, both dealing with the ramifications of what they had seen. Both knew full well who they worked for and what their business entailed. They'd seen the drugs and hookers regularly around the place but had developed a practical myopia. Denial versus ignorance.

The *Times* ran headlines every week about what they were calling "Gangland Slayings." The turf war raging between Italian, Irish, and Jewish mobs had become bloody. It had also become the major focus of Mayor LaGuardia and Herbert Hoover at the FBI. The public was being urged to contact the police if they had information that could help lead to arresting mobsters. And now Allan and Ira were witnesses to a gang murder, warned by their own employer's gang lieutenant to keep quiet. One last nail in the coffin of a less than stellar 1935.

Their shared knowledge weighed on both of them. They were loath to discuss it, yet the shared experience haunted the room like a specter when they were together. Soon, they begin to hang out less frequently. Allan also noticed that Lucchese's men were treating Ira with increasing disrespect and watching him more closely than normal. Allan found himself dealing with both his guilt and the loss of closeness with his only real friend.

Two weeks later, Allan found himself at an after-hours club in Harlem with Daisy and a group of her friends. The sun was already up on a cold Sunday morning. They found a little hash house and had breakfast, hoping the food would take the edge off their hangovers. As they were preparing to leave, Allan felt a compelling need to be alone. He begged off staying with Daisy and her crew, much to her disappointment.

Harlem was quiet at a little before ten on a Sunday morning. As he approached 137th Street, he began to hear music in the distance. Like a bee to honey, he homed in on the sound and arrived at a church, from which the most glorious Black gospel music emanated. He stood there, letting it wash over him. It felt as if it were cleansing his spirit.

Three massive doors beneath several large windows faced the street of the old stone church. Allan closed his eyes and flowed with the music. They began to sing *Steal Away*, a song he knew and loved. It was as if someone had thrown a lasso over him and pulled him in.

Entering, he found himself to be the only white face, but plenty of Black ones smiled back at him. He joined in the song and began to clap his hands with the rest. A powerful organ poured out rhythmical, enrapturing, joyful backing to a mighty phalanx of voices—a choir like nothing Allan had ever heard. The music lasted far longer than in any church he'd attended, although he hadn't darkened the doors of a church in the years since he'd left home. Finally, the music ended, and the preacher took over. His sermon was simple but powerful.

"The Lord ain't gonna forget about you unless you forget about him. We are his children, and just like all children, we want things our way even if our way ain't His way. That's when we be heading in the wrong way. Just like your children always think their way is better than what you're tellin' them to do—even though you know what's best 'cause you learned it the hard way—they ain't listenin'. That is until they fall down and bust themselves all up and come cryin' to momma. God is your father. He's gonna give you the best advice. You just got to quit listenin' to you and start listenin' to him, AMEN?!"

The pastor shook Allan's hand on his way out and asked him to come back. He told the pastor how much he'd enjoyed the music and his words. Numerous people shook his hand and invited him back. "I just might be," he told them.

In fact, on the way home he thought a lot about what the preacher had said and who he had been listening to—pretty much himself. He'd had a rough year, for sure. Things hadn't worked out as he'd hoped but he was a lot further on the road to stardom than when he'd arrived. Allan also knew he was a long way from his faith. But there would be time to settle down and have a family and get back into church. God would understand right?

—

IRA WAS WAITING FOR him when Allan arrived at Noblesse. A deck of gray clouds floated around Ira. His countenance was that of an abandoned pet. He pulled Allan into the dressing room, told him he needed to talk.

"What's up? You look like somethin' the cat drug up."

"I'm sorry, but I'm still a bit shaken. The new guy that took over for Joey? You know, Marco? He told me they're hiring a new piano player and this will be my last weekend. Something to do with not having the right 'family' way of seeing things. He said that anything I've seen here, including the murders in the alley by 'them Jew boys' is private and if he ever heard of me blabbing about any of it, I'd regret it."

"You've gotta be joking! First of all, why didn't Buddy tell you? *He* is the band leader. You work for *him*."

Ira shook his head. "I think we both know who we work for. Buddy is under their thumb, too. We all are. The things these guys are up too—drugs, hookers, gambling, extortion, murder—I've kept my head down, written it off to none of my business. I'm just the piano player, after all. But sometimes I feel like I'm sleeping with pigs— dangerous pigs. And you know how we Jews feel about swine."

"I don't know what to say," said Allan. "First thing I'm gonna do is talk to Buddy. He needs to stand up for you. Not to mention the fact that you are hands down the best piano player around. He's not gonna find anyone of your caliber on such short notice. And it gets right up my nose, all this Jewboy stuff. Just because they are at war with a Jewish mob is no reason to fire you."

Ira gazed at Allan. "You obviously think we're dealing with rational people. These are the scum of the earth, evil, murderous...I actually think I'll feel better not being around all their craziness. Probably sleep better too. But I'm sure going to miss you."

"Just rein up, partner. Let me talk to Buddy and Lucchese. I have a bit of pull there. Just hang in there till I can talk with them, okay?"

Allan found Buddy and braced him with what he had learned. Buddy said he didn't have time to discuss it, that he was just following orders. Next Allan tracked down Marco. The slight oily Italian reminded Allan of a salamander with the eyes of a rattlesnake.

"Listen, paisano," said the gangster. "This ain't none your business, capiche? You just keep makin' them dames happy with your croonin'. We'll run this joint."

"When is Lucchese coming in?"

"Got no idea. But I'll tell ya, this was his idea. Just like Italians stick together, so do those Hebs. We got us some big problems with that Lansky bunch. Can't be takin' no chances. Alright? Okay. I gotta tend to some things. See you on stage."

Allan's anger welled up, nearly causing him to curse Marco and take it to a hotter and more dangerous level. Catching himself, he began to admit that his moral outrage and loyalty only extended as far as his willingness to stand with Ira no matter what, including his own future. How far, he began to wonder, was he willing to go for his best friend? So far, his loyalty was sub-par.

The following night Lucchese was in attendance. Allan collared him after the first set, pouring out his disappointment and ire. He sang Ira's praises as a great musician, while assuring Lucchese of his loyalty and non-involvement with the Lansky mob. Lucchese's response was formidable.

"Listen here, you ain't got no idea what's goin' on out there. You saw for yourself those Jews mean business. You done good, kept your mouth shut. But I ain't takin' no chances. I know youze is friends, but I guess you need to figure out whose side you're on. You gotta a good deal goin' here. We like your singin'. But there's plenty of guys out that'd like a shot and would be happy to take over. I know this Italian kid, sings really good, know what I'm gettin' at here?"

Allan felt as if Lucchese had slapped him. His face burned and his anger simmered. It took a few beats for him to collect himself. One of Lucchese's gorillas was moving closer.

"This is a shock to me. He is my best friend. I'm very unhappy and I think you're wrong about him. But I gave you my word I'd stay mum about what happened out back, and I will. Let me have a little time to process this."

"Process all you like. It's a done deal." Lucchese turned and left him stewing in his roiled emotions. Had it not been for Ira helping him get that first gig at the Waldorf, Allan might still be scraping by trying for a break. He was the best friend Allan had—true, wise, and loyal. How reciprocal was their friendship? Was he willing to leave all this to show support? Furthermore, what were the limits of his turning a blind eye to these mobsters he worked for? Granted, he wasn't breaking any laws...except for a little reefer and gambling. Still, it gnawed at him. In the end, Ira, as always, came to his rescue with his insight and kindness.

"Allan, I know this is killin' you. But listen to me. I don't expect you to give up your gig because we're friends. You have a great future ahead of you, and me...I'll find another gig. Maybe not as good, not right away, but I've got a great reputation now and good piano players can always find work. Hey, we can still hang out, go to Katz, La Taverna. I'll frankly be glad to be away from these lowlife gangsters. And you be careful. You're the one who told me you can't walk in a corral and not get crap on your boots.

"I'd be lying if I didn't tell you I've been worried about some of the changes I've seen in you since we've been here. You lost your gal to the stuff they deal in, you've got a problem with the cards, and you are no slouch with the broads and the party. You're a good kid. Don't let these slimebags rub off on you."

Chastened, Allan considered Ira's words. That same niggling, small voice spoke aloud through him. In the end, he decided there was nothing he could do and promised to spend time with his friend at every opportunity.

Life at Noblesse resumed the usual rhythms. Allan continued his favorite indulgences. In fact, it seemed things were looking up.

He began to win more than he lost at cards. He was starting to run with some of New York's most elite crowd and seeing three different women. The radio broadcasts were attracting larger audiences. Lucchese gave him another raise for "being like one of the family."

Over the next few months, his visits with Ira diminished. He loved the guy but, honestly, he had so much on his plate that there was scant time left for his visits with Ira. In late November, they met for dinner at La Taverna. Allan was bit uncomfortable with having to see Angelina, but it was tradition for them to meet there. As expected, she waited on them. Pleasant, yet reserved, she took their orders with most of her conversation focused on Ira.

"I feel a nip in the air," said Ira, "and I don't think it's weather."

"Well, Ira, as I told you, we had a lovely little fling. But I haven't followed up and gotten back with her and you know how dames are. I'm juggling three gals as it is. She's a beauty and will have no problem finding a guy."

"Yeah. Just not the guy she wants. I've watched this little drama from the beginning. She's something special, not just another dame. And you're something special, too. She set her cap for you the first time she saw you. You can't really blame her for feeling hurt. But, you're a big boy and it's really none of my business. Just making observations."

"Yeah, well...fair enough. I guess I've been a bit of a cad. It's like the dames are pouring down on me like a waterfall. You really can't blame a guy. I mean you've seen them. High society, well connected, classy. I'll admit an unusual fondness for Angelina. She is special, deep, honest, and, of course, gorgeous. But I guess I'm just playing the hand I've been dealt."

The meal as always was marvelous, in spite of the ambient chill from Angelina. Ira always made him laugh and always made him think. Allan appreciated anew his friend's perspicacity and advice. Even as he absorbed it, however, he knew he would ignore it at the first opportunity. The world, as they say, was his oyster...and he planned to enjoy the banquet.

Chapter 19

The spring of 1937 was glorious. Not only was the weather perfect, but Allan's fortunes had picked up a head of steam. Lucchese arranged a meeting with a new record company owned in part by Marazano. Sales of recordings of popular artists were growing again, after falling during the early Depression years. The big bands with jazz-flavored swing dominated record sales, as did the vocalists fronting those bands. Perhaps it was his time to move up to the elite echelon of singers.

Palace Records was enthusiastic about Allan. Marazano's influence greased the wheels and a deal was struck. Ernie did a fair job at negotiating it, and if the record got plenty of airplay and sold well, Allan wouldn't be worrying about gambling debts or a new Buick anymore. A producer was assigned and Buddy's Band was, of course, enlisted. But this would not be Buddy Adler featuring Allan Dale. This was to be his launch to the status of a major singing star.

Over the next few weeks, songs were chosen and a recording date set for May 6. Allan felt like an eagle being lifted high by thermal updrafts. And then, on the day recording was to begin, the radio buzzed with live news of the Hindenburg's tragic explosion. Not perhaps the most auspicious omen, but Allan paid it no mind.

He had strained with impatience as the weeks rolled on. The process of picking the right songs, creating proper arrangements, bringing extra musicians, including strings, absorbed all his spare time and energy. Walking into the recording studio for the first time was both inspiring and intimidating. He'd imagined it so many times, but in the hush of the soundproof room, surrounded by great musicians, it was a reverential moment.

Allan had developed a good working relationship with the producer, Charles Vandiver, as they'd prepared for this day. A highly respected graduate of the increasingly famous Juilliard School of Music, Vandiver was a talented jazz clarinetist and seemed ideal for the task. Charles was standing in the midst of the band chatting with Buddy and going over arrangements. As Allan approached, Buddy presented a sardonic smile. "Ah, here is our star," he said. "Charles and I have been fine tuning things for you."

A subtle tension between the two had emerged since the firing of Ira and the sudden promotion of Allan as a rising star. His displeasure at being braced by Allan for the firing of Ira and now the attention focused on "his" vocalist grated on him. But the extra dough salved his emotions.

Charles, on the other hand, was an enthusiastic and encouraging volcano of energy. "Allan! Perfect timing. I believe we're ready to get this ball started. We're beginning with *Georgia on My Mind*—love the way you sing that, and you've been doing it for so long it should be easy to get it down today. I've brought in a couple of my friends for the string work." He gestured to the musicians. "Bob, Ted, meet Allan. You're gonna love this guy's voice."

Allan expected the process to be seamless and quick but it was anything but that. Charles was a perfectionist. He stopped repeatedly to re-do a particular passage if he didn't like the sound. Allan grew restive, having to sing numerous takes of a song he'd done for years. It was late afternoon before the producer seemed satisfied.

"Hey guys, great work today. I think we may have it. I'll work on the mix with the engineers tomorrow and see if there are any bits that need redoing. But I'm satisfied we got this much done. How 'bout it, Allan? You happy?"

"Yeah, I guess. I'm amazed it takes so long to lay down one song. And that is one of the easier numbers. But you know what you're doing, and I look forward to hearing the final mix."

"Cool. See you guys at eleven in the morning. Don't wear out your chops tonight. Save some for tomorrow."

Allan stood by the door and thanked all the musicians. Buddy gave him a perfunctory nod. Just as Allan was leaving, Charles patted him on the back. "You sang very well today. I think we got a good take. I'll know when I get in the mixing booth and give it a good hearing. If we need to clean up a few bits, we'll do it tomorrow. Takes longer than you thought, doesn't it?"

"Honestly, I'm amazed. At this rate, to get down all ten songs, it could be a week or two."

"Or a month or two. Once it goes to the pressing plant, there are no do-overs. It HAS to be perfect, or as close as humanly possible. I know I irritated Buddy and some of the boys with my demands. But understand, that's my job. The guys at Palace Records told me to take as long as needed, and not to worry about studio time. If they're willing to put out the dough, I'm willing to put in the time. Cool?"

"You bet, Charles. I'm in for a penny, in for a pound, as they say. But I'm flat tuckered out. I'm going to grab some dinner and catch a nap before I have to sing tonight."

"Save some energy for tomorrow. You'll need it. I've set up some of the sessions for nights you're not performing so all of you can be fresher. That means, of course, that it will take longer to finish, but it will sound better. Tomorrow will be your last session after a gig for a week. See you at eleven."

Allan drove to Katz for a quick bite. He felt as if he'd done eight hard rounds on a heavy bag. The concentration and performance had drained him. He was stunned by how much more demanding this was than singing at the club. But this was what he'd been working for, and this was going to be worth it.

—

CHARLES BEGAN THE FOLLOWING day by playing back what they had recorded and pointing out several places that needed fixing. There were a few frustrated sighs, but they were all making good money for the session, so they went to work. And work it was. The days blurred, became weeks, and Charles gave everyone a break in early June.

Allan's eagerness for completion was tempered by an invitation from one of his friends at the club to listen to the broadcast of the heavyweight championship fight. The bout was between James Braddock and Joe Louis, June 22, from Chicago. Louis had lost the previous year to the German Max Schmeling. The fact that Louis was Black also figured to make the audience largely with Braddock.

The opportunity to get away from the music and spend time drinking scotch, smoking cigars, and listening to the fight in Arron Eiger's penthouse was just the tonic Allan needed. The fact that the crowd included some ravishing beauties added to his excitement. By the time the fight began, all were well into their cups, eager for it to start as they gathered around the radio.

The fifteen-rounder started with a first-round knockdown, Braddock catching Lewis with an uppercut. The room erupted with cheers. But Lewis came out in the following rounds throwing lethal leather. A minute or so into round eight, the announcer's shocked call of a left to the body and a straight right to Braddock's chin, knocking him down, hushed the room. The count seemed to be in slow motion, but when it hit ten and Louis declared the winner by knockout, the room fell silent.

Allan knew that everyone in the room except him had serious money on Braddock. The losses wouldn't hurt them, but Allan, for whom recent gambling hadn't been going his way was riding high. He celebrated his change in luck in booze and a willing brunette.

He awoke the next morning feeling like he'd been rode hard and put up wet. Shooing the girl out the door, Allan headed for a little hash house two blocks away. Sitting over his coffee, he thought about the fight and how the underdog had surprised everyone.

He had been the underdog growing up. Now he had a shot in the ring to prove to everyone, especially his mother, that he could achieve greatness. He felt so close to success—he just wanted to get the record done and on the radio so people could hear it and buy it. That was how Crosby and the rest struck gold.

A guest vocalist was filling in for him at Noblesse, so he had all day to recuperate. Church bells rang in the distance. Maybe, he thought, he should go to that church in Harlem again. But if he was honest, he felt a bit guilty, considering what he'd been up to the night before.

———

ON A STEAMY DAY in mid-August, the final mix was completed and the record went to press. The album cover featured a dramatic headshot of Allan with heavy shadow falling on his right side, accentuating his strong, cleft chin and heavy brows. An artist's rendering of a New York skyline floated over his shoulder. At the bottom of the cover, stylized script read in bold yellow letters on a black background: *ALLAN DALE....with The Buddy Adler Band.*

Seeing himself on the album cover brought him to the realization of how close he was to breaking through. Meeting with Ernie and Frank Bellini from Palace Records brought him back to earth. Though they were enthusiastic, they were also cautious. The process of getting airplay, promotion, generating publicity and good reviews, was like preparing a battle plan. Frank assured him that Marazano was very supportive and could "grease the wheels" with cash and contacts. Frank assured Allan that Palace was making him a priority. They were trying to get him a guest shot on The American Album of Familiar Music. Young up and coming stars were invited on the show featuring Donald Dame and Frank Munn. It would be a great shot if they could get him on.

But one thing Bellini said rankled him. He mentioned the practice of paying cash "under the table" to some of the radio people in return for playing his record. Allan knew it was at the very least unethical, possibly illegal. When questioned, Bellini said not to worry, it happened all the time. Just the price of doing business. Allan wondered what price he was willing to pay. He decided he had to leave it to the record people to do it the way they saw best. It was his job to sing, not worry about how people came to hear him and to buy his record.

It had all been such a rush, producing the record while still working at Noblesse, that he was a bit worn out from it all. He'd been as busy as a four-fingered guitar player with a twelve-string guitar.

The first few weeks out of the studio had been a relaxing change of pace. But by October, he was getting restless. His birthday in September had made him aware that time was rapidly bolting on. Still, there was no airplay as yet, and record sales weren't happening. He called Frank Bellini who assured him they were out there talking to all the right contacts and things were looking up. He was told to hang in there, it would all work out.

Feeling less than cheered one Sunday evening and not in the mood for company, he turned on the radio. It was as little after eight on October 30. The Mercury Theatre on CBS was a popular show featuring the actor Orson Wells. Allan was listening and pouring a drink. A Latin orchestra was playing, when an announcer broke in and began reporting the crash in New Jersey of some large metal object which fell from the sky. Allan sat down and listened as the story began to unfold. The earth was under attack from something from outer space. Outside his window, he could hear traffic picking up on the street below. Soon, sirens started to sound. He couldn't believe what was happening. Looking out the window he saw people rushing about in a state of confusion.

He sat mesmerized by the unfolding attack by creatures from Mars. Then, to his unmitigated relief, an announcer said that this was only a dramatization of the H.G. Wells book, *War of the Worlds.* Even as he was breathing a sigh of relief and laughing at his own reaction, the rising cacophony of traffic, sirens, and raised voices continued. Satisfied that the world and his career would survive, he picked up his guitar and sang a few songs for the sheer pleasure of it.

Opening the paper the following morning, Allan was shocked by headlines describing the widespread panic created by the radio program. Welles was now a household name, having created the most profound public reaction to a radio broadcast in history. It struck Allan that radio was a far mightier force than he had ever considered. He was intrigued by the power of the medium, not just for music and entertainment, but for the ability it had to motivate people at a deeply emotional level. Now he wanted to be on the radio more than ever.

—

WITH THE SLOW PROGRESS on the record's success Allan was getting restive. Everyone assured him that progress was being made and it would all break for him soon. In early November, Ernie, with a little Italian help, got him an appearance as a guest vocalist with The Sonny Ellis Band broadcast on Mutual Broadcasting Station WOR. Through affiliates, the broadcasts were heard coast to coast. That meant Allan would be exposed to many potential fans, increasing his fame.

The broadcast was live from the Grand Island Casino in New Jersey. Buddy Adler was none too pleased with his star vocalist performing with the famous band while he had to use a fill-in singer. Taken together, his simmering displeasure over Allan's first billing on the record, and the tensions over Ira, made the atmosphere less than amicable. Allan ignored Buddy and focused on the next step up.

He enjoyed rehearsing with Sonny's band and felt as if he were already destined to be their new vocalist. The broadcast turned out to be perhaps his best performance ever. The band was superb, the crowds loved him, and the reviews raved, while mentioning his new record.

Ernie was ecstatic over the possibilities. For the first time, Allan knew he was getting ready to step into the national spotlight. He had always been impatient. Perhaps his dad was right...things develop slowly, then happen suddenly.

By the end of November, Allan was slated for several more live broadcasts on Mutual's WOR and affiliates. Record sales had begun to increase, and Allan was approached for interviews by a couple of critics. He began to miss more performances with Buddy's band as he was doing occasional guest shots and broadcasts. And the money began to roll in. According to Ernie and the guys at Palace Records, the dam was getting ready to break and flood them with it.

To celebrate, Allan had two new suits tailored at Brooks Brothers. Then he went and finally bought the very last Buick Roadmaster left at the dealership. He paid $1,250 dollars for his dream car. It was maroon, just like his Harlandale High School colors. And the beast could fly, pushed by a new 302-cubic-inch motor, producing 120 horsepower. If he hadn't arrived at stardom, he was in the stall next door.

He now found himself in demand for elegant social events, began to win at card games, enjoying the favors of two stunning lovelies. It occurred to him one morning that he hadn't seen Ira for a very long time. He wanted to share his good fortune with his old friend.

They met at La Taverna. Ira was waiting at the same table they'd shared when they first met. Angelina was pleasant but aloof. To be expected, he figured. Ira on the other hand was effusive in his joy at Allan's successes. He toasted Allan, caught him up on his regular gig playing with a band at a hotel in Long Island.

"Allan, I knew it the first time I heard you sing at the Bull and Bear. I told you, remember? But I know it's been a long slog and you aren't the best at waiting. I haven't heard you on the radio, was playing at the time, but I read the reviews, saw your picture, and I look forward to hearing your recording."

"And so you shall. I brought two copies. One for you and one for Angelina. That is, if she wants it. I mean this is where it all started, Ira! If I hadn't just stopped in for a meal, and she had not introduced us, none of this would be happening!"

"Yes, it seems God's opened up the door for you and there's no stopping you now."

"Well, Ira, to be honest, I think He's been spending more time overlooking things rather than orchestrating my success. I feel like it's happening in spite of what I do, not because of it. But come the new year, I plan to turn over a new leaf. You've always been honest, sort of like my wise advisor. I've made an art of ignoring your counsel. And with all the good times I'm having, I know there's a big hole that needs filling up in me."

"One thing I've learned about you, Allan. You're built on a solid foundation. I've seen your strength as well as your weaknesses. There is no question in my mind that you will fill up that hole you mention with good soil, from which will grow a flourishing garden. I remain your biggest fan."

"You know, Ira, I'm toying with the idea of going home for Christmas. It's been years. I've not been back since I hit the road when I was seventeen. I want them to be proud of my success. That's especially true for my mom. Like I told you, she wanted an opera star. I want her to see that I've found a way to succeed on my own terms. I know Buddy will be livid, and Ernie wants to get me on for a big New Year's Eve gig with possibly the Harry James band. They are interested. But if I don't do this now, I may not get free to visit for a very long time. The way things are picking up, I hope to be booked solid for years."

"That is brilliant. I urge you to do it. I believe that the only things of real value are relationships, time, and health. Good fortune comes and goes. Those things, they're what make the rest of it mean something. One of David's Psalms says, 'Teach us to number our days'. You can't take for granted how long your folks will be there to visit. Like I say, DO IT!"

Angelina arrived to check on them, and Allan gently reached for her elbow. "I know that I have been less than a friend to you. I hope you'll understand. I have been more than a little self-centered, what with my career and all the commitments. But I owe you a debt of gratitude. It was you who introduced me to Ira. Had you not done so, he would not have helped me get my start in New York. Everything that is happening to me is in part because of your thoughtfulness. Perhaps we can find time in the next year for me to mend a few bridges and renew our friendship. I'd also like you to have a copy of my record. As I say, you had a hand in it."

She took the record, examined it, and stared into Allan's eyes for several beats before commenting. "Well, I appreciate your words. I'm glad I could be of some help to you. I admit that I've harbored some resentment toward you. But life moves on and I wish you well. I have always believed there is a deep river of goodness running in you. It just seems to be underground right now. But sure, we can have a chat after the holidays. Anything else I can get you two? Espresso maybe?"

"Sure. And thanks for listening. Have a merry Christmas. I'll be out of town so I look forward to seeing you after." She walked away.

Ira nodded at Allan. "That was noble and well played. She is a gem although you're not the right guy to polish it, at least not now. When are you embarking on the grand Christmas homecoming?"

"I suppose the Sunday before Christmas after the Saturday gig at Noblesse. It's a long drive but, with 120 horses under the hood, my new Buick should get me there pronto." He grinned at Ira. "You're gonna love this baby. Wait till you feel the power. I've wanted one for years, promised myself I'd get a Buick when I hit the big time. Finally, it appears that's happening. It doesn't get much bigger than singing with a big band live from coast to coast and having my own record." He paused. "Well, I guess it does, but Ernie says the sky's the limit and Palace says record sales are doing very well. So let me drive you home in my new maroon chariot. What do you say, pardner?"

Chapter 20

⌢

The engine hummed a rich bass note over the soft hiss of the Buick's big whitewalls. A proper combo of contemplation supplying the lyrics to this song he was now living. *Allan's Grand Return.* The road home stretched before him, the sun behind him. His thoughts cast back over the events he'd experienced the last time he'd driven on this highway. He figured it would take two, maybe three days to get to San Antonio, depending on the weather.

Fortunately, conditions looked great between New York and Philadelphia. From there to Cincinnati, this time of year, who knew? Leaning back into the soft leather, he enjoyed the skeletal trees and the diminishing size and number of buildings. It was the first time in years he had seen open fields. It reminded him of the vast expanses of Texas that he was returning too.

Allan was stung by the thought of how little his family and home had entered his mind. New York was a different planet, like the one from Orson Wells's *War of the Worlds.* The people and environment of the city might as well be Mars compared to life in San Antonio.

Allan smiled, thinking how much he had accomplished. He could hardly wait to put his record on his dad's Victrola and watch their expressions, especially Georgia's. He'd gotten presents for all at Macy's and for the first time he could remember, he heard a carol playing in his head. One of his favorites. *Away in a Manger.* He began to sing it. Allan's spirit felt lighter than it had since he'd first arrived in New York. Turning on the radio, he found a station playing Christmas music and began to sing along. Time flew like a flock of frightened starlings, and he was surprised to see the skyline of Philadelphia looming in the distance.

Once past the city, Allan pulled into a Mobil station with the Red Pegasus flying above the roof. The attendant filled and checked the car while Allan took a break and bought a can of Pabst Blue Ribbon Beer and some peanuts to enhance his journey. He figured it would take at least two more hours to Morgantown where he'd get dinner and rest before reaching Pittsburgh that night.

As he drove, he turned the radio to WOR where Gabriel Heater, the respected news commentator, was describing the political crisis in Europe. His comments on Hitler's growing ambitions were sobering. Heater warned of the possibility of another war in Europe with Hitler invading a neighboring country.

At least things were improving in America, he thought. Heater reported the Depression continued to ease with one third fewer out-of-work Americans. Finally, some good news. He found a station playing popular music and he sang his way across rolling fields, through charming towns, and across old bridges.

Crossing the George Washington Bridge into Pittsburgh was a great relief. He was road weary. He found a hotel, had some dinner, and collapsed into a dreamless sleep.

Hitting the road at daybreak, following a stout breakfast to fuel him, and with a thermos of coffee by his side, Allan began the next leg. Hoping to make Memphis, maybe as far as Little Rock that day, he stabbed the pedal and 120 horses bolted onto the highway.

He reached Memphis as the sun was setting, glaring through the windshield into his tired eyes. Good place for dinner and a rest, he figured. Little Rock looked reachable before he ran out of steam.

For the first time that he could remember, Allan felt lonely. He'd become so accustomed to constant company and excitement that it was a novel feeling, and not one he was enjoying. Whom, then, did he miss? Ira, of course. And Allan began to consider who his friends were. What women did he miss?

He was struck by the realization that the only other person he genuinely missed was Angelina. In truth, he wasn't certain she would feel the same. More than five years in New York and, at best, two friends. Unquestionably, he had a cornucopia of contacts and acquaintances. Allan was never without an invite to enjoy the delights of the city with someone.

The paucity of his relational life surprised and saddened him. He saw himself as a popular bon vivant, sought out for his stellar company. He remembered how Ira defined real wealth — relationships, time, and health. Well, all that was fine, but without the dough? There'd be plenty of time to get all that stuff organized when he got back after Christmas. Maybe he would call Angelina and really get to know her, not as just another dame.

He passed several hitchhikers. It would be nice to have a little company but remembering the man who robbed him of everything — including his guitar, he decided discretion was the better part of valor. He turned on the radio and found WLW out of Cincinnati broadcasting The Benny Goodman Orchestra. What he wouldn't give for a shot at singing with them. Or Dorsey, or, well there was plenty to do when he got back to the city.

It was well after midnight when he finally made Little Rock. He stopped at the first hotel he found, grateful he'd not fallen asleep while driving. He thanked God, though in truth, he wasn't sure He was tuned to Allan's frequency these days. Or maybe it was the other way around. That certainly curtails a goodnight prayer, he thought, as he slid under the covers, and was away with the fairies of dreamland in moments.

Having forgotten to leave a wakeup call, Allan got a late start. By the time he finished breakfast, it was already pushing nine-thirty. He put the spurs to the Roadmaster. If all went well, he hoped to be home around midnight. He'd been making the best time he could without speeding, as he'd seen a couple of cops along the way. That was the last thing he needed. But he found himself turning the beast loose on long empty stretches, reaching more than 70 miles per hour.

He crossed the Arkansas River at Texarkana and entered the Lone Star State for the first time since leaving home. He felt a warm elation knowing he was just a few hours from the first family Christmas he would experience as a grown man with a successful career. Once he passed Dallas, he drank lots of coffee to keep him awake. Waco came and went and now only Austin lay ahead, and then the final seventy miles to home.

—

THE LIGHTS OF ROUND Rock receded in the rearview. Austin was less than an hour away. It started to rain just as the midnight hour passed and he thought of his family. He hoped the sting of Georgia's disapproval had diminished over that time, and that she would finally see that he'd made the right decision. His current success and looming stardom should make that clear. Allan's dad had understood him and would likely view him as a musical peer and relish his accomplishments.

He was keen to see how Sam and Louise had grown into adulthood. His sister was now married. Sam was out of college and starting a new career in insurance sales. He wondered how his glamorous life stories would compare with the more prosaic lives of his siblings. He also considered how much of his life he would edit out of his conversations.

A growl of guilt nipped at his heels. There was no denying the moral compromises he had come to think of as acceptable and normal.

How could they understand what life in the New York entertainment scene was like?

Bright lightning blazed nearby, followed by an almost immediate explosion of thunder. The rain was getting heavier, so Allan dropped his speed. Visibility was diminished and he gripped the wheel more tightly. Then, as if conjured by a magician, a deer appeared thirty or so yards ahead. He swerved across the center lane and onto the shoulder. A shattering impact on the left front wheel jolted the car. Allan fought for control, at last coming to a stop on the right shoulder.

He sat dazed, listening to rain beating on the roof and the counter rhythm of his racing heart. He lit a cigarette and checked his watch. Twelve-thirteen, not an auspicious time to be stuck on the roadside in a frog strangler.

Retrieving a raincoat and flashlight, Allan stepped into the deluge to assess his situation. The tire was flat, and worse, the rim was badly bent. He knew the Buick had a spare, but he'd never taken the jack out to familiarize himself with it.

With no small amount of effort, he managed to get the tire out and roll it to the front of the car. Then, getting the jack, he tried to position the light so that he could see in his attempt to put the spare on and continue. The rain pelted on him and into his eyes, making it all the more difficult. After a considerable amount of time, he removed the flat and began to mount the spare onto the hub. The tire in place at last, Allan began tightening the lug nuts.

It was then that he saw the light of a car approaching from the rear. As it neared, Allan waved the flashlight to alert the driver to his presence. Rather than swerve away, it began to drift directly toward him. By the time he started to spring away, it was on him.

The headlights loomed and Allan was flattened. The tires of the car ran over his right leg and his clothing caught on the running board. For what seemed an eternity, he was dragged down the road.

And then there was only nothingness.

Chapter 21

A solid deck of white clouds floated above him. As he focused, the clouds became a ceiling, where light bounced from unseen fixtures. Allan moved, and searing pain tore through him. His head was wrapped in thick bandages, but he could see that his lower body and left arm were encased in a cast. His legs hung from wires, suspended in traction. His mouth was as dry as the Sonoran dessert. He tried to call out, but a mere squeak emerged.

The face of a young nurse appeared and looked down at him. "Oh, my! You're awake. I'm so glad. We've been praying for you. I'll get the doctor and let him know you've come out of the coma. He'll be right here."

Coma??? Allan's thoughts rolled and tumbled like rocks in a landslide. Slowly the image of an approaching car and the feeling of terror came back to him. As he began to come to himself, he tried to comprehend the magnitude of his situation. He'd been almost home, swerved around a deer, had a flat, and been run over by a car. He couldn't wrap his head around it.

A new voice sounded. "I'm Dr. Robert Comer and you are in Brackenridge Hospital in Austin. Can you hear me?"

"Yes," Allan squeaked.

"Mr. Dale, first let me tell you how thankful we are to see you awake. You've been in a coma for two days. It has been a delicate situation and you're still not out of the woods. We have stabilized you and are giving you the best care that we can, but I must tell you, the injuries you have sustained are severe. The police say you are from New York. Do you know anyone in Austin?"

In whispers, Allan told them about his family in San Antonio and how to contact them. It took all his energy to produce those few sentences.

"We will contact them and get them here as soon as possible. Apparently, you were changing a tire and were run over by some drunken AWOL soldiers from Fort Hood. They are in the hands of Army authorities. Your car is at the city pound, but the police brought your belongings here.

"Let me be honest with you, Mr. Dale. You will be lucky to survive this. It is why I want you to think about getting your affairs in order. We are doing our best to keep you alive, but your injuries are grievous. As well as completely shattering your right leg with four compound fractures and severely damaging the left, there are numerous broken ribs, a broken left arm, and we fear, internal injuries. We are giving you morphine for the pain.

"All in all, it's a pretty wretched situation I'm sorry to say. But know this. Brackenridge is the best hospital in Austin and orthopedics is my specialty. If we can just get you through the next few days, I have hopes we can discuss your long-term prospects. In the meantime, we'll keep you as comfortable as possible. I'll leave you in the capable hands of nurse Ruth Bellamy. I'll be back for my afternoon rounds to check on you. See you then."

Allan struggled to comprehend all he'd just been told. It was inconceivable. One moment he'd been almost home for Christmas, and now he was crippled and at death's door? Could this be a nightmare?

But no, it was all too real. The smell of alcohol, an intercom calling for a doctor, his shattered body hanging there. All too depressingly real.

"Hi, I'm Nurse Ruth," said a new woman. "May I call you Allan?" Allan didn't try to speak, so she continued. "Good. I know you must be terribly frightened. That is perfectly natural. But you must be a fighter because the doctors didn't give you the chance of a snowflake in a heatwave of coming out of the coma. The doctor says it appears that you might have had polio. One of your legs is disproportionately smaller. Is that correct?" Allan nodded.

"You obviously have some experience with overcoming setbacks. I want you to know I will be here for whatever you need. Just press this little button. The doctor said you had a guitar with your effects. Are you a musician?"

Another nod.

"Well, I play the piano just for fun and, of course, at church. Maybe we can get you well soon enough to play for me. If you'll excuse me, I have to check my other patients. But I'll be back."

Tender brown eyes peered down on him. The nurse's compassion was genuine and sincere. For the briefest of moments, he felt a slight inkling of hope. It evaporated as he watched her leave.

A fog crept over him, and he passed into blissful oblivion.

ALLAN AWAKENED TO HIS mother's tearful eyes. "Sam, he's awake!" she said without turning away from him. "Hello, baby. We're so grateful you are alive. It's a miracle from what we've been told."

His father appeared at Georgia's side. "Hello, son. Heck of a way to spend Christmas season with your family. You're gonna be all right."

"Honey, your dad and I and the whole church are praying for and claiming a miracle. I know what the doctors say, but I know what God can do. I've seen what you can do as well. You're gonna get through this and we're here to help. Sam and Louise couldn't come but they told me to tell you they're praying too. Sam said he's your corner man. I know there's not much we can do but we're getting through this together, understand? We're going to visit you as often as we can, at least once a week. Is there someone back in New York that you'd like for us to get in touch with?"

The question hit him like a left hook. His whole life, his career, everything was over. Just when every door was swinging wide for him, in a matter of seconds, all his dreams torn asunder. All he could manage was to shake his head. He'd have to tell Ira and have him deliver the news to Buddy and the rest of his associates. A tear traced a line down his cheek.

"Mom," he said, "I'm ruined."

"You most certainly are not. We beat polio and we'll beat this if I have to camp out right here."

His father chimed in. "Son, your mother is right. God has plans for you yet. Believe that. Cling to it. You have always had a determination strong as Toledo steel. That hasn't changed. You hear me?"

"Yeah, Dad. We'll see."

A nurse appeared next to the bed, a new one. "I'm sorry," she said to his parents, "but you'll have to step down the hall for a little while. The doctor is coming shortly to check on your son."

Georgia stroked his face. "We'll be back when the doctor's finished, baby. Dad and I are right down the hall."

Dr. Comer literally ran into Georgia and Sam at the door. "Oh, pardon me, I'm Dr. Comer. You must be Mr. Dale's parents. I'd like to have a word with you after I check up on your son, if that would be alright. I'll meet you in the waiting area in a few minutes." He turned back to Allan. "Mr. Dale, how are you feeling? How bad is the pain? Be honest."

"It's tolerable until the morphine starts wearing off. Any chance you could increase the dose?"

"As a matter of fact, I'm actually going to slowly *reduce* the amount you're getting during the next couple of weeks. As you may know, it's highly addictive and there is a fine line between just enough and too much. Although we want to ameliorate your suffering, the fact is you are going to have to learn to live with pain. At this point, you have already surprised us by surviving such massive trauma. Our biggest concern, though, is infection under the casts. If gangrene gets a foothold, we may have to…amputate.

"The level of your rehabilitation and functionality is a big unknown at this stage. It will take six weeks in casts and traction for the bones to heal enough for you to begin physical therapy. At that point, we will know better what your potential for mobility may be and much of that will depend on whether we are able to avoid amputation.

"Part of my job is to tell you the truth about your prognosis, even if it's not encouraging. Therefore, I must be honest. If I had to place a bet, I think you are looking at the loss of the use of your legs. Amputation would mean employing the use of a wheelchair in the future or artificial prosthetics and crutches."

Allan looked away. "Gee, thanks for your honesty. I know you're telling me what you think I need to hear. But life in a wheelchair? I think I'd just as soon take the big sleep."

The doctor nodded. "That is a natural response and not the first time I've heard it. But I've seen some amazing recoveries and have been happily disproven in my expectations. For now, we'll keep you as comfortable as possible. In six weeks, we'll assess your rehabilitation protocols based on how you have recovered. Are you a man of faith?"

"Well, I have been, but I've not been practicing much. I don't think God is all that pleased with me at the moment."

"Perhaps this would be a propitious time to get re-acquainted, spend a little time praying. I've witnessed some frankly astounding recoveries from patients and their families who prayed. I'm going to tell your folks what I told you if that's acceptable. I'm sure they are praying for you."

"Of course. Their names are Sam and Georgia Ezell. I legally changed my name. I'm a singer, Allan Dale—as in "Allan a Dale," the bard in Robin Hood. Made a better stage name."

"Very well. I'll have the nurse administer your pain medication so you may sleep better. I'll see you in the morning."

The steam radiator grumbled as Allan stared at the blank ceiling. A few days earlier he might have thought it emblematic of a blank page that he was filling up with the grand adventure he was writing. Now it was as blank and empty as his prospects. Christmas was two days gone and the new year and new decade were four days away.

This would be the first time he had not sung at a New Year's Eve event in several years. The nurse and the oblivion of the poppies couldn't happen quickly enough. As if on cue, Nurse Annie Richards arrived.

"Hello, Allan. I'm here to give you something to help you with the pain. I know you must feel unimaginably distraught with what has happened to you. But I'll tell you one good thing. Your face was unscathed. In fact, it's a miracle that you weren't disfigured. Your upper body is functional…well…except for the fractured arm and broken ribs, which hurt like all get out I know. But your life isn't over and you need to remember there's always hope right up until the good Lord calls you home." She prepared his medication. "Nurse Ruth tells me you're a musician, guitar player and I believe a singer. You still can do those things again, right?"

"Wrong. Nurse, a couple of weeks ago I was singing with a famous band, live from New York, on the Mutual Radio Network. People heard me from coast to coast. I have a record that has just been released and in the process of being promoted. My career was headed for the top." He shook his head. "But all of that is gone forever. So, I appreciate the pep talk, but my hope is gone with the wind, just like the movie. Give me the shot and let's have done with it, if that's all right."

"Very well," she said. "I was just trying to cheer you up. It'll get better. Really." Allan lay quietly as the morphine was injected and descended into the land of twisted faces. His physical pain was overshadowed by the vortex of his thoughts. He pictured all his dreams swirling away down into a black hopeless void—all the years of working, striving, and succeeding flushed away in seconds. What was the point of carrying on, really? What possible future had he now? The last thought he had before Morpheus arrived was a vision of him selling newspapers on a street corner.

Allan awoke to the dancing patterns of shadows on his covers and across the walls and ceiling. Early morning sunlight crept into his consciousness. The pain was the worst he'd ever suffered. It was as if there was a fire burning beneath the casts. Disoriented, he wondered where he was and tried to sit up. Seeing his cast-covered legs suspended in traction brought him fully awake.

Spitting cotton with a raging thirst, he could hear the hospital coming to life as breakfast carts plied the hallways, dodging nurses and doctors on their morning rounds. To his great relief, Nurse Ruth arrived with his breakfast.

"Good morning, Allan. I've some lovely eggs and bacon complete with famous Brackenridge biscuits. Hope you're hungry."

"I'm parched. Can you give me water? And tell the doctor the pain has gotten much worse and it feels different, sharper, almost like it's on fire."

"Of course. In fact, I have these little pills you can take while you're at it. The aspirin will help and the sulfa is to fight the infection. Did you sleep all right?"

"I guess. Last thing I remember was Nurse Annie. Seconds later, here you are." To the extent he could, he shifted his body in the bed.

"My pain is creeping back," he said. "Could you give me just a little morphine?"

"Dr. Comer wants to wait until lunchtime for your next injection."

"You sure you can't do me a little favor and give it to me earlier?"

"Nope. You are going to have to learn to live with some pain. It will get easier over time. But the fact is that you've a long road ahead and you're going to have to strengthen not just your muscles, but your mind." She adjusted the traction and looked at him. "You strike me as a very driven and ambitious person. You've accomplished a great deal in your career from what I hear. Now you're going to need to throw yourself into getting well with the same enthusiasm that brought you success. Your body isn't the same, granted, but you are the same man inside. You could just as easily be dead but it seems the Lord wants you here—and left you with your mind intact. Focus on that, Allan. And now, how about some breakfast?"

New Year's Eve arrived. Allan asked a personal favor of Nurse Ruth—a radio with which to listen to the celebrations and live music from New York. He knew he couldn't get the local broadcast of his own band—with whoever they'd found to replace him. But Guy Lombardo's New Year's Eve event was carried coast to coast.

Ruth, with the doctor's blessings, purchased a small radio with some of Allan's funds. The doctor would allow it, she said, only if played at low volume and did not disturb patients in adjoining rooms.

Allan listened, beset by a welter of emotions and tortured by increasing pain in his legs. He pictured Times Square with the ball poised to drop at midnight, the sea of people undulating like waves, covering the streets. He thought of his friends and the people he'd have been with, the wild celebrations at Noblesse, the crowd ebullient in the extreme. Closing his eyes, he could picture it as if he were there.

Then, Angelina's lovely face appeared, and a pang of regret swept over him. He was struck with the profound revelation that all of that life had forever swept away, leaving him stranded like Robinson Crusoe, alone, shattered of body and mind on an island of broken dreams. Tears began to roll from his eyes as the countdown began. Of course, it was only 10:59 p.m. in Austin—but he was already falling behind.

Where is that nurse with my medicine? Pain wracked his body but the pain in his heart was far worse. It was, as he was discovering, an endless river of suffering he would have to navigate. He'd been hurtled over the waterfall into the roiling torrent, which would bear him to a foreboding future.

Where it would carry him? How he would battle through the unknown perils that lay before him were thoughts too daunting to contemplate.

Chapter 22

Hello suffering, my old friend, Allan thought upon awakening. He'd spent two weeks now in this bed, healing.

It certainly didn't feel like healing. His pain grew in direct proportion to the diminishing doses of morphine. Worse yet, his body was fighting withdrawal from the drug and the increase in misery from his injuries simultaneously.

The doctor was still concerned that gangrene might be setting in. His condition would be intolerable, impossible to endure, were it not for his constant companions—the radio and books. He passed the tortured hours engaged in a stream of entertainment and reading. Allan kept the small radio on the bedside table, inches from his ear, at a low volume. He couldn't take a chance on losing it.

Doctor Comer arrived with an unusually serious demeanor. "Allan, we are going to remove the cast and check on the status of infection. Your increasing pain levels have me concerned. You will be put under anesthesia. If we find gangrenous conditions, we may have to remove your legs. There is no easy way to tell you this. But I must prepare you for the possibility. The nurse will be in shortly to wheel you in to an operating room."

Allan lay in stunned silence. If he awoke with no legs, at least he would hopefully have an end to the pain. The door opened and the nurse and an orderly gently moved him on to a gurney and wheeled him down the hall. They gave him an injection and he sank rapidly into unconsciousness.

He came awake slowly, groggy from the drugs, and was afraid to look down to see if he still had legs.

Doctor Comer sat beside the bed. "Allan, let me begin with the good news. We didn't need to amputate. There was gangrene, but it has been destroyed." He paused. "But the agency by which this has occurred is frankly unheard of. And, it's an embarrassment for the hospital." Allan looked at him quizzically and he continued. "Somehow, inexplicably, ants managed to get inside your casts and began to feed on the necrotic and diseased tissues. In so doing, they actually removed the gangrenous tissues *and* the infection."

The doctor shook his head. "I have never heard of such a thing. I suspect the increased pain you were experiencing was the result of the ants at work. As I said, I've never seen anything like it and I've no idea how ants got into the hospital and your cast. But they have been removed and new casts have been put on your legs. I should imagine that your pain will be dramatically decreased—which means we can gradually end your need for morphine. I'm going to let you process all that and get some rest. I hope you will not hold the hospital responsible for the ants. Exterminators are investigating as we speak. Get some rest. I'll be back to check on you later."

Allan felt relief at his healing while being perplexed by the bizarre nature of his healing. He began to realize that the pain had indeed subsided and he experienced the first inkling of comfort he had felt for many days. He said a prayer of thanks as he relished the lack of pain. He reached over and turned on the radio, drawing him away from his situation.

Allan had heretofore thought of radio as a place to be a performer and as a source for news and entertainment programs. He had rarely listened to the comedy and drama or informational offerings that attracted millions of listeners to gather around their radios, mesmerized by what flowed from the speakers. Now it was the voices more than the music that enchanted him. The opinions of commentators sparked novel thoughts and gave context to the news reports. Fulton Lewis Junior, Gabriel Heater, and Drew Pearson challenged him to ponder the events unfolding outside his isolated room in new and intellectually stimulating ways. He began to listen to Roosevelt's Fireside Chats, a man in a wheelchair and fellow polio survivor.

He grew to appreciate the power of the human voice in a new way. As a singer, it had been his instrument. But the voices of these announcers and the actors on the radio shows awakened him to the power of the spoken word to influence peoples' emotions and ideas. He recalled the voice of Orson Welles in *War of The Worlds*. As his addiction to words arrived, his addiction to morphine departed.

Then there were the books. Nurse Ruth was an avid reader and began to bring him books from the library. He filled the time when not listening to the radio with the intoxicating adventures of the imagination. He'd read books since childhood and now, his literary tastes expanded with the discovery of new authors. Hemingway, Fitzgerald, John O'Hara, Edith Wharton, Dashiell Hammett, Tolstoy— their characters became his friends, their stories his vicariously shared experiences.

Soon the daily pattern set in: wake with the radio, go to sleep with a book resting on his chest. These things and the tender kindness of the nurses, especially Ruth, were his solace—a tether to hope and sanity.

Georgia reprised her role as encourager, used so effectively in his recovery from polio. His dad made him laugh when he felt like weeping. His brother and sister showed up at times as well. Weekly visits from his family became his lifeline to sanity and renewed glimmers of hope.

As the sixth week of his confinement ended, he was to discover that he would need those comforts and escapes more than he could have imagined.

When Dr. Comer arrived one morning, Allan turned the radio off and greeted him.

"Morning, Allan," said the doctor. "How are we feeling?"

"Well, I don't know about you, Doc, but I feel like I've been rode hard and put up lame."

"Ah…yes. It's time to talk about the next phase of your treatment. Your internal injuries have healed well, and your bones appear to have mended. That means it's time to move on to rehabilitation." He paused. "I want to be transparent with you. The process of removing the casts and traction is the easy part. The rehabilitation and therapeutic elements are going to be arduous, painful, and challenging. It will require monumental amounts of grit and fortitude. This is both a mental and physical challenge. The element of willpower is a crucial factor in how much functionality you recover.

"I would be remiss in not telling you that the best we can hope for is gaining strength in your arms and upper torso. Your right leg, already compromised from polio, is a lost cause. Your left leg can recover some muscle mass but never, I believe, enough for you to walk using crutches. The best we can hope for is competency in using a wheelchair for your mobility.

"I wish I could offer a better prognosis. However, Aaron Shahan, who runs the rehabilitation program is one of the best around in helping patients recover to the extent they are capable." He paused again. "This is Thursday. We'll remove the cast and traction and move you to a new room tomorrow. Monday, you'll be taken down to Aaron to begin your daily therapy sessions. Any questions?"

"You say there is more pain coming? Does that mean you'll be giving me morphine again?"

Dr. Comer shook his head. "I'm afraid not. You have just come through the torture of withdrawal. We wouldn't want you to go through that again, would we?"

"There's this 'we' stuff again, Doc. But I suppose you are right. Better get a good strong bit of hickory for me to chew on. I may have to use what the oldtimers did for pain."

"Very well, then. See you in the morning."

—

It was a lot to get used to, seeing his legs stretched out on the bed before him, no longer encased in casts, hanging in traction, and to see his arm free as well. His legs looked like mesquite limbs stripped of bark and scarred from an axe. His arm, still painful to move, had decreased markedly in size. In his new room, he no longer saw an oak tree from his window nor heard birdsong. And there was, of course, the anticipated rehabilitation or what the staff referred to as "rehab." It was not the most inspiring of situations.

He thought about his life in New York and realized that no one there knew what had happened to him. So completely at the mercy of his condition had he been that he only now began to think about his friends back there.

Later that day, he arranged a phone call to Ira. Revealing the details of his disappearance to his shocked friend, he asked him to help him wind up his affairs. Ira was heartbroken for his friend and agreed to dispose of his belongings, selling what he could and sending the money to Allan. He also said he would tell Angelina and all of Allan's band and business associates.

Allan made it clear that his career was over and he would not be returning to New York to resume his life. He thanked Ira for his friendship and wished him well as Ira tearfully said goodbye. He did his best to keep his spirits up, but by nightfall, he began to slip into the clutches of tortured tissues and descending emotions.

Up to this point, he'd somehow battled these foes to a standstill, more frequently prevailing with the help of the radio and his books. But as darkness fell across his room, the shadows seemed to creep into him and to whisper soft imprecations. *You will never walk again... you have lost it all...why go on? What's the point? You deserve it...it's God's punishment. Just give it up."*

Hours passed as Allan wrestled with the stark reality of his ruined body and demolished life. The more he contemplated the future, the bleaker became his imaginings. He turned on the radio, but for the first time it was unable to engage him. He turned on the lamp and tried to read to no avail. Turning off the light at last, he dropped the book in frustration. The clock read 2:22 in the morning.

He began to talk aloud to God. Up to this point, he'd avoided prayer, feeling himself both unworthy and unwelcome to do so. Now words began to pour from the deep recesses of his soul. In tears, he began to plead.

"Oh Lord, I know you probably don't want to hear from me. I sure haven't been listening to you for years. First, I know I probably deserve this. I know I asked you into my heart when I was eight and got baptized. I used to talk to you all the time and I felt you. You let me know what I should do and for that matter what I shouldn't. But somewhere along the way I just sort of slid away, stopped listening and forgot about you. And eventually you must have given up on me because your voice in my conscience pretty much went away. Guess I'm like that prodigal son in the Bible. I suppose that's what I want to tell you. Forgive me. I know you will. That is Your promise.

"I want to come home to Heaven. There is no life, no future ahead for me down here. I'll never stand up in front of a band and sing again. I've no way to earn a living, and my folks are just getting by. No woman will ever look at me again the way they once did. I'd be living in pain for the rest of my life, alone. I have no future ahead of me.

"So, God here's what I ask...no, beg...of you. First forgive me. I know that grace you promised is real. I still believe it. Please cleanse me of the guilt of all I've done to displease you over the years. But also, most importantly...Oh God, I beseech You Lord! Take me home. Don't let me live like this. You can do all things—that's what the Book says. So right now, I beg you, stop my heart from beating and bring me home."

Allan closed his eyes and waited. His breathing continued. His heart still beat. He waited—alone, bereft, defeated. Then, he felt someone take his hand. He looked up to see a stranger looking down at him. The moonlight fell on a tall fair skinned man with blond hair, wearing a grey suit. He peered down at Allan with the most penetrating ice blue eyes he'd ever seen, eyes seeming to produce their own light. He was too flummoxed to speak. Then, in a soft resonant baritone voice, the man began to speak.

"That is not what lies ahead for you. You will live. You will walk once more. You will speak and you will influence thousands of people. God loves you, has never stopped loving you, even when you turned your back on him. None of your suffering is his punishment. All your choices have consequences and things you've set in motion rebound unto you. There are tragedies that befall all mankind in this world. But you have been covered by his grace and forgiveness all along. He will strengthen you through His Spirit. The Comforter will inspire and guide you. But you must engage the Holy Spirit fully. You must believe wholly. You must proceed courageously. And from this moment forward, put all your faith, trust, and belief in what He can do through the Spirit in you."

Allan closed his eyes and shook his head, trying to take in what was happening to him. He turned to respond and answer. The man was gone.

He lay there dumbfounded. *What had just occurred?* His mind and emotions frothed with incomprehension. He began to feel a tingling in his legs. The pain began to subside. Like an electrical current, soothing waves moved up through his body. He closed his eyes and saw a vague gossamer glow, like a penumbra, surrounding what appeared to be a circular shape with pulsating colors...purple, blue, gold. Allan felt as if he were floating above the bed, wrapped in sensations of a peace he'd never experienced. Time stood still, and he felt more than heard the words, "Be here now. I am with you."

Allan awoke with sun falling across the covers, feeling more refreshed and at ease than he could ever recall. Ruth opened the door bearing a radiant smile and a tray with his breakfast.

"My, my, Allan," she said, "I don't believe I've ever seen you smile like that. What has you feeling so chirpy this morning?"

"Ruth, something happened last night. I can't...I don't know... What to, how to..."

"What in heaven's name are you going on about?"

"I think, something came in, well...Heaven's name."

"You're gonna have to be a lot more specific. You're not making much sense, dear."

"I don't know that I can. I need to spend some time processing it myself. Perhaps we can discuss it later. In the meantime, your lovely face and that breakfast are balm to my soul and stomach."

"Well, how eloquent, Mr. Dale. I always aim to please. And I am so pleased to see you in such high spirits. This is the first time I have gotten a glimpse of enthusiasm in you. It warms my heart."

"Well, Ruth, you have certainly warmed mine many a time when it felt desperately cold and abandoned. I so appreciate your sweet spirit and encouraging words. Not to mention your beautiful smile. It lights up the room—and my day—when I see it."

"I do believe you are flirting with the nurse, sir."

"One of these days I may just surprise you and take you out to dinner and then play a duet with you...on piano and guitar, of course."

"Ah...Of course. Enjoy your breakfast. I'll see you later. And Allan. Keep that smile around. It suits you."

Left alone, he reflected on the man in the grey suit. He began to talk to God again. "Thank you, Lord, for this new feeling of hope. I don't know if it was a dream, but that man was as real as Nurse Ruth. I think you sent an angel to remind me that I'm not alone, that you're always with me, within me, waiting on me to follow your guidance. You say in Your Word *I can do all things through Christ who strengthens me.* I feel that strength. I'm choosing right now to believe what the angel told me.

"For too long, I made an idol out of my dreams, made myself the center of the universe. Well, I'm not, God. I realize that now. You are my only hope to reclaim my life in this new damaged vessel. As I look back on my past, my successes never brought me joy or peace. I've been singing my song *my* way. I want to sing Your song Your way...no embellishments, just the way you write it.

"From now on, I'm doing it your way. I make you a promise starting today. Every morning when I awake, I will start my day with words from your book. *This is the day The Lord has made. I will rejoice and be glad in it.* Then I'm going read that book, pray to You, and listen for You to see if you have anything you want me to know."

The pain still gnawed at his body. Yet within, Allan floated above it. He felt himself engaging the pain, accepting it, and focusing on other things. He might not be able to erase it, but he could learn to master it. He picked up the Gideon Bible and began to read.

Chapter 23

Following Allan's visitation, his perspective truly changed. The physical pain remained, but his mental and emotional suffering were in retreat, fleeing in the face of hope, empowered by his renewed faith. He'd told no one about his visitor. He might never do so, as it likely would seem to some the deranged or fanciful raving of a severely damaged man. Allan had no need for confirmation. It was as if he had been a guitar hidden in a case, long unplayed, and was suddenly pouring out music in the hands of a master.

From that day, and in the coming weeks, Allan's faith and resolve would be sorely tested. As Ruth wheeled him down the hall to the rehabilitation wing, she did her best to prepare and encourage him.

"I know you're feeling better about things and I love your new attitude. But, Allan, I want you to be prepared for what's facing you. Dr. Comer has probably told you you'll be in a wheelchair from now on. I know you told me that you're gonna walk again, but you have to be realistic. Just take baby steps, so to speak, as you go through this. You are getting ready to experience hard work and pain that short of your accident, will likely be the most grueling time of your life. I don't tell you this to discourage you. I just figure a devil you know is better than a devil you don't know.

"But here's the thing, you can do anything you set your mind to.

I believe the same drive and ambition that took you to the top as a singer is still in you. Well, enough of my pep talk. Here we are. I'll be right back with Aaron."

Ruth returned, followed by a short bow-legged man with a pronounced limp. Thick white hair and bushy brows framed a furrowed weathered face with twinkling blue eyes. The creases spoke of countless hours under the Texas sun, squinting and smiling. He looked down at Allan and grinned, then offered his hand. "Well, howdy. Name's Aaron Shahan. I'm the foreman of this outfit and I aim to get you back in the saddle and out of here just as soon as we can do 'er. How 'bout it, pardner? You ready for the toughest ride of your life?"

"Well, what can I say to such an attractive, exciting offer? Not that I have much choice in the matter."

"Oh, you got plenty of choice, son," said Aaron. "Every day you can choose to fight or give up. Simple as that. You choose to fight, you'll feel like you crawled in the ring with Joe Louis. You choose not to fight, you get to live with yourself and chew on that rawhide from now on. I can't make you do a blamed thing. All I can do is help you win your fight...if you decide to take 'er on. Comprende?" He glanced at the nurse. "I'll take it from here, Miss Ruth."

Except for the swimming pool, the place looked like some sort of torture chamber. One man carried himself between parallel bars as his injured legs attempted steps beneath him. The sweat rolling down his grimacing face said it all. Several others worked pulleys and lifted small weights, while half a dozen people were in the pool working with a therapist.

"Let me tell you a little story before we get rollin'," said Aaron. "You might have noticed I got a bum leg. It's the best it's gonna get. But it's a long sight better than when I got thrown off my horse in the middle of a stampede. I used to be the foreman of a ranch out near San Angelo. Loved every danged day, ridin' and workin' on that ranch. But my pelvis and leg were busted up by them cows pretty bad.

"I figured my life was over. Cowboyin' was all I ever wanted to do. Well, that was a done deal. Figured I might as well just shoot myself or maybe just drink myself to death. Then a pardner of mine, oldtimer, he got holt of me and made me see there's a lot a man can do if he's a mind to.

"So, I started out at a place just like this with a fellow named Ben Johnson. He helped me climb back up on life. It took a year and a half of blood, sweat, and tears, but I walked out of there and decided I wanted to help other folks do the same. So I went to school, learned what I needed, and now instead of herdin' cows, I'm proddin' folks like you to push through the pain and get back as much of yourself as you and the Good Lord are willin' to allow."

Allan raised his eyebrows. "Aaron, that's quite a tale. Just so you know, this ain't my first rodeo. I had polio when I was a kid and worked myself up to walking with a limp, kinda like yours. But I have to say this is a lot more challenging."

Aaron looked him in the eye. "Make you a deal, son. I'll give you my best if you'll give me yours. It ain't gonna be easy. You been dealt a bum hand. But I've seen a fair few folks make liars of doctors. Fact you done been through some of this before's gonna help you. What do you say, ready to give 'er a try? But shootin' straight...you're gonna feel like you're being dragged by a horse through cactus, with one foot in the stirrup, while you're wrapped in barbed wire."

Allan shrugged. "I suppose I don't have a lot else on my plate right about now, do I?"

Aaron smiled. "Then let's get you changed and start in the pool."

Allan would not have imagined that simply holding the pool's edge and attempting to kick could produce profound pain caused by the tiniest movements. After a few seconds of moaning, he stopped. Aaron, who was standing close by shook his head. "Oh, I don't think so, compadre. I want you to say these words every time, and I do mean *every* time you don't want to do something I tell you to do. It don't matter how hard or how much it hurts. Ever hear the saying, *No pain, no gain?* Well, I got a new one for you. *If it is to be, it's up to me.*

"Fact is there's only two ways this is gonna work out. You either bite that bullet when you're hurtin' and get better, or you whine and bellyache while your body just withers on the vine like unwatered tomatoes. I may be the straw boss, but you're the one doin the liftin'... comprende, amigo? Let's see them limbs kickin'."

The pool session was followed by Aaron stretching Allan's legs with fractional movements in range of motion. Every millimeter sent gales of pain through him but he gritted his teeth and fought the urge to scream aloud. To cope, he started repeating the words Aaron had said—*If it is to be, it's up to me.*

Slowly, the mantra began to distract him. One assault followed another—holding the parallel bars while dragging his legs beneath, lifting small dumbbells and working with pulleys to strengthen his upper body and rehab his healing left arm. At the end of an hour, he was flat bushed and every tissue in his body buzzed in complaint.

"Well, son," said Aaron. "I'm proud of you. You showed some real grit. You're gonna hurt like the dickens later. All them muscles ain't had a lick of use for a long time and they're gonna let you know it. There's this stuff called lactic acid—builds up in your muscles after you work 'em, especially after they ain't been used. But the good news is it'll be a long sight better than what you just went through.

"So, here's what's comin'. We're gonna start the first week with three one-hour sessions and let your body get used to it. Then we're gonna keep addin' more bit by bit till we're doin' five days, two hours per day. And I'm gonna be rampin' up the load on you. Sad truth is, there just ain't no shortcut to gettin' you fixed. If it makes you feel better, and I know it don't, I been through it and survived. Better than that, I proved them doctors had no idea what a tough old cowboy can do. If I done it, by God, you can. I'm gonna be all over you like a dirty shirt to push you when you wanna quit. You're gonna want to cuss me and spit in my eye.

"So, I got one last question for you 'fore you skedaddle. Are you tough enough? If you ain't, I wanna know right now 'fore I waste any of my valuable time on you. Some folks got the grit, some ain't. What's it gonna be, son?"

As tired as he was, Allan managed a smile. "You weren't joking when you said it was rough. I've never had that much punishment in such a short amount of time—well, except in the accident. But as silly as it sounds, the expression you told me...*If it is to be, it's up to me,* actually helped. So, the answer is, I'll do whatever is necessary no matter how much it hurts. I know, how shall I say, in the core of my spirit...that I will walk again. Someday, maybe I'll tell you why. There it is, Aaron. Do your worst!"

The old cowboy grinned. "Together we're gonna stomp that lazy worm inside you. That no good rascal is always sayin', 'Just do it tomorrow, don't do any more than you have to, why don't you take a day off?' He never stops 'less you stomp on him and do what he's tellin' you not to do. Then you got 'sorrow skeeters' whinin' about why it ain't fair, and you don't deserve all this, and nobody understands how hard it is. They're in your head all the time. You gotta kill 'em off if you're gonna end up where you set off to be."

—■—

Aaron was a kind but demanding taskmaster. Having been through his own torturous recovery, he was both empathetic and insistent. But the pain was relentless—numerous times throughout the days and weeks, Allan wanted to throw in the towel.

But Aaron would have none of it. With sarcasm, cajoling, intimidation, and even humor, Allan was forced to push himself past what he thought were his final reserves of strength and hope.

Then, on a hot Texas morning, Allan pushed himself up from the wheelchair and with Aaron's help, placed crutches under his arms and took a step.

He was a long way from being fully mobile and walking away from the hospital, but the thrill of that first step surpassed all of his musical accomplishments. Aaron was so proud that he broke the rules and offered Allan a shot of whiskey from a leather-covered flask he pulled out of the brown leather vest that was ever part of his outfit. Allan passed on the offer but appreciated the thought.

When he returned to his room that afternoon, Ruth had another surprise for him. She had arranged to take him to Barton Springs for a picnic and to watch the sunset. Dr. Comer had okayed it after hearing of Allan's progress in recovery. Ruth wheeled him to her Chevrolet, loaded him in the front seat, and put the wheelchair in the trunk.

It was the first time Allan had been away from the hospital and as the hot wind blew on him, he took in the passing panoply of life in the real world.

Ruth found a lovely spot under a large live oak near the water at Barton Springs. Dozens of people were splashing about in the clear water as they escaped the heat. She wheeled him to a shady spot underneath long overhanging branches, with a view of the water and stone cabins built by the WPA during the Depression. She spread the blanket, laid all the accoutrements on it, and walked up to Allan.

"Okay, mister, this is a part of your therapy you probably haven't considered. It's time for you to become friends with the new public you. This is where you get to battle your old friend "pride." I'm going to help you down from the chair but you are going to have to navigate yourself across the blanket and sit with me. And here's the scary part. People are going to witness this event. It's time you began to adjust to the reality of being stared at. Okay, ready, here we go."

Awkwardly, painfully, and with much groaning, Allan guided himself to a sitting position with his back against the trunk of the tree. He was aware of numerous eyes upon them. But his self-consciousness was overcome by an overwhelming sense of gratitude for what Ruth was doing.

Humming to herself as she put barbecue sandwiches and potato salad on plates, she became someone entirely new to him. To see her out of her nurse gown and hat, smiling as the breeze lifted her auburn hair across her shoulders, brought a stirring within him that he'd not felt for a very long time. He had flirted harmlessly with her but with no real intentions. Now he took in all the little details he'd never noticed.

He'd always appreciated her ready smile. Full lips framed her perfectly straight gleaming teeth. But it was her green eyes, exuding an infectious joy and humor, that captivated him. He watched Ruth pour some sweet tea, appreciating her long articulate fingers. The loose summer dress gave little of her figure away, but her body radiated health and vigor.

She smiled. "You deserve a reward for all your hard work and progress. Besides, it's a perfect day and a perfect time for a picnic. Thirsty? Nothing tastes better with barbecue than cold sweet tea. And I've got fresh peach pie for dessert. Baked it myself."

They ate in companionable silence accompanied by splashing and laughter from children, and the trilling of the varied repertoire of a mockingbird in the branches.

It was the most delightful moment Allan could remember. Not perhaps the most exciting or elegant, considering his life in New York, but he wouldn't trade this moment for dinner at Sardi's. Nor would he have enjoyed Baked Alaska at the Ritz as much as Ruth's peach pie.

"I can't tell you how much I appreciate your kindness," he said. "I know you didn't have to do this. It's above and beyond your nurse obligations."

"Don't be silly. I want you to know how proud I am of what you have done. I've seen many with far less serious injuries give up and decide to just live with it. You're a fighter. I admire that. You're also a very fascinating man. You've lived a life I find exciting. May I make an admission? I found your record among your belongings while searching for your toiletries and I took it home out of curiosity.

"I was stunned by what a marvelous singer you are. I play piano and sing along, sometimes for friends and at church. People say I have a nice voice. But you are an exceptionally fine singer. In particular, you project emotions that I can deeply feel. I would love to see you perform again."

"Well, Ruth, I am flattered and pleased you liked the record. Please keep it. As to watching me perform again...I'm afraid that ship has sailed. There aren't any bands looking for a guy in a wheelchair or on crutches standing at the microphone. Nope, that career is over."

"But you still have such a lovely voice. And that includes your speaking voice. When we chat, I find myself enjoying how you say things as much as what you say. You think about things in ways I never would have considered. I find myself recalling our conversations hours later. I've even been admonished for spending too much time with 'that fellow in 407.' You talk about the books you read and what is happening in the world and I always walk away knowing more than when I arrived."

Allan rearranged himself against the tree. "I'm beyond flattered. I too enjoy our time together. I grew up in a house where music and ideas were always in play. As I told you, Dad is a musician and a reader. Mom read to us from the time we were tots, engendering in us a love of literature. Our dinnertimes were filled with opinion and debate, as well as humor and laughter. It was what I was most looking forward too on my first trip back home for Christmas. But we know how that ended."

"What are your plans when you leave this hospital and re-enter life?"

"Ah, that is the great unknown, isn't it? As you can imagine, I have pondered this at length. Lord knows I've plenty of free time. During the hours I've spent listening to the radio, I've realized that the world has been irrevocably changed with the war, as much as I've been changed by the accident. I would like to help our country in the war effort, but obviously I'm not equipped to fight. It is something I've been praying about. I know without question that God has plans for me. He's made that abundantly clear. Now I'm working to get myself as functional as humanly possible and to make myself available. In the meantime, I'm waiting for His orders."

Ruth nodded. "I'll join you in those prayers. I know He has a plan for you and I've seen with my own eyes how determined you can be." She paused. "Would you mind if I take a dip in the springs? I have a bathing suit under my dress. You can watch over our little picnic and have some more pie."

"Wish I could join you, but the thought of trying to make my way to the water is inconceivable. Have fun."

Allan enjoyed watching Ruth pull the butter yellow dress over her head, revealing a toned, curvaceous body atop lithe long legs. She winked at him when she noticed his interest, turning and gamboling off to swim.

Peace washed over him, borne on a southeasterly breeze, which played through the branches like brushes on a snare. A mockingbird supplied the melody. In public for the first time since the accident, Allan felt hope and happiness.

The feeling was so unfamiliar, he hardly recognized it. Leaning back against the tree, he began to hum, then to sing to himself. No one was near, so he sang loudly. The mockingbird joined him and tears rolled from his eyes with the sheer joy of making music once more. He'd forgotten the rapturous release found in singing for the sheer joy of it.

He was lost in the song with his eyes closed when Ruth returned. It wasn't until he finished that he opened his eyes to find her listening with her eyes closed and a soft smile on her face.

"Yes, Allan," she said, "you have a special gift. God will put it to use one way or another." She straightened the blanket and sat down again. "I'm going to sit in the sun and dry off and then I have to return you to your room by seven. Doctor's orders."

On the drive back, their conversation was as warm and familiar as that of old friends. When they arrived at the hospital, she reassumed her nurse role, getting him to his room and settled before dinner arrived. With a peck on the cheek, she was gone, and he was alone again.

—

ALLAN TURNED THE RADIO to WOAI in San Antonio as the evening news came on. The news was dire as Americans were still recovering from the attack at Pearl Harbor on December 7. Italy had joined Germany in their march across Europe. Already France and Poland had been occupied, as had Denmark and Norway. The bombing of Britain, the Blitzkrieg, they were calling it, continued to rain down terror upon the island. It was indeed a "world" war—the second in the century.

Young men were joining the armed services in droves. Rubber was being rationed and blackouts and air raid drills had been staged in the big cities. And here he sat, as Aaron would say, useless as teats on a bull.

Tiring of the dirge of unpleasantness, he turned the dial to KNOW, the Austin station, to find the Light Crust Doughboys playing western swing. Allan wasn't sure how he felt about this new hybrid musical style. It was an odd amalgam of western cowboy, Dixieland jazz, and a little polka. The guitars and fiddles, including pedal steel guitar, were played through electric amplifiers, giving them a unique twangy sound. It was lively and it put Allan in a better frame of mind. The music was replaced with the ten o'clock news report. The local news led, then the coverage of national and international news. The war dominated the report, and it was not encouraging.

Something in the local newscaster's delivery grated on Allan. It was like a wrong note played in a piece of music. Then it struck him. It was the announcer's nasal voice and nascent Texas twang. Having spent so many hours listening to the great cultured voices of the network announcers, it irritated him. Surely, they could hire better talent than what he was hearing.

Then, slowly, a smile spread across his face. A seed of hope began to sprout within him. Why couldn't *he* do this? Allan knew he had a good speaking voice. He'd read all his life and could no doubt read news copy well.

Sleepy, Allan thanked God for the amazing day he'd had and asked again for guidance and direction in how he could re-join this tumultuous world. How he would fulfill the promise in those words of the mysterious man in the gray suit. Perhaps radio was in his future after all.

When Ruth arrived the next morning with breakfast, Allan asked if she had a few minutes to spare—that he had something he needed to share. She smiled and said she would love to hear whatever he wanted to tell her. Her sweet spirit filled the room like the smell of gardenia on a gentle breeze.

"Last night, I was listening to the Austin station. The news came on and the newsreader was, well, to put it nicely, not all that great. I analyzed why it bothered me and realized I have been listening to the greatest voices on radio for years. And it dawned on me that I could do a much better job. You told me you like to hear me talk, like the sound of my speaking voice as much as my singing." He looked at her earnestly. "This is something I know I could do and do well. This is the first time that I have had a vision of how I can re-invent myself. My singing days may be over but there may be a future for me in radio yet."

Ruth grinned. "That is so exciting! Your face was beaming the whole time you were telling me this. You are right. You have a very rich, unique voice. You sound like an actor, maybe like Orson Welles a little bit. I know you can do this.

"And there's another benefit to this dream. For you to accomplish great things, you gotta have big dreams. That means big challenges. Think about it. Until now your goal, your motivation has simply been to become mobile. But this vision gives you a far greater goal to achieve. Now all the rehab, all the pain and effort, become a means to a far greater end. And I will be your biggest supporter and fan."

"Ruth, I just had a thought. Since I need to become adept at reading aloud, would you consider letting me practice on you? All these great books you bring me from the library...Shoot, I could read them aloud and not only become a good reader—we could share reading the books together. Of course, I wouldn't want to impose on your free time. I mean you spend your entire workday in this place. Perhaps it's asking too much for you to come back here when you could be pursuing your private life and activities."

Ruth thought for a moment. "Hmm...tell you what. I can spare one evening, I know. How about Sunday evening? I rarely have anything to do. Yes, actually, I think it would be a delightful way to finish the weekend. You've got a date. Dinner is served at six. How 'bout six thirty?"

"It's a date. Oh, well, not a 'date,' but an appointment. And you've given me something wonderful to look forward to." He smiled at her. "You've no idea how much your friendship and kindness have done for me. You're breathing new hope into me where a few months ago, all I wanted was to be done with this life."

"That's what a nurse is for, isn't it? But to be honest, you've become far more than my patient. You're becoming my very dear friend. I anticipate the time I get to spend with you. Which I'm afraid is ending now as I have breakfast to deliver to my other patients. See you later."

Listening to the radio now became far more than an entertaining distraction. Allan began to listen closely and critically to Gabriel

Heater, Edward R. Murrow, and many other announcers. He studied actors on shows like *The Adventures of Nero Wolfe, The Lone Ranger,* and of course, Orson Welles's *Mercury Theatre.* He began to read his books aloud, putting dramatic inflections in as needed, and speaking each character's dialogue in the appropriate dialect and accent. When his parents came to see him on Saturday, he shared his vision and asked if he could read to them. They enjoyed listening and the role reversal of him reading to them.

By the time Ruth arrived that Sunday evening, Allan was in full sail, sheets to the wind, following the joy of reading and acting out the words for his parents. When she arrived, he gave her three books from which to choose. She chose *The Big Sleep* by Raymond Chandler, saying that she was in the mood for a good mystery and had heard Chandler's detective book was a gem.

Dropping into character Allan began. *It was about eleven o'clock in the morning, mid-October, the sun was not shining, and a look of hard wet rain in the clearness of the foothills…*

For the next two hours, Ruth sat spellbound as Allan inhabited the characters' marvelous dialogue and Chandler's crisp, economic prose. When she happened to look down at her wrist, she sat up smartly, realizing the time. "Oh, my, it's almost my bedtime. I can't believe it. When I closed my eyes and listened it was like watching a film in my mind.

"Oh, Allan! I believe you've found your calling. I could listen to you for hours. You're as good as any of those guys on the radio. Now I have a different problem. I have to wait a week to hear what happens to Phillip Marlowe and Vivian and Carmen. I'll be pondering that all week. Thanks for the most entertaining evening I can remember. That includes going to the movies. This may even be better. Sweet dreams, my handsome radio actor."

Allan lay back, savoring what Ruth had said. In truth he had enjoyed it as much or more than she. He had always been borne away on the music when he sang. It was a truly transcendent experience. But tonight, reading and acting out the book, he'd become so completely absorbed that he'd lost himself in the words. Different, yet not unlike when he sang. He chuckled to himself. *I have to keep my eyes open to read.*

By the third Sunday's reading date, Ruth suggested they do Wednesdays as well. And then she surprised him with another request.

"I told Nurse Annie about our little Sunday reading time, and she asked if she could join us. Her boyfriend has signed up with the Army and she doesn't have much to do. Would that be all right?"

"Really? You don't think she'll get bored? I mean not everyone is a big reader."

"When you read, it's like I've been hypnotized and transported to another world. I doubt Annie will get bored. What do you say?"

He shrugged. "Sure, if you don't mind the extra company."

"Annie's a great gal. We're good friends. It'll be fun."

"All right, then. You're on."

After she left, Allan felt both flattered and a bit disappointed. He had grown fond of Ruth. But as yet, he'd been careful not to overplay his hand. He knew the cards he'd been dealt didn't augur well for sweeping a girl off her feet and he had virtually nothing to offer. But if it made Ruth happy and Annie too, so be it. Plus, it would be more practice in front of an audience.

Ruth was a rapt listener and Annie, it turned out, was even more drawn into the drama. Gasps, laughs, groans, and even tears poured from her, so caught up in the reading was she. When the first session ended, they were both effusive in their praise and eager for the next chapter.

It was only the beginning. A week later, Dr. Comer arrived unexpectedly. Allan prepared for a prognosis or recommendation for therapy. The doctor, indeed, had a recommendation—but of a different sort.

"Ruth and Annie have told me about your little reading sessions," said the doctor. "They rave about your dramatic interpretation of the books. It occurred to me that it would be great therapy for both you and some of the patients if we were to turn it into a regular event. I know that may be asking a lot. You are working so hard and progressing so well, I'm loath to interfere with your rehabilitation. Would you give it some thought? We can use the cafeteria since dinner is over and it's empty. Like I say, just think about it."

"Wow, Doc," said Allan. "That's a bit unexpected. Let me think about it. Can I let you know tomorrow?"

"Sure, Allan. I'll see you later on my rounds."

Allan was stunned. Funny, he thought—singing in front of a huge audience was easy for him. But the thought of reading for a small group of fellow patients made him nervous. But then, what better way to get used to a large audience? Perhaps this was just the training he needed.

The Brackenridge Book Group became a much-anticipated event on Sunday evenings. He began with Dashiell Hammett's *Maltese Falcon*. He'd read that the film starring Humphrey Bogart was coming out soon, so it seemed a great way to let them hear the book, then compare it to the film. The evening was a grand success and word spread. The group grew to include patients as well as staff, frequently numbering more than twenty listeners.

He was still making strides, though not great ones, with Aaron and the rehab. Now he was walking thirty feet with crutches under his arms and a brace on one leg. It still hurt like all get out, but he wasn't about to give up now. Aaron continued to push him—cajoling, demanding, encouraging, and sometimes even cursing. No slack was granted by the tough old cowboy.

Then, one afternoon, following a particularly grueling session, Aaron sat down beside Allan for what he called a little "jawboning." "You done real fine today, son. I think you're gettin' pretty close to walkin' out of here and gettin' shed of me. From what I understand, you had it pretty good 'fore that wreck. You was a good singer, and you don't seem to spook the gals. It all came pretty easy for you seems to me.

"But I'll tell you somethin' real as dirt. When you get everything you want all at once, you don't appreciate it. It's the things you have to earn the hard way that come to mean somethin' to you. Them's the only things you value, only ones you own. You've earned a whole passel around here and I'm mighty proud of you. Yep. You're a stand-up man. Oh, and you made yourself stand up." Aaron chuckled. "Now, that's funny."

Had Allan been handed a gold bar, he could not have been more appreciative. That tough old boot had been kicking him around with kindness and helping find the courage to forge a new image of what he could be. Aaron leaned over and uncharacteristically laid his arm over Allan's shoulder.

"By the way, been hearin' 'bout your little readin' club. Might come by and give 'er a listen. See you tomorrow, pardner."

———

ALLAN'S PARENTS ARRIVED FOR their Saturday visit and were surprised and encouraged by his progress. Seeing him lift himself from the wheelchair and walk on crutches for nearly forty feet showed the substantial progress he'd made since their last visit.

It was a special occasion as well. The upcoming Wednesday, September 9, was Allan's birthday. Georgia had baked a cake and brought fried chicken, biscuits, potato salad, and lemonade with mint leaves.

"Oh, baby," she said. "You are looking so well, and I can't get over your improvement. To see you upright makes my heart leap for joy. We're gonna have a little early birthday celebration. Where would you like to do this?"

"There's an empty table under that big pecan tree over there. That ought to do."

"I'll roll your chariot over," joked his dad. "You supply the theme music."

"Good news is this chariot isn't *comin' fore to carry me home* much longer. They're fitting me with a new brace for my bad leg. Once I get used to it, I'm ditching these crutches for canes. Once I master them, I'm walking out of here."

"Well, baby, you can stay with us for as long as you want," said his mother. "You know we'll take great care of you. Plus, Sam and Louise will love to have their little brother back. Oh, and you can meet your nieces."

"Thanks, Mom and Dad. But I'm working on getting back on the radio. I know no band is going to hire a guy with canes to stand up and sing with them. I've accepted that my singing days are over. But I've been developing my reading and acting skills. I've begun a reading group. More than twenty people show up as a rule to listen while I do a dramatic reading of a book. Currently, we're halfway through *The Maltese Falcon* by Dashiell Hammett. I'm getting lots of encouragement on becoming a radio announcer or actor. What do you think about that?"

Georgia busied herself in laying out the lunch before answering. "Allan," she said, "I've regretted that you took the path you did and it came to grief. I still believe you would not be here if you'd taken my advice. Nonetheless, here you are, and I know it's been a cruel and bitter experience for you to have failed in your dreams of stardom. I'm just concerned that you may be setting yourself up for yet more disappointment. You've no training in radio. You don't have any contacts in the business nor experience. Why don't you think about something a little more practical?"

Allan bristled. "Thanks so much, Mom, for that little pep talk. As you've already seen, I make my own decisions. Let me remind you that were it not for the accident, I was also on the threshold of big things in New York. I know you've never agreed with my choice to become a popular singer but it's time to move on. I could use a little support."

As was his habit, his dad had kept his own counsel during the exchange but now he unexpectedly spoke up. "Georgia, I've lived with your regrets about this for a long time and kept to myself about it. But it's high time I had a say.

"First off, every man has to plow his own furrow and live with the results. I've been proud of Allan for having the gumption to head off and follow his dream. You might remember that my dad wasn't too happy about my music. He'd have rather I studied to become a lawyer. I'm glad I didn't listen to him. And I'm glad Allan didn't let you buffalo him into something he might have regretted in the long run.

"A man becomes a man by learning to make hard choices and living with the outcomes. The only real knowledge, the only true wisdom, is earned through experience. And some of the best experience is how to get knocked down, pick yourself up off the canvas, and fight on. Our son's proving to be a fighter." He looked at Allan. "Whatever you decide, son, we're with you. I see a strength in you I've never seen before. I know God has plans for you if you in include him in yours. Right, Georgia?"

Allan's mother blanched. "Well...yes...of course, dear." She looked at Allan. "We just want what's best for you."

"Believe me, Georgia," said his father. "He's man enough to figure that out. Right, son?"

Allan smiled at his dad. "Yes, sir. You give me time and I'll prove to you what I'm capable of. I know for a fact God has a hand in all this. Hide and watch. We'll all be amazed with what He's got in store."

The birthday celebration was cordial following his father's declarations. Ruth spotted them and stopped by to say hello and wish him a happy birthday. She extolled Allan's talented reading as well as his rapid rehabilitation. After his father wheeled him back to his room and they bade him farewell, Allan savored his father's supportive words. He was yet more emboldened in his plans.

And he figured his mother would one day come to see that *all things work together for good, for those who love the Lord and are called according to His purposes.*

That's what he read in his Bible and that was his new motto.

Chapter 24

A couple of weeks before Thanksgiving, a moment worthy of giving thanks arrived. Fitted with a hinged brace on his bad leg and supported on two canes, Allan walked the length of the rehab area, all one hundred feet of it. He got a "Yee Haw!" from Aaron and applause from those in the room, including Ruth. Allan felt a greater sense of accomplishment than he'd ever experienced, more even than getting a record deal or singing on the radio, coast to coast. The journey of a thousand miles was well and truly underway.

The pace of that journey began to accelerate. Aaron and Dr. Comer agreed that Allan was nearing the time he'd be released. Because the accident was the fault of the drunken soldiers, the commander of Fort Hood saw to it that all the bills were taken care of. That included storage and servicing of Allan's Buick Roadster. This meant that Allan still had a comfortable cushion of cash with which to launch himself into this new chapter of his story. But he'd have to wait to figure out how to drive and manage shifting the gears. He knew he'd figure it out.

Getting his affairs settled and saying farewells came suddenly after his nearly two years at Brackenridge Hospital. And the hardest of those goodbyes was to Ruth.

Allan knew that he was infatuated with her. She was always sweet and supportive but had never given him a sign that it was more than a friendship. Still, he figured that just like every other challenge he was facing, if he didn't attempt to succeed, he was certain to fail. She walked in as he was packing his suitcase. "Well, how is our miracle man?" she said. "Feels good to be getting sprung from this joint, I'll bet."

"Well, Ruth, there's not much I'll miss about the place, but there's one thing I will miss terribly. You have been my steadfast supporter, my cheerleader, my inspiration, and my dear friend. You will never fully understand what you've meant to me. But all that is speaking in past tense. I'd like to continue our relationship outside this place, in the real world, like normal people."

She gazed at him. "Thank you so for your lovely words," she said. "I too have enjoyed our time together and my belief in you and what you can accomplish in your new life is limitless. As to the personal element, well, I am and always will be your friend—and I hope a close one. But I have met a soldier, a medic actually, in the Army and we are seeing one another. I hope you understand."

His heart sank but he managed a smile. "Of course, I'm happy for you. Tell the good folks in the reading group how much I enjoyed our time together and how I will miss them. Perhaps you'll let me take you to lunch after I figure out what I'm going to do with myself."

"I would be delighted. I hope you will always remain my dear friend."

A long hug, a short peck on the cheek, and Ruth left the room to get the wheelchair and an orderly to help get his belongings downstairs where his family awaited. She was back shortly, wheeling him down for a final signoff from Dr. Comer. The doctor rose from his desk as Allan was wheeled into the office.

"There's my miracle patient! Thanks, Ruth. Allan, there's so much I'd like to say to you but first I would like to thank you for proving me wrong. When they wheeled you in here on that gurney,

I was absolutely certain that if you managed to come out of the coma and survive, you'd be bedridden or, at best, wheelchair-bound for the rest of your life. What you have accomplished is astounding. You've fought and won a war of monumental proportions. I can only pray our country is as determined and successful in winning this war we are fighting overseas.

"Now, I'd like to give you an idea and maybe a helping hand in your next step to establishing yourself in your new life. I have a close friend, Andy Rosenberg. He is the station manager at KNOW Radio. We were fraternity brothers at the university. I have listened to you read to your group a couple of times and have been struck by your rich voice and powerful delivery. And I know you worked in radio in New York." He paused. "I was talking to Andy the other day and he mentioned that they have need of a newsreader and announcer. With the war on and so many men enlisting, he's having a devil of a time finding someone. So, I took it upon myself to tell him about you. He would like for you to call him to set up an audition. I hope you don't think that's presumptuous of me, but I feel you'd do well at this."

Allan could only shake his head and laugh. "That is amazing. The Lord really does work in mysterious ways. As a matter of fact, Doc, I have been planning to get a job in radio. You could not have given me a better going away present. I can't begin to thank you for this and all you have done to help me heal."

"I was just doing what I'm trained to do. You put the time and effort into it. And as to the radio, there are no guarantees but Andy's a good guy and he knows about your…ah…handicap."

"Well, Doc, as far as I'm concerned, I don't have a handicap. I just walk a little slower than other folks. But I can do things they can't. I've had lots of time to examine my situation while I've been here. I came to the conclusion that no one gets to choose the circumstances that happen to them in life. The only choice we get is our perspective. Depending on how we choose to look at things…through fear, or through faith, determines our experience of life. I've decided on viewing through the lens of faith. I'm taking one step at a time the way I'm being led and leaving the outcome to God. I'm just gonna keep on a keepin' on as Aaron would say. Oh, by the way, where is that old cowboy?"

"I believe he's waiting out front to see you off." The doctor opened his desk drawer. Here is Andy's card. Call him. I wish you the best, Allan. I believe I will hear great things about you in the future. And hear you on the radio. God Bless."

Aaron was indeed waiting for him under the porte-cochere at the hospital entrance, talking with his parents. Ruth wheeled him to their car and Allan climbed out of the wheelchair for the last time. Aaron came and threw his arms around him.

"Well, son, you done it. You made a liar outa Doc and a champion outa yourself. As I've been tellin' your folks here, I've been workin' with busted up people for more than ten years. I ain't never had nobody as ready to listen and take all the torture I could dish out and keep 'er a comin' as you. Son, I don't know what's waitin' round the next bend, but you dang sure got what it takes to stay aboard and keep a ridin'. I ain't got no young'uns, but I'd be mighty proud if you was my son. Hope your daddy appreciates what a good'n you are.

"In a rodeo, you get a belt buckle when you stay aboard for eight seconds. Shoot, you done more than that. So, here's a buckle for you for bustin' every bronc I put you up on." Aaron looked away. "Gotta get back to my folks. Best of luck, pardner."

Allan saw the tears in Aaron's blue eyes and looked down at the buckle. It was an oval of silver with a figure of a man riding a bucking bronco. Words were engraved below the image...*Macho Hombre*.

—

ALLAN'S PARENTS THANKED THE staff and helped him into the back seat of their car. As he watched his friends and perused the hospital that had been his home, he felt the odd sensation of being completely on his own for the first time in nearly two years. The wind whistled at the windows as they headed for the reunion delayed by his accident.

Basking in the freedom of being once more a part of regular life, he gave thanks for his healing, thanks for his family. It helped keep his mind off the constant pain that still nagged at his legs. Both Dr. Comer and Aaron had warned him that pain would always be with him when he moved his legs in certain ways. His muscles were sore from learning to carry his weight with his upper body as he supported himself on the canes.

They drove through San Marcos forty-five minutes later, and he rediscovered the beauty of the rolling hills and trees. He'd forgotten how much he loved this part of Texas, as the song *Deep in The Heart of Texas* said.

His childhood had been filled with exploration of it. During vacation periods, when both the school and the symphony were closed for summer, the family spent weeks driving the backroads, exploring and camping out. Even now, he could see his father in a hammock reading or playing the violin under a cypress, while his mom stirred a Dutch oven over a campfire. Those enchanted family times, woven with laughter and love, had helped form his worldview and character as well as his faith. Sundays, his dad would play the guitar as they sang hymns and Negro spirituals, followed by his reading from the Bible and discussions about what had been read. "Home church" on the road it was, and he had missed it.

How very far away from those roots he had drifted in the years of chasing his dreams. Now, with only the sound of engine, tires and the breeze, Allan reflected on the indulgences and compromises he'd embraced, how deceptively easy it had been to slide into darkness. No, if he were honest, he'd call it what it was. Sin.

And then a peace drifted over him, and he remembered that he was forgiven and therefore could forgive himself. Like Satchell Paige said, "Don't look back. Somethin' might be gainin' on you." Allan had been reborn in the crucible of tragedy and pain. They harden steel by heating it and banging it into the proper shape. He was ready to discover what kind of tool he'd become.

—

PULLING UP IN FRONT of his childhood home, Allan waited after his dad turned off the engine. He sat listening to the clicking of the car as it cooled.

Tears ran down his face. The feelings that gripped him were a far cry from what he'd envisioned when he'd left New York. No longer the pompous conquering knight. Now, a humbled and grateful penitent. Opening the door, gathering his canes, and locking his brace straight, he stood with painful groans, and walked carefully, still mastering the process, to his old front door.

His brother and sister, waiting in the living room, turned with surprise at his earlier-than-expected arrival. His brother Sam and sister Louise leaped from their chairs and smothered him in embraces. Georgia joined with his dad as they gathered around him. They stood wordlessly, each lingering in the deep familial joy of reunion with the prodigal son.

His dad whispered, "My boy's home at last."

Then his sister broke the spell. "Let me take him to meet his nieces."

A small girl sat on the floor beside a toddler playing with dolls. "Mary Lou, this is your uncle, Allan. He's been gone a very long time, since before you were born. And Allan, this is Nancy, her baby sister."

Allan grinned. "And beautiful big girls they are too. Oh, Louise," he said, "they're gems. Where is the man who stole your heart? I've yet to meet him and give him my okay."

"E.W. is having dinner with his family, but he'll be here later. He's a great guy. You'll love him."

They all gathered around the table set with the family heirloom china and silver. They joined hands and his father began to pray.

"Oh, Lord, never has our Thanksgiving celebration been filled with more thankfulness. Father, you have saved and restored our son, your son, saved him from death, healed his injuries and, miracle of miracles, helped him to walk again. Our family is made whole this day. May this be the beginning of a new and blessed season in his life. Thank you for this family and this food. Oh, and thank you for our lovely Louise for cooking this feast. In Jesus's name, Amen." His father opened his eyes and stood. "All right, I'll carve this bird. Pass the potatoes."

Allan watched through tears of gratefulness, joined once more with his family at home, sharing this grand tradition. The food was the best he'd had since leaving home, including any cuisine he'd had in New York. He tasted the love in every bite. At last came his favorite dessert, one he'd not tasted since the last Thanksgiving at this table so many years before—pumpkin pie.

Allan was overwhelmed with their questions and had many of his own. After dessert, his brother Sam suggested they go for a drive and catch up. Excusing themselves they walked out to Sam's green 1937 Chevy coupe. Settling behind the wheel as Allan arranged himself on the bench seat, Sam offered him a cigarette.

"Thanks, but no. I quit while I was in the hospital and kinda lost my taste for them. So where are we headed?"

"Remember that place on the river near the Mission Concepcion where we used to go fishin'? I thought we could go there and tell a few lies. I'm mighty curious about your adventures since you ain't been big on writing letters. I'm powerful interested, since I heard my little brother on the radio and the folks played your record for me. Bet the gals were all over you."

"Were is probably the right choice of words. As you can see, I'm a mite damaged. Don't think my prospects for romance are quite the same these days."

After stopping by an icehouse for some Dr. Pepper and fried tortilla chips, they drove to a bucolic spot under cypresses and oaks beside the San Antonio River. Sam pulled a blanket from the trunk and a couple of cane-fishing poles, as well as a carton of worms. He spread the blanket, arranging it so Allan could lean against a tree trunk.

"Looks like everything's squared away. Let's bait these hooks and see if we get lucky. All right then, little brother, let 'er rip. I've got all afternoon to hear 'bout your wild life in the big city."

As they fished, Allan wove a tale that sounded as if he were describing a strange character from a book. Sam had always been his trustworthy confidant so he held nothing back, even the more sordid elements. For every success, Allan had several compromising stories to share. He could read the perplexity in Sam's expressions. The more he spoke, the more the choices he'd made grated on him. He'd been loyal to his own ambitions and desires and devil take the hindmost. When at last he finished, he looked at the old limestone mission.

"Saying it all like this doesn't make me particularly proud. In fact, pride is the one thing I need a whole lot less of, because that's what got me into most of my trouble. Pride and its ugly stepsister, desire. I was running with a very fast crowd, Sam, and pretty much anything was Okay, long as you didn't step on the wrong toes. I've had a lot of time to think about it and I don't really miss most of it. Only the music, the singing."

"That right there is quite a story. Can't say I blame you for the dames. I mean you're only human and it sounds like you had 'em swarming like hungry mosquitos. As to the other stuff, especially the drugs and mob business, I'm dang glad you got out in one piece."

"One rather broken piece, but I've come to look at things in a very new and unexpected way." He took a deep breath. "I'm going to tell you something that's going to make you think I'm loony. It's something I've told no one, and you have to keep this strictly between us. But perhaps it will help you understand where I am now and how very differently I see things now. What matters is something bigger and more important than me and my ambitions."

Allan told Sam about the mysterious visitation by the man in the grey suit. He left nothing out, including his belief that it had been an angel and that he believed what he'd been told. The way events in his future would unfold was an unknown. What Allan *did* know, believed with every fiber of his being, was that he would accomplish what the man foretold. In fact, he had already managed to walk again as promised. It was only the beginning.

His brother had sat silently through the story. "My word, Allan, I don't know what to say. You gotta admit it sounds crazy. I mean could it have been some kind of delirium or the drugs they were giving you for pain? Not that I don't believe you, but..."

"I had gone through withdrawal days before when they took me off the morphine. He was as real as you are, Sam. And I blinked and turned my head and that fast," Allan snapped his fingers, "he was gone. Nope it was real and now that I'm back on my feet, I'm going wherever this takes me. God has a plan, I believe in Him, and it's my job to put as much effort into whatever presents itself as I did when it was all about my dreams."

Sam shook his head. "I've already seen you beat your polio and walk, and then accomplishing all you've done since you left...shoot brother, my money is on you. "

"Enough about me. First let me apologize for not writing or calling but I really am interested in what you've been doing."

"Well, compared to you, it's pretty tame. Finished college, got a girlfriend, went to work selling insurance, got engaged, rented a little place down near St. Mary's. Oh, and I'm thinking of enlisting in the Army. Guess that pretty much covers it. Hey, looks like you got somethin' on your line!"

The next three hours of brotherly reunion was the most enjoyable time Allan could remember. They re-established the bond as if they'd never been apart. On the drive home, Sam filled him in on the rest of the family and the general lay of the land. After dinner and warm family conversation, Allan experienced sleeping through the night in his own bed for the first time since the accident.

After breakfast the following morning, his mother asked Allan to join her in the study. The smell of old leather furniture and aging carpet filled him as he followed Georgia and sat in his favorite chair. She sat on the couch across from him and put her cup down on the coffee table between them.

"Son, I hardly know where to begin. When this accident happened and I saw you in that bed in a coma—and the doctor said you were not likely to make it…I'm sorry for these tears. Anyway, I started to pray for God to save you like I've never prayed for anything. And then, He brought me to the realization that I needed to lay down a burden of unforgiveness and resentment toward you, a burden I've been dragging around like a bunch of dirty laundry since you left home.

"As you know, I was dreadfully angry and wounded that you spurned my advice and my dreams for you. I even hoped for you to fail and return to your senses, or I should say, my *opinion* of what made sense. Not a day went by that I didn't grumble and stew in my resentment. I am ashamed to admit these things. I had no right to impose my will on you. As your father has rightly told me, each of us must choose our own path in life if we are to find fulfillment.

"Darling, I want you to know how proud I am of what you have overcome and accomplished. You are truly an amazing young man and wherever God leads you, whatever path you choose, I will be your biggest supporter and fan. Please forgive this foolish old woman."

"Oh, Mom, I don't know what to say. I have to admit that I harbored my own resentment toward you for not supporting and encouraging me. But in a strange way, it actually became a motivation. A part of me was whispering, 'I'll show her.'" His smile was warm. "Right now, though, let's lay these burdens down and start anew. I feel a great weight has been lifted, Mom. I love you and appreciate your words. I don't know what God has in store, but I know with all my heart it's going to be something grand. Something better than what I would have accomplished had I continued on the path I was on. I've got a possible opportunity to get back in radio, not as a singer but as an announcer. Dr. Comer has recommended me to a friend at the radio station in Austin. I have a good feeling about it. So, you can join me in praying for favor and guidance on the path ahead.

"And Mom, thank you for the countless hours you spent helping me through the ordeal of my polio and teaching me how to overcome. It's the reason I have overcome this accident and learned to walk again. You are a hero to me. You helped put the grit and determination in me and I promise you I will make you proud of what I do with my life from here on."

Georgia came to him and threw her arms around him. After a good cry, she recommended he find some music he liked on the radio.

Chapter 25

Thanksgiving at home had filled Allan with an abundance of family, familiarity, and, of course, food. Three days later, he was feeling impatience to get on with his life. His parents, in particular his mother, wanted him to stay with them, let her take care of him for a while and continue to rehabilitate his injuries. It was clear that he must craft a new path for himself, and he knew the first step in doing so.

He retrieved the card Dr. Comer had given him, took a deep breath, and dialed. He asked for Andy Rosenberg and the receptionist put him through. "Mr. Rosenberg, my name is Allan Dale. Dr. Robert Comer gave me your card and suggested you might be looking for an announcer or newsreader. If you have a few moments, I'd like to tell you about myself and find out if I might fit the bill."

"Oh...right. Bob told me about you, spoke very highly of you. He mentioned you'd worked in radio in New York and had been recovering at the hospital. He says that you are partially handicapped. Obviously, that might present a problem, but if your voice and delivery are good, being handicapped shouldn't matter."

"Well, I can walk actually—brace on one leg and a couple of crutches. But my voice and reading skills are in grand shape."

"Your voice certainly is. Bob told me about your little reading club, I would imagine that is about the best training one could have for reading dry news copy or ads. I've got some time around three. Are you free to come in for a chat?"

"Actually, I'm at my parents' house in San Antonio at the moment. I came for Thanksgiving and to sort things out. But I can be there any other day."

"How about Thursday at four. Would that work?"

"Yes. Thanks for the opportunity."

His parents were excited with the possibility of Allan getting a chance to start over in radio and were happy to drive him to Austin for the interview. They dropped him off at the radio station and went for a cup of coffee while he had the meeting.

Allan liked Andy Rosenberg from his first firm handshake. His crooked smile and quick wit put him at ease. Andy was very impressed by his singing success, but pointed out that the job would not entail any musical elements. He had Allan read several pages of news copy and a couple of radio commercials. Then Andy sat back, ran a hand through his curly black hair, and laughed.

"Have to be honest with you. When Bob told me about you, I figured I'd be doing both him and his patient a favor by taking the meeting. Turns out it was Bob doing me the favor. You already sound like a network voice. I've had a time getting guys without a strong Texas accent and good pipes who can read well. You ticked off those boxes, for sure. I do have to ask, though, how difficult is it for you to get around. The studio is upstairs and there is no elevator. Would that be a problem?"

"I'm sure I can manage stairs. I've never tried them, but I'm willing to give it a go. Want to watch my audition?"

"I like your style. That's pretty bold of you."

"We might as well find out if I can do it together."

Allan stood at the bottom, staring up the steps which appeared stories high. He felt his heart beating and his respiration increasing. Could he really pull this off?

Using the railing with his right hand and supporting himself on his cane with he left, he began the climb. It was not unlike walking with parallel bars except doing it uphill. Very cautiously, very deliberately, he made the ascent, fighting gravity and anxiety. Reaching the landing winded, but thrilled, Allan turned to see Andy smiling and holding his thumb up.

"Great. Now why don't you get yourself back down here so we can talk about your duties and how much I can afford to pay you. You can get back down, right?"

Allan took a breath. "We're getting ready to find out right now." It was trickier coming down, but Allan managed it. He felt a newfound confidence, having taken this chance and mastered the stairs. Figuring out the rest should be easy. Returning to Andy's office, he was offered a full-time announcing job. However, the pay was less than he was used to.

"I can offer you $175 a month. And two weeks of vacation, although in this business we usually have to work holidays."

"Gee, Mr. Rosenberg, I really appreciate that. But having been in the business, I had friends who were announcers that made three times that. I realize it was New York and this is Austin, but I'm starting over and I have a lot to get settled. How about two hundred a month? It's way less than scale and only twenty-five bucks more. Believe me, I'll make it the best investment you can imagine. All you asked me to do is read news copy and commercials. I'm a pretty good writer and voice actor. You may find all sorts of ways I can help this station."

The station manager leaned back in his chair. "You're a pretty good salesman too. Who knows, maybe I'll put you to work selling airtime. I appreciate your pluck. To tell you the truth, with the war on and so many men joining up, it's getting hard to find talent and I must say you have plenty of that. So all right, it's a deal. How soon can you start?"

Allan thought for a moment. "Well, I have to get my car, find a place to live, and get settled in. Can you give me a week?"

"Got by this long without you, so I suppose we'll muddle through. See you in one week. And I'm Andy from now on, okay? Look forward to working with you."

Allan felt pain from the exertion of his assault on the stairs all the way to the car, but his joy banished the suffering. His parents were thrilled and wanted to celebrate. They went to a great barbecue place Allan knew and made plans for helping get him to his car and making sure he was able to find a place to live.

The next day, his brother Sam drove Allan back to Austin to pick up his car. He'd spent extra time with Aaron working on the articulation of his right leg so he would be able to work the gas pedal with the brace on his right leg and the brake and clutch with his left. He had read that Oldsmobile had come out with an automatic transmission and he planned to trade in his beloved Buick for one of those. He figured since his Buick had very few miles and he had a good amount in savings he could easily afford it and it would make driving far easier.

By that evening, with his brother's help, Allan had managed to trade his Buick for a 1940 Oldsmobile with their patented Hydra-Matic transmission. Allan was thrilled with the ease with which he was able to drive it to the motel. Sam said his goodbyes and Allan promised to come home for a visit the first chance he got.

After he got checked in, he thought of Ruth. Maybe she was free for dinner. Knowing her hours, he figured she would still be at work. He'd hoped he'd never have to darken the doors of Brackenridge Hospital again, but here he was pulling into the parking lot. Even if Ruth wasn't free for dinner, she would still be thrilled at the good news. For that matter, he should thank Dr. Comer for the introduction and tell him the outcome of his kindness.

He found Ruth at the nurses' station getting ready to deliver dinner to patients. Taken by surprise, she smiled and threw her arms around Allan's neck.

"Well, howdy, stranger. I hoped not to see you back here. Everything okay?"

"Better than okay. Ruth, I just got hired to be an announcer and newsreader at KNOW Radio. I'm going to be living here in Austin. I wanted to know if you're free to celebrate with some dinner tonight when you get off."

"Oh, my, I'd love to! I'll have to get home and change. Can I meet you in an hour and a half? I'll be ready by then."

"You bet. Our usual Mexican?" He glanced around. "Is Dr. Comer still around?"

"Should be. Check his office. I believe he's finished his rounds for the day. I'll see you there."

Allan found Dr. Comer pouring over paperwork in his cramped, untidy office. "I hate to interrupt, but do you have a moment?"

"Allan, what the devil are you doing back here? You *do* realize that when we sign a patient out, the idea is they stay gone."

"I'm here for a very good, non-health-related reason. Because of you, I'm the new staff announcer and newsreader at KNOW Radio. In fact, your friend Andy said he needed to thank you. But I wanted to thank you first. You have seen me through the most difficult time of my life and helped heal me more than you can know. And now you are helping me to get back in the game of life. I owe you more than I can repay."

A big smile appeared on Dr. Comer's face. "Allan, that is the most gratifying news I could hear. I went into medicine—orthopedics in particular—because I wanted to help mend broken people. I must say you have been my most challenging and most rewarding patient. Your will of steel has helped you surmount injuries that would have destroyed the majority of people. That same indomitable spirit will no doubt take you far. I'm honored to have been of help. I wish you all the best. Before you go, you should drop around and give Aaron the good news. He's a tough old boot, but I think he's got a real soft spot for you. Best of luck. I'll be listening for your dulcet tones on the radio. And I'll make sure all your friends from the reading group know as well."

Allan made his way to the rehab area to find Aaron pulling his Straw Boss routine on an unsuspecting patient. He cracked a slight grin and indicated he'd be done in five minutes and nodded toward the bench. Finishing his physical terror session with the sweating patient, Aaron limped over to Allan.

"Well, lookee here, a stray maverick. Didn't expect to be seein' you around this place again."

"I just wanted to share a bit of good news with you and thank you again for all your kind cruelties. I just landed a job on KNOW Radio as an announcer and new reader. Be sure to be listening. It's 1400 on the dial."

"Shoot, I know where it is. They got good western swing on sometimes, Bob Wills and them. I'm mighty glad to hear that, pardner. You deserve a good hand, 'bout time you got dealt one."

"I know you're working, but thanks again for all you did. And if you're ever of a mind to visit and solve a few of the worlds' problems you can find me at the radio station. Since I'm going to be reading the news, I should be an expert on the worlds' problems."

"Best of luck to you, son. And I will take you up on it, sure as shootin'. Adios, and *buenas suerte vaquero.*"

By the time he finished his visits, Allan had only twenty minutes to kill before meeting Ruth. He was doing his best to adhere to the fine line of friend versus girlfriend, knowing she had a boyfriend. It in no way lessened his attraction to this tenderhearted and lovely creature. But gentleman he would be, even if it killed him.

He parked near Congress Avenue and passed the time and listened to the radio broadcast from his new station, feeling a sense of belonging and purpose he'd not enjoyed since being part of a band. He took a few minutes to express his gratitude to God for orchestrating it all and leading him there. He also asked for his guidance and favor in helping him become successful in this new career.

He checked his watch and left to meet Ruth. She was waiting for him when he pulled up, looking ravishing in a light gray wrap, red blouse peeking over the collar, and black pencil skirt. Her hair was up in a fashionable twist, and she wore red lipstick that matched her blouse. He was smitten.

They went into Cocina Merida near the Colorado River Bridge. The view was grand, the food excellent, and the conversation eloquently entertaining. Her happiness at his good fortune matched his own.

Allan added a twist of flirtation. Mariachis serenaded at their table, time seemed suspended, right up until Ruth looked down at her watch. "Oh, dear, I've been having too much fun. It's later than I thought."

"There's a lot I've never done, but I've never had too much fun. Are you sure you can't stay a little longer?"

"Behave, young man. I have a boyfriend as you know. But I'm flattered as always. And I promise to be your biggest fan. I can hardly wait to hear your voice on my radio. Now put me in my pumpkin and let Cinderella go home. She's gotta be at work by seven."

Allan woke early and lay in bed pondering his amazing good fortune, encouraged about the future of his career. But he was discouraged about the future of his personal life. An unavoidable question nagged at him. What woman would want to take on a life caring for a man than walked with canes? It was a bitter pill to swallow, but one he chewed on while thinking about Ruth.

—

ALLAN FOUND AN AD in the morning paper for a guest cottage, and it turned out to be ideal. The one-bedroom cottage sat behind an old, large limestone home. The older couple who met him were Texans in the historical mold, real as dirt, friendly as family, and unashamedly probing in their questions. They made it clear they wanted a sober, civilized, and responsible tenant. He assured them that, considering his condition, he wouldn't be rowdy, drank sparingly, and though single, was not a womanizer. He even joked about not being very good at "chasing women."

Tom and Betty Martin liked him immediately and sealed the deal. The rent was amazingly low compared to New York and well within his budget. He arranged to move in that weekend.

Allan marveled as he drove back to San Antonio in his new Olds with the Hydra-matic transmission at how his life was beginning to take shape. It seemed his luck had truly changed. But the more he thought about it, the less he believed luck had anything to do with it. He felt like Hansel and Gretel following breadcrumbs and he was certain who was dropping them to guide him along the path. Christmas was but three weeks away and he looked forward to finally sharing it as he'd originally planned two years before when he'd left New York. This would be dramatically different than the Christmas reunion he'd envisioned.

While crossing the Comal River in New Braunfels, he turned on the radio. KNOW was fading but a quick turn to the left brought him to the powerful signal of WOAI in San Antonio. It was one of a handful of stations in the U.S. with a "clear channel," not sharing the 1200 AM frequency with any other station and booming over numerous states with 50,000 watts. The news was on, delivered by a polished newsreader. Allan studied his delivery and style, listening for guidance in his new profession.

The news was far from sanguine. The war dominated and even with the obvious positive spin to keep up morale, he surmised it would be a long hard slog with no guarantees as to the outcome. With the draft and volunteer recruitment, at least the armed forces were getting ample manpower for the war effort. His brother was planning to join up and a part of Allan wished he were able to as well. But someone had to fill those jobs that were being abandoned and he was blessed to be one of them.

He considered the fact that with all the young men going off to war, the odds of finding a young woman were improving. While he pondered his prospects, he was haunted by his past. A brutally honest appraisal of his past liaisons was anything but flattering. It grated on him to admit what a self-serving playboy he had been. He'd taken whatever love was offered and gave only what was needed to get his desires satisfied. In fact, the only one who'd shown any true depth and tenderness had been Angelina and he'd treated her badly. The rest seemed like faces he'd seen in a movie, far removed from any tangible definition of profound, lasting love. That said, he figured he'd gotten no more than he deserved. As he contemplated his romantic future, that niggling question returned. Who would want to be with a man in his condition? All things are possible, he reasoned, deciding to table the quest for love while he focused on his new career.

—

ALTHOUGH ALLAN'S FOLKS WERE overjoyed by the good news of his radio job, they were less so by the fact he'd be moving away to Austin. With rationing in place, there'd be fewer trips home, but Allan was falling in love with Texas again. He'd thought New York was the pinnacle of living, but the steadfast and fearless honesty of Texans beat the sly chicanery of New Yorkers. The contours of his emerging new life were shaping themselves around him and he liked the way they fit.

He would not get Christmas Day off as it fell on a Friday and the news still had to be reported. But he'd be there to spend the weekend, open presents, and eat Christmas leftovers.

It took Allan all of an hour to organize his meager belongings in his new home. Having done his moving, he took a book and sat in a rocker by his new front door and listened to the breeze sigh through the trees.

Betty, his landlady, showed up around sunset with a covered dish, a welcoming and housewarming for her nice young tenant. She left him to his reading with the promise that he'd let her know if he needed anything. The Martins seemed to be the quintessential happy older couple—comfortable in their marriage, home, and their own skin. He laid down the book and offered up thanks for where he had arrived. And, in advance, for where he believed he was heading.

Chapter 26

The first things that hit Allan when he arrived in the station were the smell of old carpeting, cigarette smoke, the clatter of typewriters, teletype machines, and the broadcast coming from on air monitors. Andy welcomed him and introduced him to his news and production director Burt Tucker. Allan cautiously followed Burt up the stairs to the studios. After he'd shown him around, Burt took him into his office. Teletype wire copy and scripts covered his desk. Only a dirty coffee mug and typewriter peeked out from the paper hills. Rheumy gray eyes stared at Allan from a baggy, basset-hound face. Burt's jowls wiggled as he spoke, his balding head shining in the harsh overhead light.

"Andy told me all about you. He seems mighty pleased. I understand you were a singer. Know anything about writing news copy?"

"To be honest, no. But I devour books and listen to a lot of news. I love words, but I have a lot to learn."

"Well, Andy was right about your voice. Nice rich timbre. Understand you have some experience reading to people in a group, that right?"

"We had a reading group at the hospital. I read two entire novels to them over the course of several weeks. I think my skills will be adequate for a news segment."

"Let's talk about writing, then. I'm an old newspaper man. Been a reporter, writer, editor. Worked for the *Houston Chronicle* before coming here.

"Secret to writing news is keep it simple. People want to know particular things about whatever event you're reporting on. Every story has to answer these questions. Who, What, When, Where, Why, and How. Avoid conjecture. Your job is to report, not opine. Crisp, clean copy means keeping it simple. Shakespeare said, 'Brevity is the soul of wit.' He had that right.

"I'm going to give you several pieces of wire copy to look at. Then I'm going to show you how I edited them down to half their size to fit the time allotted in the newscast. Take a good look, and then I'll give you another bit of wire copy to cut down from a two-minute to a forty-five-second read. Use that desk in the corner; you've got fifteen minutes."

Allan sat down and poured over Burt's copy. He thought he saw how the original story had been edited down. Then the news director handed him a story about the war in North Africa, recently joined by American troops. He puzzled his way through marking out sentences he felt superfluous. At last, he had what appeared to be fewer than half as many words. He spotted a stopwatch near the ink blotter, grabbed it, and began to read. It was still ten seconds too long. He cut down a couple of sentences and read as he would on the air. He heard Burt chuckling as he walked to Allan's desk.

"Not bad at all, son. I think you're going to be just fine. Only way to learn is by doing it. We got a five-minute newscast coming at the top of the hour. You have thirty-five minutes to edit these stories and read them on that microphone over there when the light comes on. Think you can do that?"

"I know I can."

In what seemed a matter of seconds, Burt was leading him to the news studio and settling him behind an RCA microphone with a KNOW plaque attached. The engineer waited behind the glass. Allan felt as nervous as he had the first time he had sung before a large audience. The engineer signaled one minute to go and pointed at the headphones laying near the mic. Slipping them over his head, he held the first story in his sweaty hands and waited. The engineer pointed, the red light came on, and he was off.

"Good morning, this is Allan Dale with the KNOW headlines at ten." He read without flubbing any stories and tried to put the inflections in the proper places. The light went out, and Burt came over.

"Decent for your first time. We'll work on the writing, and you'll get the hang of it. As to your delivery? Stiff as saddle leather. You have a nice voice, but you were reading *at* me, not *to* me. I know you think there are hundreds, maybe thousands of people listening, and there are. But each of them is one person. I want you to imagine you are reading to that one person. Make it someone you know, maybe your girlfriend. In your imagination, tell it to her, as if she is sitting right there in front of you a foot or two away.

"You see, radio is very personal, even intimate. Listeners invite you into their minds. They imagine what you look like, what you're wearing, even what you think and feel, all from the sound of your voice. So be strong, authoritative, yet intimate. With that rich baritone of yours, you'll be completely believable. The next newscast is in fifty minutes. Let's check the teletype and I'll show you how to decide which stories to cover, lead with, and skip. Then you can rewrite them for the eleven o'clock news cast."

When he took off the headphones after finishing the five o'clock newscast, Allan's brain felt like scrambled eggs. He'd forgotten about lunch, so busy was he editing, writing, delivering, and being lectured to about news. He let out a long sigh as Burt walked out from the engineer's booth. A wee smile lifted the corners of his mouth from the folds of skin.

"How do you feel? You look bushed."

"You know, Burt, I am. Who would have imagined that something as simple as writing and reading would take so much out of you?"

"It's hard work, son. All mental, lots of concentration. Maybe not as tiring as digging trenches but tiring in a different sort of way. I have to say you did well. I think you're going to make a fine newsman. Next step is teaching you how to cover a story and write what you report."

Andy Burst into the studio beaming. "Great work, Allan. You've gotten better with every news cast. I didn't want to intrude until you were done, but you make KNOW News sound like a major market operation. You're as good as any of the guys on WOAI already. Come on, let me buy you dinner after your first trial by fire."

Allan breathed a long satisfying breath of relief and satisfaction. He'd driven the first nails into the structure of his new life.

—

THE MONTHS UNFOLDED IN a blur. Each day there was a fresh crop of stories that were as difficult to hear as to report. The nation was in lockstep to win the war effort at home. Rationing increased as everyone felt a unified spirit to win the war. As their sons shipped out to an uncertain fate, people felt a unanimous spirit of hope and patriotism and that victory lay ahead.

Allan had easily mastered rewriting and reading news copy pulled from the teletype machine. One day while at lunch, he watched three young boys with a wagon going door to door asking people if they had any old items to donate for the war effort. They wanted to collect anything of value, sell it, and contribute to the war effort. All were under ten years of age, but bold and fearless in asking people to help.

An idea struck him and he called the boys over. Allan interviewed them and found their patriotism and ambition inspiring. When he got back to the office, he wrote a story from his notes about the boys showing their pluck in doing what they could to help. The news report resulted in numerous phone calls complimenting the station on the story. Burt was thrilled. Old news dog that he was, he saw the local, human-interest appeal. He commissioned Allan to dig up and report more local feature stories.

In the days that followed, Allan began to discover and report more such stories and the response was dramatic. Burt suggested creating a program called "Home Front," devoted to such stories. Listenership, glowing newspaper reviews, and advertising revenues all increased. Soon Allan had become the voice of Austin. He was encouraged by the response and began to enjoy the creative process of interviewing people and capturing their essence in a story.

One day, he invited people to the station to record interviews with them telling their own stories. Hearing the voices of local people doing their part created yet more interest and listenership. He was rapidly becoming a popular and respected newsman. Burt and Andy were thrilled.

Allan began to expand the show by bringing local and state politicians and community leaders in to interview. He poured himself into finding new angles for telling the stories of how Texans were fighting the war in personal ways. His interviewing and writing skills continued to develop, helped by his love of words and his ear for the music of language. Although limited in his mobility, he was able to cover vast distances editorially. As the war unfolded, so too did creative ways to report and capture the local, human element of these historic events.

New Years 1942 was a subdued event. The world was caught in a downward spiral of destruction with no surety as to what lay ahead. U.S. troops were fighting the Japanese in Bataan, even as the hangovers from New Year's Eve were fading. As events unfolded Americans sought news, entertainment, and escape, as they gathered in front of their radios. The major networks supplied the worldwide picture. KNOW delivered the local perspective, with Allan becoming the voice of authority.

He became consumed by his career. Each day was a new opportunity to capture the patriotism, passion, and enterprise of ordinary people doing extraordinary things. Never had he been so completely inspired by something other than his own ambitions. Unlike his singing career, the adulation he was receiving was for doing something that focused outside of himself. He wasn't just performing—he was informing, encouraging, and influencing an audience on matters larger than themselves. He felt a sense of purpose he'd never known.

So focused on his work was he that Allan forgot about his personal life. Then, one day, Ruth called him. As he answered the call, he was surprised to realize he'd not thought about romance or relationships since he'd been at the station.

"Hey there, Mr. Newsman," she said. "It's your friend Ruth from the hospital. Remember me?"

"Of course. What a surprise. How are you?"

"Honestly, I spend a lot of time thinking about and praying for Jim. He's the man I told you about. He's overseas in the Pacific. I'm still working at the hospital and watching the world go mad. I just wanted to call and tell you how proud I am of what you have accomplished. I watched you go from a lost cause to a news celebrity. I know you're probably very busy but if you'd ever like to grab a meal and visit let me know."

"Ruth, I would love that. You pick the time and place, and we'll do it. I'm off on weekends so that is probably best for me."

"How 'bout Saturday night at our Mexican place? Would six work for you?"

"You bet. I so look forward to catching up. See you Saturday."

Allan felt the unfamiliar warmth of connection. He hadn't realized how alone he'd become through his focus on work. Other than the people at the radio station, he had no friends. The thought of spending time in Ruth's delightful company excited him, reminding him of a critical element missing in his life. Even though she was not available as a romantic interest, her lovely feminine presence would be a balm to his soul.

He arrived to find Ruth already sitting in a booth waving and smiling. He'd forgotten the glow that emanated from her guileless smile. After greeting her, he unlocked his brace and slid onto the bench, leaning his canes against the wall. "Well, don't you just look fitter and more handsome than I've ever seen you!" she said.

"And you as lovely and delightful as I remember. Ruth, I can't thank you enough for getting me out of my cage. I've gotten so focused on the news that I've gotten out of touch with the pleasure of good company."

The waiter arrived, took their orders, and returned shortly with drinks. After a toast to friendship, they resumed their conversation. Over the next hour and a half, they rediscovered the easy, convivial joy they found when together. They managed to avoid the dire state of the world, for the most part, focusing on personal observations spiced with shared wit and laughter. Although Allan still found Ruth alluring, it became clear to him that theirs would always be a platonic relationship. Accepting this, he began to appreciate her in a new and deeper sense. He needed a friend and he needed the balance and insight that only a woman could supply.

He found Ruth gazing at him. "Allan, I've witnessed something in your recovery that to me is difficult to explain. I've seen injured patients give up hope, accept defeat, find escape in various ways. But never have I seen someone rise above their circumstances and spit in the eye of fate like you have. You are different from anyone I've ever known. God gave you extraordinary gifts, that is obvious. I have listened to your recording numerous times. Your talent as a singer is amazing. But I am coming to see that your gift with words is even more so. When you first began, your powerful voice was so infectious, natural, compelling. More even than when you sing. These stories you are doing about everyday folks and the effort they make to fight the war…it's so encouraging."

"Wow, that is high praise indeed. It confirms a feeling I've been getting but couldn't quite articulate. For the first time in my life, my purpose isn't getting people to love my singing and adore me. All around us, there are common, anonymous people who have heroic spirits. As they began to tell their stories, I found myself deeply moved and inspired by the selfless goodness of the invisible people. In this time of radio and movie stars, I'm beginning to see the warp and woof of the fabric that has made America unique. All the different colors, textures, origins of who we are. There has never been anything like America before. A constitutional republic, based on the consensus of the common man, and now we are committed to defeating the tyranny of the powerful few, with the gifts with which we have been blessed. And somehow, innately, we are coalescing into what our forefathers wrote about. One nation unified in vision, while retaining our individual purpose and freedom."

"Allan, do you have any idea how powerful the words that just came out of your mouth truly are? You thought your gift was music. And it is. But by far your greatest gift is words. There's power to move people with the words you speak and how you speak them."

He sat back in his chair, keeping his eyes on her. "May I share something with you? I have been infatuated with you. I know it's not uncommon for male patients to get a crush on their nurses. Yet I am beginning to see that you are the most honest, insightful, and inspiring friend I've ever had. Your soldier is a fortunate man to have you as his girlfriend. But I believe I'm equally blessed to have you as my wise friend. The fact that you are a woman gives you an insight I will never have. I will cherish this friendship. I hope that you will become my adopted sister."

They parted with a new depth between them, promising to see one another more regularly. As he watched her walking away, Allan felt a void within himself being filled in part, with the friendship of a woman. But not the *love* of a woman. He considered again the likelihood of finding someone willing to become his wife and accept life with a disabled man. The prospects weren't encouraging.

—

ALLAN BEGAN TO DO a commentary that ran several times throughout the day. Just as he'd heard the great Gabriel Heater, Fulton Lewis and others do on the networks, he gave his opinion on and gave context to the daily struggle of living through greatest challenge the world had ever faced. The popularity of *Home Front* increased, as Andy and the station owners reaped the revenue from radio spots. However difficult the war had been for the country, 1942 was proving to be the most rewarding of his life. When Allan struggled with the chronic and sometimes excruciating pain from his injuries, he was bolstered by the ameliorating sense that he was doing something that was more important and greater than himself.

So caught up in his career had Allan become that it hit him one day that he'd not been home to see his family in months. An occasional phone call was the most he'd been able to find time for. They had visited a few times, but the encounters were brief.

Then, suddenly, Thanksgiving was once more looming. He decided that he would go to Andy and ask for a special favor of getting both Thanksgiving and Christmas off. Because of the popularity of his broadcasts, he felt he had the leverage to ask.

To his great relief, Andy's answer was yes, if he pre-produced reports to run in his absence. That would double his workload, but it would be worth it to spend time with his family.

Time with Ruth became ever more enjoyable as their friendship blossomed. He was able to share his deepest thoughts with her.

She reciprocated and began to open his eyes to the essential and mysterious nature of women in ways that amazed him. He came to appreciate them with a perspective he'd never had, and to understand how essential they were to a complete life for a man. He shuddered, remembering his callous, arrogant attitude toward women in the past and vowed that he would never see them as anything other than the greatest and most important element in his life.

Preparing for the drive home for Thanksgiving, Allan was humbled by how much progress he had made. Bit by bit, any leftover resentment or disappointment about the accident and all he'd lost were dissolving. Though less the person he had been physically, he felt he was becoming more than he'd ever been intellectually and morally. This new man was someone he was getting to know. How would his family come to see him?

When he walked in the door, one would have thought Allan had just gone around the corner to pick up something from the grocer. It was as if he'd never left. He was greeted with warmth and appreciation. The beauty of his family was that no matter who he was to the world, in their world he was still just Allan.

The canaries and parakeets twittered away as Georgia fed and watered them. The screened-in back porch was still her aviary. She had created a small business raising and selling the birds to supplement their income. Allan sought her out in her duties. She threw her arms around him as he walked through the door. "Oh, baby, it's so wonderful you could come. I'm just finishing up. Come on then, let's all catch up in the living room."

It was like sliding into a warm bath on a frigid night. He felt peace and a sense of belonging gently displacing his feelings of isolation. The unconditional love of his family washed away all sense of inadequacy. The intuitive connection, shared humor, unquestioned acceptance animated them. Allan drank the healing flow of togetherness like a parched man consumes water. Washed in laughter as they shared their memories and plans, he felt the sting of knowing he would likely never have a family of his own to carry on such traditions.

Thanksgiving that year was as Norman Rockwell would have painted it. Following the pumpkin pie and a conversation with his dad, brother, and brother-in-law E.W., Allan sought out his mother—pulling her away from time with "her girls."

The last deep conversations they'd shared had been as healing to his heart as therapy had been to his body. With the roots of bitterness banished between them, they recaptured the warmth they had shared before he'd left home. "Mom, this is the best Thanksgiving of my life. I know that may sound odd considering my condition. But everything that has happened since the day I walked out that door has led me to this time and place. I know you must ponder as do I, what might have happened if I had followed the path you had planned for me. You poured yourself into my healing and recovery from polio and had your own vision for developing my talent as a singer.

"I appreciate all you did for me. I understand the ambitions you had for me. But every choice I made has brought me to this point. And Mom, it's been a turning point. I was headed in a direction that would have perhaps given me everything I thought I wanted and likely would have left me bereft of all the things that matter.

"As wretched, as painful, as disappointing as this accident has been, it has also been enlightening. My focus on fame and adulation led me down some dark paths. The accident has changed my entire perspective. I am coming to realize that making my life all about fulfilling myself, about being admired, about achieving my grand visions of stardom are empty goals. I've been given a new lease on life. I realize how fragile and precious it is. I don't want to waste a second of it chasing my own pleasures and accomplishments.

"Mom, I believe we both had wrong plans for my future. I think I have an even greater gift than music. The gift of words and helping others express their words."

"I hardly know what to say. Yes dear, I was very determined on your behalf. I foresaw you being a great baritone and creating a grand life as a famous opera singer. And hard as it is to admit, I relished the pride I would have as the mother of an opera star. As you know only too well, it galled me no end when you spurned my direction and went off with those jazz musicians.

"But all you need to know is that I am prouder of you for what you have become than if you were the star of the Metropolitan Opera in New York. I see something new in you. You've become both stronger and softer at the same time. In spite of the fact that your body has been compromised, I see a strength in you I've never witnessed. I see you becoming something better than what you might have if you'd followed my guidance."

Allan's heart grew lighter with every mile on the way back to Austin. The healing conversations with his family inspired him. He had a new canvas upon which to paint the rest of his life. It was both ironic and illogical that he would feel happier than he had before his accident. A lightness of spirit lifted him, and he began to sing to the accompanying road noise for the sheer joy of it.

Chapter 27

The time spent working at the radio station was the most rewarding period of Allan's life. His popularity as a news commentator had eclipsed both Andy and Burt's expectations. Allan Dale had become "The Voice of KNOW" and was promoted as such on air in newspaper advertisements. One writer even called him the Gabriel Heater of Austin.

The accolades were rewarding but Allan kept it all in perspective. His dad had told him when he left with the band those long years before, "When it comes to the critics, believe half the good stuff and half the bad stuff they say about you. It'll help keep you from taking yourself too seriously."

As 1943 was drawing to a close, the news from overseas gave increasing hope that the war would be ending soon.

Following a weekend visit with his family, Allan returned to work to find several phone messages on his desk. One of them was from a man named Frank West in Wichita, Kansas, asking him to call back "collect." He pondered the mystery, knowing no one in Wichita.

He had so much to catch up on that he forgot about the strange call for two days. Then glancing at the number on the paper, he decided to find out who this person might be. He picked up the phone and placed a call.

He was surprised when the receptionist answered with the greeting, "KFH, Kansas's Greatest Radio Station." He told her his name and that he was returning Frank West's call. She put him through immediately.

"Allan, this is Frank West," said the voice. "I'm so glad you called. I was visiting friends in Austin a few weeks ago and heard some of your broadcasts, in particular your commentaries. I was quite impressed." He paused. "I'm the Program Director here at KFH. We have the most powerful signal in the region and a widely-listened-to station. We're heard in five states clearly and three others fairly well. Although we have a good staff of announcers, we have no keystone personality. I think that you would be a great addition to our staff. What sort of contractual obligations do you have at your current station?"

A frisson ran down Allan's spine. "Well, Mr. West, let me first say how unexpected this is. I'm very flattered by your kind words and interest. As to a contract, I have none. I *do* have a great deal of loyalty to the folks here, however. I'm from San Antonio, so my family is nearby which makes living here attractive as well."

"I can understand that. But let me tell you, we are prepared to offer you an opportunity and salary that is most attractive. Because of our wide reach, we have many national sponsors as well as the usual local and regional ad buys. We are one of the most profitable stations per capita in the country. I believe you would give us the network level presence we need. If I may—I don't know what they are paying you but I'll wager we can double it."

It was Allan's turn to pause. "Mr. West, I'm a little surprised, and greatly flattered. But there's something I need to tell that may factor into this. I was run over by a car a few years back. I walk with canes and a brace on one leg. It has no effect on my radio work, but I'm not as mobile as most. Since all I have to do is sit, write, and talk, it poses no problems."

"That makes this even *more* amazing. After all, the president is in a wheelchair. It's your words and your voice I'm after. I'm prepared to offer you $450 a month to start and depending on your success, performance bonuses, as well as guaranteed annual raises. I would want a two-year contract. How does that sound?"

"It sounds most generous, Mr. West. This has all taken me by surprise and that's a lot to process. May I have a day to think and pray about it?"

"Pray about it? Allan, I like you better already. You bet. I look forward to hearing from you. God bless."

Allan sat back in his chair. A tornado of thoughts whipped up in his head. The numbers stunned him. His current salary had increased to $2,600 a year. Frank was offering $5,400. With the average national wage somewhere around $2,200, that was a huge number for a non-network or major market station. He needed to talk to someone about this, get another perspective. He needed to talk to Ruth.

They met at their favorite Mexican restaurant that evening. She was excited by the news but not entirely surprised. "I half expected this, to be honest. I have watched...well...*heard* the growing mastery of your writing and delivery. People tune in to your broadcasts religiously. They talk about them at work and church. You tell us what is going on, give us things to contemplate, and, most importantly, you always give us encouragement and hope. With the Depression, and now the war, it's much needed. I don't blame this fellow for wanting to snag you."

"Ruth, the money is more than twice what I'm making with raises and bonuses and a two-year contract. But Andy gave me my break and has been so helpful. Plus, you are dear to me and my family is just down the road. That's a lot to give up."

"Losing your company would be a bitter pill for sure. But I have always believed that you are destined for great things. You are one of the most inspiring people I've ever known, and I want whatever is best for you. Honestly, I think you should do it."

"Well, I'm going to pray on it and sleep on it...that is, if I can sleep."

The answer to his dilemma became clear at three a.m. as he lay among scattered bedclothes. He'd talked and talked to God about it, and finally, as he drifted into the nether consciousness before dreams, it came. Not a voice, but a thought so precise and certain that there was no doubt as to the rightness of it. So it was that the first week of the new year, Allan was on the way to Wichita, Kansas.

Everything he owned filled the Oldsmobile with room to spare. He felt a twinge of loneliness already. He'd made some friends at the station, and he would sorely miss Ruth, who he hoped would be a lifelong friend.

Light snow began to fall on the windshield as he traversed the panhandles of Texas and Oklahoma. Weather was not the only thing that was going to be different. From the sound of Frank's enthusiasm, much was expected of him. He found himself surprisingly confident, felt the rightness of it, and trusted that this was the path he was supposed to travel.

KFH stood for Kansas's Finest Hotel. Three- and later four-letter call signs beginning with the letter W or K had begun in the early days of radio. There was WLS in Chicago (World's Largest Store— for Sears), WIS in Columbia, South Carolina (Wonderful Iodine State), WGH (World's Greatest Harbor—Norfolk, Virginia). The KFH studios were in the Lassen Hotel downtown. Allan had a suite waiting for him when he checked in. It was his until he found a place of his own.

There were at least two inches of snow on the ground when he arrived. A large neon KFH sign graced the corner of the eleven-story red brick structure. A doorman stepped to the car and helped him in. The suite was spacious and elegant even by New York standards. The bellboy helped him put away his things and Allan realized he was famished.

He ate a delightful meal in the elegant dining room, accompanied by his thoughts, imagining how this new verse in his song would play out.

Frank West met him the next morning for breakfast, then took him to the studios and began introducing him to people whose names he promptly forgot. The sound stage for live music performance was four times the size of the one at KNOW. The newsroom was equally impressive.

Frank showed Allan around and then took him back to his office, where Allan signed the contract. Frank explained what was expected and a bit about the overall programming and staff he'd be working with. Finally, he led Allan to his own office—the first he'd ever had. The news director Bill Nielson showed up and Frank left the two of them to get acquainted.

Allan liked him immediately. Tall, raw boned, blond and blue-eyed, he was textbook Scandinavian. Bill was overjoyed that Allan was part of his team, having heard recordings of his work on KNOW. It was Thursday and he told Allan he could start on Monday so he had time to get his bearings and maybe look for a place to live. Bill warned him that housing was a bit scarce with Boeing building B-29s and Cessna and Beechcraft factories building planes as well. Wichita was booming with the war effort.

—

ALLAN'S FIRST DAY WAS nearing an end. His broadcasts were well received and Frank and Bill were effusive in their praise.

KFH was labyrinthian compared to KNOW. In this larger market, there was so much to report that the hardest part was deciding what to cover and how to comment on it. He took a few minutes to organize for the next day and make an appointment to look at a place for rent.

Turning down a long hallway he thought lead to the reception area, he heard a woman singing with a big band through the speakers and stopped dead still in the hallway. Closing his eyes, he felt the same wave of emotions that had carried him away the first time he'd heard his father playing a violin solo with the symphony.

Allan was transfixed by her rich contralto. She was creating intoxicating melodic textures reminiscent of a painting by Renoir. The song ended and he was disoriented, having lost track of time and location. He walked a little further where a large soundproof window gave a view in to the soundstage. His breath seized.

The band was putting down their instruments. The singer before the microphone had the posture and bearing of a ballerina. She remained before the mic with eyes closed, her right hand over her heart, and a tear shining like a diamond at the corner of her eye.

He only now considered the song she'd sung, *Embraceable You*. He'd sung it many times, sung it well, and loved it. But she'd made something completely new of it. There was a splash of Sarah Vaughn and a bit of Judy Garland, but the interpretation was hers alone.

She opened her eyes at last and found herself staring directly through the glass into his. He smiled and nodded in appreciation. She returned a demure smile and turned away toward the band.

"She's a humdinger, ain't she?" said a voice behind him.

"Oh, yeah, she is an exceptional singer."

"Yep, that's our Peggy. My name's Dave Callens. I'm with The Green Prairie Boys. I play guitar. We're on the broadcast at seven. We play every Monday."

"Good to meet you, Dave. I'm Allan Dale. Just started here today. I'm doing news and commentary. I used to be a musician, singer, in big bands before I got busted up. I still play guitar for fun."

"Hey, maybe we can pick and grin sometime."

"Tell me about that singer in there. She is as good as anyone I heard in New York when I worked there."

"Her name's Peggy Jones. Local gal. She's the staff vocalist with the KFH band. She ain't just the best singer you ever heard. She's the best lookin' filly in the stable and she can act too. Does some on the radio plays we do here."

"She is every bit as lovely and talented as some of the Hollywood stars. Bet she'll go far." Allan pointed down the hallway. "This leads out to reception, right? I'm a bit turned around, first day and all."

"Yep. Just through that door, and first right after that. Good meetin' ya'. See you around."

Allan made his way to the car and followed the directions to a potential rental. He couldn't get the song or the singer out of his thoughts. When their eyes met, a brief arc of light seemed to connect them, and it shimmered yet within him. He had to find a way to meet her.

Then the familiar echo returned. What woman would find him attractive? Especially one as stunning and talented as Peggy Jones. Perhaps like he and Ruth, they could become friends.

The address for the rental was a few miles outside of town on what appeared to be a farm, complete with a barn and grain silo. An elderly couple met him at the door and showed him what had been the hired hand's quarters but had been converted into a small cottage. He liked it, they liked him, and the rent was fair. Considering his new salary, it was cheap. He agreed to move in over the weekend.

He was officially a resident of Kansas.

Chapter 28

Each day Allan grew more focused on the news and more compelling in his commentary. There was a sense of hope following the landing of Allied forces at Anzio on January 22 and the bombing of Berlin on March 6. Allan attempted to leaven the news with encouragement even when the reports were less than inspiring.

The response was astonishing. Midwesterners adopted him as their own favorite regional voice of the people. Following the D-Day invasion on June 6, the station added a morning report to Allan's noon and afternoon broadcasts. He had never been so busy, so inspired, nor so rewarded. But despite making friends at the station, he'd found his life becoming a solitary affair with a rare after-work social event from time to time.

He'd just reported Roosevelt's re-election to an unprecedented fourth term and was heading out for lunch when Peggy Jones stepped into the elevator. They traded polite smiles and rode down in silence. As the door opened and she stepped out, he finally spoke.

"Pardon me, Miss Jones. I have been hoping to run into you at the station. I simply want to tell you what an exceptional talent you are. Having been a singer myself, I appreciate how very rare your gift is. Your delivery is like finely acted drama. You inhabit the lyrics with such feeling that one has no choice but to be moved." She looked at him quizzically. "Oh, pardon me," he said. "My name is Allan Dale. I do news and commentary at the station."

She smiled. "Oh, my. I listen to you faithfully. I'm amazed we've not met. You've been here for months. Thanks so much for your kind words. They are especially gratifying considering the source. But you said you were a singer? I thought you were a newsman."

"Well, you probably noticed that I'm a bit banged up. Before my accident, I sang with big bands in New York. Did a recording. Ancient history. Just wanted to tell you how much I enjoy hearing you sing. The first time I heard you was my first day at work. You sang *Embraceable You,* and I watched through the window. It's one of my favorites."

"I remember now. You were looking at me and smiled and nodded. Did you say you sang in New York? Love to hear about that sometime. I hope to go there or perhaps Hollywood to pursue my career in singing and maybe even acting."

"Anytime. What are you doing for lunch?"

"I was just going to grab a sandwich at Woolworth's."

"Could I interest you in lunch at the hotel restaurant? It's actually quite good. My treat? I'll agree to talk only about music and movies and none of the disturbing subjects that I report on. What do you say?"

"Why, I say yes, Mr. Dale. Lead the way."

Having stayed at the hotel for a short while and being a daily regular, he was warmly greeted and seated at a table by the window. They ordered and sat quietly, Peggy looking at the view from the window, Allan assimilating the view before him. Such lovely long fingers, ideal for piano. Such erect posture, head held high, a profile etched by strong square jaws, and a perfect straight nose resting atop full lips framed by ready laugh lines.

Peggy turned and caught him staring. She smiled self-consciously. "So, tell me about New York. I grew up listening to the big bands and all the singers. Since I was a little girl, I sang along with them. I knew all the songs. Then I started taking voice and piano." She stopped.

"Oops, sorry. I came to hear about *your* career."

Over lunch, Allan covered the highlights of his career. He gave as much detail as he thought would be insightful for the planning of her own career. Peggy was surprised and greatly impressed by what he'd done. She asked many salient questions, listened attentively, and after he gave a truncated version of the accident and what followed, she sat silently and looked at him.

Her blue eyes held his as they had the first time he'd seen her, this time with a look of curiosity. Her full lips parted. "You are a wonder. How could you possibly have suffered such a tragedy, recovered, learned to walk again, and gotten back in radio to become who you are? I am truly speechless." She looked down. "I volunteer at the hospital. I've seen some tragic situations, especially boys returning from the war. There is a look in their eyes—it's one of hopelessness and acceptance that their lives, their hopes, their dreams are forever destroyed. Yet...I look in your eyes and I see joy, peace, and confidence. How is that possible?

"Peggy, all the things I told you about my success, the attention, the taste of fame, singing on the radio coast to coast, that was all I lived for. My entire existence was about me—my fame, my reviews, my fans. And the whole time there was a wordless nagging, as if there was a hole inside of me that none of those things could fill. In effect, I became my own universe, and everything revolved around me. Yet nothing satisfied." He paused before continuing.

"I'm sure you've heard the Bible verse, *All things work together for good for those who love The Lord and are called according to His purpose.* Now, I don't believe God caused the accident for my punishment. I'd been living a wild life. I'd been drinking the night it happened. I should have pulled further off the road. But, because of the accident, I have discovered what matters, what's bigger than me. I've been given a new path and a new purpose and, as crazy as it sounds, I'm happier and more fulfilled than I was in New York."

Peggy gazed at him through tear-filled eyes. She said nothing for several minutes. Then through choking words, she replied. "I can truly say that I've never met anyone like you. It's strange how one envisions how someone they hear on the radio might look. You don't look anything like the slightly older bookish fellow I pictured. You are handsome, youthful, and beaming with energy. I am so glad you invited me to lunch, Allan. I feel like there is so much more I'd like to hear about you, learn about you. Could we do this again some time?"

"I am flattered, and I would be greatly honored. When are you free again?"

"Oh, golly, let's see. I'm singing with the band for a private party at the Cessna Plant this evening. I have to do the broadcast tomorrow night, of course. The weekend's very busy. How about lunch again on Monday?"

"It's a date...er...I mean not a date...lunch."

She grinned. "Oh, Allan, it's a date all right. Meet you here Monday around one. And thank you for the most unusual and enlightening conversation I can remember having for, well, maybe ever."

He watched her walk away with the grace of a gazelle, her grey wool skirt clearly outlining her lithe athletic body. She wasn't a tall woman, yet she carried herself with the erect elegance of one of the models he'd known in New York. Allan was unable to process what had just transpired between them. The old voice cautioned him not to get his hopes up. His condition didn't bode well for a fairy tale romance.

—

On Monday, Allan was already seated when Peggy walked into the hotel restaurant. She moved like a lynx, yet her face held the gentleness of a doe. She spotted him, and her smile caused his heart to accelerate. When she walked to the table, Allan grabbed his canes and began to rise.

"That won't be necessary, though the gentlemanly gesture is appreciated. In the future, I'll take it for granted that you are cultured and genteel." Peggy seated herself.

"Very thoughtful of you under the circumstances. You look absolutely ravishing. More formal than one might expect at this early hour."

"We are performing at the Boeing Plant for the celebration of beating their B-29 quota for the month. It's a few hours away but why go home and change?"

The waiter arrived and after a brief chat, they ordered. The conversation flowed with easy spontaneity. She grilled him with questions on the New York music scene, one query leading to the next. Laughter punctuated their meal and by the time their plates were removed, there was a budding melody and harmony in the composition they were creating.

They sat quietly in the midst of the noisy restaurant, gazing at one another. Allan had looked into the eyes of many beautiful women. He'd seen desire, longing, lust, and love—but what resided in Peggy's clear blue eyes was unique. They radiated peace, innocence, a joy and wisdom beyond her years. With the clarity of a flawless diamond, she possessed a quality he found indescribable. It beckoned him to know her, even as she sought to know him. Time vanished in their absorption in one another. Neither had ever felt so lost in such a powerful and mesmerizing moment.

The waiter broke the spell as he delivered the check. They came to themselves slowly and began to smile, then laugh, at the wonder of what had passed between them. "I haven't words for...what just happened," Peggy whispered.

"Only one word comes to mind, and it seems presumptuous and premature to use it."

"How very gentlemanly and diplomatic of you, Mr. Dale. I believe this needs more study, a deeper exploration, don't you?'

"I completely concur. What would you think about my asking you on an official date?"

"Depends on what you have in mind, I suppose."

"Tell you what, the film *A Song To Remember* is opening Friday. Perhaps we could have a nice dinner and see it. Since 'song' is in the title, a couple of singers should enjoy it."

"Oh, that's lovely. I've been wanting to see it. Merle Oberon and Paul Muni are the stars. I read a review and it sounds grand."

"I'll find out the show times and, since you're the local gal, you can choose where we dine. Pick your favorite—I'll eat anything that isn't moving. I have to get back and work on the evening report. Will you be at the station tomorrow? We can make arrangements then."

"I will indeed. I look forward to it. Thanks for this captivating lunch. See you tomorrow."

Allan found it difficult to focus when putting the news report together. He felt a lightness lingering. Meanwhile, the news gave him renewed sense of hope in the clear change of momentum in the war. Germany was in retreat on all fronts and the war in the Pacific was improving as well. There was a heartening sense of victory in the air.

Perhaps there was a brighter future looming. Could that include Peggy? It was perhaps too much to expect. He'd come to accept his limitations. But she felt like so much more than a friend. They were going on an actual date and so far, she had shown no indications of being put off by his obvious physical limitations. His motto came to mind. *I can do all thing through Christ who strengthens me.* It had worked so far.

—

THEIR FIRST DATE WAS far from their last. By the time the buds of spring were showing, their romance was in full bloom. Not everyone was pleased, however. Several of the male staff became most unfriendly. The younger ones were disappointed that the desirable Peggy Jones was off the market, while older staff had an avuncular protective attitude. Why would she get involved with this disabled fellow when plenty of healthy ones are available who could look after her better? And then there were her parents.

Virgil and Bess were cordial, but the thought of Allan's disability and what that would mean for their daughter was the elephant in the room. Peggy tried to cheer him up and tell him they'd come around, but the problem was, he understood their reticence. Although she was oblivious to his disability and saw only the qualities in him that had caused her to fall madly in love, Allan felt the weight of the practical obstacles they would face because of his disability.

With Peggy, he experienced the joy of courting a woman and the chaste nature of romance writ large. He loved the slow simmer of it as the months passed, as opposed to the quick conflagration of passion. Their love was like a wood stove warming all night rather than a bright quick match. That is what he focused on, ignoring the opinions of others. It still amazed Allan that she found his disability irrelevant. All she cared about was, as she put it, "the prize not the packaging." His prayers became primarily long dissertations of gratitude.

Early summer was filled with picnics by the river, duets with Allan on guitar or Peggy on piano. They celebrated Peggy's twenty-second birthday with friends and her family. Her brothers, Dick and Bob, were warming to Allan, but her parents still had reservations. Nothing, however, was able to diminish their love or delight with one another.

On May 8, 1945, Allan reported the most momentous and glorious news of his career. Victory in Europe was announced, as Germany surrendered. Jubilation unlike anything America had ever witnessed broke forth from coast to coast. For a few glorious hours, all past misery was banished, all concerns about the continuing battle with Japan were forgotten. The Depression was past, the war in Europe over, the defeat of Japan looming, and a future of untold possibilities lay ahead.

It was the most glorious summer imaginable. Their love grew and their future together became ever more solidified. Peggy's dreams of a singing career and Allan's growing popularity fueled their hopes with the implication of permanence whispering just off stage.

Peggy recorded her first record and entered it in a nationwide talent search seeking an unknown to star in *The Fabulous Dorsey Boys* movie. She recorded *Got the Sun in the Morning and the Moon at Night,* and *What's The Use of Wondering?* She laughingly said that was the perfect song for the lark of entering the talent search.

Allan reported the bombing of Hiroshima on August 6 and Nagasaki two days later. This felt like the punctuation at the end of the war story they all had been awaiting.

He began to consider buying a ring and asking Peggy's father for her hand. It seemed incomprehensible to him that he might actually live the rest of his life with the most glorious woman on the planet. He decided to make haste slowly. He began a serious charm offensive with her parents and brothers and started saving for a serious rock to place on her finger.

At the same time, they both got far busier. She was in ever more demand as her regional fame grew. He was now producing his usual reports as well as a special series on the impacts of war and prospects for the future. Finally, he felt he was ready to spring the question and began to plan how he would go about it. Then, suddenly, everything changed. Allan remembered his old friend Ira's expression: *Man plans. God laughs.*

In 1946, Peggy received a telegram informing her that she was one of six finalists for the starring role in the Dorsey Movie. She was to be flown to Hollywood and booked into the Hollywood Plaza Hotel for a week. She would meet with the director and perform for the Dorsey brothers. She would be screen-tested and if chosen, star in the movie and become the permanent vocalist for the Dorsey orchestra.

Peggy was in shock. "I didn't expect to win any position. I just made a record for the contest and that was all I thought about it," she told the newspaper reporter when interviewed.

Allan was happy for her, as supportive as he could be. But his emotions were roiled at how this could change everything. If she became a big singing star, moved to Hollywood, and got involved in that life, he would likely be replaced by some dashing actor.

He saw her as often as possible, but suddenly, she was boarding a plane and waving from the window as it taxied away with his dreams.

Chapter 29
Peggy

Photographers were waiting on the ground for Peggy's arrival. She was whisked away in a limousine to meet the director Al Green at the Charles Rogers Studio where the film would be produced. After their meeting, they went to the Brown Derby where they were joined by members of the cast—Joel McCrea, Diane Clark, Janet Blair, and William Lundigen. Her head was spinning.

Nothing in Peggy's experience had prepared her for the sheer power and opulence of the Hollywood movie culture. Although convivial and charming, everyone radiated an air of sublime loftiness. Like her, the other finalists were over-awed and obsequious. Each of them was navigating this skewed playing field with similarly unsophisticated backgrounds and perspectives.

They did their best to be friendly to one another, while knowing only one of them would get the part. Simultaneously, they sought to make themselves charming to the Hollywood royalty who held their fate and future in their hands.

The assistant director met with each of them, assigning times for screen tests and interviews with the director and casting director. Then they were all taken back to the Hollywood Plaza Hotel to check in and prepare for a cocktail party at the Beverly Hills Hotel Polo Lounge.

The bucolic life Peggy knew had given her scant preparation for the frenetic phantasm enveloping her. As she unpacked, her thoughts turned to Allan. She felt a twinge of guilt for not having thought about him sooner. He had become the center of her life. He understood her career and he supported and advised her with his entertainment background and encouragement. Peggy had never felt as loved nor complete.

She stood before the large, beveled mirror studying her reflection framed by the background of the opulent suite. For the first time, she considered what she might do were she to be selected. Would Allan give up his career and join her in Hollywood? Could he find work doing radio? It would completely skew the landscape of their relationship.

It was too much for her to process, so she turned her attention to getting ready for an elegant evening with Hollywood's elite. She slipped into her most alluring dress, the one she wore for really big performances. She applied makeup as if she were going to be on stage. In a way, she *would* be performing.

They departed at seven in three limos with two contestants per car. The young woman sharing the ride was taciturn and withdrawn when Peggy attempted conversation. She turned her attention to the passing cavalcade of the palms lining Sunset Boulevard. Sooner than she expected, they pulled into the circular driveway of the Beverly Hills Hotel. The verdant foliage surrounding the entrance seemed like something from a Tarzan film. Who knows, she thought, Johnny Weissmuller might be inside. It *was* Hollywood, after all.

The group was led through the ornate lobby to the Polo Lounge — where the power brokers and stars made connections, cut deals, and pursued liaisons. A man in the corner played soft jazz on a white baby grand piano with just enough volume to compete with the ego-driven hubbub of the crowd. Numerous eyes appraised them with the attention of cattle buyers at an auction.

They were led to booths with views of a green lawn leading to the pool, bathed in dramatic subdued lighting. The air was permeated with competing scents of perfume, tobacco smoke, and booze.

The director and actors engaged the aspiring starlets with enthusiastic encouragement, while at the same time, taking readings on the potential star power of each of the girls. Bill Gordon, who produced the *Dorsey Mutual Show*, spent time with Peggy, sharing suggestions and thoughts on what she could expect for her screen test. Orders for drinks were taken and menus handed out. Peggy was torn as she didn't drink. She decided not to follow the rest and ordered a Shirley Temple.

—

ALLAN WAS FAR FROM relaxed and was even depressed. The more he thought about what Peggy might be doing out in Hollywood and what the future held for her, the more dire the possibilities seemed. He berated himself for not asking her father for her hand, buying the ring, and proposing before all of this occurred. Now, with merely the signing of a contract, all could be lost.

What could a disabled news commentator in Wichita possibly offer to compete with Hollywood stardom? He turned to the one thing that always brought him solace—prayer. He determined to do what he could to focus on the things he could control and leave the rest up to God. He did, however, fervently ask for guidance no matter what eventuated. He wanted what was best for her, but he also wanted it to be best for them.

—

THE SCREEN TEST, THOUGH intimidating, turned out to be easier than she'd expected. Peggy had been acting in plays since junior high and recently on the radio. Her faculty with remembering lyrics and lines was impressive. She memorized her lines from the short scene she was given the night before. She delivered what felt like a good performance. The director was complimentary, and she felt she'd done her best. This was followed by a session with one of Hollywood's top photographers. They were then driven to a palatial oceanfront home in Malibu for a pool party.

The relaxed atmosphere and abundant liquor set a much more nuanced tone. Peggy found herself with a Shirley Temple in one hand and a handsome actor at her elbow. She'd noticed that a couple of the other contestants had disappeared with some of the men. Andrew, as he introduced himself, spent the next twenty minutes telling Peggy about the film he was co-starring in. He was certain it was the right "vehicle" to propel him to the A-list star level. She knew she'd seen him in something but couldn't remember what. Then he suggested they head to the bungalow for some "more private time to get to know each other." All alarms went off simultaneously and Peggy firmly sent him packing and walking away in a huff. She felt a gentle touch on her elbow. She turned to find a man in a black coat and white collar.

"Hello, I hope you don't mind. I'm Father Michael. I couldn't help but observe the exchange you just ended. You demonstrated admirable restraint. Unlike, I might add, several of your fellow aspirants. I hope you don't mind, but considering that I'm a priest, reading people is a large part of my life. This probably seems an odd place to find a man of the cloth. I work with the studios on questions of moral guidelines in scripts. I have a sense about you. You are different from most aspiring actresses that I've observed. What's your name?"

"I'm Peggy Jones. I appreciate your kind words. It's just that I've been raised as a Christian and don't believe in doing things I'd be ashamed of. I have a fine gentleman back home to whom I am devoted. I hope to win, but I will not compromise in any way to achieve that."

"That is exactly the sort of thing I expected you to say. Peggy, I am a chaplain to many stars. I have seen more than I want to of what this town does to young women. It devours them the way a whale goes through plankton.

"There is something pure in you. You don't fit here. That doesn't mean you can't be successful. But you may be asked to give away parts of yourself that you'll never get back. Hidden in all the beautiful scenery are snakes, awaiting tender flesh to sink their fangs into. Tread carefully, my dear. I don't think you belong here."

Peggy was speechless as the priest walked away. Yet his words resonated within her. She felt something dangerous in the air—not unlike the atmosphere before a Kansas twister. She was perplexed by what her life might look like as a movie star as compared to marriage and a family, hopefully with Allan. Of course, he'd not popped the question—but it sure felt like it was coming. She decided that the visit from the priest was a whisper from God. Probably best to leave it in his hands.

Chapter 30

Allan slept fitfully, his mind tortured by visions of Peggy on the arm of a movie star. As he drank his coffee over a half-eaten breakfast, he felt as helpless as he had the morning he came out of a coma in the hospital. He'd overcome monumental obstacles to arrive where he now found himself. But fighting his way through the pain and rehabilitation was a systematic and tangible challenge. His effort achieved concrete results based on determination and effort.

This situation was completely out of his control. It had seemed he was on the threshold of achieving all he could dream of. He'd found the most wonderful woman he'd ever imagined, who—wonder of wonders—overlooked his disability and loved him for who he was. He'd pictured a life with children running around a lovely home, while he and Peggy sat on a veranda drinking iced tea and holding hands. If only there were something he could do.

He was wound as tightly as a guitar string. Then suddenly, as if struck by an arrow, an idea sprung to life within him. Why not propose now? It sounded foolish, but as he pondered the idea, it began to seem plausible. Why not declare his intentions and give her a clear alternative? No matter what she might be offered, at least she'd know that she had another offer waiting. He took out a pen and began to write a telegram.

> Offer lead opposite me in new romantic play
> / Peg and Allan / To start soon on Main Street
> of America / Script full of Love, Fun, some
> heartaches / Music by Wagner and Mendelssohn
> / Play set for a lifetime run /
> Advise.

Allan drove to the Western Union office on the way to work and sent the telegram to her at the Hollywood Plaza Hotel. He knew it was a bold, non-traditional way to propose. No matter. She had to know how desperately he wanted to spend his life with her. He could only pray she would choose the role he offered.

—

THE TELEGRAM AWAITED PEGGY when she returned from the party that night. She suspected it was a word of encouragement from her family, but perhaps from Allan. Worn out from her frenetic day, she laid it aside, took off her makeup, changed into her pajamas, climbed into bed and, at last, opened and read it.

She re-read it twice more.

Her heart leapt with joy at the proposal but her mind was staggered at the magnitude of the decision. So much was riding on things outside her control. Would she get the part? If she did, how would marrying Allan work, with her living and working in Hollywood? If ever she needed guidance, it was now. She offered up a prayer asking direction and wisdom, but sleep was slow to come. Her thoughts were cast about in a tempest of indecision.

The studio kept the group entertained and busy during the next few days. Meanwhile, discussions went on as to who would get the part. On the day the choice was to be announced, Peggy was told that it was down to herself and one other. The rest of the girls were sent home. Peggy was interviewed again by the producer, director, and two men introduced as investors and co-producers. Riding back to the hotel after the meeting, she was jumpy as a grasshopper. So much was riding on a decision that was out of her control.

She stepped into her room and saw the telegram on the bedside table. She picked it up and clutching it, walked to the window. Gazing down at Hollywood Boulevard from her ninth-floor suite, she watched the crowds below through a mist of tears. Her thoughts turned to her ambitions, the hours of practice, all the possibilities the world she gazed upon offered her. She wanted all that this magic place seemed to promise.

Her heart, however, was playing a different melody. Never had she known a man of such depth and tenderness. His strength of character in overcoming the challenges he'd faced was astounding. She loved Allan's humor and insight, the way he listened to her with his whole being, his enormous talent, his voice, and, of course, his handsome face and hypnotic eyes.

How could she possibly live without him? It seemed an insoluble problem. Her love burned within her like the red orb of the sun she watched, sinking behind the Hollywood hills. No matter what the future held, she could not live in it without him. "Oh, Lord, please, show me what I must do."

Her prayer was interrupted by a radio playing loudly in an adjoining room. It was a song she knew well. The lyrics from the refrain rang out...*Peg of my heart, I love you, we'll never part, I love you...* The verse followed...*When your heart's full of fears, and your eyes full of tears, I'll kiss them all away.* She was dumbstruck. *Peg of My Heart* was Allan's song to her. He'd played his guitar and sung it to her often.

She would often follow up by singing her song to him: *You Are My Sunshine.* She turned to look out the window and saw the last crescent of sun slide behind the Hollywood hills. She thought of the lyrics. *You'll never know, dear, how much I love you. Please don't take my sunshine away.* She opened the telegram again and re-read it. Tears of joy slid down her cheeks. Could God have made it any clearer?

She knew now with every ounce of her being, that no matter the outcome of the movie decision, she could not live without Allan. That was the most important role she must accept. If she was offered the film role, then they would decide together how to proceed. But Peggy now knew without question that she would rather live a simple life with Allan, than have all the stardom in the world without him.

She laughed at the irony of it. She'd arrived at the threshold of achieving her most ambitious dreams, only to leave them behind if she had to. The decision resolved, and an early meeting set for the morning, Peggy went to bed and awoke the next morning having enjoyed the most refreshing sleep she could remember.

Peggy arrived at the Charles R. Rogers Studio at nine. She was shown into his office, and he rose to greet her with a slight, unreadable smile. "Please sit, Peggy. We want you to know that you have impressed us all with your amazing singing, your stunning beauty, and your acting abilities. Your screen test was fabulous. We have already released the rest of the contestants.

"It has been a struggle, rather divisive at times, to arrive at our final decision. As you can imagine there are a number of factors to consider. When we began this talent search, we hoped to find an unknown to develop into a star. You certainly have that star quality. You were my choice for the part. However, other factors and considerations have been brought to bear from some involved in the production.

"The consensus has been to go with Janet Blair. She wasn't one of the contestants. But she is a rising film star who can sing fairly well—not, I might add, anywhere near as well as you.

"Peggy, between us, this was a fixed deal. The financing, the director, her agent's influence all led to this choice. I disagreed as vehemently as I could, but in the end was overruled." He looked at her sadly.

"However, having said this, and understanding your natural disappointment, I would like to make you a counter-offer. I believe you are an exceptional singer and have the potential to be a big star. I would like to offer you a management contract. I believe that I can develop you and create a highly successful career for you.

"As with all such arrangements, I would get fifteen percent of all income from performances, recordings, films, and any other related entertainment opportunities. I will put the full force of my abilities into your development. I would expect a five-year contract, renewable at my discretion. Does that take some of the sting out of it?"

Peggy sat in stunned silence. The sound of the traffic below and the ticking of a large grandfather clock held her suspended in time. Had she been faced with this choice before her decision to accept Allan's proposal, she would have been disappointed in losing but encouraged by his offer.

"I know this is a lot to take in," he continued. "You needn't give me your answer immediately. However, I would appreciate an answer no later than tomorrow. I have another singer, Patti Paige, who is my second choice. We've spoken and I've expressed interest but made no offer to her."

Peggy shook her head in amazement and smiled. "Mr. Rogers, I can give you my answer now. I've been given a better offer. I do so appreciate all you've done for me, and for the interest you've shown in helping me in my career. I know you'll do a fine job with Patti. I'm scheduled to fly home this afternoon so I may not be seeing you again. Thank you for everything."

They shook hands and Peggy left with an unshakeable sense of the rightness of her choice. She was surprised that she felt no disappointment. All the tension drained from her as she stepped into the limo for the ride back to the hotel. She found herself humming, and the lyrics were close behind. *Please don't take my sunshine away.* She would accept Allan's proposal in person, she thought, and sent a telegram with her arrival time the next day, asking if he could pick her up.

She dined alone that night in the hotel, then took a stroll down Hollywood Boulevard, the last she might ever take. Peggy noticed how many attractive young women filled the sidewalks. The dream of stardom was a spell that captured and pulled them from small towns and big cities across America. Only one in millions would ever achieve stardom. Yet she had been offered the chance to be what all these young women dreamed of. Peggy felt not the slightest tinge of regret.

—▪—

Allan was as anxious as a man in a room full of alligators. He'd hoped to hear back from Peggy with her answer to his proposal. He'd already bought the ring—a real beauty—which he'd paid dearly for. Now, as he drove to the airport to meet her, he rehearsed his speeches. The "ring presentation and acceptance response speech" and his "best friends speech," the one he hoped he would not have to deliver.

Her plane was an hour late, which gave him sixty minutes to swing in the winds of uncertainty. Then, at last, Peggy walked down the ramp and across the tarmac to the terminal. Allan's heart pounded like a kick drum. She saw him and rushed, beaming, into his arms. Her perfume mingled with her own scent and her breasts pressed against him.

She whispered into his ear. "Hey, handsome, did you miss me?"

"More than I imagined possible. I'd rather be tied to a whippin' post and beat for a week than to be away from you again." He held her away from him. "Lord, Peggy, California put a glow on you. You are more lovely than I've ever seen you."

"You know what they say about absence making the heart grow fonder."

"I don't believe my heart has any fondness limits when it comes to you. So darling, may we sit down for a moment? I've something I want to say to you."

"Of course."

They sat on a bench near the gate. Allan reached in his pocket. "I would prefer to do this on my knees, but circumstances preclude the traditional approach. You got my telegram as you said, but I would like to formally propose and put this ring on your finger, asking that you sign for a lifetime run of our production."

Peggy held out her left hand and he opened the box for her approval. A brilliant half-carat diamond glimmered where it rested upon a gold band. "Oh, my word, Allan! It's huge! Of course, I will marry you."

"I took the liberty of asking your father for your hand and your mother for your ring size. He agreed, somewhat reluctantly, but gave me the okay anyway."

The ring slipped perfectly onto her finger. The two sat savoring the moment, lost in each other, as passersby smiled at the striking young couple so clearly in love.

—

THE MORNING OF THEIR wedding day—October 13, 1946—Allan still had to produce and deliver the live morning and noon newscasts and record the afternoon broadcast. Fortunately, after that, they had a week off for their honeymoon.

He'd finished the morning report and was busy writing the script for noon when he was interrupted by a delivery. A Western Union boy rushed in and nervously handed the respected radio man a telegram.

Allan thanked and generously tipped the shy young man.

Who in the world would be sending him a telegram? Maybe it was a congratulatory note from an associate or professional acquaintance. He opened the envelope and read:

Accept lead in play / Will meet you today at
church at four o'clock to sign contract / Peggy

He laughed and wept and turned his face up, giving thanks for everything that had led to this glorious day. Carefully folding the telegram, he put it in his coat pocket and returned to the task of writing and recording the news.

Two hours later, Allan Dale straightened the stacks of paper on his desk and leaned back in his chair. He reflected on the long and twisting road he'd traveled. He felt gratitude, not only for where he'd arrived, but for every event that had led him there.

The man he'd become and the man he hoped to be had been formed in a crucible of pain and disappointment. His recovery, his rebirth, the renewal of his faith, were not in spite of but *the result* of his greatest tragedy and loss. The promise of his future, as melodic strains of a prelude, swelled to the heights.

The lifetime run of *Peggy and Allan* was about to begin.

Coda

☥

We sat silently in the musty room after he finished his tale. What was there left to say? I rested my hand on his.

"I believe it's time for a nap, son. I am so proud of you and your brothers. The men you became. Pull the curtain for me when you leave. I love you."

I kissed him on the forehead, pulled the sheet up over him, and closed the curtain. Once outside, I stood, as if in a trance, watching the Spanish moss blowing in the cypress trees, streaming like the hair of Valkyries in the fresh January wind. I walked down to the lake and sat on a tree stump. The scent of northern latitudes began to override the smell of the lake. The corners of lily pads near the shore lifted in the breeze, floating on a million prisms of sun-kissed ripples. A Great Blue heron hunted in the shallows while a Florida gator watched from the far shore.

The conversation with my father and his revelations reverberated within me. I was torn with the thought of losing him while, at the same time, understanding his desire to be freed from his suffering. To dance in the arms of Mom—and be home at last. I began to cry.

And then I smiled. *What a father. What a man. What a woman. What a life.*

"And Now the Rest of The Story…"

— Paul Harvey, Radio Commentator

Allan and Peggy Dale were married on October 13, 1946, at four o'clock on a lovely fall day in Wichita, Kansas. Shortly thereafter, Dad was approached by an old acquaintance with an offer to take over the management of radio station KURV in Edinburg, Texas. It was there that I was born on a muggy south Texas day on September 10, 1947. My brothers Terry and Tim followed over the next three years.

This book is based on the revelations of Dad's wild musician's life before the accident and meeting Mom. He revealed things he'd never told me in the days before he went home to the Lord. The rest is based on stories my parents told me, anecdotes from their families and friends, and my own experiences growing up in radio with them.

Unfortunately, priceless recordings, press releases, photographs, and other memorabilia were lost when a microburst destroyed the building in which they were stored. I had to create the pre-Peggy years of the story from Dad's revelations about his wild life as a singer on the road and finally in New York. The characters with whom he associated, the clubs where he performed, are fictional. Many historical figures are, of course, as portrayed. I suppose you could call the pre-family days "fact/tion."

The main characters, though—Peggy, Allan, and their families— are as presented. The Tommy Dorsey contest and outcomes are accurate, the people mentioned are real. Patti Paige would go on to have a wonderful career. One can only wonder what Peggy might have achieved had she not chosen to marry a man who walked with two canes—and become a mother and homemaker.

Dad began the next phase of his radio career in south Texas at the time when records and popular music formats displaced live music and entertainment radio. Television gradually replaced radio dramas and comedies, although many dramatic radio shows continued into the fifties. Then, rock and roll came along and changed radio forever. Dad, having been a musician, quickly recognized the trend and adapted. His success in increasing listenership and ad revenue led him to KSOX in Harlingen a short time later.

It was there that he began an experiment with what would one day blossom into an entirely new type of medium—"talk radio." Remembering Roosevelt's fireside chats and the great commentators like Gabriel Heater, a seed germinated in Dad's mind. What if the radio audience could not only listen but have a conversation with the man on the radio? Much as the oldtimers sat around the Cracker Barrel on the porch of the Country Store discussing current events like rocking chair philosophers, would listeners enjoy expressing their opinions on the events of the day?

With the help of his engineers, he set up a call-in line and began a daily show of his opinions on the news of the day, inviting listeners to call in and express their viewpoints. He was already a master at commentary—now he developed the specialized skill of actively listening and responding to what his audience had to say. People loved it.

So much did they like *The Allan Dale Show* that in the mid-fifties, he was hired to manage KEYS in Corpus Christi. While managing a Top-40 rock and roll station, he continued his call-in talk show, and the ratings were tremendous. Dad was becoming a phenomenon in his own right with this new talk radio concept.

In the late fifties and early sixties, FM began to fundamentally change radio broadcasting, overtaking AM due to FM's higher power and better sound quality. Suddenly AM music stations began to lose audiences to FM rock stations. Dad saw the handwriting on the wall. He believed that the only way to compete with FM was asymmetrically. Instead of doing the same format less effectively, why not offer something that FM didn't?

He believed in the idea so strongly that he took the biggest gamble of his life. Risking his successful career at KEYS, with a wife, three boys, and a mortgage, he approached WOAI in San Antonio with his concept. He presented the station manager and owners with a way to beat the FM "rockers." Based on the proven success with his novel talk show, he proposed that they offer the audience an alternative.

Rock and pop music primarily reached the younger demographic. Most of the disposable income was in the hands of those 35+, making them an attractive target audience for advertisers. WOAI was a clear channel, with no others on the same frequency at 1200 AM, and having a 50,000-watt signal, it reached hundreds of miles in the daytime and thousands of miles at night, reaching from Canada to central Mexico.

The folks at WOAI liked what they heard and decided to offer Dad a chance to prove his theory. He could try out this new talk radio format in the mid-morning slot for three hours. They would give him two ratings periods—or "two books" in radio parlance—roughly six months—to prove it would work. Taking the greatest gamble of his life, Dad agreed.

So he quit his job at KEYS, sold our home, and moved us to San Antonio. Unbeknownst to us, he was putting everything on the line. If the concept didn't produce the audience he promised, he was out of work. I'm glad I was too young to understand that.

The risk was not only successful, but *The Allan Dale Show* took off like a Titan rocket. While Rush Limbaugh was still in school, my father became the voice of South Texas and a talk radio pioneer. The popularity of his talk show led the brilliant Lowry Mays and Red McCombs, who had acquired WOAI, to expand the idea, making the station a full-time news/talk format. The listeners flocked to talk radio. Ratings and revenues increased.

Mays and McCombs began to expand their Clear Channel company, buying radio stations across the country and replicating the news/talk format. The company continued to expand at light speed.

Clear Channel went on to become one of the largest broadcasting companies in the world.

Dad left WOAI to do his show on KITE in San Antonio in the early seventies. He retired with Mom to Florida in the late seventies. Then, in the mid-eighties, Dad's life and mine joined up. I'd followed him into radio and television and was working in Corpus Christi as a weatherman. I got a call from a friend who was starting a news talk station in San Antonio to compete with WOAI. Larry wanted to know if Dad would come out of retirement and be the anchor of the morning show. I told him I'd call Dad and find out if he was interested.

"Absolutely," Dad said. "I'm bored out of my mind."

KRNN (*K-Radio News Network*) came to life with *The Allan Dale Show*—and Radio Free Texas was born. Shortly thereafter, Larry twisted my arm into leaving TV, in which I had been working for more than twelve years, to host the afternoon talk show. And so, I went to work with my father, the master and a pioneer of talk radio. It was the sweetest and most rewarding period of my broadcasting career. We came to know and respect each other as fellow broadcasters, even as our father-son relationship, always warm and loving, grew apace.

KRNN was sold in the late eighties and Dad retired for the last time, while I headed to New Zealand to work in radio and TV.

Dad was a force to be reckoned with. His authoritative conservative style made him, as one columnist wrote, "San Antonio's answer to Walter Cronkite." Among his many unique accomplishments was a live interview with President Ronald Reagan aboard Air Force One, the first ever done while a president was airborne. While Dan Rather and other network reporters awaited Reagan's arrival on the hot tarmac, Dad had a long and informative interview with the president. You can read the transcript and learn more from the Reagan Library, and Wikipedia.

I've called this little roundup at the end *"The Rest of The Story..."* in honor of Paul Harvey, a fellow radio broadcaster of the time. But, let me tell you the *best* of the story.

Think for a moment about what kind of woman would look past the obvious physical disabilities of a man hobbling around on two canes. Not just *any* woman, mind you, but a gorgeous songbird with the voice of an angel—a woman who was offered a contract with the studio producing the Dorsey movie and passed on a career that would have likely been a big success—all to marry and spend the rest of her life helping do things that must be done when one lives with a disabled person and raises three rambunctious boys.

Mom still went out and sang during my early childhood. I remember the first time I saw her in an evening gown, getting picked up by the band for a gig. Chanel No. 5 still triggers memories of her.

She poured her soul into being the most engaged and loving mother three boys could have been blessed with. Our days were filled with music while she did housework. Some of it from her jazz and classical records, some during the breaks she would take. Every so often, she would sit at our blond upright grand piano. She would play and sing songs that would have done justice to the finest piano bars in New York. Once, I asked her why she sang all the time. Her answer? "God respects me when I work, but He loves to hear me sing."

When we were young, Mom would read us stories by the hour and dress the wounds that only three wild boys can fall victim too. When Dad returned from work, she delivered a delectable dinner— lots of it—for the four ravenous males at the table.

Peggy Jones was every bit Allan Dale's equal. Although most of our friends and neighbors would never know or appreciate her great talents, nor what she gave up to marry Dad, we came to understand this as we grew into men.

The "angel in the grey suit" was correct in his words. Allan Dale proved the doctor's prognosis wrong. How? Because he believed, not in what he saw, but what he could not see as the final outcome, because his faith defeated his fear, and because he lived by the words of Philippians 4:13: "I can do all things through Christ who strengthens me." He did, as prophesied, go on to touch thousands of people's lives through his talk show, his newspaper column in *The San Antonio Light*, and his book, *Cracker Barrel Comments*.

Allan and Peggy Jones Dale are still the most inspiring and loving people I have ever known. Everything I am is the result of their love and the values they taught and lived. Mom went home to the Lord on October 17, 1994 at 72. Dad passed on January 17, 1996, at 84.

The day before he passed, as I sat on his bed, he said, "You know, son, that accident was the greatest blessing of my life. Had it not happened, I would have never met Peg, never had you boys, and never lived the great life God gave me."

He winked at me. "By the way, Peg came to visit me last night and said she'd be back to take me home. You know the first thing I'm going to do when I get there? I'm going to dance with her for the first time."

I pray their story will encourage you to live with a faith that defeats all fear. To know that whatever trials you face on this fallen planet, if you are His child, the power of the Holy Spirit lives in you and can empower you to overcome your challenges.

And who knows? Maybe through this book, Allan Dale will continue to touch thousands of people's lives.

DORSEY PICKS KFH VOCALIST AS ONE OF SIX

Peggy Jones, staff vocalist at KFH, has been selected as one of the six singers from over the nation in the Tommy Dorsey contest to find a vocalist for the Tommy Dorsey band.

"It just can't be hapening to me," Miss Jones said several times during her interview this morning.

Miss Jones, who has been staff vocalist at KFH for the last five years, entered the contest when she was in California two weeks ago.

"I didn't expect to win any position," she said. "I just made a record for the contest, and that was all I thought I would hear from it."

When she got home Sunday evening, the telegram was waiting for her. She will have to be in Hollywood from August 16 to 20. All expenses will be paid, and she will stay at the Hollywood Plaza hotel. The screen test she will be given will be given by Charles R. Rogers.

If Miss Jones is selected as the national winner she will play the part of the vocalist in Tommy Dorsey's band in the picture, "The Fabulous Dorseys," that will soon begin production. The winner of the contest will also become the permanent singer of the Tommy Dorsey band.

Miss Jones is a graduate of East high school, class of 1941. Her parents are Mr. and Mrs. V. E. Jones, 1514 Hydraulic. The songs Miss Jones recorded while in Hollywood were, "What's the Use of Wondering?" and "Got the Sun in the Morning."

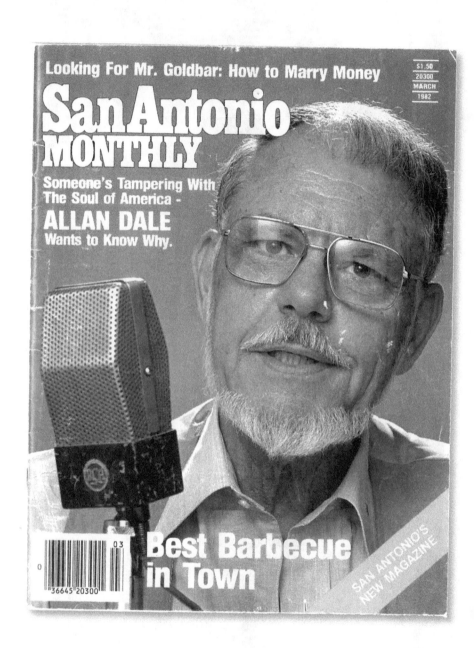

Looking For Mr. Goldbar: How to Marry Money

$1.50
20300
MARCH
1982

San Antonio
MONTHLY

Someone's Tampering With
The Soul of America –
ALLAN DALE
Wants to Know Why.

**Best Barbecue
in Town**

SAN ANTONIO'S
NEW MAGAZINE

0 3

0

36645 20300

Acknowledgments

I believe that the greatest wealth is relationships, time, and health. I am blessed to have some bright and honest friends who were kind enough to read my manuscript and give me honest feedback. It was incredibly helpful. Thanks to Cheryl Every, Pagan Gilman, Matt Padula, and Charles Welch for their insight.

My brilliant editor, Rowe Carenen was invaluable with her suggestions and hard work. She had to help me navigate not only grammatical minefields but technical ones as well. Her title, "Book Concierge," is truly indicative of her marvelous service.

And special thanks to Vally Sharpe at United Writers Press for her guidance and wisdom in helping deliver this baby.

Everyone needs mentors and encouragers. The highly respected author John Carenen has been that for me. He kindly checked on my progress. Gave sage advice and read my manuscript, giving me honest feedback. By all means read one of his excellent books. Heck, read them all!

Thanks to my best friend, business partner, and co-host of "Common Sense Talk," Phillip Allan. His constant encouragement throughout was like a fresh breeze in my sails.

Of all the people who helped me, the most essential, invaluable and encouraging of all is my priceless Pernilla. She went over every word with a critical eye and imparted great wisdom in helping me shape the story. My wife is the greatest relationship of my life and God has blessed me beyond my ability to praise Him adequately.

Printed in the USA
CPSIA information can be obtained
at www.ICGtesting.com
LVHW011306311223
767822LV00018B/2137